GLORIOUS RIVALS

LOVE IS A DANGEROUS GAME.

Also by Jennifer Lynn Barnes

The Inheritance Games Saga

The Inheritance Games

The Inheritance Games
The Hawthorne Legacy
The Final Gambit
The Brothers Hawthorne

The Grandest Game

The Grandest Game
Glorious Rivals
Coming next: *The Gilded Blade*

Games Untold

The Same Backward as Forward

The Naturals

The Naturals
Killer Instinct
All In
Bad Blood
Twelve: A Novella

The Debutantes

Little White Lies
Deadly Little Scandals

The Lovely and the Lost

GLORIOUS RIVALS

#1 *New York Times* bestselling author
JENNIFER LYNN BARNES

LITTLE, BROWN AND COMPANY
New York Boston

Copyright © 2025 by Jennifer Lynn Barnes

Cover art copyright © 2025 by Katt Phatt. Cover design by Karina Granda. Cover copyright © 2025 by Hachette Book Group, Inc. Interior design by Carla Weise.

Little, Brown and Company
Hachette Book Group
1290 Avenue of the Americas, New York, NY 10104
Visit us at LBYR.com

First Edition: July 2025

Little, Brown and Company is a division of Hachette Book Group, Inc. The Little, Brown name and logo are registered trademarks of Hachette Book Group, Inc.

The publisher is not responsible for websites (or their content) that are not owned by the publisher.

Little, Brown and Company books may be purchased in bulk for business, educational, or promotional use. For information, please contact your local bookseller or the Hachette Book Group Special Markets Department at special.markets@hbgusa.com.

Library of Congress Cataloging-in-Publication Data
Names: Barnes, Jennifer Lynn, author.
Title: Glorious rivals / Jennifer Lynn Barnes.
Description: First edition. | New York : Little, Brown and Company, 2025. | Series: The grandest game ; [2] | Audience term: Teenagers | Audience: Ages 12 & up. | Summary: "Players move into the next round of the Grandest Game, where millions of dollars in prize money are on the line—and new relationships, motivations, and threats come to light." —Provided by publisher.
Identifiers: LCCN 2025004359 | ISBN 9780316481311 (hardcover) | ISBN 9780316481519 (epub)
Subjects: CYAC: Contests—Fiction. | Puzzles—Fiction. | Riddles—Fiction. | Romance stories. | Mystery and detective stories. | LCGFT: Romance fiction. | Detective and mystery fiction. | Novels.
Classification: LCC PZ7.B26225 Gl 2025 | DDC [Fic]— dc23
LC record available at https://lccn.loc.gov/2025004359

ISBNs: 978-0-316-48131-1 (hardcover), 978-0-316-48151-9 (ebook), 978-0-316-59711-1 (international), 978-0-316-58765-5 (B&N exclusive edition)

Printed in Virginia

LSC-H

Printing 1, 2025

For Lisa Yoskowitz

GLORIOUS RIVALS

LOVE IS A DANGEROUS GAME.

Prologue

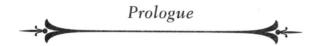

The Grandest Game had to be allowed to reach its conclusion. Of that, she was certain. Carefully laid plans depended on it. Of course, what that conclusion was mattered a great deal.

It was a delicate balance, steering the tide without revealing her hand. But then, *delicate* was a specialty of hers.

Alice had seen to that.

Chapter 1

LYRA

Kissing Grayson Hawthorne felt like stepping out of time. Nothing else existed. Not the ground beneath Lyra's feet. Not the ruins or the cliffs. Just *this*. Every place their bodies touched. His lips and hers. A jagged breath—*this*.

The right kind of disaster just waiting to happen, Odette's voice whispered in Lyra's memory. *A Hawthorne and a girl who has every reason to stay away from Hawthornes.*

As if he'd heard Lyra's thoughts, Grayson pulled his lips slowly back from hers. "I usually have more control than this," he said, his voice achingly low.

"I usually have better sense," Lyra replied, keenly aware of just how close her lips still were to his—and how close the two of them were to a repeat performance. That kiss, their first, their only, had been earth-shattering.

It had also almost certainly been a mistake.

The wind off the ocean picked up behind Lyra, sending her

ponytail flying into her face—and his. Grayson tamed her long hair, pushing it back, and as he did, the wind calmed, too, so suddenly and completely that Lyra couldn't shake the illogical thought that *he* had calmed it through sheer force of will.

An alarm went off in the back of Lyra's mind. This was *Grayson Hawthorne.*

And even if he wasn't the cold, above-it-all, asshole rich boy she'd thought him to be twenty-four hours earlier, he was still a Hawthorne. His blood wasn't just blue; it was practically cerulean. And soon enough, the Grandest Game would be over, and promises or not, Lyra and Grayson Hawthorne would go back to being what they'd always been: little more than strangers...with *every reason* to stay away from each other.

Neither one of you knows what you think you know. Another of Odette's warnings echoed through Lyra's memory, but even that couldn't distract her from the fact that she was still so close to Grayson that she could feel his every breath on her skin.

"We should try to get some sleep before phase two," Lyra said. The words came out throaty and low. She'd been aiming for *practical.* They'd been given twelve hours to recover from the first phase of the game. So far, Lyra hadn't managed anything resembling respite.

"We should," Grayson agreed, but instead of putting even a modicum of space between them, he brushed the knuckles of his right hand lightly over her cheek, stealing her next breath like a born thief. "I meant what I said, Lyra. We'll figure this out—the game and all the rest."

The rest. That was the understatement of the century, and even just thinking the words had others ringing through Lyra's mind. *A Hawthorne did this.*

A Hawthorne.

Omega.

There are always three.

Lyra took a step back. Maybe with a little more distance, she'd be able to breathe, to think, to focus on what came next. The two of them were standing on what had once been the cliffside patio of a glorious mansion that was nothing but ruins now, a charred and visible reminder of the way even the grandest things could be reduced to ashes.

"Someone sent me here." Lyra focused on that. "Someone put me in this game, and whoever that person is—they know about my father. I'm someone's pawn." Lyra looked away from Grayson's pale and piercing eyes. "Or a weapon. Or a bomb."

That was the logical conclusion, wasn't it? That the person who'd sent her that ticket had put Lyra in the Grandest Game *because* of her history with the Hawthorne family? Because of her father's death.

Because of Alice Hawthorne's role in it.

"You are no one's weapon, Lyra," Grayson said, his tone making it perfectly clear just how rarely he lost arguments of any kind, "bomb or otherwise, and you are certainly not a pawn."

"Then what am I?" Lyra retorted, her gaze returning to his like a homing missile.

"You are lethal," Grayson said quietly, "in the best possible way."

Where did he get off saying something like that and sounding, for all the world, like he meant it? Lyra went to take another step back, but Grayson reached for her shoulder, and the next thing she knew, he'd reversed their positions. Now Grayson was the one standing with his back to the cliff's edge, and Lyra had the magnificent ocean view.

He'd just put himself between her and the drop-off. "I don't need your protection, Hawthorne."

Grayson arched a brow. "Agree to disagree."

The wind off the ocean picked up again. *A front rolling in.* A slight shiver passed through Lyra's body. Eyeing her, Grayson undid the top button on the jacket of his fits-like-a-glove suit. The middle button was next.

"What are you doing?" Lyra asked. She wasn't just talking about his suit jacket, and he was perceptive enough to know that. *What are* we *doing?*

"I would think the answer apparent." Grayson undid the final button on his jacket, and then...

The jacket came off, and Lyra's body remembered: *My lips and yours. A jagged breath.*

"You'd better not be planning on offering me that jacket." Lyra steeled her voice.

"You're cold." Grayson's lips curved. "And I believe that I have already acquainted you with the fact that when I encounter a problem, I solve it."

This was about so much more than the damn jacket. It was about his family and hers and an unknown threat. It was about the fact that Odette Morales, the one person who might have known some fraction of the big picture here, had given up her spot in the Grandest Game—and her chance at millions—because of the danger that Lyra and Grayson somehow represented.

The right kind of disaster just waiting to happen.

"I don't need your jacket," Lyra told Grayson.

"Perhaps *I* need to give it to you," Grayson suggested. "Chivalry. It's a coping mechanism."

"I'm warning you, Hawthorne: If you try to put that jacket

around my shoulders, I'm taking mine off and giving it to you." To make her point, Lyra lifted a hand to the zipper on her own athletic jacket—which, to be fair, was more of an outer shirt.

Grayson took a moment to assess whether or not she was bluffing.

Lyra was not bluffing.

"Consider me warned," Grayson replied archly. He slipped his suit jacket back on.

Lyra narrowed her eyes. "Why do I feel like I lost this argument?" she said.

"Because," Grayson replied, "I'm still standing between you and the edge of the cliff."

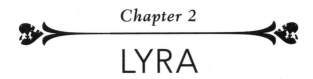

Chapter 2

LYRA

Once upon a time, Lyra might have had it in her to let another person protect her, but that was *before*. Before the dreams had started. Before she'd realized that her entire life had been a lie.

For years, her parents had let her believe that she was normal. They'd let her just go on like the defining trauma of her life had never happened, like her biological father hadn't abducted her from preschool on her fourth birthday, like she hadn't witnessed his suicide. And once Lyra *had* remembered, it was like nothing about the life she'd lived fit anymore, like the person she'd been had never even been real. She hadn't wanted anyone to know why she'd changed, so she'd pretended that she hadn't. She'd faked it for as long as she could.

But there was no faking anything with Grayson Hawthorne. And these days, when it came to the possibility of being hurt in any way, Lyra had to face it head-on. She had to protect *herself*, and Grayson made that so very hard. He was a hand on the back of her neck, pulling her from the darkness, telling her that she did not have to be fine.

But she did.

So instead of letting Grayson escort her back to the puzzle-filled mansion on the north point to get some sleep, Lyra warned him not to follow her and took off on another run.

Even though she'd already pushed her body to its limits.

Even though she needed her mind sharp for what was to come.

Lyra ran because her thoughts were a mess. She ran to stop her body from remembering his. She ran because she *could*.

Grayson must have sensed that it *really* wouldn't be wise to follow, because he didn't, and eventually, once Lyra had pushed herself hard enough and long enough, the ghost of his touch left her, and the only thing that existed besides the burning in her muscles and her lungs was the island.

Lyra felt it like an extension of herself: wild and free, scarred and ruined, beautiful, sharp. Hawthorne Island was full of rocky shores and steep drops, native grass and soaring trees, cliffs upon cliffs, the occasional narrow slice of beach, all of it surrounded by ocean.

The day before, Lyra had been drawn again and again to the burned forest. Today, she stuck to the southern and eastern shores—the roughest terrain on the island by far. Uneven ground. Thorns. And very little else. Objectively, it didn't resemble the place where Lyra had grown up, but somehow, Mile's End and the most untouched parts of Hawthorne Island *felt* the same to her: unchanging, real in a way that nothing more developed ever was.

Lyra let that feeling fill her as she ran, her sense of purpose crystalizing. She'd entered the Grandest Game to save Mile's End. Everything—and *everyone*—else could wait.

When Lyra finally reached the point where she could risk not running, where she could let herself stop, she stared up at the lone, breathtaking structure on the southeastern shore. Out on the water, massive stone arches that looked like they'd been lifted straight from ancient Rome cast outsized shadows on blue-green waters. Beneath those arches, there was a dock.

Breathing heavily, Lyra made her way onto a large boat slip that stood perpendicular to two smaller ones, a platform in between. Her body very nearly spent, she walked to the end of the dock, and as she stared out at the water, an odd feeling hit her, like calloused fingers skimming her shoulder blades. Lyra turned, casting her gaze back toward the island.

Nothing. She was alone.

Exhaling, Lyra turned to face the ocean. She tried to make out the mainland in the distance and couldn't. The real world was out there somewhere, but Lyra couldn't see it. She couldn't see anything other than water and shadows and a light fog on the ocean.

And still...

Still. As Lyra stood there, staring out at the Pacific, she had the strangest sense that she was being watched.

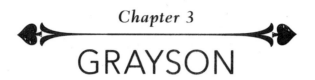

Chapter 3

GRAYSON

G rayson looked down at the smartwatch on his wrist. Given that each remaining player in the Grandest Game had been given one, it doubtlessly did more than tell time. A thorough assessment, however, revealed that the only thing Grayson could do with the watch at this juncture was toggle between the time and another symbol.

A spade.

In phase one of the game, the players had been divided into teams: Hearts, Diamonds, and Clubs. Grayson's mind made quick work of this fourth symbol. *Spades—for the people behind the scenes.* From the beginning, Grayson had been able to feel his brothers' and Avery's touches in every detail of the Grandest Game—including the fact that they'd made him a player. Grayson had fully intended to have a *conversation* with all four of them about that, but now there were more important conversations to be had.

Grayson tapped the spade. A text box and keyboard popped up, a way to send a message to the game makers. Grayson chose his words with care, a simple anagram that Avery and his brothers would recognize as a Hawthorne request—meaning that it really was not a *request* at all.

ZEN DROVE US.

Grayson waited for a reply, and eventually, he got one. *NORTH-ERN SHORE.*

Grayson knew from experience that, when it came to his brothers, a *rendezvous* could take a variety of forms. Some involved explosions. Some involved helicopters. Sword fights, mud wrestling, karaoke, and fisticuffs were all on the table. But the brother who joined Grayson on the northern shore of Hawthorne Island wasn't prone to most of those.

"Nash." Grayson kept his gaze trained on the ocean and greeted his eldest brother moments *before* Nash stepped into his peripheral vision.

"Thinkin' about a swim?" The oldest of the four Hawthorne brothers nodded his head toward the waves.

"A bit cold for that," Grayson replied.

"Never stopped you before."

"Assignment from my therapist," Grayson said evenly. "Apparently, I swim as an exercise in punishing perfectionism with the goal of exhausting myself to the point where I cannot feel. It is, supposedly, healthier to let the thoughts and the feelings come."

Thoughts like: *Some mistakes are worth making.*

Thoughts like: *Why not me? With her, right now—why not me?*

But Grayson hadn't called for a rendezvous to discuss his

feelings. "There's a threat," he told Nash. "Or at the very least, the potential for one. Lyra Kane received her ticket to the Grandest Game from an anonymous third party. Someone sent her here."

Nash chewed on that. "Now why would an anonymous third party do that?"

Exactly. "As it happens, our family was implicated in Lyra's father's death." Grayson's voice sounded, to his own ears, far more measured than he felt. "Suicide. She was four. She was *there.*" Just thinking about what the memory of that night did to Lyra made Grayson want to wage war on behalf of the child she'd been—and that wasn't even touching on the woman she was now.

In his entire life, Grayson had kissed four people, counting Lyra. And when he'd kissed her, for the first time in his life, he'd let the feelings come. All of them.

Lyra Kane kissed the way she moved: with heightened bodily awareness, with grace, like kissing was a matter of whole-body coordination.

"How big a threat is she?" Nash asked, his tone casual. Grayson wasn't fooled. A threat to one of them was a threat to all of them, and Nash was a man who defended what he loved.

"Lyra is not the threat." Grayson hadn't meant to issue that statement as a warning, but there it was.

Nash cocked his head. "Exactly how far gone are you, little brother?"

"It's only been one day," Grayson replied, the answer automatic.

Nash rocked back on the heels of his boots. "I knew almost immediately with Lib."

Libby Grambs—Libby Hawthorne, now—was Nash's wife. Grayson lips quirked upward just thinking about his sister-in-law and the babies she was carrying. "How is Libby?"

"Full of cravings. A little cranky." Nash grinned. "Wholly incandescent." He turned his head to shoot Grayson a knowing look. "I'm going to ask again, Gray: How far gone are you with this girl who's not a threat?"

Grayson fixed his eyes back on the horizon. *Let it all come.* "Far enough."

Nash let out a low whistle. "Jamie was right. This is gonna be fun."

"Delighted to amuse," Grayson said dryly. "But I didn't call you here for *fun*. What do we know about the blackout last night?"

During phase one, the power had gone off—generator and backup generator both.

"Xander says the culprits appear to be squirrels," Nash replied. "The collective noun of which he insists is also *squirrel*."

"A squirrel of squirrels?" Grayson tone made it clear: His skepticism was not limited to Xander's linguistic assertion.

"Island's locked down tight," Nash said.

"Either it's not locked down as tight as you think or Lyra's sponsor has another player in the game." With characteristic efficiency, Grayson proceeded to tell Nash about the notes someone had left for Lyra in the burned forest, bearing her dead father's names—his *aliases*. "You'll also want to have someone keep tabs on Odette Morales now that she's exited the game. She knows something."

"What kind of something?"

Grayson saw no reason to dissemble. "The kind that involves our grandmother not being nearly as dead as advertised."

Nash responded to that bombshell with trademark calm, removing his worn cowboy hat and running his thumb slowly over its edge. He'd done the exact same thing the one and only time Grayson had ever taken a swing at him.

"You're going to want to get in a sharing mood real quick, little brother."

Grayson narrowed his eyes, but ultimately, he allowed Nash to get away with pulling rank. "As of fifteen years ago—several years after our grandmother's supposed death—Alice Hawthorne was apparently alive and well. She came to the old man, revealed herself, and asked him for a favor." Grayson paused, thinking about the grandfather he had known, the Tobias Hawthorne who'd come out on top of every challenge, every confrontation. The one who'd trained them to do the same. "Also fifteen years ago," Grayson continued, "one of the last things that Lyra's father said to her before putting a bullet in his own head was: *A Hawthorne did this.*"

"*A. Hawthorne. Alice.*"

"You'll tell the others." Grayson did not phrase that as a question. "There may be more than one game being played on this island."

"Do we call it off?" Nash said, steady as ever. "This year's Grandest Game?"

"No." Grayson didn't even hesitate. "Either there is no true threat and calling the game off would be premature, or there *is* one—and we need to take this opportunity to identify it."

The first step to neutralizing an opponent was to make them show their hand.

"So you're playing," Nash said. "Phase two."

"I'm playing," Grayson confirmed. *Not to win—but for her.*

Nash ran the back of his hand over the five o'clock shadow on his jaw and smiled slightly. "What does she need the prize money for?"

Grayson's brothers had all always been too perceptive for their own good. "She wants to save her family home." Grayson thought about Lyra refusing his jacket and threatening to give him hers. "Suffice it to say, the lady will not accept a dime from me."

Lyra needed to win the money. Grayson needed to do whatever he could to help her.

"She got a nickname for you yet?" Nash cocked a brow.

Grayson's lips twitched. "I'm pretty sure it's *asshole.*"

"I like her already." Nash grinned and put his hat back on. "And speaking of family, I have something to tell you, and you're not gonna like it. When we went to escort the eliminated players off the island, Gigi never showed. Little sis is MIA—and so is Xander's boat. Seems Gigi took it and left a note. And apology Twinkies."

Grayson frowned. "We're on an island. Where did Gigi get Twinkies?"

"My understanding from Xan is that it was more of an IOU."

Grayson kneaded his forehead. That sounded *exactly* like his sister, and Grayson didn't need Nash to tell him that Gigi had taken being eliminated from the Grandest Game hard. "I should have checked on her."

"Alisa's already working on tracking down the boat. We'll find little sis. In the meantime, you've got a game to play—and another sister to watch out for."

Savannah. Nash's reminder had Grayson thinking about his sister's roughly shorn hair—hair that looked very much like it had been cut with a knife. And then Grayson thought about the player with whom Savannah appeared to have allied herself in this game.

The person who had, in all likelihood, *borne* the knife.

"Savannah doesn't want me looking after her," Grayson commented with all the calm he could muster.

"The ones who need the most looking after never do." Nash slapped Grayson on the back. "And on that note, we fixed a room up for you at the house." He held out a large, bronze key. "Find it and get some shut-eye, little brother. Phase two is not for the weak of heart."

ROHAN

Rohan never slept deeply. He hadn't since he was a child. Memories lingered in deep sleep, like shadows with a mind and hunger of their own, so Rohan slept lightly—always aware, always listening, always on guard.

And yet...

He woke in Savannah Grayson's bed to find himself alone. *Let your guard down, did you, boy?* the Proprietor's voice said somewhere in his mind. The formidable Ms. Grayson was nowhere to be seen—and neither was Rohan's room key.

He knew immediately what Savannah was up to. *The sword.*

The weapon in question was a longsword with words etched along its silver blade: *From every trap be free, for every lock a key.* Each team in phase one had been given its own sword—just one. Rohan had made a point the night before of keeping possession of the one he and Savannah had been given. They might have been allies, but theirs was an alliance with a ticking clock.

Ultimately, the Grandest Game could have only one winner, and for Rohan, everything was on the line. He *would* win. Savannah just hadn't realized it yet. She'd doubtless stolen his key to search his room for the sword and claim it as her own.

Propping himself up on his elbows, Rohan smiled wolfishly. *Good luck with that, love.* He decided to return the favor, searching Savannah's room while she was gone. With skilled hands, he tested every floorboard, pressed at every molding with fingers both dexterous and strong, removed pillows from their cases, sheets from the bed. He flipped the mattress, searching it for slits. When that turned up nothing, Rohan made his way into the attached bathroom.

Sitting on the marble counter was a mask made of swirling, silvery blue metal. Three teardrop diamonds hung from the corner of each eye. The design had suited Savannah at the masquerade ball the prior evening. Rohan ran the pad of his index finger over the delicate strings of diamonds. *Precious gemstones, frozen tears.*

But Rohan knew: Savannah Grayson didn't cry.

Wondering how long it would take her to admit defeat in *his* room, Rohan turned on Savannah's shower. While the water heated up, he gathered his clothes from the floor of the bedroom and slipped a pair of glass dice out of his pocket.

The indomitable Ms. Grayson had a lot to learn. If she'd been playing long games for as many years as Rohan had, she would have stolen his dice and *then* gone to look for the sword.

Stepping into the shower, Rohan laid his red dice on a marble shelf and gave his body up to the scalding spray. Rohan had never minded heat. The cold was a different matter—cold water, especially.

The past will drown you if you let it, boy. The Proprietor's voice echoed through the twisting halls of Rohan's mind. *Like stones tied to your ankles.*

Rohan stepped farther into the scalding heat of the spray, taking in it a distinct kind of pleasure. His focus was sharpest in moments like these. *I am going to win the Grandest Game.*

Power came, always, at a cost. Pain was a reminder of that. And heat reminded Rohan: *I was not made to shiver or drown.*

Whatever he had to do to win, he would do it.

Footsteps. Rohan marked the sound of them and the length of the stride—Savannah, incoming. Soon enough, she was standing right outside the shower curtain.

"I didn't say you could use my shower." Savannah Grayson's voice was a socialite's voice, its sharpness the sharpness of diamonds, not glass.

"And I didn't say you could try to steal my sword," Rohan replied lazily. It was too bad, really, that her shower had a curtain instead of a glass door. He would have liked to have seen the expression on her delightfully angular face the moment he called her out.

"The sword isn't yours."

Didn't find it, did you, love? Rohan's smile deepened. "Agree to disagree."

"Get out of my shower," Savannah ordered.

Rohan, magnificent bastard that he was, was happy to comply. He turned off the water, swept the red glass dice from the shelf with his left hand, and curled the fingers on his right hand around the curtain. "Careful what you wish for, love."

Savannah threw a towel over the rod. *Hard.* Rohan made use of it, toweling off, then wrapping it around his waist before stepping out from behind the curtain. "I do hope you put my room back as you found it after you failed to find that sword."

Savannah's gaze roved over his body—chest, abs, down to the place where the towel hugged his hips. "I hope *you* weren't expecting what happened to mean anything," she replied.

Ruthless. Rohan appreciated that in a woman—in anyone, really. "I expect you to hold up your end of the deal in this phase of the game, Savvy, and that is all."

Per their agreed-upon terms, the two of them would continue playing the Grandest Game as a team until—and *only* until—the competition had been effectively dispatched.

"There's no need for concern." Savannah arched a pale brow at him. "When I promised to work alongside you and *then* destroy you, I meant it." She turned toward the mirror, examining her own reflection—an attempt, Rohan was certain, to keep from further examining *him.*

He brought one hand to rest on the towel around his hips and smirked at her.

"Grayson is going to be a problem," Savannah commented coolly.

All business. "How fortunate, then," Rohan said, "that I excel at taking care of problems." *And how fortunate that the Hawthorne brother in question has developed a weakness.*

Savannah raised her chin, her newly shorn hair making her pale eyes look that much larger, her cheekbones that much sharper. "What do you know about the girl?" she asked.

Lyra Kane. Savannah had zeroed in on Grayson's weak point with admirable efficiency.

"What do you know," Rohan countered, "about how Lyra Kane's father's name ended up plastered all over the burnt forest?"

"What are you suggesting?" Savannah could play the ice queen to perfection.

"You have a sponsor, love." Rohan didn't pull his punches. "You're very likely not the only player with one, and I doubt any of them are above playing dirty." He gave her a look. "Tell me I'm wrong."

"If I wasted my time pointing out your every misapprehension, we'd barely have any left to strategize." Savannah gave a deadly, elegant little shrug. "I will, however, point out that *you* are the one more positioned to know other players' secrets—assuming, of course, that the Mercy is as powerful as you claim."

An eighteen-year-old American girl couldn't even begin to fathom the power, the wealth, the reach of the Devil's Mercy, the organization that had raised Rohan, the organization that he was determined to rule. He'd been given a year to come up with the buy-in, a year to obtain ten million pounds and claim his rightful place as the next Proprietor.

Unless and until he did so, as far as the Mercy was concerned, Rohan was *nothing*.

"You claim that you want to win more than I do." Savannah shifted her gaze back to his. "You never told me why."

"Imagine that," Rohan replied.

Savannah narrowed her eyes at him. "You know why I'm here."

Rohan stepped forward, his body brushing hers. "*I'll never pause again*," he quoted, "*never stand still, till either death hath closed these eyes of mine or fortune given me measure of... revenge.*"

Rohan gauged Savannah's response to that final word in the slow rise and fall of her chest.

"*Henry the Sixth, Part Three*," he clarified.

"I am well aware," Savannah replied. She didn't take the bait, didn't say a word about her motivation for playing this game—or her plot for revenge. "Perhaps you should be going." She picked up Rohan's clothes and tossed them at him. "We have hours yet before phase two, and there's no reason for you to spend them here."

No reason. Is that right, love? "You mentioned strategy." Rohan lowered his voice, a move aimed at forcing her to lean slightly toward him. "Here's a tip, Savvy: divide and conquer." Now it was Rohan's turn to lean forward ever so slightly. "And here's another one: The fewer players there are left in a game, the more important it becomes to control the board."

"The board," Savannah repeated, intensity in her tone. "The island."

"The island. The house. The objects." Rohan held Savannah's gaze a moment longer, then brushed past her and stepped into the bedroom. "Think fast, love." He tossed something back over his shoulder at her.

He heard her catch the glass dice—the *white* dice, hers, lifted from her pocket, along with his room key—as he'd passed.

"And that," Rohan called back, as he sauntered out of Savannah's room, "is why I'm the one in charge of securing our sword."

Chapter 5

GIGI

"Good. You're waking up. You've been out for hours."

The first thing Gigi was aware of was the voice—male, quiet, a little rough.

The second thing was the feel of a fur throw beneath her body, soft and warm.

And the third thing was ABSOLUTELY EVERYTHING ELSE, including and especially the fact that there was a distinct possibility that she had been kidnapped.

Gigi blinked rapidly. *No need to panic!* she told herself sternly. *I'm sure it was a completely amiable kidnapping.* Maniacal optimism in the face of danger was a real strength of Gigi's—and so was taking in every last detail of any situation.

The room around her was large, circular, and dimly lit. Light crept in through cracks in the stone wall, tiny, concentrated beams shining in the air like stars in the sky. Somewhere up above—the building was at least forty feet tall—there must have been windows, but Gigi couldn't see them, only the faint light they let in, which cast shadows on a twisting staircase made of stone.

Absolutely nothing to worry about here, Gigi assured herself. As far as she could tell, there was nothing else in the room except for herself, the criminally soft blanket beneath her, the staircase, a door...

And the person blocking the door.

"I'm not going to hurt you." He made that statement sound less comforting than matter-of-fact.

"That's my line," Gigi replied, trying to buy herself some time to study her captor. Blond hair hung in his face, partially obscuring eyes so dark brown they looked nearly black. She knew from their last meeting that he had a scar through one eyebrow, but she couldn't see it now—not with his hair in his face, not from this distance, not in this light. Instead, Gigi's gaze was drawn to the tattoos on his arm, thick, black, semi-jagged lines that looked like nothing so much as claw marks.

"I'm not going to hurt you is your line?" He may or may not have been amused by that. His stone-cold expression and utterly flat voice made it hard to tell. "Glad to hear I'm not at risk of bodily harm."

Oh, you definitely are. Gigi considered the merits of an unexpected flying tackle, but she'd obtained a head wound during the Grandest Game, and it was pounding just a teensy bit. A thing like that could really throw off a person's tackling calculus.

"Actually," Gigi informed him, adjusting her legs to sit crisscross, "my line is *You're not going to hurt me*—said with a smile."

"You say everything with a smile."

"Not everything. Observe." Gigi pointed an emphatic, jabby finger at her captor. "You knocked me out! And kidnapped me! You broody-faced muscle-goblin!"

She really hadn't meant to say anything about his muscles.

Can't say I wasn't warned, Gigi thought with an internal sigh. A year and a half earlier, her brother had warned her that this mysterious stranger—Code Name: Mimosas—was Very Bad News. Grayson had told her to run the other way if she so much as saw the guy. And what had Gigi done when she'd realized Mimosas was on Hawthorne Island, interfering with the Grandest Game?

She'd gone looking for him.

"*Kidnapped* is a bit harsh, sunshine. I'm just doing damage control. As soon as the game is over, I'll let you go."

"What are you up to, Mimosas?" Gigi narrowed her eyes. "What is *Eve* up to?"

Gigi didn't know all that much about this guy's employer, but she knew that Grayson considered Eve dangerous. She knew that Eve had resources—and a personal connection to the Hawthorne family.

"*Mimosas?*" her captor said.

Gigi did not dignify that question with a response. Instead, she plotted. Mr. Very Bad News had made a key error in taking her. In addition to being an Olympic-level optimist, Gigi was also very skilled at the art of interrogation.

Unveil evil plot first, tackle later, she thought. "What does Eve want with me?" Gigi smiled her most endearing smile. "And on a scale of one to ten, how dastardly are her intentions and/or yours with regards to the game?"

No response.

"Fine," Gigi said, as agreeable as agreeable could be. "On a scale of one to *twelve and a half,* how—"

"Eve doesn't know I took you." Dark, dark eyes stared at her from behind the blond hair in his face. "I didn't do it for her."

Gigi suddenly flashed back to the moment he'd knocked her out, to his voice in her ear. *Easy there, sunshine.* Gigi swallowed. "Did you take me to protect me *from* Eve?"

Maybe that was overly optimistic. Maybe not.

Mimosas was silent for the longest time. Finally, he crouched, bringing his eyes level with hers, his forearms braced lightly against his thighs. "What makes you so sure that Eve is the only threat I might be protecting you from?"

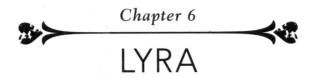

Chapter 6

LYRA

The dream started, as ever, with the flower. *A calla lily.* Then came the candy necklace. *Only three pieces of candy.* Somewhere in Lyra's consciousness, Odette Morales said: *There are always three.* But in the dream, Lyra was small. In the dream, there was no Odette. There was only a shadow and a gun and a man's voice saying, *"A Hawthorne did this."*

Only this time, Lyra saw the man's face. She saw his eyes, her *father's* eyes, amber just like her own.

And then everything was dark.

And then her feet were sticky with blood.

And then she was running barefoot on pavement, out into the night.

Lyra's eyes snapped open. She forced herself to exhale the breath trapped in her chest, forced the muscles in her body to relax, one by one. She reached for the feeling she'd had running the island, that clarity, and rolled out of bed and into a stretch, lifting her knee to her chest. After a few seconds, she rotated her hip and extended her leg back and up—and up and up, until she could feel a low, familiar ache in her hips and back. She switched legs, stopping only when the watch on her left wrist began to buzz.

A message appeared on its screen: *DON YOUR ARMOR.*

The night before, it had been gowns and masks. Today, it was *armor.* Lyra couldn't help wondering what that said about phase two. She tapped a red circle that had appeared beneath the words, and in response, the back wall of her room began to part.

Within seconds, Lyra was staring at a hidden closet—*hidden* no longer.

A single rack held two outfits, identical but for their color. One was white, the other black. At first glance, Lyra thought she was looking at body suits, but a closer inspection revealed three separate pieces for each outfit: tank top, outer jacket, and pants. The fabric looked almost like leather, but touching it ruled out that possibility. Whatever the fabric was, it breathed. It *stretched.*

Lyra knew instinctively that a person could dance in this fabric—or run or climb or *fight.*

She donned her armor—black. The clothes felt like nothing she'd ever worn, the fabric molding to her body. There were pockets on the outside of the jacket and more in the pants. Lyra made use of them. *Room key. Glass dice.* Grayson had their longsword, but Lyra had kept possession of the opera glasses Odette had given her as a parting gift. Picking them up by their diamond-encrusted stem, Lyra tucked the opera glasses through the belt loop of her pants, securing them directly over her hipbone. Then she retrieved the key-shaped pin she'd been given in phase one of the game and affixed it to her left sleeve, just above the place where her wrist met her palm. Finished, she turned her hand back over and looked back down at her watch.

The message about donning armor had been replaced by a timer—*2:17:08*.

Lyra watched as it counted down, second by second. Prior to the first phase of the game, there had been a masquerade ball—and a challenge. With more than two hours to go until the start of phase two, Lyra had to assume that this night would follow a similar pattern.

So what's the challenge?

Bringing her index finger to the face of her smartwatch, Lyra tried to scroll but quickly realized that there were only two screens, the timer on one and an isolated symbol on the other. *A spade.* Lyra tapped it and was presented with a keyboard.

"Feels like a test," she mused. Lyra thought about the only piece of instruction she'd been given: *DON YOUR ARMOR.* And then she thought about Grayson Hawthorne, telling her that she was no one's weapon.

That she was lethal in the best possible way.

If nothing else, Lyra was a competitor. She chose her reply to the game makers. *READY FOR BATTLE.*

Lyra hit Send. Within a minute, she'd received a message back—a map.

Chapter 7

LYRA

The map led Lyra down to the north shore and around to the western bank. If the tide had been much higher, she would have had to walk through ocean to squeeze past the base of yet another cliff and around to a thin slice of sandy beach. Rock formations out in the water broke enormous waves as they came crashing in from the west—from open ocean as far as the eye could see.

There was only one person standing on the hidden beach. *Avery Grambs.* The Hawthorne heiress stood with her arms loose at her sides, staring out at the Pacific horizon and the setting sun. She looked almost nothing like the girl on all those magazine covers— the billionaire, the philanthropist, the angel investor, the beauty. This Avery was wearing faded jeans that were torn at the knees and a men's sweatshirt that hung down nearly that far. Her hair was braided back from her face in a loose, messy braid that matched the utter lack of makeup on her face.

As Lyra walked to stand next to Avery, she couldn't help thinking that this version of the Hawthorne heiress felt real, the way that parts of the island did.

"Looks like I'm the first to arrive," Lyra said in greeting.

"You were the first to reply to our text." Avery smiled slightly, her gaze never diverting from the Pacific view. "It's beautiful, isn't it?"

"The ocean or the sunset?" Lyra replied, and then her gaze was drawn back to the massive rock formations, which called to mind nothing so much as a circle of standing stones, like a Stonehenge on the water. "Or the rocks?"

"All of it. Look right there." Avery pointed, and Lyra's gaze followed the heiress's finger to two of the stones, jutting out over the waves, with maybe a foot between them. "Do you see that gap?" Avery said. "It's called the Sunset Gap. This time of year, the sun sets exactly there. And when it first begins to set, when the sun touches the water, the way it will any minute now, if you're looking right between those rocks, it's like nothing else in the world."

Part of Lyra wanted to do nothing more than wait for the magic moment, but a bigger part of her was restless—about phase two and whatever challenges awaited, about the mysterious benefactor who'd brought her here.

About *Alice* and *omega*.

Some people just weren't wired to stand around waiting for something marvelous to happen. Lyra looked away from the Sunset Gap, concentrating on their surroundings instead. In a recessed area beneath the cliff, there was a mound of branches, arranged just so.

"Are we having a bonfire?" Lyra asked. *A fire. On Hawthorne Island.* That was a choice.

Avery cheated her gaze toward Lyra. "Has anyone ever told you that you have a very expressive voice?"

Lyra didn't have it in her to feel abashed. "Given the history," she said, "why host a game here at all?"

The heiress took no visible offense to that question. If anything, Avery's expression softened. "My aunt died on this island. In the fire."

Lyra hadn't known that.

"I never knew her, obviously," Avery continued, "but my mom grieved what happened here. Deeply." Avery wound her arms around her waist. "And the thing is, I never even knew she was grieving, because my mom had this incredible, ridiculous way of finding joy in the most unlikely circumstances. Anything could be a game. There was always a reason to laugh. And when she loved someone, she loved hard. No reservations. No regrets."

And now she's gone. The muscles in Lyra's throat tightened. Grief recognized grief, always and in deeper places than Lyra had ever realized, back when she'd been normal.

"Joy in unlikely circumstances," Lyra repeated quietly. "And anything can be a game." Lyra had read a lot about the Hawthorne family and the Hawthorne heiress over the years, but nothing she'd ever read had explained the enigma that was Avery Kylie Grambs even half as well as what the heiress had just told her.

Beside her, Avery trained her gaze back on the Sunset Gap. Lyra didn't even try to resist doing the same. The sun was nearly touching the water, and already, it was breathtaking.

"Have you thought at all about what I told you before?" Avery asked. "About the game?"

Lyra couldn't even blink for fear of missing the moment when the setting sun would fully fill the gap. "Sometimes," she said, repeating back what Avery had said to her the night before, "in the games that matter most, the only way to really play is to *live.*"

The sun sank farther, and suddenly, a thousand shades of orange and yellow and pink filled the air, reflecting off the ocean's surface, completely filling the Sunset Gap. *Like nothing else in the world.*

A full minute passed before Avery spoke again. "Do me a favor: Don't hurt him."

Grayson. Before Lyra could reply, before she could so much as say *I couldn't if I tried,* Avery glanced back over her shoulder—and up.

"Incoming," the heiress warned.

Lyra turned to see three figures climbing down the face of the cliff without protective equipment of any kind. Like Avery, the trio of Hawthornes was dressed in jeans and sweatshirts, but never in the history of the world had jeans and sweatshirts looked like *that.*

"I'd tell you that you get used to it," Avery said beside her, "but you really don't." The heiress caught Lyra's gaze one last time. "Good luck, Lyra."

With that, Avery strode toward the base of the cliff. Jameson Hawthorne dropped a good eight feet to land beside her. Nash and Xander followed suit, and Lyra couldn't help thinking that there was just something about the four of them.

About all of them.

The same thing that had made Lyra look away from the Sunset Gap before made her look away now. She glanced back the way she'd come, and suddenly, like she'd dreamed him into being, Grayson was there. He stepped onto the hidden beach dressed in black, his *armor* a perfect match for hers. It fit his body better than any suit possibly could have, showing the breadth of his shoulders, the way his waist narrowed in, even the muscles of his thighs.

Lyra saw the exact moment Grayson registered *her* outfit. He crossed the beach in six long strides. "You slept." In typical Grayson Hawthorne fashion, that wasn't a question.

"I dreamed," Lyra replied.

Grayson's expression made it clear he took her meaning. "We will find answers," he promised. "After the game."

Lyra couldn't let herself believe in *after.* "That kiss." The word *kiss* tried its best to lodge itself in Lyra's throat. "It can't happen again."

"And here I'd had you pegged as a realist." Grayson gave her a look. "But if it's our ability to focus you're concerned about, logic dictates we need only wait until the game is won—until *you* win it."

He acted like the two of them kissing again was a foregone conclusion, as inevitable as her victory in the game, and Lyra couldn't even resent his arrogance, because she couldn't shake the absolutely maddening feeling that Grayson Hawthorne dealt in facts.

That some things really were inevitable. That some people were.

"It's not fair, really." Lyra returned his look with one of her own. "You're a Hawthorne. You have the advantage here." She was talking about the Grandest Game—and she also wasn't.

"My brothers and I were not raised to play fair," Grayson admitted. "And on an unrelated note, it seems our competition has arrived."

Lyra didn't see evidence of that until a second or two later when the remaining three players began to make their way onto the hidden beach, one by one. Savannah was the only one of the three in white. Brady held his own longsword in his right hand. And Rohan...Rohan moved over the sand like gravity was an issue only for lesser mortals.

"Now that the gang's all here..." Xander Hawthorne jubilantly inserted himself between Lyra and Grayson. "May I borrow you, Lyra?"

Lyra had enough sense to be concerned. "Borrow me for what?"

Grayson's youngest—and tallest—brother grinned. *"Gallus Gallus Domesticus en Garde."*

Lyra glanced at Grayson. "Do I even want to know?"

"GGDEG," Xander clarified helpfully. "It's a time-honored Hawthorne tradition and not at all a way of getting to know you while Gray here is otherwise occupied."

Grayson narrowed his eyes. Given that he was *not* currently occupied, Lyra didn't blame him.

"Gallus gallus domesticus," Grayson informed her, "is the scientific name for *chicken."*

"Chicken," Lyra repeated. *"Chicken...en garde..."* She turned to look incredulously at Xander. *"Chicken fight?"*

"Don't mind if I do!" Xander wasted no time whatsoever hoisting Lyra onto his shoulders, and Lyra decided pretty early on in that process that resistance was futile. As Xander straightened to his full height, Grayson went flying.

From her spot on Xander's shoulders, it took Lyra a moment to register what had just happened—or rather, who. *Jameson*. He'd just tackled Grayson.

And now, Lyra thought wryly, *Grayson is otherwise occupied.* "Is a flying tackle what passes for a greeting in your family?" she called down to Xander.

"If you can call that a flying tackle," Xander scoffed, and then he let out what could only be described as a hefty battle cry. "Who among you shall stand against the mighty team-up of XanLyra? Nash? Avery? You!" Xander pointed at Rohan. "Can you get him on your shoulders?"

Lyra snorted. The *him* in that question appeared to be Brady Daniels. Xander seemed to be taking it for granted that Savannah would not be chicken fighting *anyone*, but she took one step toward them, then another.

"I'll tell you what," Savannah called out, raising her chin. "I'm in if Avery is."

Chapter 8

LYRA

After a lengthy, ocean-side chicken fight—during which, remarkably, no one got wet or injured—came the lighting of the bonfire. By that point, Grayson and Jameson were nowhere to be seen, and Lyra was starting to suspect that there was no *challenge* forthcoming on this beach tonight, no hint to be won for the game to come.

This was just a part of the experience, a memory in the making.

As the first flames began to catch, Savannah took up position beside Lyra. The resemblance between Grayson and his half sister really was remarkable, and as the bonfire surged, Savannah spoke in her brother's even tone. "He won't choose you."

"Excuse me?" Lyra said.

"Grayson," Savannah replied, her voice high and clear and utterly certain. "Part of you is already falling into the Hawthorne trap, believing in all of this, thinking about what it would be like to be a part of it, to be one of them." Savannah paused, giving Lyra a chance to deny that—though not much of one. "But you need to know, when all is said and done, when it matters most, Grayson won't choose you."

"I'm not asking him to," Lyra retorted.

"Yet. You're not asking him to choose you *yet*." Savannah stared through the flames at Avery, who was laughing with Xander and Nash. "You'll save yourself some heartache if you realize going in that he'll choose them every time. He'll choose *her*."

Avery. Lyra thought about the heiress telling her not to hurt Grayson.

"She's not what you think," Savannah warned, and without waiting for a response, without so much as allowing for one, she turned and walked away.

Lyra just stood there blinking for a moment. *What the hell was that?*

"I'd watch out for Savannah, if I were you."

Lyra turned toward the owner of that voice—Brady. His locs were tied back, and his thick-rimmed glasses might have made him look unassuming had it not been for the way his armor accented his strong, muscular build.

"It's a competition," Lyra replied. "Pretty sure that means I should be watching out for everyone." Fun and games aside—*bonfires* and *chicken fights* and *sunsets* aside—they were all here to win. She cut to the chase. "I'm Lyra. You're Brady. We haven't technically met."

"*Lyra*." Brady said her name wrong, the way Lyra's stranger of a father had during their one and only meeting. *Lie-ra*. "It's a constellation, you know." Brady studied her like he was reading some kind of esoteric book. "The constellation *Lyra* contains one of the brightest stars ever visible to those of us on Earth—southern hemisphere, northern sky."

Southern hemisphere. Lyra knew next to nothing about her biological father, but she knew he'd claimed whatever heritage suited him, many of them South American.

"My name is Lyra," she told Brady flatly. *Leer-a.*

"It's possible I know too much about constellations," Brady admitted. He inclined his head toward the night sky, and Lyra found herself doing the same. "I know a lot about a lot of things," he continued. "I could be a useful ally to you in phase two."

"Careful with that one, Ms. Kane." Rohan appeared out of nowhere. "He left Gigi Grayson bleeding on the rocks. Anything in the name of the win, isn't that right, Mr. Daniels?"

"Divide and conquer." Brady met Rohan's gaze. "An expected strategy." With one last glance at Lyra, he made his way to the other side of the fire.

Lyra preempted Rohan before he could even try to get inside her head: "Don't."

"Wasn't planning to." Rohan had a charmer's smile. "You might ask yourself, though: Where *is* your Mr. Hawthorne?"

Chapter 9
GRAYSON

Follow the Leader, the way Grayson and his brothers had played it growing up, had led—no pun intended—to numerous concussions and two-and-a-half broken arms. But when Jameson had issued the challenge—in the form of a flying tackle, followed by the requisite hand signal—Grayson had accepted.

He'd followed Jameson all the way up the vertical wall of the cliff, out of sight of those below, well aware that his brother was up to something. Grayson knew Jameson—better, perhaps, than he knew anyone else in the world. They'd been born three hundred and sixty-four days apart, one day short of a year. For the entirety of their childhoods, they'd been formed in contrast to each other, in competition with each other.

Jameson was a master of the Hail Mary pass, a sensation seeker, a risk-taker. The more Grayson had pushed himself to be what their grandfather wanted him to be, to be *perfect*, the more risks his brother had been forced to take, and the better Jameson had gotten at choosing his risks, the more formidable Grayson had been forced to become.

And somehow, despite it all, theirs was a rivalry that ran only half as deep as their bond. It was that connection that told Grayson, long before they finished the climb and Jameson took up position on the very edge of the cliff they'd just scaled, that something was wrong.

When it came to his family, Grayson took no risks. "Speak."

"I love it when you give me orders, Gray. It makes me feel so seen and loved. An order's the next best thing to a snuggle, I always say."

Grayson's immunity to Jameson's sarcasm was absolute. "Jamie? Speak." *Tell me what's wrong.*

"I'll do you one better. *On Spake.*" Jameson issued the phrase like the trump card it was.

There was a set of rules that Grayson and his brothers had agreed to from the time they were children, traditions that none of them could break without significant penalty. On Spake— an anagram for *no speak*—was one. From the moment Jameson had invoked the phrase, Grayson *could not* say a word, not until Jameson called, at which point, it would be up to Grayson whether or not things would come to blows.

The question was why Jameson considered whatever he was about to say to be *fighting words*, worthy of invoking On Spake to begin with.

"Lyra Kane is a threat," Jameson said, "whether you see it or not."

That assertion could not stand. Only a lifetime of control kept Grayson from making that point out loud. Instead, he relied on his face to make it for him. *Tread lightly, brother.*

"I would tell you to stay away from her," Jameson continued, "but I have eyes and rather remarkably no death wish at the moment, so instead, I will say this: Be sure that she's worth it, Gray." Jameson locked his eyes on to Grayson's. "Make damn sure that she's not Eve."

The moment Jameson said the name *Eve*, Grayson unzipped his jacket, removed it.

"If you think I'm looking for a fight," Jameson said, "you're wrong."

People find plenty of things they are not looking for, Jamie.

Jameson responded as if he'd spoken out loud. "I'm not done, Gray. You said something to Nash about our grandmother being alive. She's not. Do you understand, Grayson? *She is not.*"

Grayson did not, in fact, understand, but he was sure as hell going to.

"I mean it, Gray. Don't even say the name."

Grayson noted that his brother had not—Jameson had not once said the name *Alice Hawthorne.*

"Don't breathe a word of whatever it is you *think* you know," Jameson told Grayson. "And don't ask."

Don't ask me why. Jameson's message was loud and clear. *Don't ask me a damn thing about Alice Hawthorne.* Seconds passed. "Now I'm done." Jameson held Grayson's gaze. "I call."

By the rules of On Spake, Grayson could speak now. Also by the rules, it was up to him to decide whether or not they were going to fight this out.

"You know something." Grayson stated the obvious.

"I'm a regular fount of knowledge, but when it comes to this, I know nothing. I'm not even curious. And, like you, I am *not going to ask.* I'm not going to pull at a single thread."

Grayson stared at his brother. Jameson had been born pulling at threads, hunting for secret passages, and throwing caution to the wind. *Something is very wrong.*

"How dangerous is this?" Grayson demanded.

"I don't know what you're talking about," Jameson said blandly, his hands hanging loose by his sides. "And I called, Gray. Judgment's yours."

The option of *forcing* Jameson to talk was not without appeal, but Grayson also suspected it was little more than wishful thinking. In a physical fight, Grayson would come out on top, but not by much and not for long enough to make a point.

"I don't want to fight you."

"You never do," Jameson said. "And yet..."

By the rules of On Spake, Grayson had to actually make the call, one way or another. "She's not a threat." Grayson didn't even say Lyra's name. "And she isn't Eve." *She's something else.* Grayson let the thought come, let Jameson *see* it wash over him. "If Lyra's in danger, I need to know."

"I called." Jameson's tone made it clear: He wasn't backing down here. "You know the rules, Grayson. If we're going to fight, the first swing is yours."

"We are not going to fight," Grayson said, pausing slightly between each word to add weight to that declaration. "But, Jamie?" Grayson took a step forward, placing himself firmly in his brother's personal space. "You have as long as it takes for the Grandest Game to conclude to get a handle on this—whatever *this* is. Find the threat and contain it or be prepared to tell me everything you know."

About whatever secret you're keeping. About Alice.

"Why, Grayson Hawthorne, has anyone ever told you that ultimatums really bring out your eyes?"

Grayson snorted. "You're going to have to deal Nash in on whatever's going on here. You know that, right?" Their oldest brother didn't have a temper, but he *did* have a protective streak a mile wide.

"Let me handle Nash," Jameson said—famous last words. "You just worry about playing the game. Phase two is really something."

Chapter 10

ROHAN

It was quite some time into the evening before Rohan allowed himself three seconds to relish the sight of Savannah in form-fitting white. A thick metal chain, won earlier in the game, was wound around her body, just above her hips. Rohan could almost tell himself that his interest *was* the chain—but then, in his line of work, *almost* was never enough.

The Proprietor's voice echoed in the halls of his mind. *What are distractions, Rohan?*

Even in firelight, Rohan could make out every line of Savannah's body beneath her so-called armor. *Weakness*, Rohan thought, the word a murmur in his mind. Distractions were weakness, and Rohan was many things—but never weak.

Instead of allowing himself to dwell further on his one and only ally in this game, he turned his attention to the competition. Lyra Kane was sitting near the bonfire. Brady Daniels stood at the darkened ocean's edge, longsword held at his side.

And then there was the Hawthorne of it all.

Only a lifetime spent in shadows allowed Rohan to pinpoint Grayson's exact location. He tracked his quarry's progress back down the cliff, then looked for Grayson's brother, the Hawthorne that Rohan knew best.

Jameson was nowhere to be seen.

"Notice how one of the game makers pulled Grayson aside?" Savannah and that white *armor* of hers slid in beside Rohan. "And Grayson and Lyra were the first two down here tonight. A cynical person might say this game appears to be rigged."

"All games are rigged, love." Rohan continued tracking Grayson's progress. "In the long run, the house always wins. If you've gotten this far without realizing that nothing in life is fair, then evidence suggests that perhaps you *are* the house." Rohan's voice was like silk in the night air. "Perhaps you always have been."

Savannah had a trust fund. She had a mother—an excellent one, based on Rohan's pre-game reconnaissance, not to mention a sister who was all things good and light.

Savannah's jaw hardened. "You're thinking that my ticket to this game was handed to me."

Rohan noted that she did not specify the person who had given her that ticket. In fact, by Rohan's accounting, Savannah had not said the Hawthorne heiress's name once since the night before and that tantalizing confession of hers. *Avery Grambs killed my father.*

Rohan doubted that very much, but he was not in the business of correcting false beliefs that he could use. "Frankly, love, I'm less interested in how you received your ticket to the Grandest Game than I am in knowing who got to you immediately thereafter." Rohan knew exactly how to pitch his voice to ensure that he was not overheard. "That sponsor of yours."

"Your *interest* is of little concern to me," Savannah said tartly.

In the distance, Grayson made it to the base of the cliff, and Rohan allowed himself to turn and drink in the sight of Savannah once more, his gaze going slowly to the thick platinum chain just above her hips. "That's going to slow you down."

"Is that why you didn't bring our sword?"

Their sword—or more accurately, *Rohan's*—was well hidden, and it would stay that way until its use in the game became apparent. Being weighed down was a liability, a risk. *Weakness.*

"There is limited utility," Rohan advised Savannah, "in the kind of weapon that other people can see." With a magician's flourish, he produced a photograph seemingly out of thin air, one he'd helped himself to earlier as he'd brushed past Brady Daniels. Zippered pockets provided little protection against an accomplished thief.

"What is this?" Savannah asked, less question than demand.

In the photograph, a teenage girl with heterochromia—one blue eye, one brown—drew an arrow on a longbow.

"The scholar had it in his jacket pocket," Rohan told Savannah, allowing her a moment longer to look before he made the picture disappear as easily as he'd stolen it in the first place. "*For every lock a key,*" he quoted, his lips twisting into a not-so-subtle smile. "Weakness and motivation are often one and the same. The girl in that photograph is Brady's."

His weakness. His motivation.

Savannah took a second to reply—only one. "You knew about this girl coming into the game."

Rohan had made it his business to gather as much information as he could about all of the other players, which made the things he did *not* know that much more enticing. "Puppy love, tragic endings, etcetera, etcetera," he told Savannah. "The girl is missing, presumed dead. Has been for years."

Rohan didn't tell Savannah that the girl's name was Calla Thorp or that Calla's father had sponsored one of the eliminated players, Knox Landry, in this year's game. Even without those details, the lovely and merciless Ms. Grayson zeroed in on the appropriate question with admirable efficiency.

"Does Brady have a sponsor?"

"Not that I know of," Rohan replied. He neglected to point out that this lack of knowledge was itself significant because it suggested either that Brady Daniels was not much of a threat at all... or that his sponsor was a very big one.

Discretion, Rohan had learned over the years, was not merely the better part of valor. Discretion—flying below notice at will—was a blade.

Chapter 11

ROHAN

Five minutes to go. Rohan tracked the game makers. Soon, the four of them began to assemble in front of the bonfire. Backlit, Avery Grambs and her Hawthornes stood shoulder to shoulder.

"Listen up, y'all," Nash said. The fire crackled as the players went instantly silent. "There are a few things you'll want to know before those timers on your watches hit zero," Nash continued, and then he glanced at Avery, and she took over.

"If part one of this year's game was the Grandest Escape Room," the Hawthorne heiress announced, "you can think of part two as the Grandest Race—clue to clue to clue."

"No shortcuts," Jameson declared, his left hand finding its way to Avery's right. "Each puzzle you solve will lead you to a new clue. Before you take possession of any such clue, you'll have to sign for it. You'll find an electronic ledger at each stop. Hold your watch up to the ledger, and your name will appear on the page."

"You must sign the ledgers—all of them—in the order in which they appear in the game," Avery said. "First one to sign all of the ledgers, make it to the end, and complete the final puzzle wins."

What Rohan heard Avery saying was: *It would be unfortunate if any player were to lose their watch.*

"For any friends of Machiavelli among you..." Xander Hawthorne raised one eyebrow to ridiculous heights. "Allow me to stipulate that there is to be no watch-thievery, watch-tampering, or watch-shenanigans-not-otherwise-specified of any kind."

Friend of Machiavelli. Rohan had been called worse.

"If an emergency arises"—Jameson, again—"you can use your watch to contact us. Touch the spade, and you can send the four of us a message at any time."

"You'll be wanting to make as much progress as you can before midnight," Nash advised, and Rohan flashed back to the cowboy drawling other words. *It's not gonna be you.*

Our games have heart, Nash Hawthorne had told Rohan. *It ain't gonna be you, kid.*

"What happens at midnight?" Savannah asked.

"What *doesn't* happen at midnight?" Xander replied. "But hypothetically, if you receive a message from us at around that time, you'll want to do exactly what it says."

It was nearly seven now. Midnight was a little over five hours away. *Less than a minute left on the countdown.*

"Look around," Avery told the players. "Only one of you can win this year's Grandest Game, but in a very real sense, none of you are in this alone." The heiress lifted her arm and Jameson's over their heads, their fingers intertwined, and Rohan noticed a ring on Avery's right ring finger bearing a symbol he knew all too well: a lemniscate. *Infinity.*

"You'll find your first clue in the Great Room," Jameson announced. "In three..."

"Two...," Avery said.

One. As the countdown hit zero, Rohan took off, a bullet through the night, fully confident in his ability to win this race. Lyra Kane was a distance runner, made for endurance, not sprints; Brady's solid build would slow him down; Grayson would hold back to guard Lyra. *And Savannah...*

As Rohan edged back around the base of the cliff, Savannah tore right through the water at high speed. Within two breaths, they were both running, full-out, along the shore. Rohan knew that it did not matter, in theory, which of them got to the Great Room first, so long as they beat the competition to their destination. And yet...

He could not quite restrain himself from cutting her off. "I have four inches on you, love. Enjoy the view from behind."

Up the cliff. Around the front. Into the house. Rohan made it to the Great Room less than five seconds before Savannah did. He'd fully intended to allow her entrance then lock the others out, but the door to the Great Room had been removed.

Coming to a standstill at the threshold, Rohan took in the sight before him.

"Dominoes," Savannah said, scanning the pattern: thousands of dominoes, made of gold and positioned just so, lines and loops, a complicated design covering the entire Great Room except for a narrow path that went from the door to a round table that stood at the center of the room. All other furniture had been removed.

Savannah stepped foot on the path, just as Brady hit the foyer.

"Tread carefully, love." Rohan eyed the dominoes.

Savannah didn't so much as look back or break her stride. "Don't call me *love*."

Rohan took to the path himself, and Brady followed Rohan, and in less than a minute, all five of the players were standing around the circular table. Its top was made of rings of metal—bronze around the outside, then silver, then gold. On it were five crystal champagne flutes bearing deep red liquid.

Rohan plucked one into the air, examining the design of the flute. Cut into the crystal, there was an *H*. His mind already fast at work, Rohan made a show of taking a sip. "Tastes of pomegranate. Mythologically speaking, I might be stuck here now."

A pomegranate cocktail. A round table. A crystal H. Rohan's gaze slid over the complicated, swirling lines of dominoes on the floor as the other players each claimed a glass.

The moment the last glass was lifted off the table, the first domino fell. The click of golden tile against golden tile became a roar as one line of dominoes triggered two more triggered two more, until all around the room, swirls and loops and lines were going off at all once.

Like fireworks.

The metal rings on the tabletop began to move. They split down the center, separating to reveal a compartment underneath. In it were five golden objects. *Darts.*

Savannah moved to grab one, but Rohan intercepted her, his touch stilling her hand as he took the lay of the land. The five darts were arranged like a flower or a star, needle-sharp tips in the center, flights to the outside. Around the display, words had been carved into the wood of the table, curving around the darts.

"Every story has its beginning . . . ," Rohan read aloud. *"Take only one."*

Chapter 12

GIGI

Gigi's interrogation could have been going better. Her target had the silent, broody thing down. She was having about as much success as she would have cheerfully interrogating a tangerine.

A tangerine with an eyebrow scar, jagged tattoos, and pecs of steel. That last bit was an extrapolation, but Gigi had great faith in her ability to extrapolate about chest muscles. All muscles, really. Fortunately, she also had faith in the power of persistence.

Eventually, Code Name Mimosas would break. They all did, sooner or later.

"Let's play a game," Gigi said, like her captor hadn't been very effectively ignoring her for hours. "It's called True or False."

Based on the total lack of light coming from the cracks in the stone wall, Gigi knew that it was dark outside—and had been for a while now. The only reason she could even still *see* Mimosas was that when the last of the light from the outside had faded, he'd lit a candle, which was now sitting on the floor in a heavy silver candleholder that looked like it had been plucked straight out of the eighteenth century.

"I don't play games."

He responded! Now that Gigi's target had cracked open the metaphorical window, all she had to do was limbo in, Reverse Heist style.

"Okay," Gigi chirped. "Then let's play a game. It's called Negative or Affirmative."

"That's the same game."

Gigi smiled winningly. "In fairness, I reversed the order. But fine, if you want to be that way, then let's play a game. It's called Yeppers or Nope."

This time, her kidnapper leaned back against the door and said absolutely nothing.

Challenge accepted. "I can do this all day, tangerine. Let's play a game. It's called Computer. You're the computer. The game is in binary. Zero is no. One is yes."

"Stop." Well, that tone was ominous! But possibly a good kind of ominous?

Really, Mimosas was probably going to come to regret—if he hadn't already—assuring Gigi that he wasn't going to hurt her, because Gigi believed him wholeheartedly. She figured she had a couple of hours, max, before one Hawthorne or another came riding to her rescue, and she considered it her solemn duty to put that time to good use.

"Let's play a game. It's called Stop or Go. You gave me the idea for this one! I'll say something. If it's true, you say *go*, and if it's not, you say—"

"Stop."

"Very good!" Gigi grinned. "What's your name?"

"That's not a yes or no question."

Gigi shrugged. "I'm a cheater. I've never met a Monopoly bank I didn't rob. True or false: Your name is…Sebastian? Aaron? Damon?" She paused. "What I'm hearing is that you *want* me calling you Mimosas, capital *M*, and/or tangerine, lowercase *t*, indefinitely."

"Slate."

Now, she was getting somewhere! "Your name is Slate?"

"True. And false. And that's as much of your game as I'm playing."

Gigi replied like *he* had just posed a question: "False."

Slate—like the rock, like rock-hard abs—was not amused. "Hasn't anyone ever told you that it's a bad idea to argue with the guy with the knife?"

Gigi's gaze went to Slate's hand. Based on what she could see in the candlelight, he was indeed holding a knife—but she was ninety-four percent sure it was sheathed, and if *Slate* thought he could scare her, he was wrong. Gigi Grayson was made of sterner and far less sensible stuff than that.

"Is that the knife that spent most of last night strapped to my thigh?" Gigi asked. "Because if so, that knife and I are friends. And frankly, Slate, people tell me lots of things are bad ideas. It's kind of hard to keep track."

Now that Gigi had gotten *an* answer out of him, proper interrogation technique said to nudge the conversation toward what she actually wanted to know, in this case: (1) what he and Eve were up to, (2) what role the Grandest Game played in their nefarious plans, and (3) what Slate had meant when he'd very clearly implied that Eve was not the only threat out there.

"True or false," Gigi said, "Eve has a player in the game." That was a guess, but it was a logical one. Gigi had been told that there was a group of wealthy individuals who had made the annual Grandest Game into a game of their own. Maybe Eve was one of them. Maybe she was in this to prove that she was more formidable than anyone gave her credit for being.

As much as Gigi hated to admit it, she could understand that. "True or false: Eve has a deep-seated psychological need to win the admiration, respect, and/or affection of others."

No response from Slate.

"True or false," Gigi continued brightly—and *mercilessly*, "Eve's player in the Grandest Game has not been eliminated yet. If they had been, you wouldn't have cared that I found the bug." Gigi gave into the urge to randomly finger-gun. "Setting aside my siblings, that leaves Brady, Lyra, and Rohan—and your brood just got significantly broodier when I said Brady's name."

Honestly, Gigi wasn't sure what to make of that.

"Furthermore…" Sherlock Gigi was on the case. "My well-honed instincts are telling me that Rohan's shoulders are far too broad for him to be anyone's lackey—like I'm talking almost *supernaturally* broad in proportion to his waist."

"Anyone ever tell you that you're a bad judge of character?"

"All the time!" Gigi smiled through the sting of Slate's assessment. Even just saying Brady's name had reminded her of how badly she'd misread that situation. Gigi had trusted Brady Daniels—and she shouldn't have.

"Is it Lyra?" Gigi asked. "Because I really hope for Grayson's sake that Eve's player in the game isn't Lyra."

More silence.

Time for another subject change to keep him off guard. "The marks on the sheath of your knife—what do they mean?" Gigi knew from having counted them during the game that there were thirteen total.

"Maybe they're people I've kidnapped. Or horrible things I've done."

That second option had the ring of truth—not that Gigi could claim to be particularly good at realizing when someone was lying to her. "Let's play a game. It's called Yes, No, or Maybe."

Slate took an audible step toward her. "Okay, sunshine. Let's play." His hair wasn't in his face anymore, but with so little light, Gigi still couldn't make out the scar through his eyebrow.

Time to make this question count. "Is there someone else on Hawthorne Island?"

"Define *someone else.*"

"Not the players. Not the game makers. Not you. Not Eve."

"Maybe." Slate was staring directly at her now.

"Last night," Gigi said, "when the power went out—was that you and/or Eve?"

Slate looked down at the knife in his hand. "No."

Finally, she'd gotten some real intel out of him, an actual piece of the puzzle. When he'd suggested that there was another threat out there, he *had* meant on Hawthorne Island, interfering with the game. *Another sponsor?*

Gigi's sixth sense for broody boys told her that that she'd gotten about all she was going to get out of Slate—for now.

Her gaze drifted of its own volition back down to the knife in his hand—*definitely sheathed*—and she had to ask: "How many horrible things have you done?"

"Counting this?" Slate slipped his knife from the sheath. "Counting you?" He used the edge of the blade to add a notch to the leather. "Fourteen."

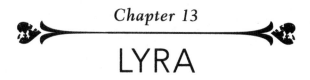

Chapter 13

LYRA

Lyra's hand closed around a golden dart. *Five darts. Five players.* For an elongated moment, all of them stood there, each holding a dart and taking measure of the others.

The game was on.

Lyra looked down to the words carved into the table. *EVERY STORY HAS ITS BEGINNNING...* The game makers had said that phrase before. It was even engraved on the players' room keys. *That has to mean something.*

Across the table, Brady lifted his dart up even with his eyes. To Lyra's right, Savannah started disassembling hers. Rohan took a sip from his champagne glass, then pointed the tip of his dart at Grayson.

"You have the look of a man who knows something," Rohan declared.

"I don't know anything." Grayson rotated his own dart in his fingertips, studying every golden inch of it. "Yet."

Lyra kept her eyes on the competition as her fingers began to explore her own dart. Etched lines encircled its shaft, each forming a complete ring. At intervals, other marks slashed across the rings, diagonal lines, scattered on all sides of the shaft.

Brady suddenly closed his fist around his dart and walked out of the room.

"And then there were four." Rohan made a show of lifting his champagne flute to his lips once more, seemingly unconcerned with his dart—or anyone else's.

The darts might not be the clue. Lyra processed that. The promised *first clue* in the Great Room could be the champagne flutes or the dominoes or the words scrawled across the table.

Rohan lowered his flute and turned his attention wholly and noticeably to Savannah. He looked at her like looks could do more than kill—like looks could *touch.*

"Rohan." Grayson's eyes narrowed slightly. "I'd like a word."

Rohan met Grayson's gaze and offered up a dauntless, taunt-the-devil smile, and then he set his champagne flute on the table and lifted his right hand to Savannah's face.

From what Lyra knew of Savannah Grayson, that seemed like a good way to lose a hand, but Savannah allowed it.

Rohan slowly trailed his fingers along Savannah's jaw and down the lines of her neck. *"Ambrosial,"* Rohan said. *"Sybaritic. Voluptuary.* That's three words for you, Mr. Hawthorne."

Sensing danger, Lyra felt compelled to return a favor from the night before. She lifted her hand and placed it on the back of Grayson's neck, silent encouragement for him to refrain from murder.

"I, too, know words," Grayson told Rohan, his tone contemplative—and chilling. "I'll allow you to imagine which ones I'm thinking right now."

"Alas, my imagination is without peer." Rohan twirled his golden dart through warm brown fingers, then picked his crystal champagne flute back up with the same hand that held the dart and raised it toward Grayson in a silent toast. "And so is your sister."

The muscles in Grayson's neck tightened under Lyra's touch, but his ironclad control held.

Rohan pushed his luck and winked at Grayson, then sauntered out of the room, raking his gaze over the fallen dominoes as he did. Savannah went to follow, and Grayson placed himself directly in his sister's path.

"Savannah? Do be careful."

"I could tell you the same," Savannah replied, "but you're male, and it's my understanding that men never have to be careful. Anatomy is fascinating that way, is it not?"

Lyra snorted. In other circumstances, she might have liked Grayson's sister.

Head held high, Savannah stepped around Grayson and exited the Great Room without ever breaking her stride.

Grayson turned to Lyra. "I assure you, I would have given either of my younger *brothers* the same warning."

"Have you always been this overprotective?" Lyra asked.

"I have always been precisely as protective as I need to be."

Lyra thought about Grayson putting his body between hers and the cliff's edge—and then she forcibly redirected her thoughts. "The clue might not be the dart."

Grayson eyed the golden dominoes that littered the Great Room floor, then moved to kneel over one section in particular. "This one's a Fibonacci spiral. Xander's work, no doubt." Grayson studied the spiral for a moment, then held up his dart. "But *this* has Jameson's name written all over it."

Jameson was the brother with whom Grayson had disappeared at the bonfire. "How so?" Lyra asked, as she came to stand over Grayson and the spiraling domino pattern on the floor.

"Jameson is...competitive. Intensely and frequently reckless. Fearless to a fault. Our mother always referred to him as *hungry*." There was an undertone to Grayson's voice that Lyra couldn't quite pin down. "Jamie's specialty has always been wanting things with an intensity that puts the sun to shame—every win, every answer, every rush."

And you never let yourself want anything at all. Lyra crouched beside Grayson, picking up a golden domino and turning it over in her hand to reveal its face: five dots to one side of the line down the center and three on the other. Lyra flipped another domino and found the same combination. *Five and three.*

Lyra reached for her jacket pocket—and her glass dice. She rolled them and then looked meaningfully at Grayson. "Five and three."

Grayson produced his own pair of dice, red to her white, and rolled them. "Six and two." He turned over a domino to reveal the same combination of numbers.

Five and three. Six and two. "What does it mean?" Lyra asked, thinking out loud. "The fact that the numbers are the same."

Grayson stood. "In my grandfather's games, we called them *echoes*—details or motifs that repeated themselves from game to game or within games. Some echoes meant nothing. Some were the lynchpin, the single most significant thing in an entire puzzle sequence. You never know what kind of echo you're dealing with— until you know." Grayson glanced toward the Great Room door. "Shall we remove ourselves to somewhere with a bit more privacy?"

To work the puzzle, Lyra told herself. *And that is all.* She gathered her dice, her other hand holding the champagne flute from which she'd yet to take a single sip. "Where to?"

"My room." Grayson pocketed his own dice, plucked his champagne flute off the table, and made his way to the edge of the Great Room and around to a place on the wall where they'd discovered a hidden door the day before. From the same pocket into which his dice had just disappeared, Grayson produced a bronze room key seemingly identical to Lyra's own. He held his key flat against the wall, and the hidden door swung open, revealing the darkened staircase beyond.

"They couldn't have just assigned you to one of the eliminated players' bedrooms?" Lyra asked wryly.

"Hawthorne logic," Grayson replied. "Making me find the room was half the fun." Nodding toward the stairwell, he bowed at the waist and met her gaze. "After you."

Chapter 14

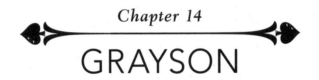

GRAYSON

As Grayson descended the darkened staircase, listening for the sound of Lyra's footfalls ahead of him, Jameson's warning echoed through his mind. *Lyra Kane is a threat, whether you see it or not.* Grayson took the lead at the bottom of the stairs, trying to shift his focus to the present: the metal chamber, the theater, door after door, the feel of Lyra walking in his wake.

Be sure that she's worth it, Gray. Make damn sure that she's not Eve.

Grayson came to a stop at the threshold of the mosaic ballroom. In its center, there was now a single piece of furniture: a king-sized bed. *Black frame. Black pillows. Black sheets.* Grayson's mask and tuxedo from the masquerade ball had been laid out across those sheets.

"*This* is your room?" Lyra asked.

"For the duration of the Grandest Game." Grayson crossed the dark, glittering ballroom and knelt at the foot of the onyx bed. He set first his key, then the champagne flute and golden dart, on the floor, then withdrew a longsword from beneath the bed, placing it beside the other objects. "At the start of a game," he told Lyra, "it helps to lay out all of the pieces of the puzzle that you've been given." Grayson produced the glass dice he'd found zipped into the pocket of his jacket when he'd put on his outfit for phase two. He added them to the other objects and studied the entire collection.

"Your turn," Grayson told Lyra.

With effortless grace, she sank to the floor, laying out her own objects, and then she flipped over her wrist. Grayson's gaze landed on the pin she'd affixed to her sleeve.

He stopped her from removing it. "The pin isn't a part of the game. We gave them to the top ten players last year, too."

Once a player, always a player, Avery had said then. From the moment she'd conceived of the Grandest Game, Avery had wanted the players to feel like they were a part of something, like having played the game meant something, even if you didn't win.

Grayson and his brothers had given Avery a pin once, too.

"I'll take your word for it." Lyra picked up Grayson's room key and her own, comparing the two, rotating them in her fingers. Grayson saw what she saw: The same words were engraved—front and back—on both keys.

EVERY STORY HAS ITS BEGINNING... TAKE ONLY YOUR OWN KEY.

"An echo," Grayson told Lyra. "The wording is nearly identical to that on the table upstairs."

Lyra tilted her head slightly to one side and then she went for the opera glasses that hung over her hipbone. Lifting them to her face, she examined the words on the keys anew.

"Anything?" Grayson asked.

"No." Lyra lowered the opera glasses and slid them back through her belt loop, and Grayson's thoughts went to their original owner. *Odette Morales.* The old woman knew something—more than she'd told them—and Grayson had spent much of his childhood being taught how and where to apply pressure to get results. But for now...

"Your instincts were good." Grayson nodded toward the opera glasses on Lyra's hip. "Those will give us an advantage at some point in all of this."

"All of this." Lyra's amber eyes gleamed with something like anticipation—or determination or both. *"Clue to clue to clue."*

"A true Hawthorne game," Grayson replied. "Nearly every puzzle sequence my grandfather ever designed started with a collection of objects just like this." Grayson paused, his gaze lingering on the objects, one by one. "Keys were a favorite of the old man's."

Keys—and knives. Rings. Glass. Grayson thought for the first time in years about a specific object in a specific game: a glass ballerina.

"Did your grandmother play the same kind of games?" Lyra asked.

Alice. "I wouldn't know," Grayson said. That was the truth, but it was also dissembling as a matter of precaution. Jameson had been very clear that any talk of Alice was a liability.

"My dreams are starting to feel like one of your grandfather's games," Lyra said beside him. "Like my father laid an array of objects and riddles out before me, right before he died. Omega. *A Hawthorne did this.* A calla lily. A necklace with three pieces of candy." Lyra's eyes found his like flames cutting through night. *"Three,* Grayson."

There are always three. Grayson let that thought come.

"With a Hawthorne game, how do you know what any of it means?" Lyra pressed.

Grayson felt the pull to delve into this mystery with her, but he had given Jameson until the end of the game, and his word was his bond. "The only way to ever really know what any element of a Hawthorne game means," Grayson said, reaching for his champagne flute and redirecting Lyra's attention, "is to play." He lifted the crystal to his lips, taking a taste. "Pomegranate—and a hint of elderflower liqueur."

Lyra mirrored his action, taking a sip out of her own flute.

Grayson did his best not to dwell on the shape of her lips. "The drink. The glass. The dart." He paused, just a fraction of a second, holding her gaze. "The numbers from the dominoes and the dice. The sword. The key."

Grayson saw the exact moment that he had her—here, now, focused on the game, *safe*. And still, he knew that this victory was temporary.

Lyra Catalina Kane was not the type to back down—from anything—for long.

Chapter 15

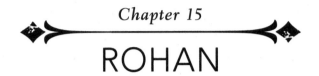

ROHAN

R ohan surveyed the room around him. The fifth-floor library was circular, its curved shelves stocked with what had to be at least a thousand books. Rohan trailed his hand along spine after spine, committing the titles of the books to memory and waiting for Savannah to say it.

"Use me again to get to my brother, and you will find yourself flat on your back and seeing stars." The lady did not disappoint. Rohan admired her restraint, given that she'd waited until they were well and truly alone to issue those words in that cut-crystal voice of hers.

"Is that a promise?" Rohan replied, his inflection just wicked enough to make it clear that the prospect of being *flat on his back* was not altogether unappealing. There was, after all, more than one way to see stars.

He began to circle the room, and Savannah blocked him. "What are we doing up here?" She punctuated that question with a hand on Rohan's chest.

He shifted his gaze from the books on the shelves to the champagne glass in Savannah's other hand. "You should try it." He nodded to the liquid in the flute.

"If I work up a thirst, perhaps I will. My question remains."

She wanted to know what they were doing here. Rohan obliged her. "Stained glass on the ceiling. Shelves. Books." He held Savannah's silvery gaze for a moment longer, then side-stepped her and continued his circuit of the room. "Ever work a maze, love? Start at the beginning and there might be dozens of wrong turns you can take, dozens of dead ends. But start at the end of the maze and work your way back, and you'll find far fewer. In a game that goes from clue to clue, each puzzle's solution must point to the *location* of the next clue."

"Landmarks." Savannah's icy blue-gray eyes narrowed very slightly, emphasizing the equally slight widening of her pupils.

"Landmarks—or notable objects." Rohan finished his circuit of the room. "A finite number of solutions, no matter how dazzlingly complicated the puzzles. Perhaps there's a book on those shelves whose title relates somehow to darts—or targets. Perhaps not. But the fact that we've been up here, that we've reminded ourselves of the contents of this room, will open our mind to possible answers—for this clue and the next and the next."

With that, Rohan headed for the spiral staircase. They had more ground to cover. "For the record?" he said, beginning his descent. "I wasn't using you to get to Grayson downstairs. I was allowing you to use me." Rohan had overheard Savannah's warning to Lyra at the bonfire, and he'd inherently understood that Savannah had not just been talking about *Lyra* falling into the Hawthorne trap.

When Savannah had said *he won't choose you*, she'd been speaking from experience.

"Your brother hurt you." Rohan took his life in his own hand by daring to say that out loud. "Badly."

"Half brother, and I've told you before: I do not do anything badly." Savannah's control was absolute. "Steps," she noted pointedly. "A railing." *Possible end points to clues.* They came to the fourth-floor landing, and Savannah continued, "Seven bedrooms. A clock."

"Not just a clock." Rohan took note of the minute and hour hands, the Roman numerals showing the time. "It's thirty seconds faster than our watches."

"And that means...?" Savannah had a way of making every question sound like a challenge.

"Nothing yet," Rohan replied. "Perhaps nothing in perpetuity." He hopped up on the railing and slid the rest of the way down to the foyer. He landed on the marble and immediately crouched to run his hand over the floor. "The dining room, study, and Great Room all played a large role in phase one," he noted, "which makes them lower-value targets for our purposes, excepting the new additions to the Great Room."

"The dominoes. The table. The darts and champagne flutes." Savannah sank into a crouch next to Rohan, seemingly for the sole purpose of staring him down. "I would wager, however," she said, "that our first puzzle won't lead to another clue in the same room, which means the Great Room is out. In fact, I would wager our next clue isn't in this house at all. We're dressed for the elements."

Indeed you are, love.

"What would we find if we went down another floor?" Rohan challenged.

"Two doors." No one did *unimpressed* like Savannah Grayson. "One covered in gears and the other made of white marble, struck through with gold."

"Awfully fond of gold in this game, aren't they?" Rohan said, producing his dart.

"Golden dart, golden door." Savannah stood. "Too obvious. Besides which, the door in question has a three-tiered dial on it. We'll know when a clue leads there, because the answer to the previous puzzle will be three numbers."

"In that case, love..." Rohan rose to his feet beside her. "Shall we see what the great outdoors has to offer? Race you to the place where we first met."

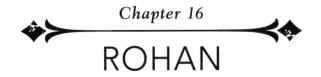

Chapter 16

ROHAN

"What do you see?" Rohan posed the question from the top of the flagpole.

"A starry night and not much else." Savannah gave herself a moment to take in the view from fifty feet up.

Rohan removed his right hand from the pole and brought his fingertips to lightly brush Savannah's temple. "What do you *see*?" he repeated. His own mind laid out every detail of the island over the darkness of night. "The ruins. The burned forest, the living one. Stone arches with a dock beneath. Thorny brush. The helipad. The house. And beneath one of the many cliffs on this island, a bonfire I would wager no longer burns. What else?"

Rohan had been trained to miss nothing, but the point of having an ally was, in part, a matter of additional perspective.

"A stone staircase," Savannah said in the darkness. "Another dock. Evidence."

"Of?" Rohan prompted.

As ever, there was no hesitation in Savannah Grayson: "What Hawthornes can get away with by being Hawthornes."

She was talking about the devastating fire, decades past—and about her father. *Is it the Hawthornes you blame—or is it Avery Grambs?* Savannah's anger was a many-layered beast. From Rohan's perspective, it was both a strength and a weakness.

Use the strength now. Exploit the weakness later.

"Channel it, love."

"You seem to be confused." Even in darkness, Savannah could make the arch of her brow *heard* in the tone of her voice alone. "You aren't the teacher here, British. I'm not your pupil. I am here for a reason, and it is not you."

Rohan smiled. "I'm a magnificent bastard, love. I'm not anyone's reason." Their limbs were very nearly entangled on the pole. Rohan brought his face closer to hers, his lips to her ear. "Picture in your mind a golden dart. Don't think. Don't hesitate. Don't even breathe. What are we looking for, Savvy?"

Answers flew through his own mind.

"A dartboard," Savannah said. "Or a tar—"

Rohan's well-honed senses sent up a warning. "Eyes," he told Savannah. "On us."

They had company. In the darkness of the night, it took Rohan a moment to locate the company in question. *Hello, Mr. Daniels.*

"In a game like this one," Rohan told Savannah, "some contenders play the game, and some play the other players. The logical alternative to solving the puzzles is to track your competitors as *they* solve them."

Rohan really should have known better than to say something like that to Savannah Grayson. In an instant, she was flying down the flagpole. Rohan followed but held back slightly, interested to see how she would play this.

"The girl you're playing for." Savannah addressed Brady with that high-society voice of hers, diamonds and iron. "The one you lost. What was her name?"

Brady didn't so much as blink. "Her name is Calla."

Is, Rohan thought. *Present tense.*

"You're playing this game—and trying to win—for *Calla*." Savannah didn't make that a question. "Money can move mountains. Or maybe your sponsor can?"

Right for the jugular.

Brady stared at Savannah for a moment. "You're nothing like your sister."

Savannah had succeeded in getting under his skin. Brady was trying to do the same to her. Gigi was a weak point for Savannah—one of very few.

But in response to Brady's words, Savannah showed no weakness. "I was born first. It would be more accurate to say that Gigi is nothing like me."

Chapter 17

GIGI

"For the last time, stop asking questions and *go to sleep*." The borderline growl in Slate's voice meant that he was probably getting close to breaking. Gigi could tell.

"But sleep deprivation is so much fun," she replied, laying back on the fur throw he'd so thoughtfully provided for her. It was the little details that really made a kidnapping. She folded her arms behind her head and stared up into the darkness of their mysterious abode like she was stargazing. "One time, I stayed up all night and had so much coffee that I hallucinated a mouse in overalls sitting on a non-hallucinatory policeman's shoulders." Gigi smiled beatifically. "But if *you* want to get some sleep, go right ahead."

"Nice try, sunshine. I won't be sleeping tonight." There was the slightest flash of light in the darkness. *His phone.*

"Expecting a call?" Gigi asked. "From someone Eve-il, perhaps?"

"I'm not talking to you about Eve."

Definite growl this time. Progress!

"I know who her father is." Gigi propped herself up on her elbows. Sometimes, the trick to getting someone to talk was just to refuse to stop talking until they complied. "Grayson let it slip. Eve is Toby Hawthorne's biological daughter—Toby, of course, being Grayson's mysterious uncle, who is totally not dead anymore."

"Not a Hawthorne anymore, either," Slate pointed out.

Grayson had once told Gigi that the situation in question was *complicated.* "Once a Hawthorne, always a Hawthorne," she replied.

"Yeah, well, tell that to Eve."

That's what this is about, Gigi realized, suddenly as sure of that as she was of her own name. Eve wasn't interfering with the Grandest Game as part of some broader competition with a bunch of other rich sponsors. This was personal.

"Daddy issues?" Gigi guessed. "I know them well."

Slate reverted to broodier-than-thou silence, and Gigi decided to change tactics.

"Tell me, my blond, nefarious friend, do you ever feel compelled to do the right thing? The heroic thing?" Gigi adopted a stage-whisper: "Blink once for yes and twice for no."

"There's almost no light in here. You can't see my eyes. And we aren't friends."

"Yes, we are, and as it happens, I'm sporadically psychic. My powers of intuition tell me that you aren't blinking at all." If Gigi could find the goodness in him—if *he* could find it—maybe she could talk him into letting her go.

It hardly even counted as having gotten yourself kidnapped if it lasted less than eight hours.

"You want to know what I think about doing the right thing, sunshine? About trying to be a hero?" There was no growl in Slate's voice now and no emotion, no emphasis at all. "I think that I'm always at my most dangerous when my intentions are good."

Like right now? Gigi's fingers gently stroked the soft fabric beneath her. "You could let me go," she said quietly.

"You could go to sleep."

Not likely, bucko. "Returning to the topic of Eve and daddy issues," Gigi said grandly, and then suddenly, she stopped—because suddenly, a half dozen different details came together in her mind.

Details like the necklace that she'd worn in the game, which had turned out to be a two-way communication device that had almost certainly been meant for someone else. A *female* someone.

Details like the fact that when Gigi had considered potential candidates for Eve's player in the game, she'd focused on only three of the five remaining players.

Details like THE SECRET that Gigi had been keeping for the past year-and-a-half.

This is personal.

Daddy issues.

"You okay?" Slate asked. Apparently, he didn't trust her silence, but Gigi barely even heard him.

All she could do was think about was the fact that more than a year earlier, when Slate had first approached her, Gigi had been searching for her father, and Grayson had been trying to make sure she didn't find out the truth.

THE SECRET.

What if Slate knew? What if Eve did? Gigi's heart pounded in her throat. *Daddy issues.*

"Eve's player in the game." Gigi didn't want to ask, but she had to. "Is it my sister?"

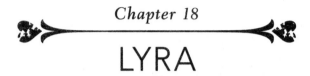

Chapter 18

LYRA

An H cut in crystal. Five and three, six and two. A golden dart. Lyra drained the last of the liquid in her champagne flute. Grayson had been right, there was a floral taste—a little bitter, a little sweet. Like honey and roses.

"Tune out everything but the dart," Grayson said beside her on the mosaic floor.

"Is that a suggestion or an order?" Lyra replied.

"Do you take orders?" Grayson asked archly.

"Not very well."

"And do you think that fact has escaped me?"

Lyra gave a little shrug. "Probably not."

"Then I suppose," Grayson told her, "that logic dictates it was a suggestion."

Lyra picked up her golden dart. "The design," she said, running her thumbnail along the shaft of the dart, stopping when she hit the first slash she'd felt back in the Great Room. "Rings cut through with diagonal lines."

Grayson made quick work of inspecting his own dart. "There are ten diagonal slashes, equally sized, dispersed around the dart's circumference. What's the pattern?"

There's always a pattern, isn't there? Lyra closed her eyes, rotating the dart in her fingers, feeling for the slashes—ten of them, just as Grayson had said.

"You are forever doing that," Grayson commented. "Closing your eyes."

"I'm not a visual person." For Lyra, that was an understatement. "I need to feel things." With her eyes closed, Lyra couldn't even summon an image of Grayson's face to her mind, but the way the contours of his body *felt* against hers, the way he smelled faintly of cedar and fallen leaves—

"One mark every four rings." Lyra clipped her words and opened her eyes. "That's the pattern."

"Four rings. A diagonal line." Grayson's voice shifted. "Tally marks."

Twisting the dart in her fingers, Lyra saw that he was right. Viewed from any one perspective, she could see what looked like hashmarks: four lines with a fifth cutting through the diagonal. "Five, ten..." She stopped counting and leapt straight to the answer. *"Fifty."*

"Bull's-eye," Grayson said beside her. "In darts, the only way to get fifty points with a single throw is to hit the bull's-eye."

Adrenaline flooded Lyra's veins. "So we're looking for a bull or an eye or a target."

"A target."

Lyra's heart leapt in her chest. "What do you know, Hawthorne?"

"Where on this island have we seen a target?" Grayson replied.

Lyra pushed down the urge to grab him by the front of the shirt and request he get on with it. "I told you, I'm not a visual person."

Grayson laid his dart to the side and picked up his champagne flute. "The answer's right here, a very Hawthorne kind of hint." He reached for Lyra's hand, and she allowed him to bring both his and hers to touch the champagne flute, tracing their thumbs in a slow circle around the *H* cut into the crystal.

Lyra had told him that she needed to *feel* things. He'd listened, and right now, eyes wide open, she felt far too much.

"An encircled *H*," Grayson told her, "is the typical marking for a helipad."

Lyra thought back to landing on Hawthorne Island. She couldn't see the helipad in her mind, but she remembered thinking that Jameson Hawthorne had touched down dead center.

Right on target.

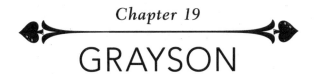

Chapter 19

GRAYSON

Grayson wondered if this was what it had felt like for Jameson and Avery, solving the old man's puzzles. A thrum of energy was palpable in the air as he and Lyra stepped foot on the helipad. Strips of light burst to life all along the edges of the concrete.

There, in the center of the helipad, was the landing target.

"The bull's-eye," Grayson said. He and Lyra moved toward it in perfect synchrony. At the center of the target, there was a circle roughly the length of Grayson's arm from shoulder to fingertip.

Bull's-eye. Grayson knelt to run a hand over its surface, feeling the concrete beneath his palms, pressing at it with his fingers, looking for…

"A latch." Grayson found it and pried it upward. There was a click. He pulled, and the edge of the bull's-eye came up just far enough for him to slip his fingers beneath it. Bracing his body with his legs, Grayson tightened his grip on the concrete.

Lyra slid in beside him, placing her hands next to his. "On three?" she said.

Her voice killed him. *She* did. For once in his life, Grayson truly understood what it was like being hungry, wanting answers, wanting *everything*. "Three," he said.

They put their weight into it, and the disk moved, and soon, they'd removed it altogether, uncovering a circular sheet of metal down below.

"Bull's-eye," Grayson murmured. The metal was smooth, nothing engraved on or cut into its surface, except at the very center, where there was a slit.

Less than two inches wide but not by much, Grayson noted. *No more than two-tenths of an inch high.*

Grayson pressed his hand against the metal, feeling around the slit. The closest thing he had to a flashlight was his watch, so he brought his wrist down to the metal, then lowered his head, trying to look through the slit to whatever his brothers and Avery had hidden below.

"No hinges," Lyra reported, having finished her own assessment. "The metal can't be lifted up or moved. It's locked into place."

Locked. Having played Hawthorne games for as long as he had, Grayson knew exactly what that meant. "We need a key."

"A key," Lyra repeated, and then her eyes lit up, electric in a way that Grayson felt to his core. "Grayson. *For every lock a key.*"

He looked back to the slit in the metal—just large enough for the blade of a sword.

Chapter 20

ROHAN

Rohan smiled in the darkness. Lyra and Grayson may have reached the target on the helipad first, but that meant nothing now.

They need their sword. Rohan kept his voice low. "Stall them, Savvy." He and Savannah were close enough to have heard every word Grayson and Lyra had just said—and far enough away from the light not to be seen themselves. "I have a sword to retrieve."

And one to steal, if I can.

"If you'd worn the sword," Savannah retorted, her voice muted, her gaze on their adversaries, "this wouldn't be an issue."

Rohan let his gaze go down, down, down, to the place where he knew her chain rested, hugging her hipbones. In the dark, Rohan could barely make out anything about her body, but he had an *excellent* memory.

"To each their own, love. I don't believe in weighing myself down."

Rohan didn't bother telling her *how* to stall the other team. She was Savannah Grayson. She'd figure it out.

Rohan hadn't hidden the sword in *his* room. He made it back to the fifth floor of the mansion, to the library with its circular shelves, in record time. Rohan had always had a soft spot for libraries.

He'd also always had an unerring sense for knowing when he had company.

"I'm a bit busy at the moment, Mr. Hawthorne." Rohan didn't so much as glance back over his shoulder. There was an art to cultivating an air of omniscience.

"And here I had you pegged as the stop-to-smell-the-roses type," Jameson quipped.

Rohan locked a hand around the mahogany bookshelf at eye level and began to climb. "Ask me if I've ever incapacitated a grown man using nothing but a rose."

"I would ask," the Hawthorne he knew best said, "but you'd probably lie."

"I probably would," Rohan agreed. Once he'd made it ten feet up, he let go of the shelf with one hand and used that hand to lean an entire row of books forward in one motion. Reaching past those books, Rohan locked his fingers around the hilt of the sword.

"If I told you that someone in this game is a threat..." Jameson didn't bother to mask the sound of his footsteps as he closed in on Rohan. "What would you say?"

Rohan dropped to the floor, longsword in hand, then straightened to meet Jameson's gaze head-on. "Honestly? I'd say that the odds are fairly good it's me."

"You're playing for the Mercy." Jameson did not phrase that as a question.

"You seem confident about that," Rohan replied.

"I'm confident to a fault—and better at math than I look. Two possible heirs. One dying old man. How *is* the duchess?"

Jameson Hawthorne and Avery Grambs had been allowed into the hallowed halls of the Devil's Mercy not as members but as guests. But that had been enough for them to acquaint themselves with Rohan's rival for the throne.

The duchess was rather memorable.

At the moment, however, that was neither here nor there. "You need something, Mr. Hawthorne, and I have somewhere to be." There were few things that Rohan recognized as immediately and innately as the kind of opportunity provided by another person's *need*. "What exactly is it that you would like to know?"

Information was currency, and Jameson clearly hadn't come here in the middle of the game to talk to Rohan about the succession of the Devil's Mercy.

"Lyra Kane." That was all Jameson said.

Rohan had to admit: He had not seen this coming. "The plot thickens."

"Get me something I can use to disqualify her and send her home." Jameson's voice was low in a way that made Rohan think the words cost him.

Your brother won't thank you for that. In the labyrinth that was his mind, Rohan could feel the corridors rearranging themselves. There was a particular room—more a vault, really—where Rohan kept bits and pieces of information that he knew *would* matter a great deal, even if he did not yet know why.

This request—and that tone in Jameson's voice—certainly qualified.

"And what if Ms. Kane has done nothing wrong?" Rohan queried, testing his opponent. "What if she is not the threat?" Rohan's mind went to Savannah, but he could not afford for Jameson's to do the same, so he provided another outlet for Jameson Hawthorne's suspicions. "Brady Daniels."

"Is he working with a sponsor?" Jameson said immediately.

"Would you like for me to find out?" Rohan replied. "Assuming, of course, that it would be to my benefit to do so."

"Any player disqualified from the game is one fewer player for you to worry about," Jameson pointed out, and then he smirked at Rohan. "I assume this is the part where you tell me that you are not the kind of person who *worries*."

"This is the part," Rohan said, "where I tell you that specificity is your friend. If you're worried about a *particular* sponsor..." Rohan leaned very slightly toward Jameson. "Do share the particulars."

"Cue the part where I tell you that *I* don't worry."

Not feeling forthcoming, Hawthorne? Rohan lackadaisically swung the longsword in his hand up to hold it vertically, directly between them. "If you have nothing else to tell me, then I'm afraid *this* is the part where I ask you to get out of my way—politely, of course."

"Of course," Jameson replied, stepping to the side.

Rohan strode past him toward the spiral staircase.

"If you lose," Jameson called, "does Zella automatically win the Mercy?"

Zella. The duchess. Jameson probably thought he was pressing on a sore spot, but Rohan refused to think about the aristocratic, high-society insider who would have no trouble coming up with the Proprietor's ten-million-pound buy-in should Rohan fail to win the Grandest Game.

"Irrelevant," Rohan called back, projecting his voice to surround them both. "You should know by now, Jameson Hawthorne: I don't lose."

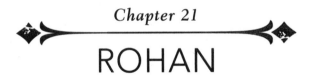

Chapter 21

ROHAN

Rohan abandoned the idea of searching for the other swords and headed straight back to the helipad, but he considered the slight delay and the accompanying shift in his plans to be well worth it. *There's a threat of some sort, and Jameson Hawthorne believes it centers on Lyra Kane.*

"Took you long enough." Savannah was waiting for him at the edge of the landing pad, and she was alone.

Rohan leapt up beside her. "How long did it take your brother to realize you were faking an injury?" That was a guess as to the method's she'd employed.

"Half brother," Savannah corrected. "And long enough. I see you have the sword."

Rohan spun the hilt in his hand. "Shall I do the honors?" Rohan asked. "Or will you?"

Savannah grabbed the hilt directly above Rohan's hand. *The barest brush of skin.* He let her have the sword. There were benefits to letting your adversaries win battles that didn't matter.

As Savannah strode toward the very center of the helipad, Rohan took his sweet time joining her, arriving at her side just as she gripped the hilt with both hands and plunged it into the slit in the metal.

Rohan placed his hands above hers and twisted the sword. Almost immediately, the metal beneath them began to give way, splitting, seams becoming visible for only a second before the entire circle folded in on itself like fanned-out cards being swept back into a single deck.

Rohan jumped for solid ground. Savannah did the same. The taste of anticipation was sweet—almost as sweet as the moment Rohan's gaze landed on the sole object in the hidden compartment they'd just uncovered.

A ledger, bound in leather. Rohan's mind went briefly to another ledger, a very valuable one that would be his once he won the Mercy, but the second he retrieved the Grandest Game ledger, he returned to the here and now. Opening it, Rohan found a single page. *A screen, designed to look like paper.* He pressed his watch to the page.

Like magic, his named appeared in cursive, as if scrawled by his own hand—a neat little digital trick, that. Savannah went next, and her name appeared directly below his. Almost immediately, she was on the move again, and Rohan realized why.

Two more sections of the landing pad had popped up. *Two more hidden compartments, revealed.* One Rohan's. One Savannah's. *Sign the ledger,* Rohan thought, *get another clue.*

Savannah claimed one of the compartments, and Rohan strode

toward the other. Removing its concrete top, he stared at the rectangular cavity underneath. It was perhaps a foot deep and filled with water. Through the liquid, Rohan could make out two objects resting at the bottom of the compartment: a delicate bracelet and a metal charm. Rohan pushed up his sleeve and reached down through the water to claim them. As he did, a voice spoke, the words coming from all around him.

"From every trap be free, for every lock a key." The voice was Jameson's. The phrase was repeated in Avery's voice when Savannah retrieved the objects from the bottom of her compartment. The tilt of Savannah's chin gave away her feelings about *that.*

Deciding against prodding at her, Rohan turned his attention to the charm. *A miniature sword.*

"A charm bracelet and a charm," Savannah summarized tartly.

Turning that over in his head, Rohan stood. Water dripped from his hand onto the helipad. *Drip. Drip. Drip.* The sound—or possibly the sensation—gripped him like a fist tightening bit by bit, and for an instant, Rohan felt his body soaked to the bone, felt air much colder than the November night cutting into his skin like a thousand icy splinters.

Slamming his mental walls back into place, Rohan forced a lazy smile onto his face. *"From every trap be free, for every lock a key."* He relished quoting the words, because when he was relishing anything, taking pleasure or pain in anything, there was only the now. "Repetition."

"We already know that the inscription on the sword meant that it *was* a key." Savannah walked back toward the hidden compartment. She tossed the ledger in, then gripped the longsword's hilt with two hands and twisted it counterclockwise.

Like a deck of cards being fanned out once more, the metal sheet covered the compartment, obscuring the ledger as Savannah pulled the *key* from the *lock*.

Locks and keys. Charms and swords. "A chain," Rohan said out loud, looking from the bracelet to the chain around Savannah's waist. "And a chain." Perhaps that mattered. Perhaps it did not. His mind had a way of moving through multiple trains of thought at once, like a half dozen steam engines going full speed ahead on parallel tracks. "And this isn't the first time the game has repeated a key phrase."

"From every trap be free, for every lock a key and…" Savannah moved toward Rohan. *"Every story has its beginning."* It was clear, just from the way she moved, that she could have done some real damage with that sword.

"Every story has its beginning," Rohan echoed, and suddenly, his brain reached the end of one of those tracks. "A key phrase, in more ways than one."

Rohan slipped his room key out of the inside pocket of his jacket. Savannah reached for her own. The designs on the heads of their keys were identical, a combination of four shapes: a diamond, a heart, a club, and the infinity symbol—or, tilted sideways, the number *eight*. Words had been engraved into the stem of the key on either side.

EVERY STORY HAS ITS BEGINNING… TAKE ONLY YOUR OWN KEY.

Upon adding their names to the ledger, they'd been given a charm bracelet and a charm. But what if neither of those things was the next clue?

"The water." Rohan crouched next to the compartment from which he'd retrieved the bracelet and the charm. "There's a reason for it." He closed his eyes and breathed in. The smell was faint, but it was there. "This *isn't* water."

He opened his eyes in time to see Savannah crouch beside him. "I am splendid, am I not?" Rohan said.

"You don't want me to answer that," Savannah told him. Her lips curved as she dropped her key into the compartment. Immediately, the liquid inside bubbled and began to shift colors.

"A chemical reaction," Rohan noted. He gave it a full minute, then thrust his hand down into the liquid, locking his fingers around Savannah's key and pulling it out. Certain letters now jumped out of the phrase that had been engraved on the front of the key, nearly luminescent.

EVERY STORY HAS ITS BEGINNING...

Rohan turned the key over to see one more luminescent letter.

TAKE ONLY YOUR OWN KEY.

Rohan turned the key back and forth in his hand, focused on the letters.

V

I

I

I

L

Adrenaline was an old friend of Rohan's—and so was victory. "Fair warning, love, I'm about to become insufferable."

"You're already insufferable," Savannah said. Rohan could feel her presence beside him, feel the moonlight shining down on them both like warmth on his skin.

Savannah not-so-gently grabbed Rohan's jaw, angling his face toward hers. "Tell me, British, why are you about to become even more insufferable than usual?"

"Because I know exactly what a *V*, three *I*'s, and an *L* spell." Rohan let that sink in, and then he continued, "A finite number of answers. I know where we're going next." He brought his lips within a centimeter of Savannah's, and this time, his smile was downright wicked. "Do you?"

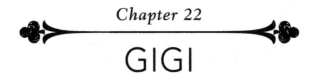

Chapter 22

GIGI

No matter what Gigi said or how she prodded at Slate, he wouldn't tell her whether Savannah was Eve's player in the Grandest Game. Gigi's mind churned with every attempt to get an answer out of him, because the only way she could imagine her take-no-prisoners, make-no-errors twin sister in league with anyone was if Savannah *knew*.

Gigi's twin didn't take orders, not even Grayson's, and Gigi was pretty sure that Grayson could order a solid brick wall to crumble and sprout daisies and it would comply.

"What did Eve tell Savannah?" Gigi demanded, her voice hoarse from talking and talking and talking—with no reply. She stopped beating around the bush. "That our father is dead?" Gigi put a little more pep in her voice. "That he was a murderer? That he died trying to kill Avery Grambs?"

She'd never said any of that out loud before, and the moment she did, THE SECRET was just a secret. *I wanted to keep it.* Gigi couldn't fight the thought—or the tears pricking her eyes. *I wanted to be the one who protected Savannah for once, instead of the other way around.*

Savannah, who'd been their father's favorite.

Savannah, who did not believe in forgiveness.

Savannah, whom Gigi loved more than anyone else in the world.

"For what it's worth, I advised against all this." Slate had retreated far enough into the shadows that Gigi wasn't even sure where he was standing—or *if* he was standing. All she knew was that he'd finally spoken, and his words were confirmation enough.

Savannah knows. Gigi pulled her knees to her chest. For as long as she could remember, her specialty had been choosing happiness, choosing to smile even when everything was wrong. She'd been a happy baby, a happy little girl, *happy* even when she wasn't.

"Did Eve lie to her?" Gigi's voice was small. She'd thought, she'd *really* thought, that she'd been the one pulling back from Savannah these past months and that the rest of it was just distance. Savannah was in college. Gigi wasn't. Savannah was moving on with her life.

Gigi wasn't.

Slate's voice came to her again through darkness, gravelly, quiet, and sure. "There's nothing you can do, either way."

You want to bet? Gigi thought. This interrogation was *over*. She was about eighty percent sure she'd pinpointed his location, her head injury only hurt a *little*, and there was officially no time for a flying tackle like the present. But before Gigi could pounce, there was a buzzing sound. It took her a moment to realize that it was Slate's phone.

The next thing she knew, there was another sound. *A door, opening.* Gigi leapt for it—but not fast enough. By the time she landed, Slate was on the other side, and the door was closed.

There was another sound: a key turning in a lock.

Setting aside any emotional devastation she may or may not have been feeling about Savannah, Gigi pressed her ear to the crack between the frame and the door.

"Yeah?" That was apparently how Slate believed a person should answer the phone. There was a pause and then: "No, *you've* talked about phone manners. I've tuned you out. What do you need?"

Eve? Gigi wondered.

On the other side of the door, Slate spoke again. "No updates." Another pause. "What makes you think I'm not?"

Not what? Gigi wondered.

This time, there was an extended pause, and then: "That's going to be a problem, Eve." Slate said those words like a person who was used to taking care of problems.

Problems, Gigi thought slowly, *like me*. She pressed her ear harder to the door, but Slate must have stepped away from it, because whatever he said next was muffled.

What is she asking you to do? What are you telling her? Gigi liked to think that she'd been a good sport so far. She hadn't panicked even once. But even Gigi's common sense and survival instincts could only be put on mute for so long. Backing away from the door, she took advantage of Slate's absence and grabbed the closest thing she could find to a weapon: the candle in its old-fashioned iron holder.

Did Gigi *want* to set anyone or anything on fire? No, no she did not. But *would* she, if she had to?

Possibly.

Maybe.

Probably.

Settling on that last one, Gigi did the only other rational thing she could think of: She put some distance between herself and her dark-eyed, blond-haired captor. The only place to go was up. Candle in hand, Gigi took to the stone staircase. The steps were, at most, two-and-a-half feet wide—no railing. Even with the candle, Gigi couldn't see much more than a step or two ahead, but that didn't stop her from climbing.

Eventually, the staircase twisted at a ninety-degree angle. Gigi kept going. Down below, she heard the door open, and she picked up her speed. She glanced back just in time to see a small beam of light cut through the darkness—the flashlight on Slate's phone.

The second he realized where she was, he cursed.

Busted. Gigi heard him stalking toward the stairs, and she went from walking up the steps to running, hugging the wall as she went. *Another twist of the stairs.*

Another.

Slate was gaining on her when she made it to the top. A small ladder hung down from a room overhead. Tightening her grip on the candleholder, Gigi stepped onto the bottom rung.

"What the hell is your plan here, sunshine?" Slate called.

Gigi was an expert at ignoring questions like that. She pulled herself up and into a circular room. In the center of the room there was...*A very large lantern?* Gigi approached it to get a better look, then glanced up to see windows surrounding her on all sides. Outside, the night sky was velvety black, lit only by a scattering of stars and a partial moon—just enough for Gigi to make out the moon's reflection on *water.*

Suddenly, she knew what this building was. "A lighthouse." Neurons firing at warp speed, Gigi looked to the candle in her hand, then back at the lantern. *If I'm going to set something on fire...*

"Don't even think about it." Slate climbed into the room.

"Because someone might see the light?" Gigi retorted, her heart pounding in her chest. "A literal beacon to your evil lair—and my location?"

"Because this thing obviously hasn't been functional in decades," Slate replied. "Maybe even a century. You could burn the whole place down."

He turned his flashlight off and tucked the phone into his back pocket, leaving them with only candlelight. *And freeing his hands.*

"Burning things down sounds more like a *you* kind of thing," Gigi said. "Or are you a strict non-arsonist when it comes to taking care of problems?" There was an audible note of hopefulness in her tone.

"I'm not a strict anything."

Gigi frowned. "Why do you sound like that?"

"Like what?" Slate took a step toward her.

Gigi took a step back. "Sad?"

"I don't do sad."

"That's the saddest thing I've ever heard."

"Oh really?" Slate's tone never changed. "You do remember that you were bugged during the game, right? You made it pretty clear to your teammates that you don't do sad, either, even when you should."

I might, Gigi thought. *When I get out of here, when I see Savannah, when I talk to her—I might be sad.*

Slate took another step toward her, and Gigi backed up until she hit the wall of windows. Slate closed in. Standing right in front of her, he lifted his hand to the candleholder, covering her fingers with his before Gigi could attempt to so much as fling it at the glass.

"Fine," Gigi said. Her heart was *still* pounding—harder now. "Neither of us do sad. That's why we're platonic kidnapper-kidnappee soulmates, and that's why you're letting me go."

Slate relieved her of the candleholder—and the candle—and looked her dead in the eyes. "I need you to know that no one is coming for you." The flame flickered between them. "No one is looking for you, no one is watching for your signal, because you aren't *missing*. As it happens, you stole a boat and left a note."

"Whose boat?" Gigi asked immediately. "And what kind of note?"

"Xander Hawthorne's. And you left an IOU for apology Twinkies."

"*Apology Twinkies,*" Gigi gasped with no small amount of horror. That sounded *exactly like her*! "You bastard!"

Slate shrugged. "Step up from muscle-goblin."

"No," Gigi informed him, narrowing her eyes. "It's not."

"I'm going to need you to go back down the ladder now, and then you will walk very carefully down the stairs, staying close to the wall."

"Rest assured"—Gigi lifted her chin—"I am always, never careful."

Slate eyed her. "Can't have you getting hurt on my watch, now can I?" he said. Relief shot through Gigi, but it was short-lived, because the next thing she knew, Slate had picked her up and tossed her over his shoulder.

"Put me down!"

"Playtime's over," Slate told her, climbing back down the ladder like holding a candle *and* a Gigi was nothing. "I have work to do."

That broody-faced, muscle-goblin bastard carried Gigi all the way down the stairs.

"For the record," Slate said, putting her down on solid ground, "*I* am always careful."

"I'm going to hit you now," Gigi announced. "With my fists! Fists of *fury*."

"Knock yourself out, sunshine." He just stood there, waiting.

Gigi did not hit him. "I don't like you," she said instead.

Slate's lips twitched very slightly. "You shouldn't." He nodded toward the fur blanket on the floor. "Get comfortable."

"Why?" Gigi demanded.

"Can't leave you with an open flame," Slate said. "Can't have you trying to scale those stairs in the dark and falling to your death while I'm gone."

"Gone?" Gigi said.

"I've got a job to do."

Gigi's mind went to Eve, to Savannah, to the island. "So you're ordering me to...what? Lay down on that incredibly soft blanket? Get some z's while you're off helping your boss manipulate my twin sister into doing something we'll probably all regret?"

"I *am* sorry about this." For once, he placed the slightest emphasis on one word over the rest. *Am*.

I am sorry about this.

"Which part?" Gigi asked, her voice coming out a little rough.

"The part," Slate replied, "where I'm going to have to have to tie you up."

Chapter 23

LYRA

$\mathcal{E}$VERY STORY HAS ITS BEGINNING... TAKE ONLY YOUR OWN KEY.

Energy surged through Lyra's body as she stared at the writing on her key. Solving a puzzle, getting the next clue—it felt like flying, like walking through fire without getting burned.

V, Lyra thought, her brain and body buzzing. *I, I, I, L.* She looked to Grayson. "These letters don't spell anything. Not enough consonants, too many *I*'s."

"Three of them." Grayson considered that. "The letter *I* is a homophone, which would give us three *eyes*." His gaze flicked up to hers. "Alternatively, letters aren't always letters."

V, I, I, I, L.

Something clicked in Lyra's brain. "Roman numerals. *V* is five. *I* is one. *L* is fifty. It could be a combination." Lyra's mind went to the second floor of the mansion, to a marble door with a multi-tiered dial. "The letters could be grouped in different ways to produce different digits, but if we need three total, the most obvious grouping is V, I-I-I, L. Five, three, fifty."

"Five and three," Grayson said beside her.

Like the dice, Lyra thought. "Grouped a different way, it's six and two," she replied, and then she thought about the dominoes on the floor of the Great Room. "Echoes."

Grayson strode back to the bull's-eye. Lyra watched as he latched his hand around the hilt of their sword. He turned it, locking away the ledger they'd both signed. When that deed was done, he withdrew the sword like Excalibur from the stone without even blinking.

"I would suggest we take a moment," he told Lyra. "A person can lose hours in a game like this one, chasing a possibility that seems promising, but nine times out of ten, when you've hit on the right answer—"

"You know it," Lyra finished. There had already been two names on the ledger when they arrived. Savannah and Rohan had the lead, which meant that Lyra and Grayson didn't have hours to lose.

Giving herself the *moment* Grayson had suggested, Lyra began pacing the outside edge of the helipad, her strides deliberate and long.

"You think better in motion," Grayson noted, longsword still in hand.

He was right, and that made Lyra remember something else he'd said to her. *You never stopped dancing. Every time you move, you dance.* She paused on the helipad's ocean side. With wind in her face and Grayson Hawthorne at her back, Lyra closed her eyes and *felt* the letters engraved on the bronze key with the pad of her thumb. She willed herself to think about only the ones in the clue.

V, I, I, I, L.

Her left hand moved of its own volition, sketching those letters at her side—and then suddenly, Lyra felt an eerie, familiar sensation, *physically* felt it like ghostly fingers on her face and neck.

Someone's watching.

Lyra's eyes flew open. The helipad was lit, but the moon had disappeared behind a cloud, and the world beyond the edges of the helipad's light was dark—the island, the ocean, all of it. Lyra tried to glance back over her shoulder at Grayson, but she couldn't move. Her head and body stayed oriented toward the ocean and the expanse of night.

The feeling lingered—*more* than lingered. Persisted.

"Where are you going?"

Until Grayson's words hit her ears, Lyra hadn't even realized that she'd just leapt down from the helipad. Grayson followed, landing beside her. Without so much as glancing at him, Lyra walked to the very edge of the light cast by the helipad, stopping before she hit darkness.

"Lyra?"

She kept her gaze focused ahead—on the water. *There's something out there. Someone.* "You're going to think I'm ridiculous." Frustrated with herself, Lyra pushed a hand back through her hair.

"Try me."

"Just now... I felt something." Lyra turned her head to look at him and realized that he'd positioned himself just a little bit ahead of her—half in darkness, half in light.

"What kind of something?" he asked. Holding that longsword, a line of shadow down the center of his face, Grayson Hawthorne looked more than human.

"It's nothing," Lyra told him.

"What kind of nothing?" Grayson amended his question very slightly, but his intonation didn't change.

Lyra shook her head, but she answered all the same. "Like someone was watching." *Was,* she realized. *Past tense.* The feeling was gone.

With a curt nod, Grayson drove the sword in his hand into rocky sand, let go of the hilt, and tapped the face of his watch.

"What are you doing?" Lyra demanded.

"Sending a message. It won't hurt for my brothers and Avery to have security do a boat run on the perimeter of the island, just in case."

"It's probably nothing," Lyra insisted. She didn't want to be coddled by anyone, let alone him. "If someone *is* watching us, it's probably just another player."

"Perhaps," Grayson acknowledged. "But you felt something *out there.*" He nodded toward the water. "And Hawthornes are raised to treat our instincts like a very close ally. *Trust—but verify.*" Message to the game makers sent, he lowered his hands to his sides.

Without warning, the light on the helipad behind them went out.

Motion sensors, Lyra told herself. In near-total darkness, she shifted her weight. Grayson must have done the same, because their shoulders brushed. A shiver went through Lyra—and not an entirely unpleasant one this time.

Beside her, she heard the unmistakable sound of Grayson unzipping his jacket.

Lyra narrowed her eyes. "Don't even think about it, Hawthorne."

"One of these days," Grayson said beside her in the dark, "you are going to let me give you my jacket."

For now, Lyra's body contented itself with the feeling of his shoulder against hers. "We should get back to the game," she said. "We've wasted enough time."

As if the universe was agreeing with her, the light on the heli-pad behind them turned back on. *Motion sensors*, Lyra reminded herself. *We have company.* She whirled to see who, but her gaze caught on a cluster of large rocks off to one side. On top of one of those rocks, she saw something. *White and green.*

Feeling like she was walking through a dream—*bare feet on pavement*—Lyra made her way slowly forward. She stared down at the flower, then watched as if from a great distance as her own hand picked it up.

A calla lily.

Chapter 24

GRAYSON

The instant Grayson realized what Lyra was holding, he reclaimed their longsword and went to her, his gaze trained on the person who'd set off the motion detectors on the helipad: *Brady Daniels. Holding* his *longsword. Crossing to the bull's-eye.*

Grayson laid his free hand on the back of Lyra's neck. "Are you with me?"

"I'm fine."

She wasn't, Grayson knew, but some people didn't know how to be anything else. *First the notes with her father's names. Now the flower.* Someone was playing mind games with her—extremely personal ones.

Up on the helipad, Brady planted his sword in the metal slit, driving it in up to its hilt. Soon enough, he held the ledger in his hand.

"Stay behind me," Grayson told Lyra, as he leapt back up onto the helipad. Lyra didn't argue, a clear sign, as she fell in behind him, that she was fighting the undertow of memory.

"Do you think it was him?" Lyra asked, her voice muted. "Watching us."

And the lily? Grayson was not yet ready to make a determination on either of those fronts, but he had no regrets whatsoever about alerting his brothers and Avery to a potential perimeter breach. Hopefully, they would act quickly and either identify or rule out a third-party presence. In the meantime...

Grayson tracked Brady's movements. Physical intimidation was not, as a general rule, a favored maneuver in the Hawthorne playbook, but Grayson was willing to entertain the idea of making an exception. He strode across the helipad toward Brady, stopping just three feet away from his target and saying nothing.

"Grayson Hawthorne." Brady's voice was deep, but his tone was mild. "Your reputation precedes you."

"A useful thing," Grayson said crisply. "A reputation. What, I wonder, is yours?"

"I'm the scholar."

"What kind of game are you playing, scholar?"

Seemingly unbothered, Brady pressed his watch to the ledger. "The same game as everyone else."

"I doubt that very much." Grayson had always excelled at fighting calm with calm. "Tell me that you don't have a sponsor, Mr. Daniels," Grayson suggested, just enough silk in his tone. "Tell me that the only game you're playing is one with clues."

Brady told him nothing and walked to the compartment he'd just revealed, removing from it the charm and the bracelet. He listened to the recorded hint, and it took him all of two seconds to drop his key into the liquid.

A scholar, indeed—either that, or he'd been spying on them all along.

Once Brady had reclaimed his key and skimmed his gaze over the highlighted letters, he finally turned his attention and calmwaters gaze back to Grayson. "I'm not your enemy. Or hers." Brady shifted pensive brown eyes to Lyra. Grayson marked the exact moment that the scholar saw the calla lily in Lyra's hand. His gaze lingered on it at least a second and a half longer than it should have.

"You were saying?" Lyra replied.

"Is that a part of the game?" Brady queried.

"No," Grayson said. "It most certainly is not." He'd played enough Hawthorne games to be sure of that. "Tell me you don't know where that flower came from."

"I don't know where that flower came from." Brady weathered Grayson's stare for three seconds, then looked away and adjusted his glasses. "I just know that it's probably for me."

Lyra stepped past Grayson, and it took every ounce of control Grayson had not to pull her back and put himself between her and Brady Daniels once more.

"Why would this be for you?" Lyra asked Brady, brandishing the lily.

The scholar's left hand reached for his jacket pocket. Grayson prepared to move should the need arise, but all Brady withdrew from his pocket was a photograph. "I have a theory," Brady told Lyra, "that everyone is playing this game for a reason."

"Like twenty-six million dollars?" Lyra said dryly.

"There are a lot of things a person could do with twenty-six million dollars," Brady agreed. He held the photograph out to Lyra, and after a moment, she took it.

"The girl in the photograph," Brady told Lyra quietly. "Her name is Calla. She would be in her twenties now."

Calla, like the lily, Grayson registered, but he read more into Brady's statement than just that. Language had a way of betraying people—her name *is* but she *would be.* Part present tense, part conditional. Whoever the girl in that photograph was, Brady hadn't seen her in years.

Whoever this *Calla* was, Brady Daniels was not entirely certain she was still alive.

"Calla?" Lyra looked down at the flower in her hand. "What was her last name?"

"Does it matter?" Brady asked.

Grayson's brain was wired to look for connections, to hunt for layers hidden from ordinary minds. A third party had put Lyra in this game, but Avery had chosen Brady as a player herself. If there was any connection whatsoever between the girl in Brady's photograph and the flower Lyra's father had given her the night he died, that was a very big coincidence.

Too big.

"If that flower was meant for you"—Grayson aimed those words at Brady with the same precision with which he'd learned to throw knives—"where did it come from?"

Who left it on that rock?

Brady gave the barest of shrugs. "My money's on Rohan. I get the sense that the Brit trades in knowledge and subterfuge, don't you?"

Grayson recognized redirection when he heard it. Brady hadn't been lying before, but he was now.

"You have a sponsor," Grayson said.

"I am not your enemy." Brady addressed that sentiment to Lyra this time instead of Grayson. "I'm not anyone's enemy. I'm a doctoral student. I'm interested in how the artifacts we interact with form us into the people we are. I like books. I like stars. I like numbers. And I am playing this game for a very good reason."

All of that, in Grayson's judgment, was true. None of it was the truth that mattered most. *You have a sponsor, and whoever it is, you think they might have left a* calla lily *for you.*

"I don't expect you to take me at my word—on anything," Brady told Lyra. "But maybe a show of good faith would help?" The scholar bowed his head toward Lyra and murmured something too low for Grayson to hear.

What are you telling her? What kind of move are you making, scholar?

With one last glance at Lyra, Brady made his way to the end of the helipad, the side of it *away* from the water. And then he was gone.

Lyra waited a bit longer before she turned back toward Grayson.

"A show of good faith?" Grayson queried.

"Roman numerals," Lyra replied.

"We'd solved that much already," Grayson said.

"He solved more." Lyra brought her amber eyes to rest on Grayson's, and he recognized the glint in them. "And when an answer is right—you know."

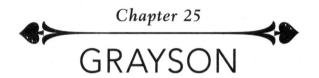

Chapter 25

GRAYSON

The clock on the fourth floor of the mansion was large, the Roman numerals on its face prominent and gold, and Grayson couldn't help thinking that his brothers and Avery had designed a shining, glittering game.

Beside him, Lyra still held the calla lily in her hand. Noting the way Grayson had just glanced at it, she spoke. "Someone sent me here, but why distract me once they did?" Lyra shifted the flower from her right hand to her left, then placed her right palm flat on the face of the clock. "First the notes with my father's names on them, then the flower, even that picture of Brady's—of a girl supposedly named *Calla*."

"Quite the coincidence." Grayson lifted a hand and joined Lyra in probing at the Roman numerals on the clock.

"What if Brady and I have the same sponsor? What if that person is trying to *make me* remember the night my father died?"

Grayson thought about the way Lyra had referred to herself as a weapon—a bomb. Given the intensity of Jameson's reaction to the mere mention of Alice, it seemed clear enough that there were secrets to be detonated here.

Dangerous ones.

"The Grandest Game." Grayson turned his head and caught Lyra's eyes. "Do you still want to win?" He felt like the lowest of the low for asking that question, for redirecting her, but he told himself that it didn't count as manipulation if he put the ball in her court.

All he'd done is ask if she wanted to win.

"Have I told you about my dad?" Lyra was still staring at the clock. "Not my father—my *real* dad, the one who raised me." Lyra's voice was even—too even. "He's great. I have always, for as long as I can remember, been a daddy's girl. And my dad—*he* never took me out of preschool and to a strange house, never told me *happy birthday* and then made me his witness to things a child should never have to see." Lyra's voice wasn't quite so even anymore. "My *dad* has always been there for me. My mom, too. And I have always—*always*—known that I was loved."

Grayson had never had parents—not really, not like that, and the old man's love had been a different kind of beast. Still, Grayson knew what *family* was, what it meant. Thanks to his brothers, he had *always* known, and Lyra had never been more beautiful to him than she was right now, talking about hers.

"I have a little brother—much younger," Lyra continued, and Grayson could hear the steel in her tone, see it in the tilt of her chin. "And we have a huge extended family on Dad's side. I've always been a Kane to them. From day one, from the moment they met Mom and me, we were theirs." She paused. "And so is Mile's End. It's been in the Kane family for generations. *My* family."

"So, yes," Grayson summarized. "We're still playing. You still want to win."

Lyra let the calla lily in her hand drop to the floor. "The Roman numerals seem to be firmly attached. We could try moving the hands on the clock?" The look of concentration on her face intensified "To eight-fifty."

Grayson saw her logic immediately: *VIII, L.* He lifted his hand, and together, they moved the massive minute and hour hands on the clock—to no effect.

"We're close," Grayson told Lyra. "I can feel it." He did his best to redirect his own mind to the game—and only the game.

"Close isn't enough." Lyra tilted her upper body sideways, raising one leg as she did until it and her torso were parallel to the floor.

"A change in perspective?" Grayson moved his hands to her waist to support her, like they were dancing—like the chandelier all over again.

"The shape of the hands," Lyra said, and if he'd thought her voice was intense before, that was nothing compared to the strength in it now. "Make it an *L*."

Sometimes, a letter was a number—and sometimes, it was a *shape*.

Lyra righted herself and swung the minute hand on the clock around, until it formed an upside-down L, the hour hand still on the eight.

VIII, L.

There was a sound like a bolt being thrown, and the face of the massive clock swung out from the wall, revealing two rows of metal drawers.

Sitting on top of the uppermost drawer on the righthand side, there was a ledger.

Grayson picked it up and opened it. Two names stared back at him, the first players to solve this particular puzzle.

The players who'd beaten them here.

"Rohan and Savannah," Lyra said. She cheated her gaze toward Grayson's. "Not Brady."

Brady Daniels had known where to go after the helipad. So where *was* he? Grayson thought again about the girl in Brady's photograph, the one the scholar had clearly—one way or another— lost. *Calla.* Briefly, Grayson's thoughts went to another girl, one whom *he* had lost, the first cut but no longer the deepest.

He really was getting better at letting it all come.

Beside him, Lyra pressed her smartwatch to the page. Her name appeared in elaborate scrawl on the ledger, third in line. Grayson went next. Two of the metal drawers popped open. Inside each, there was a silver box—and, on top of each box, a charm in the shape of a clock.

Clue after clue after clue. Grayson met Lyra's gaze. "Onward."

Chapter 26

ROHAN

Rohan wasted no time making himself comfortable on the bed. It was not, strictly speaking, his bed—or Savannah's, for that matter.

"Need I point out that we could do this in *your* room?" Savannah said crisply. "Or mine."

She stood with her back to Brady's door, above it all—or so she would have had Rohan believe.

He leaned back against Brady's headboard. "Where's the fun in that?"

Part of controlling the board was positioning yourself just so—sometimes literally. Brady Daniels and Lyra Kane might both have been keeping secrets, but *Brady* did not have a Hawthorne running interference on his behalf, and when it came to thinning the herd, the wise man always started with the most vulnerable target.

Hence, their current location.

Turning his attention to their next clue, Rohan laid the object—a silver music box—on his lap, his long legs stretched out toward the end of the bed. Savannah held a matching silver box. The two of them had already been over the music boxes and their contents out in the hall, but in games such as these, everything merited a second look.

And a third.

And a fourth.

Rohan had always done his best thinking in places he wasn't meant to be.

"Who says this is supposed to be fun?" Savannah stayed right where she was. *Don't trust yourself to come any closer to this bed, do you, love?*

Rohan gingerly opened his music box. Individual notes cut through the air, one at a time. *A waltz.* The inside of the silver box was lined with deep purple velvet. Where some music boxes might have displayed a ballerina twirling to the music, there was a flower made of white-and-gold marble.

The music the box was playing changed—no longer a waltz but a tango.

"You can pretend you're not enjoying this," Rohan told Savannah. "But you have your tells." Rohan refrained from letting his gaze slide to hers. Instead, he retrieved his silver chain bracelet and both charms he'd obtained thus far and affixed the charms to the chain, one after another. *The sword. The clock.*

The music coming from the box shifted once more, the marble flower turning and turning.

"You must get some pleasure in beating Grayson at a Hawthorne game," Rohan said. Thus far, he and Savannah had signed two ledgers, and they'd been the first to do so both times.

"In basketball," Savannah said, "there are two kinds of players on the court: the type who feels a thrill with every basket they sink and the type who cares only about the win."

"The lady makes a fair point," Rohan murmured.

Savannah's long legs took a single step away from the door—and toward the bed. "The lady is about to make another one." She nodded toward the music box in Rohan's lap. "This song—it's the same one from before. From phase one."

Rohan listened. She was right. "'Clair de lune,'" he said. After another ten or fifteen seconds, the music shifted again—back to the waltz.

Taking that as her cue, Savannah opened the lid to *her* box, identical to Rohan's in every way. It went through the same sequence, song after song.

"The flower." Savannah was all concentration. "The box. The songs." She glanced down at the bracelet on her wrist. "Perhaps the charms are meant only to mark our victories. Perhaps they'll have a use later in the game, but I would wager a good deal of money they aren't our clue right now."

Rohan did not disagree. As the music looped back to the beginning once more, he rolled off the bed and to the balls of his feet.

"What are you doing?" Savannah asked.

"Listening," Rohan replied. He'd always *listened* best when his hands were occupied. Since he doubted Savannah would welcome his touch at the moment, Rohan did a sweep of Brady's room.

The waltzed played. Then the tango. "Clair de lune."

Rohan stepped into Brady's bathroom. He checked the drawers, the shower, the tiles on the floor—and then he saw the barest hint of something tucked behind the mirror. The moment Rohan went still, Savannah crossed to stand directly behind him. Her gaze caught on the mirror. By the time she'd registered what he had seen, Rohan had claimed it for his own.

A photograph. In fact... It was the same picture that Rohan had stolen earlier. *Calla Thorp with her bow.*

"He stole it back?" Savannah said archly. "Touché."

"No." Rohan unzipped his jacket and retrieved the photo of Calla Thorp that he'd stolen at the bonfire. It was worn, like Brady Daniels had been carrying it around for years.

The one from behind the mirror looked much newer. It was creased only once.

Savannah held out a hand. "May I see them?"

Rohan acceded, allowing her a moment with both photographs. Savannah stared at the twin pictures of Calla Thorp, and Rohan could not help but note that, in comparison to Savannah Grayson, Calla had been quite plain—except for those eyes.

"There is just something about tragic love stories, is there not?" Rohan said, reclaiming the photographs.

For a moment, Savannah looked like she might fight him for the photos, but to Rohan's ultimate disappointment, she did not. "All love stories are tragic," she said.

Then she turned, her music box still in hand, and stalked back into the bedroom. Rohan tucked the photographs away and tailed Savannah through Brady's room and into the hall. The corridor was empty, the clock reset.

"Grayson and Lyra found the clue," Rohan informed Savannah. She didn't ask how he knew that, and Rohan didn't tell her. He merely watched as she stalked toward the window at the end of the hall.

The moment she opened it, Rohan knew why. "'Clair de lune,'" he said, sidling up beside her. "Moonlight."

A partial moon shone down from the night sky—and that was when Rohan saw it, down below on the beach, just barely lit. Something that had not been there before...

A piano.

Chapter 27

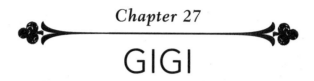

GIGI

Silk. That villainous, kidnapping cad-face had bound Gigi with *silk.* Scarves? Pieces of bedsheets? Gigi wasn't sure. Did Slate just always carry silk around with him? Who knew! All *Gigi* knew was that the fabric was soft against her wrists, which that highly vexing bicep-monster had *tied behind her back.*

He'd tied her ankles, too.

"How incredibly, utterly, absolutely dare you!" Gigi's voice echoed in the darkness. Slate was long gone. Without the candle's light, it was pitch black, and Gigi was alone.

The door locks from the outside, he'd told her flatly. *You do not want to do anything foolish while I'm gone.*

"Oh, I don't?" Gigi had no objections whatsoever about talking to herself. "Because I'm pretty freaking sure that I do!" She pulled against the ties on her wrist. As soft as the fabric was, there was absolutely no give. She kicked her feet—exuberantly and to no avail.

"Stop," Gigi told herself. "Breathe." She'd daydreamed her way through worse situations than this. She needed to go to a happy place, and then she could strategize, but for some reason, as she tried to conjure up that happy place, instead of bunnies and ice cream, what she got was Brady.

Full lips, strong jaw, velvety brown eyes behind thick-rimmed glasses. Gigi thought for the briefest of moments about chaos theory, about closed systems, about a deep, gentle, river-flowing kind of voice.

"A voice that *lied*," Gigi reminded herself. At least Slate was open about what he was: fourteen notches in a leather sheath, fourteen horrible things he'd done. Gigi would take that over someone who'd gone out of his way to *make her* trust him any day—not that either of them were up for *taking* per se. And regardless, Gigi had bigger things to worry about at the moment than her pitiable romantic history and perpetually unfortunate taste in men.

Savannah *knew.* Precisely what Eve had told her about their father's death was unclear, but Gigi was all too aware that her sister didn't see the world with many of shades of gray. There was excellence, and there was failure. There was power and powerlessness.

There was truth, and there were lies.

Savannah had always been their father's favorite, the one he'd pushed, the one who *mattered.* All Gigi had ever been expected to do was smile, and all she'd wanted, coming into the Grandest Game, was to prove to herself that she was capable of *more.*

Instead, she'd been bamboozled by a recovering physicist, gotten herself recklessly and needlessly kidnapped, and abjectly failed to see what was right before her eyes. *Savannah.* She'd been different. For months, Savannah had been different, and now Gigi knew why.

Holding her sister's image in her mind, she took a deep breath. "Enough with the wallowing. I'm getting out of here." Gigi put some pep in her words. "Step one: free my wrists."

She rolled up into a sitting position, then stood. Gigi had no idea what direction she was facing, but in a round room with almost nothing in it, that didn't matter. She hopped. Then hopped again. And again. Eventually, Gigi hopped into a wall.

"That could have gone smoother," she admitted with a wince. Her head wound throbbed slightly, but Gigi persevered, turning her back to the wall so that she could feel it with her bound hands. The stones that made up the lighthouse walls were uneven, crumbling in some places, jagged in others.

Jagged was exactly what Gigi was looking for.

It took her three minutes to find a rock that suited her purposes.

"Hello, my very sharp friend," she told the stone, and then she grinned. How long could it possibly take for a highly motivated individual to use an extremely jagged rock to cut through bindings made of silk?

Chapter 28

LYRA

n the music box, a marble flower turned and turned. *Another calla lily.* Lyra stared at it, and soon, she couldn't hear the music, couldn't see the mosaic ballroom where she and Grayson had gone to dissect the clue.

Happy birthday, Lyra. The memory of her father's voice threatened to drag her under.

Lie-ra.

Lie-ra.

Lyra fought to stay in the here and now, the way she'd somehow managed to back at the helipad, but this time, the undertow of memory would not be denied, locking its jaws around her, pulling her down—and back to being four years old.

Back to being given a flower and a candy necklace.

Back to the gunshot.

Back to the blood.

Bare feet on pavement. Running.

"Breathe." Grayson's voice wrapped itself around Lyra, keeping her from falling into a full-on flashback, but still, the *sounds* of that day—

Happy birthday, Lyra.

Lie-ra.

Lie-ra.

"Breathe for me, Lyra Catalina Kane." Grayson said her name exactly right. In true Grayson Hawthorne style, he said it like an order—or maybe a prayer.

"I'm breathing," Lyra said, but she still couldn't look away from the marble flower spinning slowly in the box.

"You're breathing," Grayson confirmed, as his chest rose and fell with hers.

Lyra managed to close her eyes, just for a second. "A *calla lily*, Grayson." Her mind echoed with a sound like roaring, screaming wind, and she gritted her teeth. "Still think the other one wasn't a part of the game?"

That question came out sounding like an accusation. Lyra hadn't fully meant for it to, but old habits died hard.

"Were the calla at the helipad a part of the game, I assure you the delivery of said flower would have been far more systematic." It was both one of Grayson's best qualities and one of his worst that he was always so damn steady, so certain. "Hawthorne games are not haphazard. There is an unassailable logic to them, and they are not cruel."

Cruel. Lyra's gaze returned to the calla lily in the shining, silver music box. She lifted a finger to touch the marble flower. "But this *was* them. The game makers." Lyra had thought before that maybe someone was trying to *make* her remember. She had to at least consider the possibility: What if it was one of them?

One of Grayson's brothers—or Avery.

"It's just a music box." Grayson placed a light hand on her shoulder. "Just a stone flower. Just a clue in a game that you are *going to win*."

"It's a calla lily," Lyra countered, putting a hand on Grayson's chest and pushing him lightly back. She didn't need comfort right now. She needed answers. "They know something—your brothers or Avery. At least one of them knows something."

Grayson let his hand fall to his side and looked down at Lyra's on his chest. "What precisely do you think they know?" he asked gently. "I never told any of them about our phone calls, Lyra— about *you*." The angles of Grayson's face were made for intensity. His was an odd sort of calm. "I told Xander the gist of your father's death but not why I was looking for him. I told Jameson about the riddle but not where I'd heard it." Grayson paused. "I told no one about you. For over a year, you were my secret and mine alone."

There was something about the way Grayson Hawthorne said *mine* that made a part of Lyra want to say *yes*—but she didn't. "There's a difference between failing to mention something and keeping it a secret," she told him.

"A secret, you think about." Grayson's lips rarely parted into a true smile; his angular face spoke only the language of slightest curves. "Even if you try to bury it deep, some secrets live with you, day in, day out."

Lyra thought about the way Grayson had reacted when he'd heard her voice the day before, when he'd realized who she was. Beneath her hand, she could feel the muscles in his chest. She could feel his heart beating. It would have been easy to just go along with what he was saying, to take it all at face value.

I was your secret and yours alone, day in, day out. Lyra let her hand drop. "Some secrets are carved into your bones," she told Grayson. Lyra had lived with that kind of secret. For years. It had divided her life into a before and an after.

And someone involved in this game *knew something*.

Lyra stared at the music box, at the marble flower. "Odette drew a calla lily last night. I never mentioned to her that my father gave me one, but after I remembered the omega symbol, after she heard me say *A Hawthorne did this*, she drew a *calla lily*. An anonymous party left one for me at the helipad. And now there's one in our current clue. That's no *coincidence*. It can't be, Grayson." She shifted her blazing gaze to him. "Do you even believe in coincidences?"

Pale silvery-blue eyes absorbed her fire whole. "I am starting to believe in a lot of things that I didn't believe in two days ago." *So damn steady. So damn sure.* "And I am asking you to believe *me* when I say that my brothers and Avery would never intentionally play with you like this."

Hawthorne games are not cruel. Lyra looked back to the marble calla, and suddenly, it was all too much, including Grayson Hawthorne and whatever it was that he was starting to believe in.

Day in, day out.

You were my secret and mine alone.

"You're about three seconds away from taking off on a late-night run," Grayson noted.

He wasn't wrong. "Going to try to tell me that's a bad idea?" Lyra challenged.

"Sometimes pushing yourself physically is the only way to push it all down," Grayson said instead. "But you only run because you will not allow yourself to dance. And I cannot help noticing that we are in a ballroom."

Lyra's mind went to the night before, to dancing with him at the masquerade ball. She could practically feel the heat of his body, feel his palm on hers, but in the silver music box, the calla lily turned and turned.

"It doesn't have to be with me," Grayson told her. "I'll give you the room and keep working the puzzle myself. You do whatever you need to do." There was no undertone to those words, no judgment. "Some of us need to be alone sometimes."

Some of us. He said that like the two of them were the same. Like there was nothing wrong with wanting to be alone.

Like she wasn't the least bit broken.

"I'll be in the Great Room." Grayson left it at that, and Lyra did her best not to watch him go.

Some of us need to be alone sometimes. And now she was. She was alone in a *ballroom*, and her body remembered—would probably *always* remember—what it felt like to turn and leap and defy gravity in every way that mattered. But dancing—really dancing, the way she used to—meant losing herself to the music, to the movements.

For Lyra, ballet meant letting go.

Instead, she paced the room like a lioness caged, the sound of the notes from the music box fading into the background until all Lyra could hear was an unintelligible whisper in her memory: a woman's voice, words Lyra couldn't decipher no matter how hard she tried.

On and on, the music played, and the marble calla lily turned.

It can't be a coincidence. None of this can. The flower she'd found by the helipad, the flower in the box, the one Odette had drawn—it meant something. All of it meant something. *Me being here. Calla lilies. Omega. Alice Hawthorne.* Lyra couldn't shake the feeling that if she could just figure out what it all meant, figure out why that night had happened, why her father had killed himself the way he had, why he'd *brought her there*, maybe she wouldn't have to be alone anymore.

Maybe she could finally stop pushing people away.

Maybe she could dance.

Refusing to hold on to that thought any longer, Lyra stopped pacing and made her way to the bed in the middle of the ballroom. She climbed onto it and looked up at the dark rainbow of tiles on the mosaic ceiling. She reached for a pillow—and felt something else.

A *piece of paper*. Lyra realized what it was a second too late, a second after she'd already taken it in her hands and begun to unfold it. The night before, to earn a hint in the game, Grayson had been tasked with drawing her. He'd kept the drawing. *Put it under his pillow.*

Lyra finished unfolding it and sucked in a breath.

It wasn't just the way he'd captured her otherworldly ballgown, the lines of her neck, the curves of her body. *Not hidden. Not downplayed.* It wasn't the fullness of her lips or the way he'd drawn her hair loose and a little wild, like she was staring down the wind. It was the look in her eyes. It was the muscles he'd drawn, along with the curves. It was the way that he'd drawn her like she was on the verge of saying something, like she was a person with something to say.

It was bad enough that Grayson had made her beautiful, but he'd also drawn her *strong*.

And somehow, that made Lyra feel—for the first time in *three years*—like maybe she didn't have to be.

I am not fine. Lyra let that be true. Just for a moment, she let it be true. She stopped fighting back the memory of a calla lily and gunshots and blood. She thought about being alone, as a child in that house with a dead body *and* now.

She let it hurt, and she breathed. She shuddered, and this time, when she heard a distant whisper in her mind—that memory she couldn't quite grasp—it wasn't quite as unintelligible.

She made out a single word in a woman's voice: *You*...

Chapter 29

GRAYSON

I n the Great Room, the dominoes had vanished from the gleaming wood floor, and a violin sat dead center on the round table. Grayson scanned the room for a bow and saw it balanced on the raised wood paneling of the wall. Based on experience, he knew better than to take that to mean that the key to solving the music box puzzle was the music.

It might be. It might not be.

Hawthorne games often contained traps—rabbit holes down which one could disappear for hours. The clue could just as easily have been the box itself. *Or the calla lily inside.*

Why that *flower, Jameson?* Grayson hadn't been lying when he'd told Lyra that the one they'd found near the helipad was assuredly not a part of the game, but the choice of a calla lily for the music box was just as certainly *not* a coincidence. Grayson had chosen his words to Lyra with care: His brothers and Avery would never *intentionally* do this to someone. Grayson would have wagered every dollar he had that the calla lily was Jameson's doing, and that Jameson had no idea that calla lilies held any significance for Lyra at all.

Thus, the real question was why *that* flower had been floating around in Grayson's brother's subconscious to begin with. *It has something to do with Alice.* That much was clear—as was the fact that Grayson was going to have to break his word. He'd given Jameson until the end of the game to get a handle on any threats, but as far as Grayson was concerned, that timeline had changed.

He would not sit back while an unidentified threat played with Lyra. *Hurt* her. Jameson clearly was not handling this—so Grayson would.

As if on cue, his watch buzzed, a message in response to the one he had sent the game makers, requesting a perimeter run.

(LITERAL) COAST IS CLEAR. FOCUS ON THE GAME.

The second part of that message had Jameson's fingerprints all over it. *Focus on the game.* Grayson had been trying to get Lyra to do the same—and for much the same reason. He resisted the urge to send another message back to the game makers. Prudence dictated watching what one put in writing.

You have until midnight, Jamie, Grayson thought, *and that is all.*

For now, Grayson claimed the violin and the bow. He brought the violin to his chin. From memory, he began to play the waltz from the music box. In his mind, an image formed: Lyra dancing, turning and turning, the lines of her body perfection. As he continued playing, as the waltz gave way to a tango, Grayson's mind conjured up a dance of a different sort. A more aggressive one.

A tango for two.

And then Lyra appeared in the doorway to the Great Room, looking like something out of a myth, her dark hair long and loose, silver music box clasped in front of her body like a bouquet.

Grayson stopped playing. "What happened?" He could tell just from the look in her eyes that something had.

"A memory," Lyra said. "A very faint one." Amber eyes flicked away from his. "Why . . ." She stopped and then started again. "Why did you draw me like that?"

It took Grayson a second to process what Lyra was referencing, what she'd found. "It was part of the game," he told her.

"No." Lyra shook her head. "I didn't ask why you drew me. I asked why you drew me *like that*." Her voice went hoarse on the end of that sentence.

Grayson did not fully comprehend the question. He was not one to take artistic license. "I simply drew what I see."

Lyra turned away from him with another shake of her head that sent her dark hair rippling down her back. "You are impossible," she bit out. "And I . . ." Her tone shifted in ways that Grayson couldn't even describe. "I am not fine."

Grayson didn't know whether or not she'd allowed herself to dance, but clearly, something had shifted in her. "It's liberating in a way, isn't it?" he said quietly. "Letting it all come."

"I wouldn't say *all*." She was still holding back.

That's a no, then, Grayson thought, *on the dancing*.

Grayson walked toward her, but before he could get too close, she turned to face him again. "We should get back to the game." Lyra looked to the violin in Grayson's left hand—and the bow in his right. "Can I borrow your bow?"

Unable to even guess at what she intended, Grayson lowered the violin and handed the bow to her. Lyra sank gracefully to the floor, set her music box down, and flipped it open. The expression on her face difficult to read, she dug the sharp end of the bow into the velvet lining of the box, tearing at the fabric.

"A hunch, I presume?" Grayson asked.

The velvet began to rip beneath her assault. "Maybe I just felt like taking a risk," Lyra said. "Or doing some damage." She set the bow down and grabbed the torn edge of the lining.

Taking a risk. Doing some damage. Grayson could not help thinking that, to Lyra, *he* undoubtedly looked like a risk, too. And the two of them together...

The right kind of disaster just waiting to happen.

There was another *rip.* "Got it," Lyra said, tearing the velvet lining the rest of the way out of the music box.

Grayson closed the space between them and looked down at the silver of the box, at what Lyra had found beneath the lining— the reward for her *risk,* the result of the *damage* she'd wreaked.

A symbol, etched into metal.

"Infinity." Lyra traced it with the tip of her finger, and then her eyes found their way to Grayson's once more. "Or eight."

Chapter 30

ROHAN

W e've searched long enough. There are no secret compartments in this piano. No symbols. No clues." Savannah
arched a brow, as if daring Rohan to argue. He did not. There was
nothing hidden in, on, or around the piano—just the instrument
itself, a bench, the beach, and strings of additional lights that had
burst to life the moment they'd lifted the piano's lid.

Rohan slid onto the bench, his fingers lightly trailing the piano's
keys. "Open the music box," he told Savannah. "Mine or yours."

A piano like this one—a grand piano, a Steinway, by the looks
of it—was meant to be played, which Rohan suspected might well
be the point.

Savannah opened her music box. Rohan listened and began to
play. He named the notes in the melody aloud as he did. "*D, E, D,
C*—"

The telltale sound of Savannah unzipping her jacket caused
Rohan to pause. He turned his head to see Savannah holding a

permanent marker, which she uncapped as she shrugged off her white jacket. Without hesitation, she wrote the letters he'd just recited down on her bare arm in a perfect, enticing scrawl.

D, E, D, C.

That marker was decidedly *not* a part of the game. "Careful, love," Rohan warned. "You never know who's watching."

They'd been told to bring nothing with them to the island.

"After I broke into your room this morning, I broke into Gigi's. The marker was hers." It was obvious to Rohan that saying her twin's name cost Savannah, but she rather expertly pretended it hadn't. "I'm guessing my sister found herself a loophole. She always does, and clearly, the game makers allowed it."

From her standing position, Savannah looked down at Rohan, seated on the bench. "Tell me to be careful again as if I am ever anything but, and I will make my irritation known."

"I assure you, love: Your irritation is *always* known." Rohan stood, closed her music box, then flipped it open again, causing the sequence of songs to start playing from the beginning. He sat back down and joined in with the melody when he reached the point at which he'd last stopped.

More notes recited out loud. More letters added to Savannah's bare arm.

Midway through the tango, Rohan shut the box again—to irritate her and to allow her time to catch up. "A truly cautious person in your shoes," he pointed out, "would not be here."

No one with the least bit of caution would go against the Hawthorne family or their heiress.

"Am I to believe that you don't know the difference between being careful and being cautious?" Savannah added the last few notes—more black ink on porcelain skin—then flipped the box open again herself.

As he waited for the music to catch up, Rohan replied to Savannah's rhetorical question. "Caution is hesitation—of which you have none."

What are distractions, Rohan?

He joined back in with the music and forced himself to keep playing, until at long last they reached "Clair de lune." He shut the box. He didn't need it. Not for this song. Rohan played straight through, bits and pieces jumping out to him as he played, as Savannah scrawled the letters onto her willowy arm, heading down toward the inside of her wrist.

D, A, G, A . . .

E, E, F . . .

D, C . . .

B.

Rohan removed his fingers from the keys. "I'm surprised you don't play," he told Savannah, nodding to the Steinway.

"What makes you so certain that I do not?"

Rohan stood, removing her ability to look down at him. "I could tell you, but where would the fun be in that?" He moved toward her, resisting the urge to run his fingers along the letters on her arm. "On the topic of caution," he said, letting his gaze do the exploring for him, "I was approached by Jameson Hawthorne."

She did not need to know the details, but for Rohan's purposes, she did need to take care.

"Jameson is wary—uncharacteristically so. It seems the game makers suspect there are larger forces of some sort at play here. Some kind of threat." Rohan shifted his gaze to Savannah's face, and she shifted hers to the ocean—what little of it they could see with such delicate light.

"Does it bother you? Being out here at night?" Savannah asked. "So close to the water?" That was a subject change—a deliberate one.

"Does it bother you," Rohan replied, "using a marker that belonged to your sister?"

Savannah didn't say a word about Gigi. Rohan didn't expect her to. But in the contours of her silence, he had his answer.

"You love her, fiercely."

Savannah kept her gaze trained on the water. "I was our father's favorite," she said. "And Gigi was mine."

Was. Rohan rolled that over in his mind. *Gigi knows exactly how your father died, doesn't she, love? She kept it from you.* Rohan couldn't help thinking that some people didn't feel pain.

Some people channeled it.

"I never did learn to swim all that well," Rohan said—tit for tat, a truth for a truth. "But well enough, I suppose." He let his gaze travel from Savannah's face back to her arm to her wrist. He lifted his hand and stroked two fingers, feather-light and daring, over the place on her wrist where he could feel her pulse.

"Is this the part where the claws come out?" Rohan said.

"The claws are always out." Savannah arched her brow. "As I'm sure you remember."

"I have an excellent memory." He stroked her wrist once more.

Savannah raised her chin. "I want the photographs. The one you stole from Brady Daniels and the one we found in his room."

"A way to divert suspicion should the game makers start to think that you might be up to something?" Rohan guessed. "One photo, a person could excuse as sentimentality. Two identical photos, on the other hand . . ." He trailed off meaningfully.

"Two is something," Savannah agreed. "May I have them or not?" She'd yet to take her wrist from him. Rohan could still feel her pulse.

He decided to oblige her—for strategic reasons, of course. He gave her the photographs. "Fair warning, love: I'll just steal them back."

"You're welcome to try." Savannah turned and started walking away. "I hope you memorized the sequence on my arm," she called back. "It's high time we both tried working this puzzle on our own."

"Rest assured," Rohan called after her, "I know every inch of it." *Every inch of you.* "First one to a breakthrough gets to make the other one grovel."

Distractions were weakness, but motivation? Motivation was gold.

Chapter 31

GIGI

As it turned out, it took a *very long time* for even a highly motivated individual to cut through silk bindings with a jagged rock, but there were two kinds of optimists in the world: those who hoped and those who madly persevered.

Gigi was the latter. At long, long last, a small rip gave way to a larger large one, which gave way to a strip of silk fabric falling to the floor. "Huzzah!"

Despite her optimism, Gigi had not thought much past step one of her plan. The obvious step two was to free her ankles, which she did, but as for step three...

Gigi felt her way to the door and tried throwing herself bodily against it a couple of times. *No go.* She changed tactics. It took her a full five minutes of crawling around in the dark, searching the wood floor with her hands to find the iron candle holder. Even without any light, she was ninety-nine percent sure that she could climb the stone stairs if she hugged the wall and took her time. And once she got to the top...

How hard could it possibly be for a highly motivated individual with a hefty metal object to shatter a few windows?

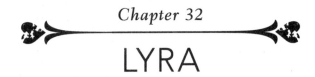

Chapter 32

LYRA

Lyra stared down at the island. Taking a bird's-eye view of Hawthorne Island to look for some kind of infinity symbol had been Grayson's idea. Using the boathouse to do it had been Lyra's. They'd already searched the mansion for anything bearing the infinity symbol—the *lemniscate*, as Grayson had called it. The roof of the mansion had proven inaccessible.

Hence, the boathouse.

Hence, the two of them at least forty feet up.

The top of the boathouse had lit up the second they'd stepped foot on it, just like the helipad.

"We could be looking for anything," Grayson said, as they stared out into the night. "Trees planted in the shape of a lemniscate, mirrors in the ground, a pattern in the grass."

"It's pitch black," Lyra pointed out. "Midnight is less than an hour away."

"Yes." Grayson Hawthorne and his *yeses*. "Try the opera glasses." He cast a sideways glance at her, and then his lips tilted upward on the ends. "Suggestion."

"Why don't I just assume they're all suggestions from now on?" Lyra reached for the opera glasses.

"If it's ever an order," Grayson told her, "you'll know."

She shot him a look. "Same." Lifting the opera glasses to her eyes, Lyra felt Grayson shift beside her, and instead of fighting her body's awareness of his, Lyra let it roll over her.

"Nothing," she informed Grayson. "Still pitch black." Her mind went to the original owner of the diamond-encrusted opera glasses as she lowered them. She glanced at Grayson and knew his mind had gone to the same place. "You're thinking about Odette."

"Odette," Grayson replied, allowing his gaze to linger on Lyra's, "is not the only one I am thinking about."

"I know." A few hours earlier, Lyra would have ignored his confession or misinterpreted it, but she couldn't unsee that drawing. "I didn't dance when I was alone in the ballroom." Lyra felt compelled to give him something true. She wasn't even sure why. "I just couldn't let myself do it."

"I know," Grayson replied.

Lyra wasn't used to anyone being able to read her. "Now it's your turn," she told him, casting her gaze back out on the island.

"My turn for what?" Grayson said.

"Your turn to tell me something else that I already know."

"You don't fall." Grayson nodded toward the edge of the roof. She was standing closer to it than he was.

"I kn—"

Grayson didn't let her finish. "You don't fall," he said again, a certain intensity in those words. "I do." It couldn't have been clearer to Lyra that he wasn't talking about balance. "I fall, Lyra."

First the kiss, then the drawing, and now this. And all Lyra could say was: "Why?"

"Why what?" Grayson returned.

Why would someone like you fall for me? He was Grayson Hawthorne. He had the whole damn world at his fingertips. Lyra sure as hell wasn't about to say that out loud.

"Why a bird's-eye view?" she deflected "Why are you sure that darkness won't be a problem?"

Grayson studied her for a moment, then answered the question. "Echoes. The kind that happen from game to game. In one of the old man's final games, there was a clue that could only be seen from above. Jameson and Avery played that game, and they're the ones who masterminded this one. Infinity—or eight—is another echo from the same sequence."

Echo after echo after echo. Lyra wondered if this one was even intentional. And then she realized: "What if the calla in the music box is another echo from one of your childhood games?" Lyra's mind churned as she walked closer and closer to the edge of the roof. "It might not even be intentional."

They already knew that Tobias Hawthorne had discovered that his wife was still alive. What else might the billionaire have known? "What if your grandfather encoded *something* in one of those games?" Lyra insisted. "Something about Alice."

Alice and calla lilies.

The night air was quiet, except for the waves breaking down below.

"*The right kind of disaster just waiting to happen,*" Lyra said. "What if that's what Odette meant? You and me. My memory and yours." She took another step forward, needing the movement, needing to think. She was right on the edge of the roof now, and suddenly, Grayson's words came back to her, haunting her the way that so many things he'd said did.

You don't fall. I do. I fall, Lyra.

There was a flash of light in the distance. *From somewhere near the ruins.* At first, Lyra thought she'd imagined it, but then there was another, not far from the first.

"Did you see that?" Lyra asked.

"I did," Grayson confirmed. "How much would you like to wager that the flashes continue and form a lemniscate? One of us should stay here and track the progression and the other should go investigate at the source."

"And when you say *one of us* should go investigate...," Lyra prompted.

"Let me do the recon," Grayson replied.

"Just to be clear, you want me to stay here in the light while you go gallivanting off in the darkness by yourself to check this out?"

"Someone has to watch for the pattern."

"That someone could be you," Lyra pointed out. "And I could do the gallivanting." There was another flash of light—this one closer to the forest than the ruins.

"Humor me. Please."

It was the *please* that did it. Lyra expelled a breath. "Fine, but prepare yourself for some very cutting sarcasm when you get back—and no moving on to the next puzzle without me if you find something."

"I'll do recon," Grayson promised with a twitch of his lips. "And that is all."

He disappeared down the ladder, and Lyra trained her gaze back on the island, keeping watch. There was one more flash of light, and then nothing. For minutes, *nothing*—until Lyra heard footsteps on the dock below.

Footsteps that weren't Grayson's. Footsteps—*coming up.*

Lyra had time to take two steps back before someone else stepped onto the roof. *Not a player. Not the game makers.* A woman. She couldn't have been more than three or four years older than Lyra, and there was something eerily familiar about her. She had hair a shade too light to be red, a heart-shaped face, a scattering of freckles—and no weapons that Lyra could see.

"Hello, Lyra." Green eyes raked up and down over Lyra's body, sizing her up. As Lyra returned the favor, she reminded herself that looks could be deceiving.

"Who the hell are you?" Lyra said. "And how did you get on the island?"

"It wasn't easy with increased security, but I had help. As for who I am..." The interloper smiled coyly. "My name is Eve, and I'm the reason you're here."

Eve. The name meant nothing to Lyra. Her mind started to race, but she forced it to slow down, holding on to every ounce of calm she could muster. "You put me in the game? You sent me my ticket?"

"You're welcome."

Lyra's eyes narrowed. "The lights—"

"A distraction," Eve replied. "My associate and I tracked you and Grayson up here, and let's just say that I know how Grayson Hawthorne's mind works. I knew he'd either interpret the lights a part of the game—or a threat. If he perceived a threat, he'd be the one to go. If he assumed it was a part of the game, there was a chance both of you would, but you would have separated eventually."

"Let me guess," Lyra said flatly, "you and your associate would have seen to that?"

"He's quite useful, my associate," Eve replied. "Very eclectic skillset. But that's not really what you want to ask your sponsor. Is it?"

Lyra eyed the ladder, but Eve was blocking it, and even if she hadn't been, Lyra couldn't have just walked away. "What is your associate going to do to Grayson?" Lyra demanded.

"Absolutely nothing. Grayson will never even know my sentinel is there."

Lyra took a step forward. "What do you want with me? Why send me here?"

"I would have thought the note that accompanied my gift to you was clear enough. I sent you that ticket because you deserve this— for everything the Hawthorne family took from you, for everything you've suffered, you *deserve* this." Eve smiled again, sweetly this time. "And I thought our interests might align."

Lyra didn't like the sound of that. "What interests?"

"You're going to do something for me, Lyra."

"I doubt that."

Eve adopted an almost wounded expression. "But I'm a friend of Grayson's—or at least, I used to be. It appears as though you're his *friend* now."

Grayson. Lyra tried to process that. *This is about Grayson?* "So you're...what? The unhinged ex?"

"I like to think of myself more as the path untraveled," Eve said. "But for your purposes, the only thing that matters is that, once upon a time, I got a look at a billionaire's List, capital *L*. Enemies. People the great Tobias Hawthorne had wronged, people he had destroyed or betrayed, mysterious individuals who'd offed themselves because of him—you get the drift."

"My father." Lyra cut through the bullshit. Grayson had mentioned his grandfather's List, but he'd also told Lyra something else. "Grayson said that Tobias Hawthorne's file on him was full of false information. Dead ends."

"Oh?" Eve replied. "How fortunate, then, that along with a great deal of money, I also inherited another man's files, which happened to detail not just that very wealthy man's rivals and adversaries but also the webs surrounding all of those individuals: their allies and friends on the one hand and their enemies on the other. You can see why you caught my interest."

Lyra had started this game *hating* Grayson Hawthorne—and the entire Hawthorne family.

"Suffice it to say, my file on your father is a bit more detailed than Tobias Hawthorne's was." Eve gave Lyra a moment to process that. "Let's play a game, shall we? I'll give you three questions about the contents of my file on your father—any three you like, which I will answer honestly, if not fully. And in return, all you have to give me is the opportunity to present you with an offer."

I'm not taking any damn deals. Eve's game, on the other hand— that, Lyra would play. "What does your file say about *omega*?"

"Nothing." Eve tilted her head to one side. "What's *omega*?"

Lyra's gut said Eve wasn't acting, that the word *omega* rang no bells for her whatsoever. Lyra took a beat to consider her second question and zeroed in on one more likely to yield results. "What does your file say about calla lilies?"

"Only that Tobias Hawthorne had some sent to your father's

funeral." Eve gave a little shrug. "A bit sentimental, if you ask me. One question left."

Tobias Hawthorne knew something. Lyra's heart rate accelerated. *He sent* calla lilies *for a reason.* The dead billionaire had clearly been a man whose every action was layered with meaning, and he didn't strike Lyra as the type to send flowers to funerals out of *sentiment.*

Putting a pin in that line of thinking, Lyra considered the fact that Eve had offered true answers but not necessarily full ones, and yet, when Lyra had asked about calla lilies, Eve had responded that her file contained *only* one thing on the topic. Lyra didn't trust her so-called sponsor as far as she could throw her, but her gut said—again—that Eve was telling the truth, that she really didn't know anything more about the calla lilies.

Not that Lyra's father had given her one the night he died. Not anything else about what that particular flower meant.

Then why send me one? Lyra wasn't about to burn her last question on that.

"I'm waiting," Eve said.

Make it count. Lyra went straight for to the heart of the matter. "What does your file on my father say about Tobias Hawthorne's dead wife?"

"Alice Hawthorne?" If Eve knew Alice wasn't dead, she gave no sign of it. "Absolutely nothing." Eve stared bullet holes in Lyra for a few seconds.

She wasn't expecting that question. If anything, Eve seemed to be wondering now what *Lyra* knew—but she got over it. "I almost feel bad about all the questions you didn't ask," Eve said finally. "So out of the goodness of my heart, I'm going to give you something—proof that you want the file that I have. Your father used dozens of last names. The man who made my List had it narrowed down to three possibilities for his real one."

Lyra didn't want that to mean anything. It was such a small thing—a last name. But after the Grandest Game was finished, a name would at least be something to go on.

A name might tell her something she'd never known about herself.

"I'm listening." Lyra's throat tightened around the words.

"Drakos. Reyes. Aquila."

Lyra filed those names away for future reference, refusing to let them mean too much.

"Now it's my turn," Eve said. "Here's my offer for you, Lyra: Lose this game and ensure that Grayson Hawthorne does the same, and I will give you two-point-five million dollars and the entirety of your father's file."

Two-point-five million dollars was more than enough to save Mile's End. It was more than enough for Lyra, period. And that file...

Lyra's jaw tightened. "Why do you want me to lose?"

"Does it matter?"

Maybe it didn't. So Lyra focused on what did. "Why would I take any deal from you? Why would I believe anything you're saying when you've been playing mind games with me since I got here? My father's names on self-destructing notes. Sending me that flower."

There was a long, barbed silence.

"I never sent you a flower," Eve said. "But I'm guessing it was a calla lily?"

"You're lying," Lyra replied, but she didn't really believe that.

"I'll admit," Eve said, "you've piqued my interest, but I can't count on this little interlude of ours lasting much longer. I had those notes with your father's names planted to remind you what you lost, what the Hawthorne family took from you. And you can trust my offer because I have no reason to fail to follow through. Two-point-five million dollars is nothing to me. That file is nothing to me."

"What's the catch?" Lyra refused to believe there wasn't one.

"Well, I suppose there is one other thing," Eve said, as she walked back toward the ladder. "If you want the money and the file, I'm also going to need you to break Grayson Hawthorne's heart."

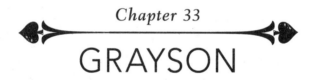

Chapter 33

GRAYSON

G rayson returned to southeastern side of the island to find Lyra exactly where he'd left her: on top of the boathouse, standing Hawthorne-close to the edge. Even from a distance, Grayson clocked Lyra's posture, the width of her stance, the tilt of her head.

Grayson would have known it was her even if the only thing he'd been able to see was the outline of her body. Picking up his pace, he made quick work of the distance separating him from the boathouse and scaled the ladder to join Lyra on the roof.

Grayson greeted his partner in crime with a question. "What did you see?"

Lyra kept her back to him and her gaze locked on the island. "One more flash after you left. No lemniscates. No discernable pattern."

Grayson walked to join her, right at the edge. "Are you going to ask me what I found?"

"If you'd found something," Lyra replied, "I would know."

Grayson was not a total stranger to being *known*. His brothers knew him. Avery did. But Grayson had never been an easy person for others to pin down. "So," Grayson said, joining Lyra in staring out into the night, "where does that leave us?"

"I don't know." The later it got, the lower Lyra's voice went, and in that deeper register, there were more layers to her tone than Grayson could count. "You never told me what you thought about the possibility that the calla lily in the music box was an echo," Lyra said finally. "Not a coincidence but not necessarily intentional, either."

Lyra was coming far too close to the truth for Grayson's comfort. *An echo—but not from one of the old man's games. From something else.* What, Grayson did not know.

"I recall no such clue in any game I ever played," Grayson said— a truth, and one he *could* give her. Something in him compelled him to give her more. "You have my word," he said slowly, "that if midnight brings us face-to-face with the game makers, I *will* ask my brothers and Avery about the calla."

Clearly, Lyra wasn't letting this go, and promising to *ask* was not the same thing as promising to tell her the answer.

"But if you want to win the game," Grayson continued, pitching his voice to cut through the night, "we can't keep circling the same drains."

Lyra turned slowly to look at him. "We can't keep circling each other, either."

Grayson really should have been expecting that. He'd told her that he was falling for her. Knowing that she might run, he had told her anyway. *And now...*

Now, Lyra Kane was reaching to grab the front of his shirt. She was pulling him toward her. "What happened while I was gone?" Grayson murmured.

Lyra's eyes glittered in the moonlight. "Maybe I just feel like doing a little more damage." She surged upward, and Grayson caught her face in his hands as her lips crashed into his.

A moment later, his hands were buried in her hair.

Grayson had known from their first kiss that there *would* be a second, but he hadn't been expecting this from her. *Here. Now.* Grayson pulled back just far enough to breathe out four words. "Away from the ledge." He moved, and she moved with him.

"I don't like being told what to do," Lyra said, her lips brushing his with every word.

"I am aware," Grayson replied. They kissed again, and Grayson let it all come. The chill of the night air. The feel of her skin. The right kind of disaster just waiting to happen.

The last thing that Grayson wanted was to *stop* kissing, to put any space whatsoever between them, but his sense of honor sent up a reminder about why he was here. He'd committed to seeing phase two through for *her*, and as often as he'd redirected Lyra's attention to the game for his own purposes, Grayson owed her the decency of focusing on the puzzle himself.

Midnight was rapidly approaching. The clock was ticking.

Parting, even a fraction of an inch, was sweet and torturous sorrow. "If we want to win," Grayson murmured—*we*, not just her. "For your family. For Mile's End. We need to play. Everything else can wait."

Even this.

Lyra looked at him for the longest time, just *looked* at him, like she was on the verge of saying something. And then, she looked back out at the island. "Then let's play."

Chapter 34

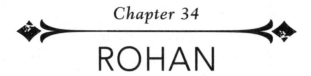

ROHAN

Rohan stood at the edge of the ocean, wave after wave washing onto the shore, stopping just short of his feet. The darkness, the water—it was like pressing on a bruise. *I never did learn to swim all that well*, he'd told Savannah.

There was a utility to pain, mental clarity in mastering it.

Gripping that clarity with both hands, Rohan willed himself into the labyrinth of his mind, sorting through information—the music box puzzle; letters scrawled across Savannah's bare arm; a pair of photographs belonging to Brady Daniels; Jameson Hawthorne viewing Lyra Kane as a threat.

Back in reality, a bigger wave broke. Rohan refused to step back as the water washed up and over his feet. In the corridors of the labyrinth, an unwanted memory reared its head.

A woman humming. Safe and warm. And then a man's voice: *"Give him to me."* Rohan could have fought the memory, could have shut it down, but he did not. It was, after all, just another bruise.

"*Please*," he could hear the woman say.

And then the man: "*We both know you're going to give him to me eventually, and if you fight me on it, if you disobey me again, it's going to be so much worse when you do.*"

The sound of footsteps pulled Rohan back to the present. Primed to fight and ready to win, he turned, and there she was: Savannah Grayson, glorious even in the dark.

"How are you at groveling, British?"

"Nowhere near as good as I am at lording my victories over people," Rohan replied. "Why?"

"You're going to want to grovel."

Figured something out, did you, love? And she'd come to him with it, as a partner should. Rohan took a step toward her. "Tell me, Savvy, what kind of groveling did you have in mind?"

Some time later, Rohan stepped into the Great Room. *No dominoes.* The gleaming wood floor was very nearly bare. Rohan noted a violin and a bow, both leaned neatly against the wall, but Savannah ignored them as she strode to the black granite fireplace. A fire now burned inside it—the first time it had been lit, as far as Rohan knew, since the start of the game.

"Is there a switch?" Rohan asked. "Or was it remotely triggered?"

Savannah didn't bother answering that. "I tried warming the music box first, to no avail. Same for the bracelet, the charms, the dice, and the lock on my chain."

"And then..." Rohan strode to stand beside her, in front of the crackling flames. "You tried Brady's photographs."

"Did I?" Savannah replied.

Yes.

As Rohan watched, Savannah held one of the photographs of

Calla Thorp—the worn one, the one that Rohan suspected Brady had carried with him for years—up to the fire. As the paper warmed, letters began to appear on the back, a message in feminine script.

Do exactly as I say.

"It strikes me," Rohan murmured, "that there is more than one kind of sponsor."

Brady Daniels had been invited to this game by the Hawthorne heiress herself. That meant that any would-be sponsors would have had very little time to approach him and make their case. In the previous year's game, resources had mattered. Sponsors had something to offer. But this year?

This year, external resources had only been a boon in the initial hunt for wild card tickets. Given that Brady *wasn't* a wild card, his sponsor had to have played this a different way.

"And the other photograph?" Rohan prompted.

Savannah held the other, less-worn picture up to the flames. Letter by letter, a second message appeared.

The game must go on. Ensure that it does.

Before Rohan could mull that over, his watch buzzed.

"Midnight," Savannah said beside him.

A message appeared on their watches from the game makers.

"*Don your tux and your mask . . . ,*" Rohan read aloud.

Savannah looked up from her own watch and finished the sentence. *"Be on the dock at quarter past."*

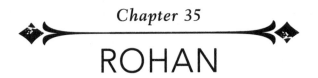

Chapter 35

ROHAN

In Rohan's room, a new wall had parted, revealing a closet bearing armor of a very different kind. *Formal wear.* Rohan let his fingers skim over the tuxedo jackets the way another person might have lightly dragged their hand through the surface of a pool or lake. He stopped when his hand hit fabric the same dark purple color as the velvet that had lined the music boxes.

For Rohan, the shade was a familiar one, calling to mind a special ink.

Ink. Rohan could feel the memory rising, like water around his ankles, then his knees, then his thighs. *Dark purple ink and a book and a quill.* This time, he did fight—and lost. The memory took him under anyway, wholly, completely, body and soul.

"Sharp, isn't it?"

Rohan is five years old, and the man across from him is a stranger— a stranger who holds a metal feather out to Rohan.

"The edges will cut you—if you let them." The man smiles. "But

you won't, will you, Rohan?" The man's smile deepens but doesn't reach his eyes. "Let them hurt you?"

Rohan might be small, but he understands that the man in front of him isn't really talking about the metal-sharp edges of that feather. He's talking about people.

People will hurt you, if you let them.

Rohan says nothing, staring angrily and defiantly back at the man, and then he turns to stare just as hard at the book the man has placed before him. The book is big. It is old. It is, Rohan knows instinctually, the reason for the metal feather and the small, silver bowl of dark purple liquid that reminds Rohan of blood in the night.

"Ah. You want to know what is in this book. An excellent question. You see, Rohan, to join the Devil's Mercy, one must pay. The price is steeper than money, steeper than blood. Don't look at me like that, child. It's not your soul I'm after." The man twists the metal feather in his fingers, a certain sharpness in his eyes. "Secrets," he says. "That is what this book contains. Horrible secrets. You have one of those, don't you, my boy?"

Rohan looks to the purple liquid in that bowl and thinks about blood.

"Do you know how to write?" the man says. "Or would you prefer I write your secret down for you?"

Rohan looks ups from the book and glares daggers at the man.

"What about your name?" the man asks. "Or just the letter R? Can you write an R, Rohan?"

Clamping his mouth closed, his voice a distant memory and rage burning inside him, Rohan nods.

"Well, then." The man dips the pointy end of that metal feather into the deep purple ink. "What if I told you that I could turn you into the type of person who never has to hurt? The type who never *has to be afraid. The type who is feared and adored the way that only those with true power can be. What if I said I could make you more than the sum of your parts?"*

The book is opened. The man sets the quill's point on the page.

"In exchange for that, would you give me your secret, Rohan? Would you tell me what you did?"

Every muscle in his little body tight, Rohan nods.

"All right then." The man bends down. "Whisper your secret most horrible to me. Tell me what you did tonight, Rohan, and I will give you the world."

Rohan has not spoken in so long that he is not even sure that he can. But he wants to be what this man is. He wants to be the one holding the quill, holding the book.

He wants it all.

Grinding his teeth, Rohan locked his hand around the purple tuxedo. He wasn't about to shy away from the color—or the memory.

"Where were you just now?" Savannah appeared behind him, too perceptive for her own good and apparently all too willing to let herself into his room.

"Plotting," Rohan answered lightly, as he lifted the tuxedo off the rack. "Your demise, mostly, with a side of...other things." He turned and let his gaze trail along the arm on which she'd written the notes from the music box, and then he let himself take in her gown.

It was as pale a blue as her silvery eyes—paler, even, so much so that at first glance, a less discerning individual might have confused it for white. It hit just below her calf. Thousands of tiny, pinprick jewels adorned its surface, catching the light from overhead, the pattern of the stitching and beadwork calling to mind snowflakes with edges as sharp and severe as blades.

The fit of that gown hid nothing and ensured that the only memory that threatened to pull Rohan back into the labyrinth of his mind now was his memory of the night before.

"I don't believe you." She arched her brow, a clear challenge.

"Best not to," Rohan agreed. "Ever, really."

Savannah studied him, intensity palpable in her gaze, and then she made her next move. "I suppose you've already deduced that my sister knows what happened to our father."

Rohan definitely hadn't been expecting that from her. "I suppose that I have."

"Grayson told her—or she figured it out. It hardly matters. Gigi found out the truth, and she let me go on thinking that he was missing." Savannah's chin tilted upward, the tension in her neck and jaw as dazzling to Rohan as her gown. "That he *left*."

Rohan recognized her strategy for what it was: This was Savannah Grayson showing him *her* truth as a demand for the same from him, a risky move on her part, to be sure, but she had his attention.

All of it.

"I'm not surprised that Grayson's loyalty lays elsewhere. But Gigi?" Savannah locked her eyes on to Rohan's. "She was my person."

Given the differences between the sisters, it was easy to forget that they were twins. Open-hearted Gigi had very likely *always* been Savannah's person.

"And now she's not," Rohan said.

"I spent a lifetime trying to be good enough for my father." Savannah's voice was like ice sharpened to a killing point. "He wanted me to dominate on the court and off it, and I did. But as I got older, I managed to find new ways to disappoint him. He wanted me to be feminine, likable, beautiful. Strong but never *too* strong."

Rohan thought of Savannah's long, long hair, before he'd shorn it. He thought of the way it had felt to pick up a knife and cut it off, thought of the look on her face as he'd done it.

"I was supposed to be perfect," Savannah said, "and I was supposed to be *liked*, and my father never even considered that it might be impossible for a woman or even a little girl to be both of those things." Savannah made her way farther into the room and took the tuxedo hanger from Rohan's hand, like she was stripping away a protective barrier between them. "Gigi was enough for our father, just the way she was—but not me. Never me. So if he *left*, well... It was clear enough that the person he was really leaving, the person who wasn't worth staying for, was me."

"Only your father didn't *leave*." Rohan said it so that she didn't have to. "And your twin sister let you continue to believe that he did."

"Gigi was my person," Savannah said, her voice breaking—just once. "And now she's not." She tossed the purple tuxedo onto the bed and took another step toward him. "Where were you just now, Rohan?"

He'd seen that question coming. He'd recognized Savannah's tactic for exactly what it was from the moment she'd started talking. And still, Rohan found himself *wanting* to answer, wanting to give Savannah Grayson just a fraction of what she'd given him. "The day I came to the Mercy."

What are distractions, Rohan? That lesson had come later, but until now, it had always, always stuck.

"Children generally aren't taken in by the Devil's Mercy for *good* reasons," Rohan said.

"Deep water." Savannah met his eyes. "Pitch black. You didn't know how to swim, and it wasn't the first time."

Keep your friends close, Rohan thought, *and your enemies closer.* In the end, they'd be enemies, he and Savannah Grayson.

"The last time," Rohan told her, "they tied stones to my ankles." Or they'd tried to. Rohan pulled off his shirt, resolved to tell her nothing else. "I have a tuxedo to put on, love, and you were just leaving."

Savannah's gaze traveled down to his abs.

"Unless...," Rohan said, letting his hands come to rest on the waistband of his pants. "You'd care to assist me?"

Chapter 36

GIGI

The windows, as it turned out, were stormproof. "Seriously," Gigi huffed, "who puts modern-day stormproof windows in an abandoned lighthouse?" It was madness! Thankfully, Gigi was no stranger to madness.

If at first you don't succeed, hit harder and refuse to stop! Somewhere around the four-hundredth time, Gigi's philosophy paid off. One of the splinters in the glass cracked all the way through.

"Victory!" Whack. *"Is!"* Whack. *"Mine!"* Gigi welcomed the shattering of stormproof glass with open arms. Figuratively—mostly. Either way, she avoided getting cut.

Even Gigi wasn't quite optimistic enough to try to scale down a sixty-foot drop in total darkness, so she moved on to the next step of her plan: She bellowed.

Gigi bellowed like she had been born bellowing, like she was training to become a pro bellower, like she was single-handedly keeping the art of bellowing at the top of one's lungs alive. She bellowed like her life depended on it.

After all, how long could it possibly take for a person with truly impressive lungs, shouting from their diaphragm, to be—

She heard a sound of a bolt being thrown, and the door to the lighthouse slammed open below.

That was surprisingly quick! Gigi edged toward the ladder and climbed down far enough to see a flashlight beam cut through the dusty air on the ground floor.

"Damn kids." Based on that voice, Gigi inferred that the person who'd just spoken was male, fairly old, and also impressively cranky.

But who was she to be picky about rescuers?

"Me!" Gigi bellowed. "Up here! I'm *damn kids.*" She took to the stairs, going down them faster than was probably wise.

"I oughtta shoot you."

Gigi slowed to a stop as the flashlight's beam found her, and she realized that her rescuer was indeed holding a shotgun. "Please don't?"

The shotgun was in his left hand. It hung by his side. That was a good sign. Right?

"You're going to break your damn neck coming down those stairs that fast."

Gigi took her new friend's concern for her neck bones to be a very good thing and resumed descending, slightly more slowly this time. "I'll be fine," she called. "My bones are bendy, and the important thing is that I've been kidnapped, and you're here to rescue me."

Gigi was used to befuddling people. To his credit, her rescuer didn't stay befuddled for long.

"I'm not rescuing anybody."

Gigi took another turn. Just ten steps left to the bottom—and the now open door. "You definitely are," she informed the man with the gun. "And you're doing a stellar job of it. Just look at how well you took the kidnapping news! If there's one quality I look for in a rescuer, it's a certain stalwart gruffness." Gigi stepped off the last of the stone steps and grinned. "I also like your beard."

That got her no response whatsoever. In Gigi's defense, it was a very copious beard.

"And frankly," Gigi added, "the rifle doesn't hurt." If Slate *did* come back before she got out of here, her bearded rifle buddy might prove very useful indeed.

"I need to shoot somebody?" he grunted.

Gigi decided it would be prudent to take that question at face value. "The broody jerk in question *did* tie me up, but I believe in redemption, so I'm going to go with an optimistic no."

Endearingly Bearded Man shifted his flashlight beam to the floor of the lighthouse. It stopped when it came to the silk bindings Gigi had so masterfully shed.

"Someone kidnapped you and tied you up?" EBM sounded, if not outraged, at least seriously annoyed.

"Indeed someone did!" Gigi replied. "Can I borrow your phone?"

"Don't have one."

Gigi blinked. Several times. "You...don't...have...a phone?" She paused. "Like, on you or—"

"Don't like phones."

Well, that answered that. "You know what?" Gigi said, stepping past him toward the open door. "I love that for you." She walked right out of the lighthouse into the November chill, pitch blackness, and sweet, sweet freedom. "Now, if you could please point me in the direction of civilization, I'll be out of your hair. And your beard."

"Civilization?"

"I need a phone," Gigi said. "Or a way to get to Hawthorne Island."

"You stay away from that place." The beard did nothing to minimize the man's scowl.

"I was just out there," Gigi assured her newfound friend. "For the Grandest Game." She knew objectively that the location of this year's game was a secret, but who was the guy who hated phones going to tell? He gave no appearance of having any idea whatsoever what she was talking about. "World-famous competition?" Gigi elaborated. "Details very hush-hush this year? Run by Hawthorne heiress Avery Grambs?"

That got a response. "Avery." His brow furrowed. "Hannah's girl?"

Gigi didn't know anything about Avery's mother, but the name *Hannah* rang a bell. "Maybe?"

Her rescuer stepped in front of her. "In that case, you really don't want to go into town."

"Agreed," Gigi said, nodding. "I want to go back to Hawthorne Island. But just for reference, which way is town again?"

Her bearded friend gestured with his flashlight.

"Excellent!" Gigi said. "In semi-related news, I need a boat. Do you have a boat?"

He glowered at her.

"You do!"

"I'm not taking anyone to that damn island."

"In that case," Gigi said solemnly, "I have no choice but to go to town." She made it two steps before the old guy cut her off. Gigi patted his shoulder. "Believe me, I am totally grateful for the stalwart rescue—A-plus—but I need a ride to Hawthorne Island, and if you aren't feeling inclined to give me one, and you don't have a phone, I'm going to town. Either way, I need to get out of here before a certain someone gets back."

"A certain someone. Who kidnapped you. And who I am *not* supposed to shoot?"

Gigi patted his other shoulder. "Correct!"

"Damn kids."

"It was incredibly nice to meet you, too," Gigi replied. "Have a nice night!" She made it five steps past him this time, and then Endearingly Bearded Man spoke again.

"Fine," he said roughly. "I'll take you to the island at dawn."

Chapter 37

LYRA

A dozen ballgowns hung in the secret closet, each more beautiful than the last. Lyra stared at them, unable to stop the pounding chorus in her brain. *Screw Eve and her deal. I have to tell him.* Except it wasn't that easy.

The money.

The file.

It was everything Lyra could have hoped for coming into this game: the ability to save Mile's End, a start on getting answers.

I'm not taking any damn deals. Lyra locked her gaze on the gown that hung dead center. The dress was blue, overlaid in gold, its skirt full and flowing, deep blue turning to a dark and stormy gray near the floor. Lyra reached out to touch the translucent gold fabric that flowed like water over the surface of the skirt. Even on a hanger, the dress looked like it was in motion. It looked like the kind of ballgown that should have had a name. *The Sky at Night.*

It looked like the kind of dress that a girl who'd caught the attention of Grayson Hawthorne *should* wear.

I should have told him already.

Lyra dropped her hand from *The Sky at Night* and forced her attention to the other ballgowns. One was silver with layers of white tulle that made it look like it had been called forth from the mists. Another was a deep, dark red with black stitching so intricate that Lyra felt like she might become hypnotized just looking at it. There was a forest-green gown, a pale silvery-blue one, lavender, indigo, glittering turquoise.

Black. Lyra stopped in front of the black dress. Compared to the others, its design was simple and understated. A fitted bodice, a loose and flowing chiffon skirt that would hit mid-calf. *More evening gown than ballgown*, Lyra thought. *More versatile. Practical.*

Her choice made, Lyra lifted the hanger from the rod and realized suddenly that the dress wasn't entirely black. As the chiffon moved, colors became visible in the skirt, obsidian giving way to purple-gray, a deep and fire-kissed pink, and honey amber. Lyra went still, and as the dress she held did the same, it looked black again—just black, the true colors of the feather-light chiffon only visible with motion. Lyra couldn't help thinking that this dress, like *The Sky at Night*, deserved a name.

Darkest Sunset.

There were no ordinary options here. Trying not to let that matter, Lyra shed her armor and downed the gown, contorting her arms to zip up the back. As she did, Eve's voice snaked its way back into Lyra's mind.

Drakos, it whispered. *Reyes. Aquila.*

Three names—none of which mattered to Lyra as much as

Mile's End. *Focus on the game,* she told herself. If she refused Eve's deal, winning would be her only option.

If?

Setting her jaw, Lyra looked back to the closet, to the end of the rack. *Luxury purses.* She chose one with a long strap. Like her dress, the bag was black, made of what looked like crocodile leather with small, glittering embellishments. *White gold. Diamonds.* More importantly, it was just large enough to hold the music box, the charm bracelet, and the dice.

Once she'd stocked the bag, Lyra made her way into the bathroom. With every step, the colors hidden in the chiffon skirt of her black gown made themselves known. With every step, Lyra told herself that she knew exactly who she was and what she had to do.

No one gets to manipulate me. Lyra looked at herself in the bathroom mirror, ignoring the way the gown accented her curves and focusing instead on the familiar face that looked back at her. *Amber eyes. Full lips. Golden tan skin.* Lyra had never looked much like her mother. She didn't sound much like her, either.

You are a kind and generous soul, Lyra Catalina Kane. The memory of that declaration had Lyra's fingers curving inward toward her palms.

A kind and generous person would have told Grayson *before* she'd kissed him. A smart person would have reported everything to the game makers while Eve and her *associate* were still on the island.

Unless that smart person was considering taking the deal.

I'm not. Holding her own gaze in the mirror, Lyra knew what her dad would have said—about Mile's End, about deals with the devil, about living life in a way that let you look at yourself in the mirror at night.

I am no one's weapon. Lyra made herself think the words. *I am no one's pawn.* And she was *going* to tell Grayson about Eve.

Eve, who'd offered Lyra millions to lose a game and break a Hawthorne heart.

There was a knock at the bedroom door.

Lyra looked away from her reflection, and her gaze fell on the exquisite masquerade mask she'd been given the night before—hers, she'd been assured, to keep. Putting it on, Lyra looked at herself in the mirror one last time, and then she retrieved Odette's opera glasses and stuck them through the sparkling, cross-body chain on her diamond-encrusted bag.

I am no one's weapon.

I am no one's pawn.

And I am going to tell him.

Lyra made her way toward the door. She could feel Grayson on the other side of it, even with solid mahogany between them, and it suddenly occurred to Lyra that knowing that Eve had sent her here might change things for Grayson. *The way he sees me. The way he looks at me.*

Clearly, Grayson had a history with Eve.

Another knock.

Lyra snapped herself out of it and opened the door, and there he was, wearing the same plain black mask he'd donned the night before, a stark contrast with his icy blond hair. This time, his tuxedo was white. Perfectly tailored—with a black silk shirt underneath.

Just looking at him, Lyra viscerally remembered stepping out of time with their first kiss and proving to herself with the second that she was no one's puppet, that whatever this thing was between Lyra and Grayson Hawthorne, it was theirs and theirs alone.

Grayson absorbed the sight of Lyra wearing *Darkest Sunset*, and he held out his hand.

Lyra took it, and she didn't say a word. *Not yet*, she told herself. *But soon.* Lyra knew what it was like for everything to change in an instant, what it was like for there to be a *before* and an *after*.

Once she told him, she might well be playing this game alone.

"Shall we make our way down to the dock?" Grayson asked, and then he smiled—a rare, actual Grayson Hawthorne smile, the kind fully capable of bringing the world to its knees.

I have to tell him. I'm going to tell him, even if it kills me. Soon.

Chapter 38

LYRA

A boat was waiting at the dock. Lyra climbed aboard, ball-gown and all. "No driver," she noted, as Grayson joined her on the boat.

"No driver," a voice repeated, "and no key."

That wasn't Grayson. Lyra whipped her head up to see Brady Daniels in the middle of the dock. She hadn't realized he was there, hadn't felt his presence at all.

She wondered how far he'd made it in the game.

"No driver," a British voice reiterated. "And no key. Now that *is* a dilemma." Rohan stepped onto the dock and into the faint light cast by the boat, and Lyra noted that Rohan's tuxedo was a deep purple to Brady's traditional black, Rohan's mask the less symmetrical of the two.

"It's only a dilemma for some of us." Savannah brushed past Rohan and looked pointedly toward Grayson. "Where is it?" she asked her brother. "The boat key."

Lyra had time to register the color of Savannah's dress—*white*—and the fact that there was something written on her arm in black ink, but that was all before Grayson responded to his sister's question by leaning over the edge of the boat—and over some more to reach the side of the dock.

Within seconds, Grayson had the boat key, complete with keychain. Lyra zeroed in on the keychain, taking in its shape. She wasn't the only one.

"Is that a narwhal giving an axolotl a piggyback ride?" Brady said, frowning.

"Let me guess." Lyra met Grayson's eyes through their masks. "This is Xander's boat."

Grayson wasted little time putting the key in the boat's ignition. "Technically," he told Lyra, "it's Xander's backup boat."

Grayson turned the key, and by the time he'd done it, all five players were on board. The boat's dashboard lit up with two blinking dots on what looked like some kind of grid.

Rohan took a seat at the back of the boat, his legs stretched out, his arms spread wide. "Who wants to bet that's another map?"

Grayson pulled the boat away from the edge of the dock and throttled it, jetting out into the Pacific. It didn't take Lyra long to confirm that on the dashboard, one dot was moving closer to the other, tracking the boat's progress through open ocean—and toward their destination.

It was a full ten minutes before it came into view.

A yacht. No amount of objectively knowing that Avery Grambs was a billionaire could have prepared Lyra for the sheer size and opulence of it. The closer they got to the yacht, the more massive it appeared. *Two-third the length of a football field? Four levels high.* Each of the yacht's four decks was illuminated with an eerie, golden glow. Blue LED lights ringed the bottom of the yacht, making the midnight ocean look somehow even blacker.

"Not bad," Rohan opined. "As far as command centers go."

Lyra supposed it made sense, given the location of the game, that the game makers had chosen a ship for their headquarters, but this wasn't just a *ship*. It was the yacht to end all yachts.

As the boat drew closer, Lyra saw Avery Grambs standing on the lowermost deck, clad in a golden gown and a matching mask. It wasn't until they'd docked and Lyra stepped onto the back of the yacht that she realized: the design on Avery's gown, the exquisite swirls of detail...

They all formed the same, familiar symbol. *Infinity*.

"Somewhere on this yacht," the Hawthorne heiress announced, "you'll find a hint or two to the puzzles you're working on."

"Puzzles, plural," Rohan noted. "I take it someone has already solved the music box."

Clearly, it wasn't him—or Savannah. Lyra and Grayson hadn't solved it yet, either. That left only one player, the one who'd *given* Lyra one answer in this game already. *Brady*.

"You're also welcome to eat, play, and rest up while you're here," a voice called down to them. "If you need it."

Lyra looked up. A masked figure stood on top of a metal railing on the uppermost deck. *Jameson Hawthorne*.

"And just like that..." Rohan snapped his fingers. "The scholar disappears."

Lyra looked around. Sure enough, Brady was already nowhere to be seen.

"After tonight," Avery told the remaining players, "you won't be seeing us again until the end of the game. No more ballgowns. No more masks. No more parties. Just puzzle to puzzle to puzzle until the end."

"Until," Jameson called down, "we have our winner." There was a tone in Jameson's voice that Lyra couldn't quite read, and this time, when she looked up, Jameson Hawthorne was staring down at her—and only at her. Unlike the rest of them, he wasn't masked.

And he wasn't smiling.

Lyra looked away from Jameson, and Savannah Grayson caught her gaze. *He'll choose them every time*, Lyra could practically hear her saying. *He'll choose* her.

Beside Lyra, Grayson was looking at Avery in that infinity gown.

I'm not asking him to choose me, Lyra thought fiercely, but she still couldn't push down the feeling of dread churning in her stomach at the thought of what was to come.

Opposite Lyra, Savannah turned to Rohan and bared her teeth in a glittering, socialite's smile. "Game on."

Chapter 39

LYRA

I have to tell him, Lyra thought. Avery and the other players had taken their leave. It was just Lyra and Grayson left on the lowermost deck now.

"There," Grayson said. "Two decks up."

Tell him. Lyra's internal monologue was stubborn as hell, but she ignored it—not forever. Just for now. She wanted, maybe even *needed,* one more moment, one more memory of this *before.*

She looked up, following Grayson's gaze. "What do you see?"

His lips curved. "Can you climb in that dress?"

Lyra pretended that there was no tightness in her stomach, no ball of anxiety in her throat. "I can do anything in this dress."

There was nothing on the third-story deck, but just off it, in the interior of the yacht, there was a lounge. The room was large and round, lined with arched doors. The carpet was deep red and plush, and set up all around the room there were game tables.

Poker.

Craps.

Roulette.

Grayson strode toward the poker table. Sitting on top of it was a stack of poker chips unlike any Lyra had ever seen.

"Made from a meteorite." Grayson picked up one of the chips. "Lined with Burmese rubies and Sri Lankan sapphires."

"Let me guess," Lyra said dryly. "The corresponding deck of cards is made of solid platinum and inlaid with fragments of Cleopatra's tomb."

"Sarcasm suits you." Grayson laid the chip down. "Though I feel compelled to point out that there are no cards on this table—or any other."

The only thing on the poker table besides chips was a trio of masquerade masks—one turquoise, one purple, one black, all divine. Lyra looked to the other gaming tables and saw more masks. Options, she supposed, for anyone who wished to trade.

Crossing from the poker table to the roulette wheel, Lyra picked up the mask that sat beside it. "Sarcasm might suit me, but this mask…" She trailed her finger across the surface of it. "Suits you."

The mask in question was a duller kind of gold, the metal of a royal knight's breastplate, battered and cracked. Smooth bronze arcs marked the mask over both eye holes, the balance of the markings uneven, the asymmetry of the mask somehow eerie and inviting all at once.

In a smooth motion, Grayson took off his black mask and picked up the asymmetrical one. "Roulette," he commented, donning the new mask, "is the only game in this entire room that we could actually play."

He reached for the small, silver ball, and Lyra instinctively spun the roulette wheel, pushing down all other thoughts that wanted to come.

Somehow, she wasn't surprised when the ball landed on the number eight.

"Did you see the lemniscates on Avery's dress?" Lyra said, and then she cursed herself silently, because it had been obvious to her from the beginning—from before she'd even ever even met Grayson—that he saw everything where Avery Grambs was concerned.

"Ask me," Grayson said in that low, even voice of his.

"Ask you what?" Lyra replied. "What the symbol means? What we're missing?"

"Ask me," Grayson told her quietly, "about Avery."

Lyra shook her head. "It's none of my business."

"I disagree." Grayson reached for the roulette ball, and, as Lyra watched, slowly rolled it around the palm of his hand. "My grandfather had a collection of watches," he said. "Extraordinary ones, clockwork marvels, each like a puzzle in and of itself. There was one watch in particular among his collection that my brothers and I all coveted. The clock face featured a tiny, mechanical roulette wheel encased beneath a crystal dome."

There was a long, weighty pause as Grayson leaned forward to roll the ball and turn the roulette wheel once more. The ball landed—again—on the number eight.

Grayson stared at the wheel for a second or two, and then, behind that cracked-gold mask, he flicked his eyes back up toward hers. "The old man didn't leave that watch to any of us. The entire collection, along with everything else, went to a stranger."

"To Avery," Lyra said. She swallowed. "But you welcomed her. You and your brothers—"

"I was not that welcoming," Grayson said wryly, "at first." After another pregnant pause, he spoke again. "My brothers and I were raised almost exclusively by the old man. Our mother was less than reliable. Our fathers were uninvolved, most of them by choice. My father, for instance, paid a private investigator to take photographs of me, starting the day I was born. He could not have been more aware of my existence, but my entire life, he never tried to know me, never even showed the least bit of desire to meet me." Grayson's voice was horribly even, unnaturally steady. "I cannot fully explain to you what Avery is to my brothers and to me, but I have confidence that I don't need to explain to you that family isn't just blood." Grayson's voice went a little lower, soft in volume and rougher in tone. "*Family* means you'd die for the person, and that you know damn well that they'd die for you. It means that no matter how lost you feel, no matter how dark things get, on some level, you *know* that there is a place and people with whom you belong."

Lyra felt those words like an ache in her soul. "Avery is your family." Lyra could understand that, and just saying the words out loud made Savannah's warning matter that much less. Life wasn't a competition about being loved more.

Love didn't work that way.

Grayson looked at Lyra through his new mask. "And speaking of my family," he said, reaching to touch her face, "I made you a promise. I have brothers to track down, and you have a hint to look for."

Tell him.

Back at the boathouse, when Lyra had kissed Grayson, it hadn't been because she'd let go and given in to this thing between them. Kissing him, in that moment, had been about reclaiming control, about proving to herself that Eve had chosen the wrong pawn.

But right here, right now, in the last moments of *before*, Lyra wanted more than that. She wanted something real. She wanted to let go, even if it was only for a moment.

She wanted *him*, even if it didn't last.

"Grayson?" His name felt familiar on her lips. "Before you go... It's a little cold." Lyra raised her chin and looked at him—just *looked* at him. "Give me your jacket?"

There was that smile again, bringing the world to its knees. Grayson undid his tuxedo jacket. He slipped it off and put it over her shoulders.

It smelled like him. *Cedar and fallen leaves.*

Grayson raised a hand to the side of Lyra's face, and Lyra let herself lean into it, let herself look at him and only him.

"May I kiss you, Lyra Kane?" That question. That voice. *Grayson Hawthorne.*

"Kiss me," Lyra said, "one last time."

"I assure you," Grayson replied, "it will not be." He brought his lips slowly down to hers, and this time, when they kissed, it wasn't timeless. It wasn't desperate or a revelation or an attempt to prove anything. This kiss was raw and long, aching and brutal, and every bone in Lyra's body said the same thing.

This wasn't a mistake.

And when it was over, when their lips finally parted, Lyra didn't even hesitate. "There's something I have to tell you." With a *before* like that, she could just almost believe in a different kind of *after*. "I know who put me in the game."

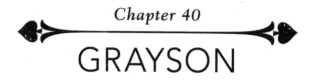

Chapter 40

GRAYSON

Eve. Grayson couldn't believe that he hadn't seen it. He'd known quite well that Eve had been given temporary access to the old man's List. And *of course* she was meddling in the Grandest Game. Of course she'd handpicked a player she believed hated the Hawthorne family.

Had Eve realized that Lyra had reached out to him, that Grayson had looked for her? It hardly mattered. Eve just couldn't let them go—any of them but especially *him.* Eve had gotten under Grayson's skin once. She didn't live there anymore. That was the thing about learning to let all your thoughts and feelings come—once you did, those thoughts and feelings were also free to *go.*

And Grayson was free to take a moment, even after Lyra had told him what Eve had offered her, to live in the now. The chill in the night air was even greater on the ocean, but Lyra was warm. *Her skin. Her breath in the air.* And she'd let him give her his jacket. She'd let him take care of her.

I told you, Jamie, Lyra isn't a threat. She isn't Eve.

"I should have told you sooner," Lyra said. "I should have told you *immediately*."

Eve had offered her everything she wanted—information about her father, enough money to save the family home and then some—and Lyra was berating herself for taking less than an hour and a half to tell him, to put her trust in *him*.

"Eve has a knack for manipulating people," Grayson told Lyra. "You did just fine."

It took three or four seconds for her to accept him at his word. "She truly didn't know about the lily at the helipad, Grayson. She put me in the game, but that calla wasn't her."

The pieces of the puzzle shifted in Grayson's mind, and he thought about Brady Daniels and *his* Calla. About Jameson's insistence that the name *Alice Hawthorne* not even be spoken. About the marble calla lily in the music box.

"We'll figure this out," Grayson told Lyra.

"I'll search the yacht for hints—and lemniscates." Lyra tossed her dark hair over her shoulders. "You go talk to your brothers and Avery."

"Was that a suggestion," Grayson said, "or an order?"

Lyra arched a brow. "Do you take orders?"

"From you?" Grayson gave her a look. "Absolutely."

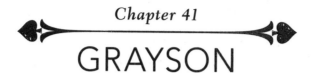

Chapter 41

GRAYSON

A spiraling black and silver staircase took Grayson from the third floor of the yacht to the fourth. The uppermost level was nothing but a deck, as close to a *roof* as one could get on a ship.

Jameson was exactly where Grayson had expected to find him: standing at the edge, leaning on the railing but not standing on top of it anymore.

"We need to talk," Grayson said.

"Ominous," Jameson replied without turning around, his nothing-risked-nothing-gained, push-the-limits tone one that Grayson recognized all too well. "Planning to explain why you requested a perimeter run of the island?"

"That," Grayson said. "And I have questions."

"No, Gray. You don't."

Those words served as a reminder for Grayson that Jameson *wasn't* pushing limits right now. He was running scared, and Grayson needed to know why. He couldn't protect Lyra, let alone give her what she needed, without information, so he said the one thing guaranteed to get his brother's full and undivided attention. "I know who put Lyra in the game."

Jameson whirled to face Grayson.

"Don't mind me, boys." Nash made an entrance, sauntered past Grayson, and took up position a ways away from them both. "I'm just here in case someone needs their ass kicked."

Grayson couldn't help himself. "How's *handling* Nash going?" he asked Jameson.

Jameson didn't take the bait. "What do you know, Gray?"

Grayson did not beat around the bush. "Eve."

Jameson blinked.

"Eve?" Nash echoed. Apparently, he wasn't *just* there for ass-kicking purposes.

"She made it onto the island," Grayson said. "Your current security measures leave much to be desired, by the way. Fire whoever Oren tasked with maintaining a decent perimeter."

Grayson knew without asking that Oren wasn't personally keeping an eye on the ocean around Hawthorne Island, 24-7. Avery's head of security would never divert his attention away from his charge for that long. And Grayson deeply suspected that Jameson hadn't told anyone in security that there was a threat.

Which raises the question of why.

"Why would *Eve* go to the trouble of finding a wild card ticket, just to send it to Lyra and put her in the Grandest Game?" Jameson pressed.

You thought it was someone else. Grayson didn't say that out loud—not yet. "It seems Eve's great-grandfather also kept files, including some focused on our grandfather's enemies. One guess as to who has those files now."

Jameson didn't bother guessing. "What exactly does Eve know?"

"About whatever you're hiding?" Grayson replied. "Nothing. From what Lyra was able to tell, Eve is in the dark about..." Grayson came very close to saying *Alice* but held back. "Matters you refuse to discuss."

Grayson recognized the glint in Jameson's eyes. That was the look of a Hawthorne, sifting through possibilities, updating any and all relevant calculations.

"We will be discussing those matters now," Grayson said.

"No." Jameson turned back toward the railing. "We won't."

"Jamie?" Nash called, his voice deceptively mild. "Climb that thing again and see what happens."

A single glance at Nash was enough to tell Grayson that Jameson had spent the duration of phase two on the edge in more ways than one. Grayson eyed his barely younger brother and made an executive decision. Turnabout was, after all, fair play. "Jamie? *On Spake.*"

Jameson didn't climb the rail then. He jumped it.

By the time Grayson and Nash made it to the railing, Jameson had already swung himself down and into a dead drop.

"*Son of a—*" Nash cut himself off as Jameson stuck the landing on the deck below.

"After you," Grayson told Nash.

The chase was on. It became apparent quickly enough that Jameson wasn't avoiding them so much as leading them into the depths of the yacht and down, level after level, through room after room until he opened a door to a stateroom.

His suite, Grayson registered. *And Avery's.* It looked like something that one would find in a Hawthorne-owned luxury hotel. Panoramic windows would have delivered quite a view in the day, but at night, the ocean was nothing but darkness. Regardless,

Jameson hit a button on the wall, and screens descended, covering the windows.

Privacy.

Almost immediately, the door to the suite flew inward. "What did I miss?" Xander asked.

Grayson didn't even have to look at Jameson to know that he definitely didn't want their youngest brother present for this.

"Xan?" Nash drawled. "Give us a minute."

"I'm sensing that my presence might be adding some stress to an already emotionally wrought situation," Xander said, holding his hands palms up. "But I think we can all agree that I really want to see this."

Jameson glowered at him and pointed to the door.

"Grumpy Charades?" Xander deliberately misconstrued the situation. "I love Grumpy Charades!"

"Gray invoked On Spake," Nash informed him.

"*Grayson* made an invocation?" Xander raised both eyebrows. "The same Grayson Hawthorne who once claimed that the sacred rite of On Spake expired when he was ten?"

"Xander." Avery entered the suite—and the fray—still gowned in the golden infinity gown.

"Milady," Xander replied.

Avery met his gaze. "Please?"

That, more even than Jameson's behavior, set Grayson's teeth on edge. *Whatever is going on here—she knows.* Avery had more sense than Jameson did, but she didn't scare easily, either.

"Xan." Nash fixed their youngest brother with a look. "I've got them." Xander was the great mediator. This was Nash telling him that everything was going to be okay. "And," Nash added, "there are scones in the kitchen."

"Foul play," Xander told Nash. "And for the record: I want photographs, plural, of any and all wrestling that ensues." With that, Xander took his leave. There was a shift in the air when he did, the slightest dissipation of tension.

Like Grayson had told Lyra, he would have died for his brothers—all of them, any of them, but Xander was the baby, and he was *Xander*. Whatever *this* was, it damn well wasn't going to touch him. *Or Libby. Or Avery. Or Lyra.*

Though clearly, the last two were already in *this* up to their elbows.

"Eve is messing with the game," Grayson told Avery, catching her up to speed. "She's the one who sent Lyra her ticket, which I know because Eve somehow snuck onto Hawthorne Island tonight and approached Lyra. And despite what Eve offered her—millions, by the way—Lyra told me." He swiveled his gaze to Jameson. "Because Lyra *is not a threat*."

Jameson opened his mouth to argue, then remembered. On Spake.

"I'm not saying that there *isn't* a threat," Grayson continued. "But the notes on the trees and Lyra's presence in the game—those were Eve. And given that Eve somehow managed to make it onto Hawthorne Island, it's likely enough that the blackout during phase one was her doing as well."

"What's Eve's endgame?" Avery spoke because Jameson could not.

"Eve is not the reason I called On Spake." Grayson directed his next words only to Jameson. "You don't want me even saying the name *Alice Hawthorne*, but the night Lyra's biological father killed himself, he said three things to her. He wished her a happy birthday. He told her *A Hawthorne did this*. And then he spoke a sentence that contained a riddle masked with a deletion code, the answer to which was *omega*."

Jameson took a heavy step toward Grayson. It was fairly clear how this particular invocation of On Spake was going to end.

Grayson was not deterred. It wouldn't be the first time he and Jameson fought. It very likely would not be the last. And he'd made Lyra a promise. "Lyra's father also gave her two things that night. A candy necklace holding only three pieces of candy. And a flower— a calla lily."

Jameson stayed right where he was, a flicker of recognition in his gaze. *You're thinking of the music box puzzle. Good.*

"Lyra is starting to see that night as a game on par with the kind the old man used to lay out for us," Grayson continued. "A series of puzzles, albeit nonsequential ones in this case. Lyra has solved three of the four: *A Hawthorne did this.* Alice. *What begins a bet? Not that.* Omega—not the beginning of the alphabet but the end. The candy necklace—the significance there appears to be the number three. Incidentally, Nash, is someone keeping tabs on Odette Morales?"

"A certain lawyer says Ms. Morales has pulled a disappearing act."

Grayson wondered who Odette was hiding from. *Not us—or not just us, anyway.* "Do you know what Ms. Morales told Lyra and me, Jamie?" Grayson turned his attention back to his silent brother, to the dark, frenetic energy that he could practically see vibrating beneath the surface of Jameson's skin. "She said that there are always *three*."

"Three what?" Nash said.

"Don't know." Grayson clipped the words—and kept his eyes on Jameson, who'd just taken another step toward him.

Avery put herself in Jameson's path, then turned toward Grayson. "Gray." Hazel eyes that Grayson knew all too well settled on his. "You need to stop."

Like Jameson, Avery clearly didn't want Grayson even talking about this, let alone asking questions. But for better or worse, Avery Kylie Grambs was a Hawthorne now in every way that mattered.

"Avery?" Now it was Grayson's turn to hold *her* gaze. *"On Spake."*

She opened her mouth and then closed it again, and Grayson got back to business. "Of the puzzles Lyra's father laid out for her that night," he told Avery and Jameson both, "that just leaves the calla lily. Its meaning is still unknown, but earlier tonight, someone left a fresh one positioned just so on a rock next to the helipad." Grayson flicked his gaze between the two of them. "I can see that I was right in assuming *that* lily was not a part of the game. Eve claimed it wasn't her doing, either. Lyra believes her, and I believe Lyra."

Grayson could tell, looking over Avery at Jameson, that were Avery not between them, Jameson would have already surged forward to grab him by his black silk shirt. Grayson's brother wasn't okay with any part of this discussion.

This *was* going to come down to a fight.

Fully accepting that, Grayson pushed on. "You can see why Lyra might have questions about the music box puzzle, Jamie. You know something. She knows that you know something. And I can't protect her if *I* don't know exactly what it is I'm supposed to be protecting her from."

Jameson lunged forward, and Avery turned, placing her hands flat on his chest, holding him back. Jameson stilled automatically at her touch, and Avery tossed a look back at Grayson, a silent *Are you done?*

He was not. "Lyra is not the problem here, Jameson. She's not the threat. *You* are." Grayson let that sink in. "Your secrets. Whatever *you* have gotten yourself and Avery into."

Jameson's eyes blazed. Grayson turned to Nash. "Am I wrong?"

"Would you believe me if I said you were?" Nash returned, calm as calm could be. "You're in deep with this girl, Gray."

"Tell me that I'm wrong," Grayson challenged.

Nash gave a shake of his head and addressed his next words to Jameson. "He ain't wrong, Jamie. Neither one of us can protect you and Avery from threats we can't see coming."

Grayson let that sink in, and then he widened his stance and met Jameson's eyes. "I call."

Jameson gently removed Avery's hands from his chest. He lowered them to her side, delicately sidestepped her—and *charged*.

Grayson didn't bother planting his feet. He twisted just before impact. Jameson anticipated it. Grayson anticipated that he would. The end result still had them both airborne. That was the thing about fighting someone you knew almost as well as you knew yourself, someone with whom you were very nearly evenly matched: No one was coming out of that kind of fight unscathed—unless there was mud involved, and Grayson had known quite well at the time that that trick would only work once.

Jameson slammed him back into the wall. "I told you not to even say that name."

"*Alice. Hawthorne.*" Grayson broke his brother's hold and reversed their positions. "When have I ever given you the impression that I take orders, little brother?" Grayson locked his arms around both of Jameson's, pinning them to his sides.

Jameson exploded, sending Grayson flying back. "You gave me until the end of the game, Gray."

As Jameson stalked toward him, Grayson saw an opening—not a big one. *But big enough.* He went for it, turning Jameson's momentum against him, but the second Grayson put Jameson on the ground, someone did the same to him, swiping his legs out from underneath him.

Avery. "Nicely executed," Nash told her. Then he hauled both Grayson and Jameson to their feet. "And that's enough, all of you." Nash let loose of them. "Start talkin', Jamie."

With a phrase like that one, it was rarely a good thing when Nash dropped his *g*.

"Telling you a damn thing could put Libby in danger." Jameson went straight for the jugular. "Is that what you want?"

"You let me worry about Lib," Nash said. "Anyone comes at her and the babies, they'll have to go through me, and personally, I don't like their chances." Nash took off his cowboy hat and set it on a dresser. "And Libby would kick your ass *herself* if she knew you just played that card."

"You don't need to know," Jameson gritted out.

Grayson shook his head. This was not going to end well—for Jameson.

"Just walk away." Jameson wasn't looking at Nash now. He was looking at Grayson. "From her. From this."

Lyra. Jameson was asking him to walk away from Lyra Kane. "No."

"We'll call off the game," Jameson said, like Grayson hadn't even spoken. "Eve's interference gives us a plausible reason to."

"You could call off the game," Grayson replied evenly, "but I guarantee you, the first thing Lyra will do is take what she learned here and start looking for answers. She is relentless, Jamie, and highly intelligent." The muscles in Grayson's throat tightened. "And she matters. To me, she *matters*. So you are going to tell me everything you know."

"I will tell you nothing." Jameson was halfway through taking another swing when Nash, who'd clearly reached his limit, intercepted it and tossed Jameson onto the bed.

Grayson stalked to stand over the bed. *Tell me, Jamie.*

Jameson's jaw stayed clamped shut.

Tell me. Grayson stared down at his brother, a promise in his gaze. There were very few times that any of them had done any kind of actual damage to another, but even Grayson's control had its limits.

Suddenly, Avery was standing between them. There was something about the look in her eyes that reminded Grayson that he'd put an end to Jameson's On Spake, but not hers.

"Avery, I call."

"I'm not fighting you." Avery held Grayson's gaze a moment longer, then turned back to look at Jameson. Grayson could feel an entire silent conversation pass between the two of them before Avery spoke again, her voice quiet and raw. "He came back that night bleeding and smelling like fire. There was ash on his skin, a cut on his neck."

Fury surged through Grayson's veins. No one hurt his family and got away with it. "Elaborate."

Avery reached out to put a hand on Jameson's shoulder, and after a moment, Jameson climbed slowly to his feet. "Prague." His voice was a hollow whisper. "More than a year and a half ago now. You want the short version, Gray? A city of secret passages. A map the old man left behind. I followed it."

Of course you did. "And?" Grayson said quietly.

Jameson closed his eyes. "I don't know." Tension rippled visibly over his brow, jagged and pained. "Not exactly. I was drugged. My memory of that night is full of holes. There are *moments*—" Jameson cut off.

Grayson put a hand on his brother's shoulder.

"*Fire*," Jameson managed finally. "*Voices*. And the feeling that I was going to die. That they were going to kill me."

"They?" Grayson said immediately. But all he could think was: *There are always three.*

"I don't know, Gray." Frustration marked every line of Jameson's face as he opened his eyes. "I do remember waking up in a rooftop garden. I had tea with a dead woman. She called me *dear boy* and made it very clear that she needed to stay dead." Jameson swallowed. "Threats were issued. My instructions were clear: *Tell no one*."

Wordlessly, Avery wrapped her arms around Jameson. Grayson's hand was still on Jameson's shoulder. For a moment, the three of them just stood there, breathing as one, and then Nash joined them, his hand planted firmly next to Grayson's on Jameson's back.

"You told Avery." Grayson stated the obvious.

"Eventually, but we never pursued it," Avery said. "We never looked for answers, never looked for *her*."

Alice. The big picture here clearly extended past one woman. Grayson didn't like it. "And the flower?" he asked Jameson. "The calla in the music box?"

"*I don't know*," Jameson said. "I told you—I remember voices. Smoke. The price of wheat. *Fire*. And being threatened. That's it, Grayson."

That clearly wasn't it. On some level, whether he could access it or not, Jameson knew more.

"You aren't alone with this now," Nash told Jameson. He put

a hand on Avery's shoulder, too. "Either of you. And it has to be asked: What about the other calla lily? The one Grayson and Lyra found."

"Brady seemed to think it might be for him," Grayson indicated. "He played it off as if he believed it to be Rohan's doing, but my money is on someone else—most likely his sponsor."

"I chose Brady," Avery said, frowning. "I gave him a ticket to the game. Why would he need a sponsor?"

"What do you know about the girl?" Grayson said. "*Calla* something."

"Missing," Avery replied. "Presumed dead." Realization hit her. "Her name—"

Silence blanketed the room. All of them had a mind for puzzles. All of them were trying to make this one make sense.

"What if Brady's sponsor is Alice?" Jameson pulled away from the rest of them. "If Alice got to Brady somehow, if she's here, if she's *watching*—we can't let on that we know. None of the rest of you are supposed to know any of this."

"We can't call off the game," Avery concluded. "We have to proceed like everything is normal. Like everything is fine."

"Why would our grandmother care about the Grandest Game?" Grayson asked. "Or Brady Daniels?"

"Why would she care about the price of wheat?" Jameson replied.

Grayson rolled that question over in his mind. "*They,*" he said finally. "Why would *they*?"

This time, the silence lasted even longer. Finally, Avery turned to Nash. "You're leaving, aren't you?" she said. "You're going to Libby."

"I'm going to Libby," Nash confirmed. "And I'm dealing Oren

in before I do. He needs to know there's a threat. We can tell him it relates to what happened in Prague without telling him how—should give him an idea of the seriousness of this. His men can search every nook and cranny of Hawthorne Island while the players are here on the yacht. Establish a better perimeter—"

"You can't tell Oren anything," Jameson said. "Nothing I've said can leave this room."

"Have you *met* Avery's head of security?" Nash asked Jameson. "And related question: How would you like John Oren to kill you when he finds out there was a clear and present threat to all of us—to *Avery*—and you never said a word?"

Jameson chewed on that for a moment. "You might have a point," he said grimly. "But Alice's name is never mentioned—not to Oren, not to anyone else."

"We don't know that it's her," Avery pointed out. "Not for sure." Her hazel eyes made their way to Grayson's. "But either way, you need to do damage control, Gray. With Lyra. You need to keep her out of this."

Lyra. Grayson pictured her, wearing his jacket.

"Keep her focused on the game," Jameson told him. "That will buy us some time to figure out how best to handle her."

It was on the tip of Grayson's tongue to tell all of them that one did not *handle* Lyra Kane, but if Alice was *that* much of a threat, for Lyra's sake and the sake of his family...

I might have to.

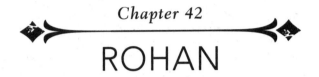

Chapter 42

ROHAN

Rohan had to admit: There were worse ways to spend a late night than exploring a yacht with Savannah Grayson. A movie theater, a spa, multiple lounges, each themed to a different jewel-colored tone—Savannah's gown outshined them all. Even in the dimmest light, it seemed to emanate an almost supernatural glow, like snowflakes in moonlight, like thousands of pearlescent mirrors, each no bigger than the point of a quill.

And even in the dimmest light, Savannah Grayson had her tells: a certain tension in the long, sinewy muscles of her arms, the length of her stride, the exact set of her pale pink lips.

Every time you see Avery Grambs, you start to grieve all over again, and you shut it down.

Rohan said nothing about the change he'd noticed in her the moment they'd stepped onto the yacht, and in return, Savannah didn't say a word about what he'd told her, back in his room. Instead, they both zeroed in—absolutely, intensely, mercilessly—on the game.

On the hints, at least two of them, hidden somewhere on this vessel.

Together, Rohan and Savannah stepped out of the interior of the yacht and onto one of the decks.

"Now this," Rohan said, sauntering forward, "is something." *Something* as in a sight to behold—and *something* as in an excellent place to hide a hint. Built into the deck, there was a large hot tub, clearly operational, and beside it, there was a pool filled to the brim with ice.

Rohan headed straight for the latter. Nestled among hundreds of thousands of ice cubes were bottles of champagne—dozens of them. Gliding over the deck with long, powerful strides, Savannah cut past Rohan to take up position between the hot tub and the pool. In the faint but warm light of the yacht, Rohan could see steam rising from the surface of the hot tub, like smoke in the night.

Rohan crouched, running a hand over the ice and then latching his fingers around a bottle of champagne. "Don't mind if I do." He helped himself to the bottle and thought back to the champagne glasses they'd been given at the beginning of the game.

The next thing he knew, Savannah had her own glass in her hand. *How?* Rohan's gaze went to the white, beaded bag dangling from her wrist. A bold move, transporting something that fragile. Savannah was fortunate it hadn't shattered.

As was he.

"Well?" Savannah demanded. "Are you going to open that champagne or just stand there, staring at the label?"

The label was blank. Rohan did away with the cork and took a swig from the bottle. "Cheers, Savvy."

Savannah shot Rohan a death glare that made him want to make her glare harder, and then she lowered herself to the ground and reached for a bottle of her own. As she prepared to pop it, she aimed the cork squarely at Rohan's chest.

"Like a bullet through the heart," Rohan told her, his voice a low and humming murmur. "And in case you were wondering, love? Yes, that's a challenge."

And yes, it was an invitation.

Savannah popped the cork. Rohan caught it.

"Show-off," Savannah retorted.

"Always," Rohan agreed, making his way to the hot tub. He crouched and sank his champagne bottle into the steaming water. Eyes on Savannah's, he pulled it out. "Voilà."

The label was no longer blank.

"The infinity symbol," Savannah said. "Just like her dress."

Still not saying the heiress's name, Rohan noted. He wondered if Savannah even truly realized that Avery was not the one she hated most, not really. *Grayson* was the one that Savannah had let in.

Family was capable of inflicting wounds the rest of the world could never match.

"Infinity like the dress," Rohan echoed, "and like one of the symbols on the head of our room keys."

Rohan reached into his jacket pocket, producing the key in question. It had played a role in the game already, but better safe than sorry. He pushed at the lemniscate on the key's head—or, viewed differently, the number eight.

Nothing happened.

He tried submersing the key in the hot tub, the way he had the bottle of champagne, and when that, too, yielded no results, he withdrew the key and poured champagne over it.

"Nothing," Rohan commented—out loud this time. He took another swig from the bottle. "Pity to waste it."

"Pity." Savannah poured herself a glass of champagne, and then she joined Rohan at the edge of the hot tub. Kicking off her heels, she sat and pulled her dress up, baring her legs to the knees. Tossing a look at Rohan, she submerged her legs in the hot tub and brought the champagne flute to her mouth.

Rohan caught her wrist, his touch light. "Look."

Luminescent letters had appeared on the flute, to either side of the *H* cut into the crystal. An *N*, an *I*, and a *G* to the left, a lone *T* to the right.

"Night," Rohan said. *Infinity. Night.* "Tricky bastards, aren't they?" he asked Savannah, ridding himself of shoes and socks, and beginning to roll up the pants on his deep purple tux. "First they drown us in details, obfuscating the actual clue in any given puzzle, and then they give us enough hints to do the same."

"More than one puzzle." Savannah's calm was a thing to behold. "More than one hint."

"Unless, of course, they're meant to go together." Rohan sat and sank his legs into the hot tub, the shock of heat nothing to him. "*Infinity. Night.* Endless night."

"Except this night isn't endless," Savannah countered. "We only have, what, four or five hours until dawn?"

With each passing minute, the two of them drew closer to the end of the game, to the moment when one person winning would require the utter obliteration of the other.

"We're losing." Savannah's tone made it clear that she could not and would not tolerate that.

"Brady is at least one puzzle ahead of us," Rohan agreed. "Perhaps two. For all we know, the hints we've uncovered are for his puzzle, not ours."

Savannah looked at her glass. "How did he pull ahead of us to begin with?"

That question might have been rhetorical, but Rohan recognized the benefit of considering every possible answer to even the most rhetorical of questions. "Based on his performance in last year's Grandest Game," he noted, "Brady Daniels particularly excels at puzzles involving symbology, mythology, and *music*."

Savannah glanced down at the writing on her arm. Rohan raised his hand to just *almost* touch her skin. Taking in the code, he moved his fingers slowly down her arm, never touching her or the ink, but letting her feel the ghost of his touch.

"May I?" Rohan asked.

"If you must," Savannah said.

Oh, I must, Savvy. Rohan started low on Savannah's arm this time and worked his way up, letter by letter. His touch light, Rohan weaved his way in and out of the writing, taking in each piece of the puzzle—each music note, beginning with the waltz and ending with "Clair de lune."

Halfway through, Savannah's breath hitched. *Like that, do you, love?*

Three-quarters of the way through, Rohan let himself imagine Savannah Grayson slipping off that dress and slipping fully into the hot tub.

As he saw his task through to the end, he leaned toward her, tilted his head down, and spoke directly into her ear. "D, A, G, A," he murmured. One section of "Clair de lune." "E, E, F." Another.

"*Adage*." Savannah's voice wasn't nearly as high or clear as her normal speaking tone. "Or *aged*. Or *fade*."

Rohan let his touch linger on the final note. "There's too many notes across the three songs for this puzzle to be as simple as spelling a word."

Savannah reached up to run her own hand over letter after letter, her gaze on Rohan. "Our next move seems clear then, does it not?"

She smelled faintly of jasmine and vanilla. "Why don't you *clarify* that move for me, love?" He added the endearment just to see her eyes flash.

"It's clear," Savannah said tartly, "that Brady Daniels has already solved this puzzle. Equally clear is the fact that he is without any allies in this game. And we have leverage on him."

Rohan thought about the invisible messages on the backs of those photographs of Calla Thorp. "Proof of communication with his sponsor. We could take him out of the game."

"Or," Savannah murmured, "we could use him."

He brought his fingers to Savannah's collarbone, lightly tracing it from one shoulder to the other. "What precisely are you suggesting, Savvy?"

Savannah gripped his jaw and angled his head back, exposing his neck. "I'm suggesting," she said, bringing her mouth down to speak directly into *his* ear, "that I convince Brady Daniels that my loyalties are . . . fungible."

Her lips brushed over an artery in his neck, and Rohan wondered if she could see his pulse, feel it.

"Your loyalties *are* fungible," he pointed out. "But if you can get something useful out of Brady Daniels before we have him disqualified, if you can string him along and keep getting things out of him . . ." There wasn't all that much of her hair left to grab, but Rohan made do, angling *her* head back. "So be it."

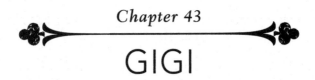

Chapter 43

GIGI

It had taken some doing, but eventually, Gigi's gruff rescuer had broken and given her his name. Now Gigi's new buddy *Jackson* was asleep in a chair at his beat-up kitchen-table-for-one, his shotgun beside him, his chair turned to face the metal door to his tiny house—which, Gigi had to admit, a less optimistic person might have referred to as a *shack*.

A less optimistic person might also have been concerned with the fact that said shack was in clear view of the lighthouse, but Gigi excelled at looking on the bright side.

Such as: Jackson had given her the bed—or technically, the mattress. Such chivalry! Such beard!

And to be honest, Cranky Men Who Hate Everyone were kind of Gigi's specialty. Besides, it was the middle of the night. Even if she did manage to make it into town somehow, everything would be closed. And even if she managed to somehow get ahold of a phone, Gigi only had three telephone numbers memorized: Grayson's, her mother's, and Savannah's. Two of the three of them were *in* the game without their phones, and the third was in Arizona, which meant that Gigi's only real option in town would have been to go to the police, and that wouldn't get her to Hawthorne Island.

It wouldn't get her to Savannah.

So waiting until morning it was. Unfortunately, all Gigi could do was lie there and think about how much Savannah was probably hurting and the lengths her sister would almost certainly go to in order to pretend she wasn't.

A whistling of wind. A creak of wood. Sounds broke Gigi from her thoughts. *Slate?* Gigi glanced at Jackson—and his gun. *It would serve Mr. I Am Sorry About This right,* she thought. *But...*

Gigi sat up and slowly made her way to the door. She didn't want Slate *dead.* Just... properly remorseful.

For what felt like a small eternity, Gigi stood on the inside of the metal door, listening, but there wasn't a single sound. Not the wind. Not the creaking of wood.

Finally, she flipped the deadbolt and opened the metal door all of an inch. There was no one there—but there was something on the ground. Gigi couldn't quite make it out with only a bathroom light on behind her, but that didn't stop her from crouching down to get a better look.

A flower. Gigi shook her head. It was only a flower.

Chapter 44

LYRA

Lyra tried to be methodical about the way she searched the yacht, but it was a *yacht*. Maybe some people were wired for yacht parties and moonlit masquerades, but to Lyra, it was like having fallen into Wonderland.

Poker chips made out of meteorites.

A ship so massive it had its own movie theater.

Bars—plural—stocked with ornate bottles, most of which looked like they cost at least as much as Lyra's diamond-studded mask.

The opulence of it all made Lyra wonder what Grayson would think if she took him to Mile's End. She wondered if he knew how to climb trees, wondered if Grayson Hawthorne had ever skinned his knees or tracked mud across a carpet.

She wondered what oh-so-proper Grayson would look like muddy.

Pushing open another door, Lyra found herself surrounded. It took her a moment to realize that the walls, ceiling, and floor were all completely lined with mirrors. There was nothing else in the room—just the mirrors.

Stepping across the threshold and allowing the door to close behind her, Lyra turned, taking in the three-hundred-sixty-degree view. As she spun, the chiffon fabric of her gown fanned out, the dark rainbow of colors on full display. *Darkest Sunset*. The mask on Lyra's face sparkled, her lips and her jawline the only features on her face not even partially obscured.

She was still wearing Grayson's jacket.

Look with your fingers, Lyra told herself, *not with your eyes*. She walked to the edge of the room, then began making her way around its perimeter, her fingers trailing the mirrored wall so lightly they left no marks.

Before she even made it to the first seam in the glass, a section of the wall across from her swung inward like a door, and Rohan stepped through. In contrast to the white jacket around Lyra's shoulders, the tuxedo that Rohan wore was a deep, rich purple.

"It's a rented yacht," he declared, his accent downright aristocratic. "But they managed to find one with a few hidden doors. How very Hawthorne of them."

"What makes you so sure the yacht is rented?" Lyra replied.

"I could tell you, but..." Rohan trailed off and crossed the diagonal, putting his hand flat on another mirrored section of the wall. "I don't want to," he finished, and then he pushed, revealing yet another hidden door.

Almost immediately, the room was hit with a visible blast of heat. *Steam*.

"Looks like I found the steam room," Rohan announced. Eyeing Grayson's jacket on Lyra's shoulders, Rohan shrugged off his own tuxedo jacket. "Mind if I take off my shirt, too?" He didn't bother with the buttons, just pulled it off over his head, exposing his abs.

Lyra rolled her eyes. "I was just leaving."

"You could," Rohan agreed, dropping his hold on the mirrored door, allowing it to swing shut and disappear into the wall once more, locking away the steam. "Or you could stay and ask me what I know."

Something about the set of her opponent's knife-sharp features and the look in Rohan's fathomless brown eyes made Lyra think that he really did know something.

"Ask you what you know," she repeated flatly, "about the game?"

Rohan flashed her a smile. "Depends on your definition of *the game*."

Lyra crossed her arms over her torso, utterly immune to his nonsense—and his bare chest. "What do you know?"

Rohan's gaze settled onto hers, and there was a subtle shift in his features, pretensions falling away like writing wiped from sand. "Jameson Hawthorne wants you out of the Grandest Game. He tasked me with finding something that would let him disqualify you."

Lyra wanted to believe that this was just Rohan playing more mind games with the competition, but she couldn't help thinking about the way that Jameson had looked down at her from the railing earlier. That Jameson had been a far cry from the one who'd welcomed her to the game.

"And why would Jameson Hawthorne do that?" Lyra replied, channeling Grayson in her tone—all control, no tells.

Rohan gave an elegant little shrug. "I was rather hoping you could tell me."

Lyra studied Rohan—the size of his pupils, the tilt of his

lips—and Brady's assessment from the bonfire came back to her. "Divide and conquer," Lyra said. "An expected strategy."

Rohan flashed her another smile. "Is it working?"

"Are you lying?" Lyra mimicked his tone, if not his smile.

"I am not." Rohan held her gaze a moment longer, then turned his attention back toward the mirrored door. "The steam room calls."

This time, Lyra really did leave. She had a hint to find—even if Jameson Hawthorne really did want her gone.

Chapter 45

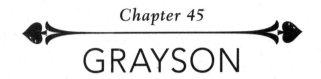

GRAYSON

T here was one more thing that Grayson needed to take care of before he could return to Lyra. Thus, his current location. He knocked on the open door to an ostentatious office, announcing his presence to the power-suit-clad woman behind the desk.

"You." Alisa Ortega greeted Grayson with a single word and narrowed eyes. She was Avery's lawyer, closer to a fixer, really, but long before Alisa Ortega had been either of those things, she'd been a girl growing up Hawthorne-adjacent, the only daughter of Tobias Hawthorne's most trusted legal counsel. Grayson had been a bane of Alisa's existence for roughly as long as he'd worn suits.

There weren't many people who could claim to have babysat the three younger Hawthorne brothers.

"Salutations," Grayson said dryly.

"You and your brothers are nothing but trouble." Alisa closed her laptop. "And don't even get me started on your sisters."

"What did Savannah do?" Grayson asked.

"Doubtlessly something," Alisa replied, "however—"

"Talking about Savannah, she was not," Xander intoned, squeezing past Grayson, a scone in each hand. Grayson knew his brother well enough to know that Xander had probably followed him here.

Scones or no scones, the youngest Hawthorne brother hadn't given up on figuring out what was going on.

It's better you don't know, Xan. And right now, Grayson had other concerns. "Gigi." He turned his attention back to Alisa. "Have you tracked her down?"

"Found her, she has not," Xander said sagely. "Gave Alisa and her people the slip, the young adventurer did."

"Yoda me again," Alisa told Xander, "and every baked good on this ship conveniently disappears. As for *your* status report..." Alisa turned her attention back to Grayson. "We found the boat Gigi helped herself to about thirty miles up the coast."

"And by *the* boat," Xander said helpfully, "you mean *my* boat." He looked to Grayson. "I was the last one to see Gigi before she took off, and I can report that she had a Gigi Plan, capital G, capital P. She was definitely up to something."

"And you didn't stop her?" Grayson narrowed his eyes at his brother.

"Gigi didn't need me to stop her." Xander took a delicate bite of each scone. "She needed snuggles and a pep talk. There were Viking epics involved."

"The two of you should not be together unsupervised," Grayson muttered, and then he turned back to Alisa. "Who do you have looking for her?" Given the magnitude of the potential threat out there, he wanted his sister found. *Now.*

"Two of my teams and a short-term contractor." Alisa wasn't exactly fond of having her methods questioned.

"Ask her who the contractor is," Xander suggested, wiggling his eyebrows. And then he preempted the question he'd just suggested. "Knox Landry."

Now that, Grayson had not expected. Knox had been a player in the Grandest Game, on Gigi's team.

"Though Mr. Landry's charms may be limited," Alisa said, "he can fit in with even the roughest locals, up and down the coast. There might be a bar fight or two in his future, but smart money says he'll find Gigi first. And he volunteered."

Grayson couldn't help thinking that Gigi had a way of endearing herself to people. Relentlessly. "Volunteer might be a bit generous," Grayson observed. "You're paying him." Alisa had referred to Landry as a contractor.

"Calls her *Lawyer Lady*, Knox Landry does," Xander said. "Bicker, they do."

Alisa pointed at Xander. "Out."

Xander grinned, but on his way out, he called back to Grayson: "If there's a threat, Alisa needs to know."

Alisa's poker face prevented her from showing any visible response to that proclamation. Like Oren, she watched out for Avery—for all of them, really. In another life, if things had gone differently for Alisa and Nash, her last name might have been Hawthorne.

Not that she would have taken Nash's name. Grayson did what he could to douse the fire Xander had just merrily set. "I can neither confirm nor deny," he told Alisa, "that there is a situation."

Be on guard, he telegraphed silently. *Be careful. And find Gigi.*

Alisa gave a curt nod. "Understood. I'll find your sister, Grayson. Will that be all?"

Grayson wasn't quite done being a thorn in Alisa's side yet. "Odette Morales," he said. "I understand she's difficult to locate." Grayson gave Alisa a *look* but did not elaborate at all.

With Alisa Ortega, he didn't have to.

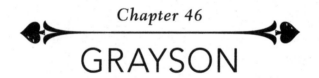

Chapter 46

GRAYSON

Grayson found Lyra exactly where he'd left her—at the roulette table, looking for all the world like she belonged there. The diamond-kissed mask on her face held back her dark hair, which was more tangled than it had been when Grayson had left her. He wondered if those tangles were a product of the wind or the ocean spray or simply the way Lyra Kane always moved like there were no limits to what her body could do.

Grayson's fingers itched to untangle her hair, but he had more control than that. *Most of the time, at least.*

"I haven't just been standing around and waiting," Lyra said, and Grayson realized belatedly that she was holding the roulette ball in her hand, using her fingers to move it back and forth across her palm. "I searched the boat."

There was something different about Lyra, the slightest of shifts.

"Technically," Grayson said, coming to stand on the opposite side of the roulette wheel, lest he forget himself, "it's a ship."

"Technically"—Lyra stared at the wheel—"it's a yacht."

"Superyacht." Grayson lips curved. "Technically."

Lyra's gaze flicked up to settle on his. "You think you know everything."

"I know that something happened to upset you while you were searching." Grayson offered no evidence for the statement he'd just made and asked no follow-up questions that might have tipped her off to the fact that he was making an educated guess.

"I didn't find anything," Lyra said, and if Grayson had been a different person, he might have believed that her search turning up nothing was indeed all that had upset her. But there was tension visible in the way she stood, her arms braced against the table, rolling that ball around in her palm. *Something upset you. Something more.*

"Look." Lyra rolled the ball and spun the wheel. "It lands on eight every time."

She was trying to distract him. Grayson just wasn't sure why.

"What did your brothers and Avery say about the lily in the music box?"

Grayson had been trained from a young age to never hesitate and never show weakness. "Jameson said that roses are overdone, sunflowers and daisies are, and I quote, *the flower equivalents of a golden retriever on uppers*, and that tulips remind him of the reason he was banned from Amsterdam." Grayson, like all Hawthornes, was an excellent liar. He picked up the ball and spun the roulette wheel again. "Hence, the lily."

"A calla." Lyra clearly wasn't inclined to let this go. The mask she wore should have dimmed the hold her amber eyes had on Grayson, but it did not.

"Xander," Grayson deadpanned, "says that callas taste better than normal lilies."

"Taste better?" Lyra repeated. "Does your brother just go around taking bites out of flowers?"

"He did for a few weeks when he was seven," Grayson confirmed. "For science. It did not end well." *That* was true.

Lyra snorted. "Weirdly enough, that tracks."

Of course it did. The secret to being an excellent liar was to selectively wield the truth. "None of us remembers anything about a calla lily in any of the old man's games." *Also true.* "That's not a guarantee that there wasn't one."

"But it *is* a dead end." Lyra was quiet for a moment. She looked away, and Grayson was hit with the sense that there were layers to this moment: The moment she was having. His. Theirs. He decided to live in the simplest of those—the one where nothing was a lie. The one where they really could focus on the game.

"What do we make," he asked Lyra, "of the number *eight*?"

Slowly, Lyra turned her face back toward his. Her diamond-studded mask served only to draw his attention to her lips. She opened her mouth, and Grayson was suddenly hit with the feeling that whatever she asked of him in that moment, he would not be able to deny her—no matter how dangerous it was.

So he didn't let her ask.

"Lyra." Grayson put a certain intensity in his voice. *"Infinity. Eight."* Grayson didn't have the answer, but making her think he'd had a breakthrough would buy him some time—not much, a minute or less, but Hawthornes had taken on worse odds.

Lyra was far too competitive not to take the bait. "What?" she demanded.

Grayson needed to stall her long enough to figure out a revelation of some sort to share. "One of the most frequent echoes in my grandfather's game was the use of keys." Another truth. "There was one puzzle in particular that was a rite of passage in our household. We were given a massive ring of keys, each more elaborate and ornate than the last. The heads of those keys bore different designs. The challenge was simple. One and only one of those keys opened the front door of Hawthorne House. The old man timed how long it took each of us to find the right key."

"And?" Lyra crossed to his side of the table. He'd succeeded in making her think he'd had some kind of breakthrough, and now he needed to deliver. He allowed his mind to work the way the old man's had—thinking in four dimensions—even as he continued stalling.

"And the trick was," Grayson continued, "that although the heads of the keys differed, the portion that went into the lock was the same on all of the keys but one."

"And that was the key that opened the lock," Lyra concluded, waiting for him to get to the point. It was clear just from the look on her face that her mind was churning, looking for the very answer that Grayson had himself yet to obtain.

Infinity. Eight.

"The old man liked to embed lessons in his games," Grayson said, aware that his distraction would soon lose its hold on her. "The lesson of the keys was twofold. First, that two things—or people—who looked very different on the surface could be exactly the same underneath."

Lyra looked down, and Grayson wondered if she was thinking about the two of them. Her breath hitched slightly, and Grayson felt that lone hitch of her breath in every single hollow place.

"And second," he continued, his hand making its way to her hair, as he finally gave in to the impulse to let his fingers begin to untangle it, "that nearly all problems are a matter of perspective."

Touching her felt right. Even when it was just his hand and her hair. Even when he couldn't feel the softness of her skin. It felt *right*—and it bought him just a little more time.

Grayson knew that he was a bastard for doing this to her, the very *asshole* that she had accused him of being multiple times. But Lyra was, in her own way, fearless, and she was dogged in pursuit of truth, and she wouldn't care that Alice Hawthorne was dangerous.

He cared. About her. About Avery and his brothers. About Libby and the babies.

Grayson Hawthorne had always—always—cared too damn much.

"A matter of perspective," Lyra repeated, then suddenly, she looked down at the roulette wheel—and then back up again. "Are you saying that maybe the symbol isn't infinity *or* eight?"

Keep her focused on the game. Grayson took Lyra's hand in his, and he drew the symbol on her palm: one loop, then another.

"I see it," Lyra said again. "Not literally, but..." She looked at the game tables all around them, at the masks scattered on those tables.

And just like that, Grayson saw it, too. Lyra Kane was remarkable. She was lethal in the best possible way, and she was right.

"What if it isn't a symbol at all?" Grayson murmured, lifting his hand to her face and feeling the delicate metal and jewels of her mask beneath his fingertips. "What if it's a very rudimentary drawing?"

"What if," Lyra said, her voice low, "it's a mask?"

Chapter 47

ROHAN

R ohan did not mind sweating—or waiting. Steam had a habit of rising to the ceiling, but when there was enough of it, it also tended to stick to mirrors, fogging them up—except where some kind of invisible coating had been applied.

The kind that was water resistant.

Four mirrored walls surrounded Rohan, and now, on each of those walls, roughly at eye level, was an infinity symbol. There was some variation in the exact placement of the symbols. *Eye level for different individuals.* Rohan stepped up to the mirror that bore the symbol at the level closest to his height. The infinity symbol was superimposed over his blurred reflection—over his face, its shape now obvious.

A mask over his mask.

"Clever," Rohan said, his voice echoing through the mirrored room, through steam growing heavier in the air by the moment. Shifting his suit jacket and shirt to his left hand, Rohan lifted his right to his own mask, the one he'd been given at the start of the Grandest Game.

An object with a specific use—just like the sword, just like the key. Rohan turned his metallic, asymmetrical mask over in his hand, then stepped into the hall to inspect the back.

And there it was, engraved in the tiniest scrawl. *A hint.* Two words, nothing vague or difficult to interpret about them.

Time Signatures

The waltz, the tango, and "Clair de lune." Three songs, three different time signatures. *Three-four, four-four, nine-eight.* How could he have played that piano and not seen it?

Not *heard* or felt it?

As with all puzzles properly constructed, the answer was simple—simpler, in a whole host of ways, than the hint.

Thirty-four, forty-four, ninety-eight. Three numbers. Rohan would have known exactly where to go with that, even if the calla lily in the music box had not been made of white marble, struck through gold—the same stone as a certain vault-like door.

"Not bad," Rohan said under his breath.

"I'm flattered." Jameson appeared at the end of the hall. He eyed Rohan's bare chest as he strolled around the corner. "Get dressed."

"Not a phrase I hear all that often." Rohan made no move to put on either his tuxedo jacket or the midnight blue dress shirt he'd worn underneath. "Lyra Kane knows you put me on her," he told Jameson.

"How would she know that?" Jameson had an excellent poker face.

Rohan shrugged his bare shoulders, like he didn't have a care in the world. "I told her."

Jameson stalked down the long hall toward Rohan. "Why the hell—"

"—did you want her out of the game and gone to begin with?" Rohan cut in. "A valid question, I agree." He looked Jameson up and down, sizing him up as quickly and neatly as he once had in a fighting ring. "Something has you frazzled, Mr. Hawthorne, and it occurs to me that it might be a *secret*."

Rohan was walking a very thin line, but he'd spent a lifetime doing exactly that, and if there was one thing that it had taught him, it was that there was never any harm in securing for oneself a backup plan. He was *going* to win the Grandest Game and, in doing so, win the Mercy. But if the worst somehow happened, there was potential in *this*.

In whatever had Jameson Hawthorne on edge. In his secret.

For that matter, there was potential here even if Rohan won. The Proprietor of the Devil's Mercy traded in secrets.

"Did you read what I wrote?" Jameson demanded.

You played my game once, Jameson Hawthorne. And to get in, you put up a secret, wrote it down, agreed to forfeit it if you lost. "The Proprietor never would have allowed that," Rohan assured his mark. "Your secret is safe—from me."

"I wasn't in my right mind," Jameson said. "Back then."

"Who among us hasn't gotten a little reckless?" Rohan replied. He studied Jameson for a moment. "It looms large in your mind, doesn't it?" he asked. "My game. The Mercy." Rohan reached for the labyrinth, for details stored, if not ever explicitly noted. "I cannot help but notice certain parallels. A lemniscate, like the one laid into the floor of the atrium of the Devil's Mercy. Ledgers bound in leather." Rohan slipped on his tuxedo jacket without bothering with the shirt. "This exact shade of purple is the color of the ink in which you wrote that horrible secret of yours that I do not know."

Even if he had known Jameson's secret, Rohan couldn't have used it. That was one of the terms of the challenge that had been laid at his feet. He could not use any information obtained while in the Mercy's employ. But that Jameson Hawthorne *had* a secret— well, that was more of a gray area.

After all, everyone had secrets.

"The music box," Rohan continued, "and keys, of course, both lifted straight from my game to yours."

"You hardly invented keys," Jameson retorted, but Rohan had an unerring sense for when he'd gotten to another person. He was fairly certain that until he'd pointed it out, Jameson very likely had not noticed how much of this game could be traced back to the Mercy, to *Rohan*.

"You have a secret," Rohan reiterated, letting his upper-crust accent shift to something with a bit more force, "and *something* has you shaken." Rohan used his discarded shirt to wipe sweat from his face and neck, his eyes never leaving Jameson's. "If you decide you require actual assistance with either of those things once the game is done—there is some possibility that I can be bought."

And there it was: A net. A backup plan. An offer from one gentleman to another.

"You need money," Jameson flatly. He did not seem inclined to take Rohan up on his offer. *Yet.*

"I do," Rohan confirmed, "and *you* are running a race against a ticking clock, because by the time this game is over, by the time I win—I won't."

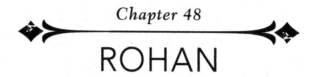

Chapter 48

ROHAN

Armed with the solution to the music box puzzle and bathed in the familiar feeling of having begun to tug certain strings just so, Rohan decided it was time to check in on Savannah—not that she would thank him for it.

But then, she didn't need to know.

Rohan exited the interior of the yacht, made his way to the starboard side of the ship, and began scaling the outside, stopping only when he reached the very top. Standing on the highest point of the ship, he scanned his surroundings, not caring that it was night. Any light was enough for someone who had spent as much time in darkness as Rohan had.

And Savannah glowed.

Rohan spotted her at the front of the ship, sitting on the helipad, her legs dangling over the edge. She wasn't alone. *Well done, love.* Rohan began the climb down. He might have signed off on Savannah's plan to offer up her *fungible* loyalty to Brady Daniels to wring whatever use out of him they could, but Rohan had never promised to trust her.

Trusting other people was always a mistake.

In less than a minute, Rohan had made his way down the side of the yacht and *past* the lowest deck. As a child, there had been days when practicing his grip had made the muscles in Rohan's fingers and palms cramp so badly that his hands had turned to claws. But nowadays, he could climb anything—vertical or otherwise.

Using raised embellishments on the side of the yacht for holds, Rohan moved swiftly. Close enough to the ocean that he could feel the spray of every individual wave, he took himself to the place in his mind that was beyond pain, beyond thinking or feeling.

He stopped moving only when he was close enough to hear.

"—double-cross your current partner?" Brady Daniels had a deep voice, pleasant enough.

Savannah's, in contrast, was high and clear, cutting through the air like a diamond-studded blade. "*Partner* is an overstatement. Rohan knows quite well that our interests only align to a point."

Rohan smiled. *There you are, winter girl.*

"And that point is...," Brady prompted.

"A matter of some internal debate. At this juncture, I could be persuaded of many things, and I have to say, Mr. Daniels, that you strike me as the debate team type."

"It's the glasses," Brady replied.

Rohan wondered if Brady was peering at Savannah through those glasses, but from this angle, he couldn't see a thing, could only hear them.

"On day one of this competition," Brady commented mildly, "you told your sister that she couldn't trust anyone in this game. You warned Gigi that I wasn't her friend."

"Was I wrong?"

"You were not." Brady Daniels left it at that.

Rohan wondered what the scholar's read on Savannah Grayson was. Obviously, he'd be suspicious of her, but did he have any idea what she was truly capable of?

Rohan hadn't—at first. *Make your move, Savvy*, he thought. *Any time now, love.*

"Gigi didn't know on day one that you were playing this game for Calla." Savannah gave that name its due. "Who was she to you?"

"Someone I knew," Brady replied quietly, "once upon a time."

"Are you a fan of fairy tales, Mr. Daniels?"

"A few of them." Brady Daniels paused in a way that made Rohan think he was studying Savannah like a handwritten letter or a broken clay pot or a piece of priceless art. "*Les Fées*, for example."

"*The Fairies*," Savannah translated.

"You speak French."

"Was that a question?" Savannah said archly.

"It was not. *Les Fées* is a tale sometimes known as *Diamonds and Toads*. Are you familiar with the story, Savannah?"

"Pretend," Savannah replied, "that I am not."

She didn't have it in her to admit to *not* knowing something, and if she *did* know—well, there were benefits to getting an opponent talking. *I see you, winter girl.*

"It's a story of two sisters," Brady said. "One kind, one unkind."

Rather brutal. Rohan hadn't thought the scholar had it in him.

"Do go on," Savannah said.

"The younger sister—the kind one—offers a poor old woman a drink, and in return, the kind sister is given a magical blessing. Every time she speaks, diamonds and jewels fall from her lips like drops of rain from the sky."

"I take it the older, unkind sister is likewise tested, fails, and gets a curse and toads?" Savannah cut straight to the chase. She was the first-born twin, the older sister to a little sister who was *very kind*.

"Toads," Brady confirmed. "And snakes."

"And it's assumed, of course," Savannah said, "that it's better to be a girl who spits diamonds than snakes."

Rohan could picture her, shaking her head in a way that would have set her braid singing, back when her platinum blond hair came down to her waist.

"But how much would you like to wager, Mr. Daniels," Savannah continued, just a hint of tantalizing anger working its way into her tone, "that no one ever really listened to either of those girls again?"

If Brady Daniels had been hoping to get the measure of Savannah Grayson—well, he had it now.

"Is that what you want?" Brady asked her. "To be listened to?"

That was *exactly* what she wanted—far too close, Rohan suspected, for Savannah's comfort. She wanted to win the Grandest Game so that she could tell the world that her father was dead and point a finger at the Hawthorne heiress on a livestream with hordes of people watching.

Or at least, that was the plan as she'd described it to him.

"I want to win." Savannah was quite skilled at masking one truth by telling another. "You obviously want the same." Savannah made another move then. *"Do exactly as I say. The game must go on. Ensure that it does.* Someone is pulling your strings. Whoever it is sounds a bit threatening, if you ask me."

Oh, Rohan wished he could see the expression on Brady's face now. *Well played, Savvy.*

"Does Rohan know?" Brady asked finally.

"About your sponsor? About the way that sponsor is communicating with you?" Savannah said. "No. Are you interested in having an ally in this game, Mr. Daniels? Because I won't be asking again."

"I'm listening," Brady said, and Rohan knew that he hadn't chosen those words on accident.

"I'll stay quiet about the photographs, about your sponsor and any rules that you might or might not have already broken. I'll aid you in the game and you will do the same for me—until the end."

"I assume the terms of your alliance with Rohan are similar," Brady said, "and that you'll continue to work with him as well, pitting the two of us against each other if and when it suits you."

"Why is it," Savannah replied, "that men can make the prospect of a woman doing what *suits her* sound like a cardinal sin? I'm making you an offer, Mr. Daniels. If it doesn't suit *you*, then by all means, decline."

A large wave hit the side of the yacht, soaking Rohan's tuxedo. As focused as he was, he shouldn't have even felt it, the same way he wasn't feeling the pain of staying in position, clinging to the yacht.

But the water was cold, and the ocean was velvety black beneath him, and he never had learned how to swim all that well.

Not. Now.

"Before we make a deal"—Brady's voice came to Rohan as if across a great distance—"you should ask me what *I* have to offer, Ms. Grayson."

Rohan listened for Savannah's voice, listened like his life and his sanity depended on it.

"What *you* have to offer?" Savannah said. "Or what your sponsor does?"

Pain seeped into Rohan's muscles as they cramped—but pain was *good*. Pain kept the memories at bay, even as it also threatened his grip on the side of the boat. Still, Rohan refused to go in, refused to move.

"My sponsor knows where the body is buried," Brady said. Rohan presumed he was talking about Calla Thorp's body. And yet...Brady had previously used the present tense in referring to her.

"The body?" Savannah said coolly.

"Your father's." Brady's voice was far too calm. "My sponsor knows how and where they disposed of his remains. *Proof*, Savannah, of what befell your father, and you don't have to be my ally to earn that information. You don't have to help me win. All you have to do is find a way to take Rohan out of the game."

Chapter 49

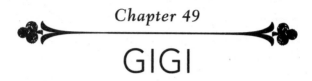

GIGI

S mile, honey."

Gigi blinked. Repeatedly. On some level, she knew she was dreaming. She had to be. "Dad?" Gigi's father was dead, but he was also *right there*. He reached out a hand to touch her hair. "There's my happy girl."

"Don't take this the wrong way," Gigi told her father, "but you're ... less than alive."

Sheffield Grayson gave Gigi an indulgent look. "You don't need to worry about that."

"Right," Gigi said, her heart twisting. "Because I'm not the one who worries. I'm not the serious twin, the one who thinks too much—or at all, right?" She swallowed. "I'm not the one who wins."

Why was she even arguing with him about this?

"And you," Gigi said softly, "are a murderer." He was dead, and he'd died doing awful things—but he was also *right there*, and this time, when Gigi's father looked at her, there was absolutely nothing indulgent in his expression.

There was a warning. "Smile, Juliet."

"Juliet." Another voice spoke behind Gigi, and she whirled. Just like that, her father was gone, and she was looking up into another familiar face. *Square jaw, deep brown skin, eyes that missed nothing.*

"Brady." For a split second, when Gigi saw Brady Daniels, she forgot how things had ended between them. "Tell me something about chaos theory?" she asked him.

"Not chaos theory." His voice was more familiar than it should have been—that deep, calm-in-a-storm voice. It wasn't until he took a step forward that Gigi remembered everything.

And that was when she saw the knife.

"Not chaos theory," Gigi repeated, her throat threatening to close in around the words.

"A closed system." Brady plunged the knife into her chest. "Nothing in, nothing out."

He lowered her body gently to the ground. "For Calla," he whispered.

"I tried to warn you, Happy." Suddenly, it wasn't Brady crouched next to Gigi. It was Knox. "I told you the players in this game were going to eat you alive."

Blood was pooling around the knife in Gigi's chest. "I'm not bleeding out," she insisted. "This is just...extreme exfoliation of the chest region."

Knox locked his hand around the hilt of the knife—*Slate's knife,* Gigi realized—and pulled it out of her chest. "Then get up," he growled at Gigi. "And *fight.*"

Gigi woke with a gasp, lying on her back on what was quite

possibly the least comfortable mattress in existence. She sat up, her eyes going straight to Jackson's chair. *Empty.*

Jackson wasn't there. Neither was his shotgun. Gigi listened, and it only took her two seconds to verify: *He's gone.* She turned in bed, her eyes going to the flower she'd found in the night.

A calla lily.

Brady's dream-voice echoed in her mind—*"For Calla"*—and Gigi physically shook her head. "That's it, subconscious," she declared. "You're in time-out."

Gigi slipped out of bed and crept toward the metal door to Jackson's abode. Her bearded friend was probably just out preparing his boat for their ride to Hawthorne Island. He definitely hadn't just left her here. Without a phone. Far too close to the lighthouse for comfort.

"Everything is fine," Gigi told herself. She cracked the metal door and peered out. *Morning twilight.* The sun hadn't quite risen yet, but already the sky was taking on an unearthly orange glow, stark against velvety purple—what remained of the night sky.

Gigi opened the metal door a little bit wider. From where she was standing, she could *see* the lighthouse. She wondered if Slate had returned in the night to find her missing. She wondered if he'd looked for her.

She wondered what he was doing now.

And then she thought about her dream, about the knife in her chest, and Gigi *stopped* wondering. She closed the metal door and flipped the bolt. Jackson was coming back. He was taking her to Hawthorne Island.

To Savannah.

All she had to do was wait.

Gigi did not excel at waiting. The next time she opened the door, the sun had just begun to peek over the Western horizon. She checked the lighthouse again. *Still nothing.*

"If I were a boat," she said out loud, "where would I be?"

Gigi eyeballed her surroundings. Wild grass grew from rocky ground—and some of that grass looked a bit worse for the wear.

A path.

It would take her away from the lighthouse and in the opposite direction of town. They were right on the coast, which meant that the path in question could very easily wind its way back toward the water.

To a boat. Gigi hesitated, which was either a sign of personal growth or an indication that she was off her game. Honestly, it was impossible to tell. But Savannah was out there. Savannah was *hurting*, and Gigi had to get to her twin before Savannah did something she couldn't take back.

"Boatward, ho!" Gigi declared. She took to the beaten path. Eventually, it *did* curve back toward the water—and a small dock, which contained exactly one boat that looked like it had been built in the seventies.

That tracks. "Jackson?" she called. She searched the boat—first above, then down below, and... *nothing*. No Jackson.

Gigi let out a long, slow breath. "How hard could it possibly be," she said out loud, "for a person with an extremely eclectic skillset to hot-wire a boat?"

With a silent promise to send Jackson apology Twinkies after the fact, Gigi turned and bolted up the steps out of the cabin—and directly into a human chest. A male one. *Black T-shirt, hard muscles.*

With a passing prayer to the Patron Saint of Chaotic Girls, Gigi calculated the best angle at which to drive her knee into a certain someone's tender bits, should the need arise.

She lifted her chin and stalled for time. "I escaped."

Slate's lips twitched slightly. "I noticed."

"Out of my way, Eyebrow Scar. I'm going to my sister, and you can't stop me. Observe the threatening look on my face as I say: I'd really hate to have to hurt you."

Slate shrugged. "You can hurt me if you want."

Gigi narrowed her eyes. She made a fist and drew back her arm—and then she kneed him in the crotch. With gusto. Misdirection for the win!

Gigi made it about four feet past him before Slate was suddenly in front of her again. Apparently, testicular damage had done nothing to his speed.

"Come on, sunshine."

Gigi liked to think the growl in his voice was just a little bit higher pitched than usual. "It's nothing personal," she told him. "I have a sister to save, and you have some private parts to ice. We can both win here!"

Slate was not amused. "Do you even know how to drive a fishing boat? Or a boat this old, period?"

Gigi folded her arms over her chest. "I can learn. The ocean is a great place for learning."

"You are a hazard to yourself."

"Thank you." Gigi tried to dart around him and ended up running smack into his chest again.

Slate caught her shoulders and righted her. "Wasn't a compliment."

"Let me go or I'll scream," Gigi replied. "And I have to warn you, Slate: My bellowing skills are second to none."

"Mattias." Beneath the blond hair hanging down over his face, the expression in his eyes shifted slightly. "My first name. It's *Mattias*."

Gigi didn't want to remember that when he'd given her the name *Slate*, he'd said it was both true and false. She also didn't want to ask: "Slate is your last name?"

"Slater, actually."

Mattias Slater. There was something about this moment—the sunrise, an ocean mist thick enough to gather on their skin, his hands on her shoulders, the fact that he'd just given her his name—that threatened Gigi's resolve.

"Mattias," she said quietly. And then she opened her mouth and screamed. Wildly. Loudly. Directly in his fuzzy face.

Wait. Fuzzy? Mattias Slater's blurry hands fell from Gigi's shoulders. Time slowed. Gigi's head pounded, and the next thing she knew, she couldn't feel her face. She went down with a thud.

Slate fell to his knees beside her.

Prone on the wood floor of the boat, Gigi belatedly realized: *the mist*. Her vision began to go black around the edges, and the last thing Gigi saw before the world gave way to total darkness—*seriously? again?*—was a pair of leather boots stepping onto Jackson's boat.

They were red.

Chapter 50

LYRA

Sunrise on the Pacific was a sight to behold. With Grayson beside her, Lyra stood at the front of the yacht, feeling like the sky had been split open. She looked down at the diamond-studded mask in her hands—at the words engraved in tiny letters on the back.

Time Signatures

Another puzzle, solved. Lyra wondered how many of the other players, besides her and Grayson, had looked at the back of *their* masks, and then she wondered what, if anything, else their competitors had found on the yacht. *We were told there were hints to puzzles, plural.* Lyra's mind went first to Brady and whatever puzzle he was working, and then to Savannah and Rohan.

Rohan. The things he'd said ate at Lyra. She knew that he'd meant for them to, that Rohan had meant for the assertion that

Jameson Hawthorne had placed a target on her back to cause problems—for her, for Grayson, for the way they'd been playing the Grandest Game. *Together.*

But that didn't mean that it wasn't true.

"What is it?" Grayson asked beside her.

Lyra ran a finger over the edge of her mask. It had been easier to hide her emotions from him when she was wearing it. But at this point, wasn't she done hiding? She'd bet on him, on this thing between them, the moment she'd let go, the moment she'd confided in him about Eve.

You either trusted someone or you didn't.

"Rohan told me that Jameson asked him to find a reason the game makers could use to kick me out of the game." Lyra looked from the broken-open sky to Grayson. "Would Jameson do that? *Did* he?"

"In all likelihood?" Grayson's eyes darkened slightly. "Yes." The muscles in his jaw tightened, and the effect was visible all through his face, his cheekbones becoming that much sharper, his brow just a shade more pronounced. "But I assure you, that won't be an issue moving forward."

"Because you won't let it be an issue?" Lyra guessed based on the look on his face.

"Because Jameson now knows that the person who sent you your ticket is Eve." Grayson turned his head toward hers. "And Eve is not a threat."

Lyra read between the lines there. "Who did your brother think sent me the ticket before?"

"There is a reason that my grandfather kept a List and a reason that we spell the word *List* with a capital *L*. My family has a not insignificant number of enemies. It might not have mattered to

Jameson which of them sent you here—only that someone had, and their motives were questionable at best."

"But Eve is not a threat?" Lyra was pretty sure Eve would have begged to differ about that.

"Eve is a known quantity," Grayson said. "And I assure you, your spot in this game is secure. You've more than proved yourself, and I would not allow—"

Grayson's words were cut off by a rhythmic roar. Lyra turned around to see a helicopter on the front of the yacht powering up, its blades spinning faster and faster.

"Nash," Grayson informed her, raising the volume of his speech enough to be heard. "My brother has somewhere to be this morning."

"Everything okay?" Lyra yelled back as the helicopter lifted off.

"Nash and his wife are expecting twins." Grayson lowered his volume as the helicopter grew smaller in the sky. "Girls."

Lyra gave herself exactly one moment to entertain the idea of Grayson as an uncle to two little girls. "Are they okay? Nash's wife and the babies?"

"They're fine, but between you and me, Nash has always been a bit of a mother hen."

"Are we talking about the same Nash Hawthorne?" Lyra asked. "Cowboy hat. Yea high."

Grayson's lips curved up on the ends. "Trust me."

I do. Lyra should have found that unsettling, but as she fixed her gaze on the ocean sunrise once more, Grayson did the same beside her, and they fell into an in easy silence, far easier than it should have been—until it was broken by the familiar thump of helicopter blades.

Back so soon? Lyra looked up. In the sky, a *different* helicopter hooked toward the yacht's helipad, coming in for a landing.

"How many helicopters does your family *have*?" she yelled.

Before Grayson could answer, Xander's voice sounded from the yacht's many speakers. "Players! Your chariot has arrived. Make your way to the bow of the ship. And if I may offer a few parting words..."

Xander paused for dramatic effect, and Lyra thought about that fact that there wouldn't be another interlude like this one. No more events. No more ballgowns. No more masks. Just clue to clue to clue—until the end.

"Live long. Prosper. Hydrate." As Xander's voice echoed over the bow, the helicopter touched down. "Make good choices. We'll see you at the finish line. Xander Hawthorne, out."

One by one, the other players arrived on the front of the yacht. The helicopter's blades stopped spinning, and the pilot's door opened. A man stepped out. He was wearing tattered jeans. Facial hair covered the bottom half of his face, a deeper brown than his hair, which had the faintest red tint to it, closer to mahogany than auburn.

She *felt* Grayson register the man's presence.

"Who's that?" Lyra asked, her voice low.

"That," Grayson told her, "is Toby Hawthorne."

GRAYSON

It was an achievement, feeling like the world's biggest liar while staring at a man who'd once faked being dead for twenty years. But Grayson had always been an overachiever—though technically, he'd dealt with all of Lyra's questions with a minimal number of lies. Each deceptive truth had come more easily than the last.

The old man would have approved. Grayson let that grating thought come as he took in the sight of his grandfather's namesake and only son: Toby Hawthorne—Toby Blake now, to the world at large. To Grayson, his mysterious uncle would have been little more than a stranger were it not for Avery, for the fact that Toby loved her like a daughter because he'd loved Avery's mother in that undying, infinite, Hawthorne kind of way.

What the hell is he doing here?

"We're one seat short in the back," Toby called, his gaze locking on to Grayson's. "You can ride in the cockpit with me."

Grayson waited until the chopper was booted back up to speak. "I take it Avery called you."

Thanks to the headphones he and Toby were wearing, Grayson's words were delivered directly to the other man's ears. A divider between the cockpit and the passenger section of the chopper provided additional assurance: No one else could hear them.

"Nash called, actually." Toby tossed a glance in Grayson's direction, pulling the helicopter into the air as casually as if he were driving a car. "Your brother seemed to be under the impression that the rest of you could use a little extra adult supervision, though he would not tell me why."

Mother hen, Grayson thought. "I'm twenty-two," he told Toby. "Hardly in need of *adult supervision.*"

"I remember twenty-two." Toby curved the helicopter around in a long arc, setting them back on the path toward Hawthorne Island. "I spent a good portion of twenty-two working on a fishing crew in Thailand. I hate boats. Hate the water." Toby's voice was gravelly in a way that suggested it didn't get all that much use. "I suppose you could say that I was trying to hate being twenty-two as much as I loathed myself." Toby's eyes flicked toward Grayson. "You just resisted the urge to say that Hawthornes do not *try.*"

Grayson had to admit: The man wasn't wrong.

"My father did a number on you boys," Toby commented, and Grayson thought again about how easy it had been for him to build a wall in his mind around everything he needed Lyra *not* to know. He sat with the discomfort of that thought until it began to dissipate—and then he changed the subject.

"Did Nash also tell you that Eve is interfering with the game?" Grayson asked.

"He did." Toby's brow furrowed then smoothed with the air of a man who'd spent far longer than Grayson had learning to let things come. "I really thought I was getting somewhere with her, but the only version of me that Eve wants is the version that has nothing to do with Avery at all."

Eve was Toby's daughter, but Avery was Hannah's, and that meant that Avery would never be *nothing* to the man. Toby had been there the night Avery was born. He'd loved Avery long before she'd known that he existed, and Grayson knew that Eve looked at Avery and saw everything that should have been hers. Toby. The Hawthorne fortune. Acceptance as one of them. Incredible, undying love.

"Avery is Eve's target." Once Grayson verbalized the obvious, it was like a line of dominoes had been knocked over in his mind. If Eve wanted Lyra to lose, that strongly suggested that she wanted a different player to win. There were limited suspects, and even fewer who could pose a threat to Avery, and Grayson knew for a fact that Eve had everything she needed to manipulate one player in particular.

He would have seen it before—they all would have—if they hadn't been so focused on Alice, on *that* threat.

"Savannah." Grayson wanted to be wrong about that. "My sister. Sheffield Grayson's daughter," he clarified for Toby. "She's the one Eve is trying to use."

"*Damn it, Eve.*" Toby's voice wasn't angry so much as rough. Out the front of the chopper, Hawthorne Island came into view. Toby turned the copter, taking another wide arc—wider than necessary. "I'd bet a lot of money that Eve led your sister to believe that Avery's the one who killed your father."

Grayson could see it all now—not just Eve's plan but Savannah's pain, her fury. He took in everything he knew about the Grandest Game and saw immediately where this was heading.

"You'll read Jameson and Avery in," Grayson told Toby, knowing that they would be able to infer the situation as well as he had. "And Alisa Ortega."

"I'll also find Eve," Toby replied, "and try to talk some sense into my daughter. In the meantime..." Toby's voice thickened. "You tell your sister that it was me. You tell her that I'm the one who killed Sheffield Grayson. *I* pulled the trigger."

"You didn't," Grayson pointed out.

"Neither did Avery," Toby replied. "And the actual truth would be harder for your sister to swallow. If Savannah needs a Hawthorne target, you damn well make it me."

They were close enough to the island now to see the house—close enough to see the section of the forest that was still charred after all these years, ravaged by a fire that a teenage Toby had as good as set.

"I gave Avery my permission to host the game here," Toby said, locking his own eyes on to the island's scars. "I don't get to be a victim of my own sins, and *this*—the Grandest Game, making puzzles, giving people the experience of a lifetime—it means something to Avery. Hannah's girl. *Our* girl. And Kaylie, Hannah's sister who died in the fire—she would have approved."

There was enough raw emotion in Toby's voice that Grayson couldn't help feeling an echo of it himself, and he had to ask: "Do you regret staying away from them for all those years? Avery. Hannah."

"I had my reasons. And now my Hannah the Same Backward as Forward is gone anyway, and I regret it every day." Toby went in for the landing. "Maybe if I'd learned to love differently, I could have loved her better." He looked at Grayson again as the chopper touched down. "I certainly couldn't have loved her more. I protected Hannah and Avery the only way I knew how."

"From the old man," Grayson said, and now his voice was the one that was thick. "From his enemies. From everything it means to be a Hawthorne."

Toby dropped his hands from the controls, but he didn't kill the engine "Nash didn't come right out and say that there was a threat, but he made it clear enough that Eve is not the only reason I'm here."

Grayson said nothing. Silence was its own kind of answer.

"You won't tell me the details. That's fine." Toby hit a button and powered down the chopper. "All you have to tell me, nephew, is whether or not the threat in question starts with the letter *A*."

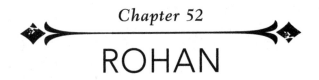

Chapter 52

ROHAN

There was a game that Rohan liked to play, one that had proven of use to him on more than one occasion, called *Who Will Betray You First?* Since becoming Factotum, he'd often been the one throwing that question out to the person in his sights, letting them wonder if they had already been betrayed—and by whom.

But long before he'd won his place as the second-in-command at the Mercy, Rohan had been a master at playing *Who Will Betray You First?* all by himself. This time, there was only one candidate, only one player in this game who *could* betray him.

And Rohan had known from the start that she would.

The only questions were *when* and *how.* Savannah hadn't said a word to Brady on the chopper ride, nor had she given Rohan any indication that her allegiances had changed. But then, with a woman like Savannah Grayson, there would be no indications, no forewarning. Regardless, Rohan had no intentions of being taken off guard.

On the yacht, he'd told her what he'd found on his mask—not so much a test as a push.

All Savannah would have to do is take what he'd given her and run, and Rohan would know: Their alliance had reached its end— sooner than anticipated, granted, but Rohan still fully intended to relish her attempts to destroy him.

Take me out of the game, love. If you can.

The doors on the helicopter unlocked. Savannah threw herself out of her seat, making it to the door first. She glanced back at Brady. "If you want me to consider your proposition," Savannah said, jerking her head toward Lyra Kane, "block her."

A second later, Savannah was out the door. "Hurry up, British."

Savannah had asked Brady to block *Lyra*, not Rohan. *Keeping up the illusion that we're a team, Savvy?* Rohan jumped out of the chopper and immediately started gaining on his quarry, his legs and stride longer even than Savannah's.

"Your brother will not allow anyone to block Lyra Kane for long," Rohan said, neck and neck with her now.

"We don't need long," Savannah retorted. "Even if they've managed to solve the music box, we just need long enough to get to the second floor and plug in the combination."

Rohan pushed past her. "Keep up, love."

Savannah kicked it up a notch and surged past him. It was almost too easy, bringing out the beast. Rohan would have upped his own pace again, but the dress was slowing her down just enough that he would have been able to leave her in the dust.

And that did not suit his purposes at all.

Within minutes, they hit the front porch of the mansion, then the foyer, then the stairs. Rohan's sixth sense for his surroundings warned him that Grayson and Lyra weren't all that far behind, but he and Savannah beat them to the marble door—just like they'd beaten Grayson Hawthorne and Lyra Kane every step along the way so far.

It was supposed to be us. A voice snaked its way through Rohan's mind, twisting and turning through the corridors of the labyrinth. *At the end of this game, after we'd decimated the competition, it was supposed to be us.*

The right kind of betrayal would have been exquisite.

The wrong kind of betrayal? Well, at least he would see it coming. At least he'd been reminded why affection was just another form of weakness.

"Thirty-four," Rohan said, setting the first dial. *The waltz.*

Savannah edged in on him, taking control of the second row of the dial. "Forty-four." *The tango.*

"And ninety-eight," Rohan finished. "For 'Clair de lune'."

There was a click, and the marble door swung open. Rohan forced himself to hold back: another test—another trap—for Savannah. She squeezed past him. She did not, however, attempt to close the marble door in his face.

That answered the *when*, in the vaguest terms at least. *Not yet.* They had some waltzing to do still, a deadly little tango, and more. Rohan followed Savannah past the marble door and shut it, just as he heard two sets of footfalls hit the top of the stairs.

Savannah practically body slammed Rohan out of the way to throw a golden deadbolt.

"They aren't getting in here," Savannah said primly, triumph and sweat both visible on her angular face. "At least, not until we leave."

"Victory is sweet, isn't it?" Rohan lingered on Savannah's eyes for a moment longer than he should have, and then he turned to the room at large to take in the lay of the land.

The room had walls made of the same marble as the door. The seams of said walls were barely visible, but Rohan marked them all the same—quite a few on one wall and one large seam on another.

On the marble ceiling, red numbers appeared. A digital clock, counting down. *Five minutes.*

"What happens in five minutes?" Savannah asked.

Rohan glanced back at the deadbolt. "My guess is that we'll have company." If there'd been anything in the room, he would have used it to block the door, but the only item in the entire room—as far as Rohan could see—was the ledger.

He let Savannah be the one to pick it up, let her add her name—right below Brady's.

To Rohan's left, the wall with the large seam parted. Behind it was a series of floating shelves, each bearing one player's name. Brady's shelf was already empty. A familiar rule had been inscribed over the shelves. *TAKE ONLY YOUR OWN.*

The game makers were awfully fond of fair play for the rich and mighty.

Rohan wasted no time in signing the ledger, then sauntered to his shelf. There were two items on top of it. He grasped the first: a charm—a music note this time. "Quite the collection we're amassing," he commented, as he hooked it on to the bracelet next to the others.

The charms would matter eventually—or the bracelet would. Rohan was as sure of that as he was of the fact that Savannah's betrayal *would* come.

He picked the second item up in his hand. *A worn leather pouch.*

"And how did our Mr. Daniels respond to your offer of an alliance?" Rohan asked the question the exact same way he would have had he not borne witness to the event himself.

Lie to me, Savannah Grayson.

"Counteroffer." Savannah kept her answer to a single word. A true one, as it happened.

"What kind of counter?" Rohan asked. He opened the leather pouch and withdrew a compass, a very old one by the looks of it.

"One I haven't decided on yet."

More truth? Perhaps. But Rohan was not in the habit of living for *perhaps.* He flipped open the compass, taking in the words written on the underside of the lid. *A riddle.*

"That's it?" Savannah said beside him, examining her own compass. "No further interrogation?"

"Wouldn't dream of it, love."

"Liar."

"We're all liars, Savvy." Rohan read and reread the inscription on the compass. "Knowing that, living it..." He glanced up at the timer on the ceiling. "That's the grandest game of all."

Chapter 53

GIGI

As Gigi came to, the world swam in front of her eyes. She liked to think of herself as a person who had a solid appreciation for duct tape. Gigi did not, however, appreciate *being* duct-taped. She blinked. Repeatedly.

The first thing that came into focus was Slate.

His head was lolled forward. Honey-blond hair hung in his face, completely obscuring his features, but Gigi would have recognized those pecs—and the tattoos—anywhere. It took longer for her memory to return, for her to realize—

It happened again. Seriously! Who managed to get themselves kidnapped *twice* in twenty-four hours? Gigi answered her own question out loud: "This girl."

She would have pointed to herself with both thumbs, but her arms had been duct-taped behind her back. On the bright side, her lips worked, and feeling was slowly returning to the rest of her body. Her torso had been bound to a metal chair, but her legs were free. Their kidnapper had bound Slate's, though.

Serves him right, Gigi thought pertly, and then, belatedly, another memory came to her—his name. *Mattias.*

"I'm going to kill him." The voice that said those words was female—and it wasn't Gigi's.

From the moment she'd woken, Gigi's world had been very small: Slate, herself, the duct tape, nothing else. But in the span of a heartbeat, her vision broadened, allowing Gigi to take in the rest of the room. It looked like some kind of meditation space: soothing colors, a few plants, cushions on the floor, and infinity-edge fountains on every wall. It was, in a word, serene.

And Slate and Gigi were not the only two people there—and, for that matter, not the only two who had been duct-taped to chairs.

"Slate. Wake up." The third person in the room was a strawberry blond who looked at most a few years older than Gigi. Like Slate, the not-quite-red-haired woman's ankles had also been bound.

Gigi was really starting to feel insulted about her own free feet. "Hello," she called to her fellow captive. She would have waved, but—duct-taped, hands. "I'm Gigi, and I hate to break it to you, but Slate and his muscles are out cold."

"I'm awake," the boy in question groaned. His body was still slumped. His hair still hung in his face. He sounded like death.

"Contrarian," Gigi accused.

"What is *she* doing here, Slate?" the strawberry blond asked.

"Hurtful," Gigi opined. "Seriously, you've been kidnapped, and your first complaint is about the company? I'll have you know I excel at being kidnapped!"

"You are horrible at being kidnapped." Slate's voice was a little more human this time. "Did either of you see anything?"

"Before someone knocked me out?" The strawberry blond was clearly miffed about that. "No. The real question is why you weren't with me to stop this from happening."

Because, Gigi realized, *he was with me.*

"Red boots," Gigi said out loud. Her companions looked at her like she'd just announced that her favorite pastime was feeding candy corn to monkeys. Clearly, a little more explanation was in order. "On Jackson's boat, right before everything went black, I saw boots. Red ones."

"I'm going to regret asking this," Slate said, "but who the hell is Jackson?"

"Old guy. New friend. Boat owner. He's got a really impressive beard, and *he* didn't tie me up, so he's my favorite right now." Gigi's brain caught up to her mouth, and she realized something.

Something incredibly obvious.

She turned her head to look at the third person in the room. "Eve?" As a general rule, Gigi believed in rehabilitation, not revenge, but she was willing to make an exception.

"What are you doing?" Slate asked.

Gigi used her free feet to scoot her chair closer to Eve. "Flying tackle," she replied.

"You can't flying tackle anyone," Slate said. "You're duct-taped to a chair."

Gigi gave him a look. *Another scootch.* "Watch me."

Eve, either not realizing or not caring that her doom was nigh, ignored Gigi and aimed an order at Slate. "Just get us out of here."

"You see a door in this room, Eve?"

At that question, Gigi stopped scootching. She scanned the room, her eyes darting from wall to wall. Slate was right. There were no visible doors.

"I told you there was something going on with the Grandest Game," Slate said, directing those words at Eve. "I told you we didn't want any part of it."

We. Gigi had always been highly attuned to uses of that word—a side effect of being a twin, of having been born a part of a pair.

"You didn't tell me," Eve said, her voice going a little quieter, "about her."

"He kidnapped me," Gigi volunteered helpfully. "It was a decent kidnapping, all things considered. Three-and-a-half stars."

Eve looked from Slate to Gigi then back again. "Is she joking?"

"Impossible to tell," Slate replied, his deadpan impressive.

Even bound, Eve managed to toss her hair. "You're fired," she told Slate.

"I'm not fired," he replied. "I'm the only one you've got."

Gigi wondered if she was imagining the slight softening in Slate's voice. She didn't think she was. *The only one she's got.* "Oh." Gigi hadn't meant to say that out loud. "I see."

"No you don't, sunshine."

"*Sunshine?*" Eve repeated incredulously.

Gigi resumed scooting her chair. "Look," she told Eve, "some people choose to be happy, and some people choose to be morally challenged smugweasels. To each their own. Now, if you could just move *your* chair a little to your right—"

"Gigi." Slate's use of her actual name gave Gigi just the tiniest bit of pause. "Tackle later. Plot now. We need to get free before whoever put us in this room gets back."

Chapter 54

LYRA

Lyra couldn't hear a thing through the marble door. She had no idea what Rohan and Savannah were doing on the other side of it. All she knew was that Grayson had been different from the moment he stepped off the helicopter. There was a look he got when he was deep in a certain kind of thought—features smooth as glass, eyes fixed straight ahead. The smaller his pupils were, the bluer and less gray his irises looked.

"You've been quiet," Lyra commented. "Is it something your uncle said?"

"I rarely even think of him that way," Grayson told her. "As my *uncle.* Toby spent most of my life presumed dead."

Lyra couldn't help her response: "Like mother, like son." She wondered if Hawthornes ever stayed dead. "He obviously said something to you."

Grayson ran his right hand around the edges of the vault door, looking for a weakness. Lyra thought for a moment that he was going to ignore her prodding, but he didn't.

"Toby is Eve's father," Grayson said finally. "He's also the closest thing that Avery has to one herself."

Lyra thought back to the mystery that had captivated the world: billionaire Tobias Hawthorne leaving his entire fortune to a seemingly random teenage girl from Connecticut.

"Let me guess," Lyra said. "It's complicated?"

"In some families, complications are par for the course."

There was a rumbling sound from behind the marble vault door then, followed by the audible flipping of a bolt. Lyra beat Grayson to the vault dial by a fraction of a second.

This time, when they entered the combination, the vault door opened.

Rohan was holding the ledger. Lyra stared him down. *Just try messing with me again.*

Rohan held out the ledger and shot her a roguish smile. Ignoring it, Lyra took the book from him, then scanned the rest of the room.

"We need to talk," Grayson told Savannah.

"I'll see if I can pencil you in after I win this." Savannah started to stalk past him. To Lyra's surprise, Grayson caught his sister by the elbow.

"I said *we need to talk*, Savannah."

"I would suggest you remove your hand from her arm." Rohan smiled. "With haste."

Grayson ignored the warning, and so did Savannah, as she wrapped her fingers around Grayson's wrist. "I have better things to be doing right now," she said tartly, "than indulging your desire to play big brother."

Grayson let go of Savannah, and though the expression on his carved-from-granite face changed very little, Lyra couldn't shake the feeling that beneath the surface, he was hurting.

"When have I ever given you the impression," Grayson asked his sister, "that I was *playing*?"

Savannah looked away first and left without another word to Grayson. Rohan followed, pausing only to cast one last knowing glance at Lyra.

"Talked his way out of it, did he?" Rohan said. "Hawthornes do have silver tongues, I suppose."

And then Rohan was gone, too.

Grayson followed as far as the marble door, then he braced both hands against it and pushed it shut, the muscles beneath his silk shirt rippling in a way that told Lyra he had pushed harder than necessary. Grayson threw the deadbolt, and a timer appeared on the ceiling.

Five minutes, counting down. Lyra opened the ledger. As expected, they were the last two to sign, which meant there was no game-based reason for Grayson to have bolted that door. As she pressed her watch to the ledger, a wall behind them parted, revealing a hidden section of the room that Rohan and Savannah had already doubtlessly explored.

As she crossed the room, Lyra pieced together Grayson's interaction with his sister, the tension in his muscles now, the way he'd gone quiet and intent after his conversation with Toby. *With Eve's father.* And just like that—just like another puzzle or riddle or code falling into place—Lyra saw it.

"Why does Eve want Savannah to win the Grandest Game?" she asked. In the silence of the vault, Lyra could hear Grayson breathing in and out, and her breaths fell into his rhythm. "Grayson?"

"You are frightening, Lyra Kane."

She passed the ledger to him. "I'll take that as a compliment."

Grayson pressed his watch to the page. "No Hawthorne has ever fallen for a woman who did not, on occasion, terrify him."

Words rang in Lyra's memory. *You don't fall. I do.*

"I'm not wrong, am I?" Lyra said. "About Savannah." The most logical reason for Eve to want Lyra to lose the game was to increase another player's odds of winning. "Maybe, if I'd been as antagonistic to the Hawthorne family as Eve had hoped I would be, she would have tasked me with aiding your sister, but—"

"It is possible," Grayson allowed, "that I have been keeping a secret from Savannah, one I'd hoped to spare her from. One that left her vulnerable to Eve."

And that, Lyra realized almost immediately, was all that Grayson was going to say on the topic. She thought about what he'd said earlier—about Eve, about Avery. *It's complicated.* From that and from the way Grayson had spoken to his sister, Lyra assumed that Savannah Grayson's motives for playing the Grandest Game weren't exactly pure.

She has a plan.

"Grayson?" Lyra's low voice echoed through the marble room. "Do you need your sister to lose this game?"

"That would be ideal."

"In that case . . ." Lyra reached for the shelf with her name on it and claimed the objects on top. From inside the leather pouch, she slid out an antique compass—bronze, just like the key to her room. She opened the compass and found an inscription inside—their next clue.

DON'T LOOK.
DON'T JUDGE.

CAN'T SEE.
WHAT YOU WANT IS NUMBER THREE.
DON'T PUT.
DON'T COUNT.
NOT WITHIN
BUT WITHOUT.

The words rang in Lyra's mind. Before, she'd been playing this game for herself, for Mile's End. Now, she was playing it for Grayson, too. The only way to ensure that Savannah lost this game was to win it.

As Grayson claimed his own compass, Lyra turned, taking in the whole of the empty room, and the oddest feeling settled over her body—part anticipation, part uncanny certainty, almost like déjà vu, like she *knew* what was going to happen before a single conscious thought had formed.

She took off Grayson's tuxedo jacket and tossed it to him, and then Lyra reached for the opera glasses threaded through the chain on her bag.

Chapter 55
GRAYSON

Grayson slipped on his tuxedo jacket as Lyra lifted Odette's opera glasses to her eyes. She truly was terrifying, Lyra Kane—the way she'd pieced together the meaning of his interaction with Savannah, the way she'd known that his conversation with Toby had affected him, when to the rest of the world, Grayson's stony mask was impenetrable. *Terrifying though you may be, Lyra Kane, there is so much that you don't know.*

So much that he could not tell her.

As if on cue, the watch on Grayson's wrist vibrated. He had sent a message to his brothers in response to what Toby had said on the chopper. Three words, sufficiently vague:

TOBY KNOWS SOMETHING.

The reply he'd just received was almost, though not quite, as oblique. *ABOUT EVE?*

The *or* on the end of that question went unsaid.

"Grayson," Lyra said beside him. "There's something written on this wall."

Taking advantage of the fact that she still had the opera glasses to her eyes—that she could not see *him*—Grayson typed back two letters, the briefest of messages. *NO.*

He trusted that Jameson and Avery, at least, would read the correct meaning into that: *Not about Eve. About Alice.* What specifically Toby knew, Grayson had not been able to ascertain, but whatever it was, Grayson's Hawthorne intuition said that Toby had known it for a very long time.

Grayson forced himself to set that thought aside and crossed to Lyra. He had to stay the course: keep Lyra focused on the game, try again with Savannah as soon as he could get her away from Rohan, and trust that Avery could get something out of Toby.

"May I?" Grayson asked Lyra. She handed him the opera glasses, and he looked at the wall. There was indeed something written there—a hint, he would wager. Unfortunately, the script that the opera glasses revealed was not nearly as clear as the writing on the compass. There were some letters visible on the wall but also disjointed symbols. *Or parts of letters.*

"Invisible ink." Grayson lowered the opera glasses and walked to the wall in question. It had an abundance of seams. *Squares,* Grayson realized. The seams divided the marble into twenty squares—*four by five.* Grayson recognized this particular trick for what it was.

"Look for a loose square," he told Lyra. "One of these will come off."

A few seconds passed as they searched. "Here," Lyra called. "This one."

Grayson slid in beside her and helped remove the piece of

marble in question—thin enough not to be *too* heavy. With that piece removed, he put a hand on one of the other sections and slid it sideways—assumption confirmed.

"It's a puzzle," Grayson told Lyra. "Slide the squares, arrange them just so, and a hint to the riddle will appear."

They got to work. It took time. The countdown overhead hit zero. The deadbolt flipped open, but no one was waiting on the other side of the vault door. *We were the last to this clue.* That didn't sit well with Grayson, but as their hint took form on the wall, Grayson knew: They wouldn't be behind for long.

Lyra did the honors, peering through the opera glasses one last time and reading the message on the wall aloud: *"Actions speak louder than words."*

Chapter 56

ROHAN

on't look." Savannah's voice withstood the wind on the cliff, the remains of the bonfire from the night before barely visible on the beach below. *"Don't judge. Can't see."*

"What you want is number three." Rohan marked the way Savannah Grayson moved as she paced the rocky terrain, like the cliff's nearby edge didn't faze her in the least. Rohan was the one who'd suggested they continue their discussion of this particular riddle out here, rather than in the house, where they might be more easily overheard.

No witnesses. That made certain kinds of traps easier to lay.

"Don't put," Rohan continued, his voice silky and pitched to surround her. *"Don't count. Not within..."*

"But without." Savannah took back over, the way Rohan had known that she would. There was an art to controlling others through the openings you gave them.

How many openings would he have to give her before she inevitably betrayed him?

"Four uses of the word *don't*," Rohan noted, and then he baited her. "It's almost like the game makers enjoy telling us what *not* to do."

His mention of the game makers was intentional, calculated to prime Savannah's anger and drive, to remind her of every motivation she had to use and discard him. But Savannah Grayson was well-used to living a lie, to burying anger and ill-intentions so deep that, to the rest of the world, they appeared as nothing more than the lightest coat of frost.

She was not as easy to manipulate as most.

"*Don't count* would suggest that this isn't a numerical puzzle." Savannah's voice remained even. "And yet, what we want is *number three*."

In the distance below, waves broke against the standing stones. Rohan had a certain appreciation for the fact that even the mightiest, wildest ocean waves *were* broken by the massive rocks, reduced to lapping harmlessly at the shore.

It would be a shame, in some ways, to render Savannah Grayson harmless.

"*Don't look* and *can't see* would imply that it's not a visual puzzle, either." Savannah turned from looking out at the water to looking at the island behind them.

"*Not within.*" Rohan walked to stand behind Savannah, directly behind her and close enough to the edge of the cliff that, should she so choose, Savannah could easily attempt to send him tumbling over its edge. "In other words: not internal, not inside of a barrier, not contained beneath the surface."

Rohan took another seemingly careless step, putting himself within an arm's length of her. *Do I look vulnerable to you, Savvy?*

"*Without,*" he continued, "is one of those handy words with multiple meanings. On the one hand: *outside, external, not contained.*"

Rohan wondered if she could hear the subtle challenge in his voice, one that said that some people were not so easy to contain. "But *without* can indicate an absence." Of all the roles he had inhabited over the years, Rohan did have a special fondness for playing the rogue. "As in without morals, without compunction, without... restraint."

Savannah turned toward him, and Rohan saw her register just how close to the edge he was. *Do it, Savvy.* She had to know him well enough by now to know that he would catch the edge. *No permanent damage.*

"You pretend to have so little restraint," Savannah said, her voice as smooth as glass, "but we both know that you are nothing *but* restraint, British. You are living, breathing, walking, talking carefully laid plans."

"Guilty as charged." Rohan allowed his broad shoulders to rise and fall in the most careless of shrugs. "Even my schemes have schemes."

As did hers.

Savannah wrapped a hand around his bicep, just above the elbow, and then she moved him *away* from the cliff's edge.

"It would be inconvenient," Savannah said archly, "if you fell." She dropped her hold on him. "So." She raised her chin. "If we can't *look* or *judge* or *see* or *count*—what's left?"

"Thinking." Rohan allowed himself to do exactly that. "Making connections. Filling in the blanks." *Perhaps it's time I fill in some of my own.* "Did you learn anything about Brady's sponsor?"

That question was not geared, of course, to finding out anything about *Brady Daniels*. It was just another little test. How much would she tell him? How far would she go?

How long did they have?

"Night." Some people changed the subject. Savannah Grayson obliterated and replaced it.

"Dodging the question, love?"

"As it happens, I'm *thinking*. We were told there were hints to multiple puzzles on the yacht. We know Brady was at least one puzzle ahead of the rest of us. What if the hint from the champagne flute was for *this* puzzle?"

"Night." Rohan decided he was done testing her for now and turned the full force of his mind to the puzzle at hand.

> DON'T LOOK.
> DON'T JUDGE.
> CAN'T SEE.
> WHAT YOU WANT IS NUMBER THREE.
> DON'T PUT.
> DON'T COUNT.
> NOT WITHIN
> BUT WITHOUT.

"You can't see at night," Rohan said out loud, his voice bordering on a purr, "except by the light of the moon." His brain churning every bit as much as the ocean in the wind, Rohan let the thrum of possibility banish all else. "There are still these." He produced a pair of glass dice. "And that." Rohan nodded to the platinum chain that Savannah had once more wore wrapped around her waist when they'd changed from their formal wear back into their armor once more.

Savannah narrowed her pale eyes—moonlit eyes, if Rohan had ever seen them. "Those are my dice, not yours." Savannah reached for them.

Rohan allowed her to reclaim the dice. "Once a pickpocket, always a pickpocket," he told her. "All's fair in love and war, Savvy."

"And which one is this?" Savannah asked, the arctic chill in her tone matched only by the underlying *challenge*. "Love or war?"

Rohan angled his head down and murmured, "War, of course."

"Well…" Savannah gave a practiced and deadly shrug. "Needs must, I suppose."

Needs must. The phrase was one Rohan had used often enough within the bounds of his own mind, but he was fairly certain that he'd never said it aloud to her. "I prefer the full proverb: *Needs must when the devil drives.*"

Rohan leaned down, bringing his lips very close to hers, telling himself that all he was doing was keeping up the illusion that nothing between them had changed.

You'll use me. I'll use you. All's fair.

"It means," Rohan continued in the kind of whisper that was meant to be *felt* as much as heard, "that to achieve a necessary end, there are times when one must do things that perhaps one would…rather not."

Needs must. Rohan brought his lips to hers. It had been his intention to kiss her lightly, teasingly, but Savannah Grayson was not one to be teased, and she was, apparently, not made for kissing *lightly*.

At least not with him.

There was more than one way for a girl like Savannah Grayson to go for the jugular. And then suddenly, her hands were on his chest. Suddenly, she was pushing him back, but not toward the cliff—and not so far that she had to let go of the front of his shirt. "*Needs must when the devil drives,*" Savannah said. "*All's fair in love and war.*"

It took Rohan a moment—just one—to hear what she was really saying. "Proverbs. Idioms."

"*Don't look* a gift horse in the mouth." Savannah let go of his shirt and let her hands fall to her sides. "*Don't judge* a book by the cover."

"*Can't see* the forest for the trees. *Don't put* the cart before the horse." Rohan offered his face up to the morning sun, because it was either that or let himself relish the way *she* looked bathed in that same light. "*Don't count* your chickens before they hatch."

"*What you want*," Savannah quoted, "*is number—*"

"*Three*. The third line." Adrenaline was an old friend of Rohan's, as was risk. And letting himself continue to do this with her *was* a risk.

A magnificent one.

"*Can't see the forest for the trees*," Savannah said. "That's the third line of the riddle. And if we're supposed to focus on the *without* of it all..." Her top lip brushed against her bottom one for just a moment, not so much a pause as the tiniest little moment of victory. "On what's missing..."

"The forest," Rohan murmured, his lips brushing hers. "The trees."

They did make an excellent team.

She will betray you, a voice very much like the Proprietor's warned Rohan. If distractions were weakness, *trust* was something far worse.

"Which part of the forest do you think we're headed for?" Savannah said.

Rohan did love a challenge. "The outer edge?" he said. "*Not within, but without.*" A double meaning, perhaps?

"Which outer edge?" Savannah pressed.

Rohan pushed back. "You tell me, love."

"This is Hawthorne Island." Savannah's gaze hardened like melted sand to glass. "They're Hawthornes. They ruin everything they touch."

Rohan smiled. "The burned part of the forest it is."

Chapter 57

GIGI

Gigi's fingernails were short, stubby, nibbled little things, but Eve's were longer and sharp—appropriately villainous nails, really, and Slate's boss had already torn one attempting to claw through the duct tape on Gigi's wrists, after Gigi had managed to get their chairs back-to-back.

Was she still planning Eve's eventual demise? Yes, most definitely. But Gigi was fully capable of prioritizing.

"This would be easier," Eve told Slate in a deceptively pleasant voice as she tried again, "with a knife."

"I already told you," Slate replied, "whoever brought us here took my knife."

Gigi couldn't help thinking that the two of them bickered like siblings—or exes. The jury was still out on that one.

"That knife was my friend," Gigi declared morosely.

"It definitely was not," Slate said.

With her back to Eve, Gigi was facing Slate. With only a few feet separating them, she could make out the exact color of his eyes, so dark the pupils almost disappeared into his irises. For once, his dark blond hair wasn't in his face, the light scar through his eyebrow fully visible.

"You don't know the first thing about that knife." That was from Eve, who tore another nail—and cursed.

"Creative use of expletives," Gigi complimented. "And I do so." She let her eyes settle on Mattias Slater's. "Fourteen notches in the sheath," Gigi said quietly. "Fourteen horrible things. And you're always at your most dangerous when your intentions are good."

Eve stopped what she was doing. For three or four seconds, she went very still. "You told her?" Eve asked Slate, and then she started in on the duct tape again—with a vengeance. "About your father?"

The duct tape tore—just a little at first, but soon, the binding had ripped far enough for Gigi to begin to wiggle her wrists out of it.

"What about your father?" Gigi asked Slate.

Mattias Slater closed his eyes. "Quiet," he ordered.

"I'm going to try not to take that personally," Gigi announced, but when Slate opened his eyes again and caught hers, she realized: He wasn't avoiding the question.

He'd heard something.

Gigi listened, but she couldn't hear anything other than the sound of gently falling water from the infinity fountains. And then one of those fountains—and the wall behind it—parted, and Gigi knew exactly what Slate had heard.

Footsteps. Heels on hard wood floor. *Red boots.* Gigi stared at those boots, then lifted her gaze. She was the only one of the three of them positioned to be able to see the hooded figure that walked toward them, clothed in a long red cloak. The hood of the cloak cast the woman's face—and Gigi *was* sure, somehow, that it was a woman—in shadow, but even if it hadn't...

There's a red cloth over her face. Presumably, their captor could see out, but that did nothing to tell Gigi who she was dealing with. *Red gloves on her hands.*

The exact shade of red was deep, the red of dried blood. *Blood-red gloves. Blood-red cloak. Blood-red hood. Blood-red boots.*

The cloaked figure walked past Slate to Gigi, who frantically tore her wrists the rest of the way out of the duct tape just in time to see the glint of a knife.

That knife is not my friend. Gigi threw her hands up in front of her face, but an attack never came. Without a word, the woman in red cut through the tape around Gigi's torso, freeing her from the metal chair.

Gigi jumped to her feet, then looked at Slate and Eve, still bound—arms, legs, and stomach—to their chairs. "Seriously. *Should* I be insulted?"

"Juliet Grayson." For a moment that was all the woman in red said, just Gigi's given name, and then she continued. "Evelyn Blake. Mattias Slater."

Gigi shifted her weight to the balls of her feet. *She might have a knife,* she told herself, *but I have the element of surprise.* Nobody expected a Tasmanian devil pounce—pretty much ever.

"Sunshine? *Don't.*" Slate bit out the words.

"I'd recommend listening to Mr. Slater," the cloaked woman said. "On this matter, at least." There was the slightest hint of an accent to their captor's carefully paced words. "I mean the three of you no harm."

"Skeptical," Gigi said. "Me. Very."

"Skepticism is a double-edged sword," the woman in red replied, her long cloak billowing around her ankles as she moved to cut Eve free as well. "Anything worth doing requires belief—in oneself at the very least."

"I believe in myself," Gigi said. *I believe that I was taught to tackle by the great Xander Hawthorne himself and—*

"Don't," Slate *and* Eve spoke in unison this time. The moment Eve was free, she stood and placed herself in front of Gigi.

"For the record, Ms. Blake," the woman in red told Eve, "you are the one who made all of this necessary. I prefer to work through more subtle means, but you? Bull in a china shop. You lead with emotion, and you lack control. I need for the Grandest Game to go on. Overt interference with the players puts that at risk. You left me little choice about removing you from the board."

The Grandest Game. Hearing that out of their shrouded captor's mouth somehow unlocked a realization in Gigi's mind, as detail after detail started adding up. "You're Brady's sponsor."

Brady was the one who'd asked Gigi not to tell the game makers about the bug she'd found in phase one. He'd told her that he needed the game to go on.

He'd been playing like Calla's life depended on it.

And once, back in the game, he'd called Gigi *Juliet*.

The woman in red issued no denials. "I am many things. For now, I am the person who came here to verify that the three of you were suffering no ill effects from being knocked out, and having verified that, I am the person who will be leaving you here in this room, where you will remain safely contained until the end of the game. Believe me when I say that this is in your best interest as well as mine."

"Bullshit."

Tell us how you really feel, Slate, Gigi thought. Out loud, she couldn't help herself. "So what you're saying is that all you're doing is keeping us safely out of the way until you've gotten what you want out of the Grandest Game?" Gigi shot a look at Slate. "My, my, my, how the tables have turned."

"You're still kidnapped," Slate informed her. "They haven't completely turned."

"You're taped to a chair," Gigi pointed out. "And I'm not. Everything else is just semantics." She turned back to their mysterious captor. "But speaking of, why am *I* kidnapped? Are we just talking wrong place, wrong time here? Unfortunate association with unsavory characters?"

Slate was the one who answered. "You were headed for the island."

"That," the woman in red agreed. "And I had a need for bait."

Bait. That word, said so calmly, sent a chill down Gigi's back. *What kind of bait?*

Their captor walked back toward the wall she'd entered through. "Lest you get any grand ideas, this door must be triggered by a remote. No amount of brute force will cause it to open. For his sake, I'd leave the boy bound. You don't want him loose when my target takes the bait. She does not react well at all to those she finds threatening."

She? Before Gigi could so much as speak that question aloud, the woman in red was gone.

Chapter 58

LYRA

When Lyra thought about the forest on Hawthorne Island, she thought of soaring evergreen trees, some living, some charred from that long-ago fire, but she couldn't picture them, and the other trees in the forest, the ones with leaves instead of dark green needles—Lyra didn't remember much about those at all. Maybe that was why the massive trees on the north edge of the forest, each with dozens of limbs sticking out from thick trunks like bicycle spokes, light shining through their branches, had an almost physical effect on her, as she and Grayson crossed into the woods.

"We could be looking for a particular tree," Grayson noted. "Something hanging from a branch or carved into bark."

"Or..." Lyra looked toward the canopy. "Something that can only be seen from a bird's-eye view?" *Echoes.* She turned to the nearest tree, fully ready to climb it and glad they'd changed back into their armor.

"Wait." Grayson looked down at an object he'd just retrieved from his jacket pocket. *The compass.* As Lyra watched, he opened it. "Nonfunctional," Grayson confirmed. "For now."

His thumb skimmed every inch of the bronze surface of the compass in a systematic search. And then, he pressed—hard—on its face. There was a click, and the needle began to spin, pointing not back at the house, but farther into the woods.

"That's not north," Lyra commented.

"No," Grayson replied, his gaze flicking back up to hers. "It's not."

The arrow on the compass pointed the way—deep into the living forest, skirting the edge of the line that marked where the fire had been stopped.

There. The handholds on the tree were a dead giveaway. They looked like they belonged on a rock-climbing wall. Lyra reached for one and placed her foot on another. Looping around to the other side of the soaring Douglas fir, Grayson did the same.

It was at least twenty feet up to the lowest branch.

Wordlessly, they climbed. The handholds stopped before they reached the branches, and for a moment, so did Lyra and Grayson.

"No ledger," Lyra noted. "And nothing that could be the next clue." She tilted her head back and her eyes up. "Do we keep climbing?"

Grayson went very still. "Give it a moment."

A moment to consider. A moment to take it all in. There was just enough adrenaline crashing through Lyra's veins to heighten her senses as she absorbed the view: the forest *and* the trees, sun-kissed…and not exactly empty.

Rohan and Savannah were maybe a hundred yards out on the other side of the divide, Savannah's white armor highly visible against the blackened trees. Lyra *felt* Grayson register his sister's presence.

"You're hurting." Lyra wasn't about to start pulling her punches with him now. "Whatever secret you were trying to protect your sister from—just *stop*."

"Stop what?" Grayson clipped the words. "I've already failed. Eve saw to that."

No matter how much Grayson Hawthorne might have practiced making mistakes, this one—whatever it was—clearly wasn't the kind of mistake he could accept from himself.

"Stop," Lyra said again, "trying to protect her." Lyra had the sense that she might as well have been lecturing rain not to fall, but she continued anyway. "I don't know what Eve told Savannah or what either one of them is up to now, but I do know what it's like to find out that you've been lied to in a way that rips the rug right out from underneath your entire existence." Lyra's parents had doubtlessly thought they were protecting her, too. "I can understand why my mom and dad did it—let memories I'd repressed *stay* repressed. I know that they were trying to give me a chance to grow up free of that trauma, but…"

"The piper has to be paid either way," Grayson said quietly. "The human brain is a miraculous thing, but it can't keep anything caged forever. You'll still pay the cost. Repressing something, pushing it down, refusing to feel it just means that you have to pay that cost again and again and again."

A ball of emotion rose in Lyra's throat as Rohan and Savannah drew closer to them. "Ask me how *protected* I felt when I found out the truth."

Grayson took an audible breath. "Our father is a murderer, Savannah's and Gigi's and mine." Lyra hadn't asked for *his* secrets, but there he was, offering them up like penance. "That's what I was trying to protect Savannah from. Do you remember seeing anything in the news a few years ago about a bomb on one of Avery's jets?"

That story had been everywhere. Lyra remembered. "You don't have to tell me this." Her voice, as quiet and low as it was, echoed through the trees.

"My father planted that bomb. He lost someone in the Hawthorne Island fire, years ago. He held my uncle Toby responsible for that, and he believed Avery was Toby's daughter. It was all very *an eye for an eye*." The muscles in Grayson's jaw tensed. "Avery ended up in a coma, but she survived the explosion. Two of the men on her security detail did not."

Lyra tightened her right hand around the handhold she was gripping, then let her left snake slowly around the trunk toward Grayson. "You didn't have to tell me that."

"I wanted to." His hand made its way toward hers. "I think sometimes," he continued, in a voice that was just a little more detached, "about what I might have inherited from my father. Do I have his perverted sense of justice? His ability to just shut morality off in pursuit of his own ends?"

"You're nothing like him." Lyra's words came out fiercer than she'd meant for them to.

"You're probably right. Of all of my brothers, I was always the one who was a Hawthorne through and through." Grayson paused. "I wonder sometimes about what that means about me, too."

Lyra could feel his mind churning again, and she knew— *knew*—that there wasn't a thing she could say to stop it.

"There's nothing up here," Grayson declared finally. "And we're about to have company."

Rohan and Savannah weren't more than twenty yards away now, compasses in hand, but as Lyra and Grayson began the climb back down the tree, Lyra caught sight of movement in the shadow of the closest, massive tree, and she realized: *We already have company.*

As Lyra's feet hit the ground, Brady Daniels met her gaze from the shadows. And then—slowly, deliberately—he angled his gaze down to the ground, to the base of the tree.

Lyra ran her foot over grass and dirt, and she realized that something had been buried there, in the forest floor. *Can't see the forest for the trees.* Lyra didn't start digging immediately, not with Rohan and Savannah incoming, but she couldn't help thinking that Grayson had been right about what he'd said before, when he'd talked about paying the piper.

Nothing stayed buried forever.

Chapter 59

GRAYSON

Grayson had not meant to tell Lyra about his father, but he was fully cognizant of why he'd done so. He'd wanted to tell her something real, something *true*, to give her a secret, even if it wasn't the one he'd been lying and not-lying to keep from her since the bonfire.

The secret he was keeping still.

Lyra couldn't have made it clearer or more explicit: She didn't want that kind of protection. Not from him. Not from anyone. But *she* wasn't the only person Grayson was trying to protect. Alice had threatened Jameson in Prague. Based on Jameson's behavior, it was a sure bet that the woman had threatened Avery, too.

Lyra Kane wanted, maybe even *needed*, truth from those she loved. And Grayson couldn't give it to her.

Knowing he'd pay for it later, Grayson shoved that thought aside, because Savannah and Rohan were *here*.

Savannah took one look at the handholds on the tree and began to climb. Grayson expected Rohan to follow, but instead, Rohan took up position at the bottom of the tree, tilted his head slightly to one side, and set his sights on Lyra.

"Figured out why yet?" Rohan asked her. Grayson levied a thousand-yard stare at Rohan, but apparently, the Brit had never encountered a warning he didn't wholly ignore. "Why your brother is so sure that Ms. Kane is a liability," Rohan clarified for Grayson's benefit, and then, without waiting for a response, Rohan angled his gaze toward the canopy. "I suppose some people just don't know when to stop."

Grayson allowed himself to be baited into looking up. Savannah hadn't stopped her climb where the handhelds ended, the way that Grayson and Lyra had. Now, she was climbing the tree with no holds, no branches—and no sign of stopping.

As loath as Grayson was to leave Lyra with Rohan, Grayson knew quite well that Rohan had assessed Savannah with remarkable accuracy. Grayson's sister simply was not going to stop.

Not at the lowest branch.

Not at any of them.

Not until she found a ledger.

"This tree is more than a hundred feet tall," Grayson said grimly.

Lyra caught his gaze. *Go.* This was Lyra telling Grayson that, when it came to handling Rohan, she could damn well take care of herself.

Grayson took Lyra at her silent word and began to climb—fast and hard, the way only someone who'd had the hesitation trained out of them could. Despite his pace, it took time for him to pull even with Savannah.

Forty feet off the ground.

"I don't need your help," Savannah told him through gritted teeth. "I never did."

The teeth gave her away. Savannah was in pain—physical pain. *Her ACL.* "There's nothing up here," Grayson told her. "No matter how far you climb, you won't find a ledger."

"You don't know that."

"My brothers and Avery wouldn't make anyone climb this high."

"I suppose I'm just expected to trust you on that?" Savannah knew exactly how to deploy every pointed arch of her brows. "Trust *them.*"

She might as well have been wearing literal armor to go along with the clothes they'd been given for the game. Grayson was not holding out hope that anything he said would pierce it, but he had to try. "I know you're working with Eve. She's manipulating you, Savannah."

"Do I strike you as gullible?" Savannah gave no sign of weakness, but her knee—that knee concerned Grayson.

"I won't let you hurt Avery. Nor will I allow you to hurt yourself. There's nothing up here, Savannah."

"You don't know that," his sister said again, her voice struck through with an intensity he recognized all too well.

"I know that you are in pain—and not just your ACL." Grayson didn't want to do this fifty feet above the ground, but either she'd listen to him or she'd head back down. Either, he would count as a win. "Our father had a bomb planted on Avery's jet. Two men died as a result, and when Avery was not among the casualties, he had her abducted. He held her hostage. He pointed a gun at her, intending to shoot her in front of Toby Hawthorne in revenge for our cousin Colin's death."

Toby's words on the helicopter echoed in Grayson's mind. *You tell your sister it was me.* But that wasn't the truth, either, and Grayson couldn't bring himself to lie to Savannah again.

"No. He wasn't a murderer. He didn't kidnap anyone." Savannah's voice shook—and so did her leg. "And he wasn't *our* father, Grayson. He was mine."

"Be that as it may, Savannah, Avery was not the one who shot him, and the person who did only pulled the trigger to save her life."

"You're lying."

"I am not."

"Are you under the impression that it would make a difference if I believed you?" Savannah asked. "If Avery's only crime was the cover-up, do you think that it cost me any less?"

"The cover-up was Toby's work—and he's Eve's father. She has more than one reason to point you at Avery instead." Grayson did what Toby had told him to do. He gave Savannah a Hawthorne target, and he did it with the truth.

"How long did it take *you* to figure out what happened?" Savannah said, her voice far too calm for either their current height or the topic of conversation. "Or did Avery tell you the truth right away, because you deserved to know?"

If they'd been fencing, she would have scored a direct hit. Avery *had* told him. She hadn't kept it from him, the way they'd all kept it from Savannah.

"I know exactly when Gigi found out." Savannah's voice echoed through the branches all around them. "Looking back, I can pinpoint the day. The hour."

"We were trying to protect you," Grayson said, Lyra's words echoing in his mind: *Ask me how* protected *I felt.*

"*We,*" Savannah repeated, her hold on the tree so vicious it turned her knuckles white. "You and Gigi."

She began to climb back down. Grayson paced her, ready to catch her if she faltered.

Savannah did not falter. "I am only going to say this once. It does not matter what lies Eve told me. It does not matter if you are telling me the truth now. Because this conversation? We both know that it's not about protecting *me* anymore. All you're trying to do now is make me complicit."

Another direct hit. Grayson had seen what keeping this secret had done to Gigi.

"What about my mother?" Savannah clearly had no intention of letting up. Acacia Grayson was the closest thing that Grayson had to a real mother himself. She had Gigi's open heart, Savannah's bulletproof resolve. "Did you even think about her? Is the whole world just supposed to go on believing that Sheffield Grayson is alive and well and living a tax-evading life in the Maldives?"

Grayson forced himself to weather every ounce of his sister's fury without a word.

"We were fine," Savannah said, the words sounding like they'd been ripped from a part of her that was already dead. "Mom. Gigi. Me. Before you came, I was holding us together, and *we were fine*. And now, there is no *us*." Savannah's breaths were audible now and laden with pain—of all types. "And the worst part of it," Savannah continued, her voice going uncharacteristically ragged, "is that Gigi chose you, but if push came to shove, you wouldn't choose her. You'd choose your brothers and Avery. *They* are your family, the way Gigi was mine."

Was. "Gigi is still your family," Grayson said as they reached the handholds. "And like it or not, you are mine as well."

Savannah didn't even look at him. "The only thing I am," she said in that same, ragged tone, "is alone."

Chapter 60

ROHAN

Rohan noted the exact moment that Grayson and Savannah made it back down to the uppermost climbing holds—and the exact moment that Savannah reversed course once more. Rohan's mind made quick work of that, and he turned his attention to Lyra Kane—not exactly an open book.

Fortunately, Rohan excelled at cracking open even the hardest shells. "You know, don't you?" he said. This time, Rohan wasn't referring to Jameson Hawthorne, wasn't even trying to manipulate her—much. He raised his eyes to Grayson and Savannah overhead. "So does he."

They knew Savannah's intentions in this game were less than pure. Grayson almost certainly knew why. And Lyra...

Rohan studied her—openly, nakedly, letting her feel his gaze. "You have a tell," he informed her. Rohan gave those words just a moment to sink in. A person could inadvertently show you quite a bit in the split second when they realized their face had already given away far too much. "It's all about the direction of the eyes," Rohan continued. "Where they go—and where they don't."

Hers went down. Rohan knelt, and before his knee had even reached the forest floor, Lyra was already there, crouched, her telltale grace exceeding even his own.

"A forest is more than its trees," Rohan noted as he pushed his fingers into the grass. "This forest, for instance, is dirt and rocks and wild grass—and *this*."

There was something there, hidden just below the dirt, barely covered.

In a single sweeping motion, Rohan cleared away enough soil for them to make out the top of a silver plaque—and the first two words.

Often . . . And right below it. *Never.*

Without a word to him, Lyra Kane began to dig out the plaque, utterly indifferent to the dirt lodging itself beneath her nails—and utterly indifferent to Rohan, or doing a good impression of it, at least.

"It really is a shame," Rohan told her, never above issuing another little mental push, "that the Hawthorne family sees you less as a person—a highly capable one, by my reckoning—than as a *threat*."

Lyra didn't so much as lift her eyes from her work, and Rohan took it upon himself to aid her in clearing away the rest of the dirt. Words stared up at the two of them—another riddle.

> *OFTEN*
> *NEVER*
> *LITTLE LATE*
> *YOU*
> *AND TWO*

TOO MUCH, TOO GREAT
NEVER, EVER
I TRAP YOU NOT
GO NOW
HOW
TO SHOOT YOUR SHOT

"A clue," Rohan noted. "But still no ledger." He lifted his gaze back up to the tree to see Grayson Hawthorne rapidly approaching. Lyra noticed the same and stood, and while she was distracted, Rohan slid his fingers around the side of the plaque, clearing dirt as he went. With the plaque free and clear, he tried subtly prying it from the ground. *Firmly affixed, for now at least.* Rohan skimmed his fingers around the outside of the metal and was rewarded when he hit a gap—a very tiny one.

Circular. A hole, a fraction of a centimeter in diameter. Rohan stood without letting on that he'd found anything at all, just as Grayson Hawthorne hit the ground.

"Savannah is not coming down until I'm gone," Grayson told Lyra.

Rohan felt something pass between the two of them as Grayson crouched to assess the plaque. Rohan could see how this would play out. Grayson would soon use his watch to inform the game makers of Savannah's intentions, if he had not already. Being intelligent individuals themselves, Avery Grambs and Jameson Hawthorne would almost certainly take precautions surrounding the announcement of this year's winner, in case Savannah prevailed and won the game.

With her original plan thwarted, the Savannah Grayson that Rohan knew would nonetheless find a way to get what she wanted.

Rohan thought back to exactly what Brady Daniels had offered her. *A body. Proof.*

Logic dictated that Savannah didn't need to win this game anymore. All she needed to do was take Rohan out.

Sidelining that thought, Rohan tracked Grayson's movements as the Hawthorne stood, having thoroughly studied the surface of its plaque—*but not*, Rohan noted with some satisfaction, *the sides*. Not that tiny hole.

So tiny, in fact, Rohan thought, the words little more than a whisper in his mind, *that it is barely any larger than the tip of a dart.*

A golden dart. Rohan knew without reaching for his pockets that he'd neglected to bring his—a result of changing clothes, a result of the fact that he'd believed the dart had already served its purpose in this game as the clue that had started them off.

Admit it. That voice was the Proprietor's. *You've lost your focus. She's stolen it from you, and you have allowed it.*

Rohan thought for a single moment of that not-light, not-teasing cliffside kiss, devoid of inhibitions—and mercy. He'd known, as he'd kissed Savannah Grayson, that she would betray him. And thanks to Grayson and his newfound knowledge, Brady's offer to Savannah had just gone from tempting to unrefusable.

Rohan played out the scenario in his mind, in all its glorious variations. Grayson and Lyra would leave to ponder the words on the plaque. Savannah would descend and read it herself. And if Rohan left her alone...well, Brady Daniels was probably around here somewhere.

Watching.

Waiting.

Savannah would take his offer now, if she hadn't already. All Rohan had to do was go to retrieve his dart and let it happen.

Chapter 61

ROHAN

The house on the north point was, to all appearances, empty. Rohan broke his own rule and entered through the front door, not even bothering to mask the sound of his footsteps. The spiral staircase awaited him, and he took it up one flight to the fourth-floor corridor.

My room. The door. It was open. Rohan slipped into silence as easily as another man might pull on a different shirt. That silence—unnatural to some but not to him—stayed with Rohan as he made his way down the hall, as he pushed the door open just a bit more . . .

Brady Daniels, it appeared, was not out in the forest after all. Not watching. Not waiting. No, Brady Daniels was currently standing over Rohan's discarded tuxedo jacket—and he was holding a golden dart.

"Mine, I assume?" Rohan announced his presence. He eyed Brady's hold on the dart, the way the scholar's deep brown fingers made a fist around its barrel.

Rohan was no stranger to breaking grips.

"You're welcome to try to take it from me," Brady said, seemingly mild-mannered to the end, but he was not wearing the jacket of his *armor*, and there wasn't a pair of glasses in the world thick-rimmed enough to mask the fact that, with muscular arms bare and his abdomen visible through a dark tank top, Brady Daniels did not look nearly so scholarly.

He did not look the least bit *harmless.*

Where Rohan's muscles were long and lean, Brady's were solid, defined enough that Rohan could make out, up and down his arms, where one muscle ended and the next began. Where Rohan's skin was unmarked with scars, Brady had several, as well as a tattoo on the inside of his left arm, a black spiral lined with writing. His shoulders were as wide as Rohan's own. *But I have the greater wingspan.*

Not that this was going to come to a fight.

"Violence would not be appreciated by the game makers," Rohan commented, sauntering just a bit closer to his target. "It might even get us kicked out of the game."

"Us," Brady repeated. "Or *you*, if I refused to fight back. I am notoriously nonviolent."

The scholar was just standing there, waiting for Rohan to attack. *You'd like that, wouldn't you? If I did Savannah's dirty work for her?*

"I'm curious," Rohan said. "How exactly did I end up in your sights—or your sponsor's?" Rohan put no heat in that question. He and Brady Daniels were just two fine and civilized men, having a little chat.

"Kind of egocentric," Brady commented, "to assume that I'm targeting only you." His grip on the golden dart never loosened. Rohan briefly wondered where Brady's jacket was.

And then his gaze settled on the lines and exact fit of the lower half of his target's armor.

"It's not a crime to be an egotist," Rohan declared. "More of a badge of honor, really, and let's face it: You always know exactly where you stand with a person who cares first and foremost about themselves. It's the ones who give away their hearts to this person or that whom you really have to watch out for. Love breeds desperation, and desperation is such a dangerous bedfellow, don't you think, Mr. Daniels?"

Rohan could practically see Brady assessing the meaning beneath those words—and this entire exchange. *Yes, I know you made Savannah an offer. And yes, I know about the messages from your sponsor.*

"My thoughts are my own." Brady did not rise to the bait. "And so is your dart."

With that, Brady went to walk past Rohan, and Rohan sidestepped just enough to ensure that Brady's shoulder hit his—solid contact, in a move so smooth that to any outside observer, it would have painted Brady as the aggressor.

Rohan feinted like he might *defend* himself, but he did not. He was too busy helping himself to something that Brady had been keeping tucked into his pants—the item that Rohan had seen, in the lines and fit of Brady's remaining armor.

Another photograph.

Rohan waited until Brady was gone to make his way into the bathroom—and up onto the bathroom counter. He rose to his full height and lifted the photograph to a light overhead. It took longer for this one to heat up than the others had, with the fire, but eventually, the words—the message—became clear.

One of three. It's time.

Chapter 62

GIGI

L et's play a game," Gigi said. "It's called True or False."

Eve considered Gigi for a moment. "I'm in."

"No," Slate grumbled. "You're not."

"You're just cranky that you're still taped to a chair," Gigi told him. "You heard the ominous lady in the red cloak: It's for your own protection." Gigi set aside any and all trepidation she felt about being *bait* and managed a smile. "My, my, my…"

"How the tables have turned," Slate finished. "Are you done yet, sunshine? Because I am your best defense against whatever walks through that door next. Both of you."

"So *now* you want to protect me?" Eve asked. "Or, excuse me, both of us."

Gigi got the distinct feeling that Eve didn't like to share. "True or false," she said. "The two of you are the kind of employee and employer who make out sometimes."

Silence. Complete and utter silence. And then came the sound of the wall parting.

Gigi whirled and saw a figure in red. *The woman.* She was back. Cloak billowing, she crossed the room, her red boots making not a single sound as she did. "Juliet Grayson. Evelyn Blake. Mattias Slater."

Her voice. That voice. It sounds...

Their captor came to a stop in front of Slate and lifted a red gloved hand to the side of his face. Slate didn't flinch, didn't even blink as she trailed gloved fingers over his skin.

Without warning, Slate slumped.

"Slate!" Eve lunged toward him, putting herself in front of him, cupping his head and feeling for a pulse on his neck.

Gigi just stood there, frozen. Taking in the details. *Silent footsteps—but before, they were audible. And her voice...*

"Who are you?" Gigi asked. *Not the same voice as before. Not the same woman.*

"I am no one," came the reply, "by design."

Gigi finally got her legs to work. She scurried to stand next to Eve. "She's not the one who brought us here," Gigi whispered.

"No," Eve said, not bothering to mute her tone. "She's not."

She's the one who took the bait. Gigi's eyes darted toward Slate. "Is he—"

"Unharmed." That came from the woman in red—but this time, Gigi couldn't help thinking of her differently. *The Woman in Red.* Not just a descriptor. A title. A name. *No one by design.*

"Who are you?" Eve turned Gigi's question into an accusation.

"So demanding. So sure of yourself." There was a frightful neutrality to the Woman in Red's voice, and Gigi thought about the way she'd rendered Slate unconscious with a single touch.

"And who are you again?" Gigi was perfectly capable of being a broken record.

"I am the one who has the right to wear this cloak," the Woman in Red said. "Unlike the impostor who took you, I am not playacting. I am not a pretender. *I* am the Lily. *I* am the Watcher." She lifted a hand to the red veil over her face, and with a single movement, she peeled back the fabric over her eyes—and only her eyes. "And I have questions for the two of you."

Chapter 63

LYRA

Lyra and Grayson ran the island, side by side. They were missing something. That couldn't have been clearer. *The ledger, for one,* Lyra thought. As she and Grayson ran, their bodies fell into a steady, rhythmic pace, and even when their feet didn't hit the ground at the exact same time, Lyra could feel Grayson's body like an extension of her own—and his thoughts as an extension of that.

His conversation with Savannah had not gone well. *We need to win the game—for his sake as much as mine.* As they hit the Eastern shore and began to loop back, Lyra let the words of their latest riddle rise to the surface of her mind once more.

Often
Never
Little late
You
And two

Too much, too great...

"Three twos," she noted out loud. *Two, too, too...*

"Technically..." Grayson's gaze stayed locked on the path they were running. "There are four."

Lyra worked her way through the rest of the riddle, looking for the fourth.

Never, ever

I trap you not

Go now

How

To shoot your shot.

And there it was on the final line—*to*. Spoken aloud, the same syllable repeated itself four times over the course of the riddle: *two, too, too, to*.

Lyra pushed her pace up, and Grayson did the same. The wind was fierce today, the kind of wind that came at Lyra from all sides, a little chaotic, impossible to ignore. Her face was starting to feel chapped, and her body ached, a reminder that they'd stayed up all night, a reminder that sooner or later, she would hit a wall.

Beside her, Grayson gave every impression of being someone who didn't even know what a wall was. "Four twos," he pointed out, "is eight."

"The dice?" Lyra let that thought take hold in her mind.

"Maybe. Maybe not." Grayson was a rhythmic runner, each stride exactly the length of his last. "It matters that we still haven't fully solved the prior puzzle."

"No ledger," Lyra said, verbalizing her earlier thoughts. "We missed something." She let the ache in her muscles crystallize her focus. "You might even say we're missing the forest for the trees."

When they rounded back and the tree line came into view once more, Grayson skirted it, looping to the south. Lyra followed his lead and started back at the beginning of their clue.

Often

Never

Little late

"Time," she said out loud. "That's the pattern in the first three lines."

"*Often. Never. Little late.*" Grayson got there in an instant. "*Time* could signify a clock. An hourglass."

"Our watches?" Lyra suggested, then she preempted his reply. "That's a stretch." Up ahead of them, light hit two giant stones at the edge of the forest *just so.* "Do you see that?" Lyra asked Grayson.

They passed the first boulder and slowed to a stop, taking in the space between the two boulders—and what lay beyond.

"A staircase made of stone," Lyra said, and then she shook her head. "How did I miss this? I ran the entire island multiple times. I should have seen it."

"There's a difference between seeing and perceiving," Grayson said. "Our minds have a tendency to fill in gaps. Sometimes, we see things that aren't there, and sometimes, you can look right at something and miss it all the same."

As Lyra looked down the stone staircase, she was hit with an ominous feeling—not the feeling of being watched this time, but it came over her body with the same visceral certainty, like her body was perceiving something that her mind could not see. Driven to pinpoint what, she descended first one step on the stone staircase, then the next. She closed her eyes with the third. Grayson followed in her wake.

His body. Hers. Step by step.

With her eyes closed, Lyra felt the connection between them that much more strongly, but that did nothing to banish that nagging sense that there was *something*—

"*Stop.*" Grayson's voice cut through the air like a scythe.

Lyra's eyes flew open, and she froze just in time to see the snake.

Chapter 64

GRAYSON

"Don't move." Grayson placed a hand on the back of Lyra's neck. The snake was within striking distance of her. Its head was triangular—and raised. If Grayson had thought he could take care of the threat with no risk to Lyra, he would have. But any movement toward the serpent, no matter how decisive or smooth, could precipitate a strike.

Even Hawthornes could only move so fast.

So Grayson stood there *with* Lyra, willing her to stay still. And with each breath they took together, Grayson saw the faces of the ones he'd failed before:

The first girl he'd ever cared for, face-down on the shore. *Dead.*

Avery, bleeding and unconscious on the pavement. *The world on fire.* In the moments after his father's bomb had gone off, Grayson hadn't even been able to run to her.

For so long, he hadn't been able to run toward anyone or anything.

Emily, dead. Avery, bleeding. But Lyra was here, and the snake was slithering off the stone steps.

Lyra was *fine*.

With great effort, Grayson let his hand fall from her neck. "You stopped when I told you to."

"It wasn't a *suggestion*." Lyra paused. "And I trust you." She was so still yet—*perfectly* still, and all Grayson could think was: *You shouldn't.*

He knew—from their conversation in the tree, he *knew* how she felt about being kept in the dark, about that kind of protection. And here he was, doing to her exactly what her parents had, lying to her and not-lying to her, deciding what risks she would and would not take.

On some level, Grayson knew that he had no right, but he also knew that he would not survive anything happening to her—not after everything else he'd lost, not when she might be his Libby, not when the reality of Lyra Kane was more than he could have dreamed when he'd thought, day after day, about a girl who'd called him on the phone.

Grayson moved down onto Lyra's step and then down again, taking the lead, and Lyra let him. No calamity struck, but Grayson walked the rest of the way down the stone staircase with his body in front of hers, shielding her as best he could.

Emily, dead on the beach. Avery, bleeding on the pavement.

"Grayson?" Lyra's voice had always been so uniquely hers: layered, honey-rich, and forever tiptoeing the line to one side of husky or the other—*raw* and *real* and *strong*.

Grayson swallowed and forced himself to speak. "About the clue—"

"You sure as hell aren't thinking about the clue." Lyra's tone made it clear: She wouldn't *let* him shrug her off.

Grayson stepped onto the rocky beach and stared out at the ocean. If he turned left, he and Lyra would ultimately end up at the boathouse. He turned right instead, onto a thin slice of shore that wrapped around the island. Following this path, they'd eventually end up below the ruins of the old house.

Once the tide rolled in, there was a good chance that this path would no longer exist at all.

"My thoughts are dark, Lyra." He walked the thin path—just wide enough that she could fall in beside him. "My mind is rather gifted at imagining in detail any potential failures on my part at protecting those who matter to me."

The stone step. The snake. If he'd been a *second* later...

"Because you've failed before," Lyra said quietly, far too perceptive for her own good—or his.

Grayson angled his eyes toward hers. "It's always straight to the heart of things with you."

Her hand worked its way stubbornly into his as they walked on. "Who did you fail? You aren't just thinking about Savannah."

No. I'm not. Grayson was loath to admit that out loud. He had moved past this. He had *worked* to move past it, to accept that he'd had no control over Emily—wild, carefree, desperate-to-feel Emily, who had never truly loved him back, who had been his first in so many things.

"There was a girl." Grayson wasn't sure why he was telling Lyra this, why he *needed* to tell her this. "I knew her my entire life. We were not particularly well suited, personality-wise, but it always felt a bit like Emily was in my blood." He exhaled. "She certainly excelled at getting under our skin." His *and* Jamie's. Grayson's voice hardened as he continued, "She died. Cliff-jumping. I was the one who took her out there."

"Emily," Lyra said. Grayson could practically see her reaching for the memory cued by that name.

"You read the article." Grayson did not specify which article. Alisa had done a good job shutting down the story, but even the best fixer could only contain so much.

"I can't picture her," Lyra said, her expression intent. "But..."

"She looked very much like Eve." Grayson was usually better at being circumspect than this. "There is some relation there."

"Do you want to talk about it?" Lyra asked.

"I am philosophically and morally opposed to talking or thinking about Eve." Grayson set his jaw.

Lyra was silent for a long moment. "Are you going to be okay?"

In his lifetime, Grayson had been asked that question so infrequently, if at all. He'd cultivated an image of invulnerability. *Okay* was not a thing to which Hawthornes aspired—especially him.

He swallowed. "I'm fine."

"Where have I heard that before?" Lyra replied.

He was the one who'd told her that she didn't *have* to be fine. He'd told her that the cost of being fine when you weren't was too high.

"Maybe some of us," Lyra told him, "need to break to be whole."

Some of us. Grayson let himself look at her—not just a glance this time. He drank in the lines of her face, the steadiness of her amber eyes, golden in the sun. "You understand," he said quietly, "why I am forever pulling you back from cliffs."

Grayson knew, though she did not, that he was not just speaking of cliffs. *Alice. The lily. Omega and three.* The snake on the stone staircase was not the only one in her path. And he *could not* tell her.

Physically—he *could not.*

"I understand," Lyra said.

You would not, if you knew. Grayson pulled his eyes away from hers as they came around a bend, and the universe gifted him with a perfect distraction—for himself and for her. At the base of the cliff upon which the first mansion on Hawthorne Island had been built, there was an opening. A tangle of vines hung down from the surrounding rocks, nearly obscuring it, but Grayson's gaze locked in on that opening with laser-like precision.

A cavern. He drew his hand slowly back from Lyra's until only the tips of their fingers were touching. Her fingers curved reflexively inward, catching his as Grayson led her onward to that vine-covered opening. He stepped through the vines. The cavern beyond was small—less than a foot taller than his own head, no deeper than eight or twelve feet. Strings of delicate lights hung just beyond vines. And beyond that...

Lyra pushed past him, never one to be held back for long. She ducked under the lights, her brow furrowing as she took in the only object in the cavern. "A bed?"

"A bed that, given its pristine state and the ebb and flow of the tide, was almost certainly placed here while we were on the yacht." Grayson examined it: an antique; wrought iron. The mattress had been made up—blanket, pillows, and all.

A bed—or a hint? The moment he saw it, Grayson began to laugh—despite himself, despite everything. "*Often,*" he said out loud. "*Never. Little late. You...And two...Too much, too great.*" The poem struck him as very likely being Avery's doing, but the bed? That had Jameson written all over it. "*Never, ever. I trap you not. Go now...How...To shoot your shot.*"

"You know something," Lyra accused. "You just solved it."

"I might have."

"Then tell me, asshole." Lyra smiled slightly as she ran a hand lightly over the wrought iron of the bed. "And not in riddles this time."

"Oh, but you see, it's *not* a riddle, sweetheart." Grayson walked to the opposite side of the bed, enjoying himself a bit more than he should have. Lyra's amber eyes caught on his, and Grayson continued, "It's a code. A very simple code."

Chapter 65

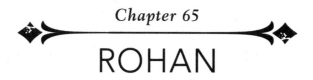

ROHAN

R ohan returned to the tree to find Savannah at its base. She said nothing about whatever words had been exchanged between herself and Grayson, and in return, Rohan said not one word about the latest invisible message he'd revealed on the back of yet another identical photograph of Calla Thorp.

One of three. It's time. The words echoed through Rohan's mind, their meaning tantalizingly unclear. The latter sentence, at least, was a sentiment that Rohan shared.

It was past time. *Time to go for my blood, Savannah Grayson. Physically, metaphorically—dealer's choice.*

"Your brother knows you're up to something." Rohan doubted she'd even need this final push, given the circumstances, but he gave it nonetheless. "And what he knows, the game makers assuredly will as well. Rather inconvenient for you that they equipped our watches for contact."

Savannah did not respond to what he'd just said, did not even correct him with *half brother*. Instead, she proceeded as if Rohan had said nothing at all. "What do you make of the words on the plaque?"

Through her white armor, every line of her body was visible to Rohan's discerning eyes. No tells, this time.

Nothing but focus.

Nothing but *her*.

Rohan refused the gauntlet she'd just thrown down. "So your plan remains unaltered? Play the game to win, hope that certain precautions aren't already being taken in case you do?"

"My plan," Savannah said, meeting his eyes with those winter-frost ones of hers, "is not now nor has it ever been any of your concern. The plaque, British."

"There's a hole in the side." Rohan purposefully armed her with that information. "Roughly the size of the tip of a golden dart. Mine seems to have gone missing."

All she would have to do to seize the advantage was pretend that she did not have hers, either. Distract him. Send him on a wild-goose chase. And Rohan would, in return, pretend that the white fabric that had melded itself to her form did not give away exactly which pocket held her dart.

"How very careless of you," Savannah said. "Fortunately, I am never careless." She withdrew her dart.

As far as pretenders went, she was flawless.

She crouched, running her hand around the side of the plaque until she found the hole he'd spoken of. Rohan let his fingers join hers, skin against skin, right before she hit the spot in question. And there it was—*a tiny hole, a hitch of her breath*.

Savannah pushed his hand aside just far enough to thrust the tip of the golden dart into the hole—a perfect fit.

But nothing happened.

"May I?" Rohan asked, fully anticipating her response: *You may not.*

Savannah Grayson, however, had the absolute audacity to give the dart to him, placing it in his hand just a bit harder than necessary but giving it to him all the same. No matter how many openings Rohan gave her, she was apparently set on doing this to her own specifications—betraying him in *her* time, in *her* way.

Rohan stood, forcing himself to keep right on looking at the way that *she* looked clad in white as he set his mind to devising a distraction that would allow him to keep her dart.

"What now?" Savannah said, and he heard the familiar intensity in her tone—not *weak* in the least.

What now, Rohan? the Proprietor asked in his mind.

Rohan slipped the dart up his sleeve as he turned. "Follow me."

Chapter 66

ROHAN

W hy are we here?" Savannah asked, her voice hanging in the humid air like a portent of things to come.

Here was the ruins, that once-grand Hawthorne mansion burned very nearly to the ground. Rohan had always been drawn to the broken and the ruined, but that wasn't why he'd brought Savannah here.

"This place is an obvious landmark," Rohan commented. "A key part of the board, yet to be used." *Just as you have yet to truly use and discard me.*

"Why are we here, British?" Savannah Grayson was not a person who enjoyed repeating herself. "The ledger is back in the forest, somewhere near the tree. It has to be."

"What would you say if I told you that we're simply giving Brady Daniels time to make his next move?" Now that Brady had possession of Rohan's dart, he was bound to show up at the tree eventually. He'd clearly already figured out the darts were needed. "Let us see what *he* discovers."

"Have I ever given you the impression that I rely on the discoveries of others?" Haughty was a good look for Savannah Grayson. The world around them was black and gray except where it was green and overgrown, wild in contrast to his opponent's icy control.

Find an excuse to leave me. Go to Brady. Take his deal. Rohan had always had infinite patience in waiting games, his next move always dictated by strategy and strategy alone, but this time, he tired of waiting.

If not now, Savvy, then when?

"If Brady has yet to prove useful..." Rohan turned slowly, making a show of taking in the view of the ruins. "Then perhaps we should take him out. I am now in possession of a third photograph."

Savannah processed that in silence. *You don't want him disqualified, do you, love? Once he's out of the game, perhaps that offer of his no longer holds.*

"What did the third message say?" Savannah asked.

Rohan offered her an abridged version: *"It's time."* He gave Savannah a look. "I tend to agree. Three photographs, at least two of which were almost certainly received while he was playing the game." Rohan gave a little shrug. "I've taken out rivals with less. And Jameson Hawthorne is predisposed to believe me."

"You're working for Jameson. For *them*." And there it was. Her anger. Her weakness. *The Hawthornes and Avery Grambs.*

"Like you, Savvy, I work only for myself."

"You are so desperate to believe that, aren't you?" Savannah said, and the lines of her body said so much more.

They said that she was ready for a fight. Aching for one. And Rohan did hate to disappoint.

"Perhaps," he said, his voice low and pitched to surround her, "the game makers will disqualify you both. Brady, for communication with his sponsor, and you, because they've discovered yours."

Go on. Fight. See me as the threat I am.

"There's nothing to link me to any *sponsor* but conjecture." Savannah might as well have announced that she was not in the business of blinking first.

"Are you so sure," Rohan said silkily, "that Avery Grambs and the Hawthorne brothers will care whether or not there is conjecture involved? Or will they care only about taking out a threat to themselves?"

Take the scholar's deal, he willed her silently. *Betray me. Hurt me. Do your worst, Savannah Grayson.* Pain only counted if you didn't see it coming. Pain only counted if you *cared*.

"Is that how it is?" Savannah closed the space between them, rendering it nonexistent in the bat of the eye. Toe-to-toe and face-to-face with him, she was anything but distant, anything but cool. "Is this your play? Once our alliance has reached its end, once the competition has been dispatched—are we going head-to-head the way we planned, or are you hoping to take me out the coward's way?"

Rohan leaned forward, so he could speak directly into Savannah's ear, his lips almost brushing skin. "No spoilers."

Savannah stared him down for an exquisite second or two, and then she took a step back. "Why are we here, Rohan?" There was a different quality to her voice now, something more guttural, something sharper—and she'd used his given name. "What are we doing?"

It was clear: Savannah wasn't talking about the ruins anymore. This thing between them had a weight to it, a gravitational pull that held them together like a binding, a fist-thick rope running from the core of him to the core of her. And there Rohan was, brandishing a knife. He'd been cutting through fiber after fiber with each push, and *damn it*—

Why hadn't it snapped? Why hadn't she? *Make your move, love. Make it now.*

"Do you know what this place is?" Savannah said in that social-ite voice of hers, the corresponding mask descending over her face as she dragged manicured fingers lightly over a stone fireplace that still stood. "To me?" Savannah Grayson was not a person who gave an opponent long to answer. "My cousin Colin died in this fire. He died *here*, before I was even born."

"Colin Anders Wright." Rohan knew the names of the victims of the fire, but his research into the Hawthorne family had only gone back so far.

"My father raised him like a son," Savannah said, that high, clear voice of hers struck through with iron. "Loved him like a son—more than he could ever love a daughter." There was the slightest of pauses and then: "Gigi looks like Colin. Our father adored her for that from the day she was born. I was different. I did not look a thing like the lost son. I was not an easy child to love. But *I* played the game."

The game as in basketball—or being exactly what your father wanted, expected, and demanded you to be? Rohan could feel himself getting sucked into the labyrinth, into the room in his mind devoted wholly and entirely to *her.*

Careful, boy, the Proprietor's voice warned, the reminder surging through Rohan's body like current through a wire.

"Are you done?" Rohan asked Savannah.

"I think sometimes," Savannah Grayson said softly, "about what it might have been like if Colin hadn't died. If Toby Hawthorne hadn't thought it was a good idea to play with fire."

"Toby." Rohan could feel the final pieces of this puzzle coming together "Your father blamed Toby Hawthorne for Colin's death?"

There was something about the way that she was standing with hands to her sides that made Rohan imagine that each of those hands held a blade. "Grayson," she said, her voice low, "wants me to believe that my father thought Avery was Toby's daughter, that my father went after *her*—for revenge."

"But you don't believe that?" Rohan pressed, stepping into her personal space once more.

This time, Savannah did not step back. "I don't believe it matters. Whatever happened to my father, however it happened, Avery Grambs and her people—they covered it up."

There was a danger in understanding someone a little too well. The bigger danger, however, was that Savannah Grayson was letting him understand her.

Letting him in.

Letting him see her bleed.

You were never enough, were you, love? For anyone. Not your father. Not even Gigi, in the end.

With anyone else, Rohan would have used the intimacy of that understanding to his advantage. He would have taken her head into his hands, brushed the pad of his thumb gently over those sharp, sharp cheekbones of hers like he was ridding her face of an imaginary tear. If she'd been anyone else, he would have made her feel like they were in this together, so that when he *did* betray her, she would never see it coming.

But touching Savannah Grayson, even *pretending* to feel for her—Rohan couldn't risk it. He couldn't risk *this*, whatever it was, a moment longer.

Take the knife and cut the rope. "Winning won't get you what you want now."

Savannah's voice went low again. "And you are so sure that you know what I want?"

She wasn't letting go. Damn it, *why wasn't she letting go?*

"I know you," Rohan said. "And that is enough." She was mercilessly in pursuit of his own ends. *Just. Like. Him.* "We're far too much alike, you and I. Best not to trust either of us, really." His British accent took a turn—less aristocratic, playful in the darkest way. "You never know when the switch might flip."

Savannah stared at him like she was Helen of Troy, staring out at a battlefield her beauty had sown. "So this is done, then?" she said, her voice going dangerously neutral. "This? Us?"

Us. "I didn't say that." Rohan told himself that he was still playing with her, that no part of him was trying to hold on—not when she was *going* to betray him.

"You're not saying anything." Savannah's neutrality began to slip away, like water dripping off a razor-sharp icicle in the sun. "A picture is worth a thousand words, Rohan, and you are nothing but smooth talk and double entendres, meaningless nicknames and never telling me anything real."

"That isn't true." Rohan felt, as much as heard, his own voice go brutally low. "I told you from the start, love: *I want it more.*"

He'd told Savannah Grayson about the Devil's Mercy. He'd told her about dark water and drowning. About the child he'd once been.

No more.

"This really is it, isn't it?" Savannah was far too calm.

"The end of the line," Rohan agreed. "Do your worst, love."

"Believe me," Savannah told him. "I will." Her expression like glass, she turned and walked away.

And just like that, Rohan flipped the switch.

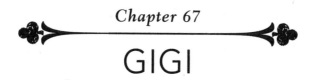

Chapter 67

GIGI

Gigi stared at the Woman in Red—at her eyes. *One blue eye. One brown.* Gigi knew those eyes. She'd seen those eyes before—in a picture belonging to Brady Daniels.

As the cloaked woman interrogated them about the Grandest Game, about the players, about the game makers, all Gigi could think about was the triangular scar at the base of Knox Landry's neck, the one the girl he'd loved had given him when she *left.*

He'd called it *a Calla Thorp good-bye.*

"You must know something else about her."

Gigi blinked. She'd lost track of the present for a moment. "Who?"

Eve shot Gigi an incredulous look. "Lyra Kane." Apparently, Eve did not believe this was an appropriate time to be zoning out, but Gigi's brain was a mess of memories and what-ifs and revelations.

Calla Thorp. Not missing. Here. Alive.

"Or we could return to discussing your brother," Calla—the Woman in Red, the Lily, the Watcher—told Gigi. "Or *his* brother."

Gigi swallowed. "Grayson has three brothers."

"Three," Calla repeated. "That is a number of some significance. Tell me why that is the case, and I will let you go—all of you."

Gigi glanced at Slate. *Still out.* If he'd been awake, he probably would have told her to just answer the question, but the number three didn't mean anything to Gigi—and those eyes did.

"You're...*her*," Gigi said. Some people loomed larger than life, even if you didn't know them, even if you'd only ever heard their name. "Calla." Gigi's heart twisted in her chest. "Brady thinks he's playing for your life. He thinks you were *taken*."

"I am not Calla." The voice that spoke those words was eerily detached. "Calla is no more, and I am no one, by design."

"You left." Gigi's mind was reeling. "That's what Knox said. You ran away, and you warned him not to follow." Gigi brought her right hand to the base of her own neck, just above her collarbone. "He has a scar right here. And Brady...Brady *loves* you."

For Brady, there had never been anyone but *Calla*.

"Brady Daniels loves a memory. He loves a dream." Calla-not-Calla reached a gloved hand out for Gigi's chin. "I assure you, Juliet Grayson, I am quite real. And I am *no one*."

No one, by design. Gigi swallowed again. "You're the Watcher. You're the Lily. *Calla*." Gigi's eyes widened. "You left that flower for me."

The Woman in Red did not deny it. "There is an order to things. There are rules. Warnings must sometimes be delivered when a person of a certain sort is being watched."

"What sort?" Eve demanded. "And what do you mean, *warnings*?"

"I am not," Calla, who was *no one*, told Eve, "talking to you."

"Maybe you should be." Eve stepped in front of Gigi once more, shielding her. "Omega." Eve let that word—that one word—hang in the air. "Calla lilies." Eve paused again. "Alice Hawthorne. Lyra Kane asked me about all of those things."

Calla went silent for a moment, and Gigi had the oddest, eeriest sense that behind the veil, the Woman in Red was smiling. "Evelyn Blake—or do you prefer Laughlin? Shane? Hawthorne?" The Woman cocked her head to the side. "Regardless, Eve, you do not disappoint."

With that, the Woman in Red—*Calla, not-Calla, the Lily, the Watcher*—turned to walk away, like Eve had given her what she wanted, what she'd been trying to get from Gigi.

"You can't just leave us here," Eve called.

"I can do many things. Mine is a higher law."

Gigi managed to free her vocal cords. *"Calla—"*

"Calla," the Woman in Red replied in that frightfully even tone of hers, "was a naive, sheltered seventeen-year-old girl in love. She was also the only great-granddaughter of Helena Thorp, and that mattered a great deal, so much so in fact that it did not matter to Helena that Calla, among all of her great-grandchildren, was the only one that had no Thorp blood at all. Calla did not know, growing up, that her father was not, in fact, her father—but Orion Thorp knew from the day she was born. Calla's eyes made her true paternity quite obvious to him, you see. For a man like Orion, an insult like that, a betrayal like that, was unforgivable— but giving his family the first *daughter* in three generations made Orion the Thorp heir. And *that* mattered more than any insult or betrayal."

Gigi felt dizzy just trying to follow that—all of it, any of it.

"After all," not-Calla continued, "it was not as if Calla's so-called father did not have a biological child of his own."

"I don't understand," Gigi said.

"You are not meant not to."

"Why are you telling us this?" Eve asked.

"I am not Calla Thorp. There is no Calla Thorp anymore." The wall parted. "And thanks to dear, dear Eve, the time for *watching* is done."

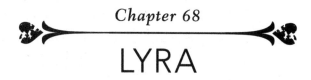

LYRA

It's not *a riddle. It's a code. A very simple code.* It took Lyra long
enough to figure it out, to look at the letters in the poem as *letters*
instead of as part of a whole. Once she stopped looking for meaning in the words of the inscription, once she forced herself to look
for the *simplest* answer, there it was.

> *OFTEN*
> *NEVER*
> *LITTLE LATE*
> *YOU*
> *AND TWO*
> *TOO MUCH, TOO GREAT*
> *NEVER, EVER*
> *I TRAP YOU NOT*
> *GO NOW*

HOW
TO SHOOT YOUR SHOT

The first letters in each of those lines—they spelled out a message, an explanation for why she and Grayson hadn't been able to find the ledger at the tree. The trick was *right there*.

ONLY AT NIGHT

"Right place," Lyra said, "wrong time. We can only move on—only find the ledger and the next clue—at night." She looked from Grayson to the bed between them, a beautiful antique setup in a damp and shallow cavern that would probably be overrun with water as soon as the tide rose. "Hence the bed."

Night. Bed.

"We're all running on fumes," Grayson commented. "And thus, the game includes a programmed break."

Lyra's brain raced. "After a night on that yacht—"

"That ensured that all players encountered the tree during the day," Grayson finished.

We were on the music box. Brady was one puzzle ahead—the compass. He must not have solved it before midnight.

"The tide will come in again." Grayson rested a hand on the wrought-iron headboard. "*This* bed is just for show."

"But we do need to sleep," Lyra said, looking at the bed, drawn to it—and to him. She tilted her eyes up to catch his. "We need sleep, and we need food."

They were only human.

"We need," Grayson said, his voice echoing through the cavern, "to go back to the house."

Back at the house, they found food and ate their fill.

"And now," Grayson said, "we sleep."

Lyra gave him a look. "You say that like it's such a simple thing."

"Control of your body. Control of your mind." Grayson returned Lyra's look. He paused, ever so slightly. "Sleep *should* be a simple thing."

But it isn't for you, either. Lyra understood that, despite his words. She thought of that moment with the snake and the way he'd looked afterward, and then she thought about Savannah and Eve, about Alice and omega and everything else.

"Should be," Lyra echoed. "But isn't."

"I fail most often," Grayson told her, "at simple things."

Lyra thought again about Grayson Hawthorne having to practice making mistakes. She thought about the girl he'd lost, the one he blamed himself for. And then she thought about herself: four years old, made a party to her father's suicide. The only witness. The only survivor.

She wondered if sleep was ever simple for survivors.

"Grayson." Lyra's voice came out rough. "Would you like to fail together?"

Chapter 69

LYRA

They ended up in Grayson's "room"—the ballroom with its mosaic floor and walls and ceiling and a single king-sized bed in the middle. Their longsword lay at the foot of it. Grayson picked it up, peeled back the comforter, and then looked at Lyra.

"You first," she told him.

Grayson set the sword down on the mosaic floor, and then he rose again and climbed into the bed. A breath catching in her throat, Lyra climbed in beside him.

Grayson propped himself up with one arm and looked down at her. He brought a hand to her temple, to her hair. "May I?"

Lyra wasn't entirely sure what he was asking, but she nodded anyway, and Grayson began slowly working his fingers through her thick tangle of hair, spreading it out on the pillow around her head.

When he finished, Grayson just stayed there, propped up, staring down at her for the longest time.

"You're not going to fall asleep like that," Lyra told him. *And neither am I.* "Lay back down."

Grayson did as she bade him, his back on the mattress, his head still turned toward hers.

Lyra raised a hand to *his* temple. "Close your eyes," she ordered.

"I'm the one," Grayson told her, "who's supposed to take care of you."

"Oh really?" Lyra retorted. At this rate, neither one of them was going to be getting any sleep. "How many hours until nightfall?" Lyra asked.

Grayson didn't even have to check his watch. "A little over six."

They needed sleep. Lyra knew that. Her body decidedly did not. "How do you normally put yourself to sleep?" she asked Grayson, staring into his eyes, thinking about arctic ice and the silver of swords. "When you can, when you succeed—how do you turn it off?"

"The world?" Grayson said.

"Being Grayson Hawthorne," Lyra replied.

His chest rose and fell, and her fingers ached to touch it in a way that might have proven impossible to deny if he hadn't answered her question.

"I imagine myself floating on my back in a pool."

Lyra flipped from her side to her back. There was maybe an inch between her shoulder and his. She closed her eyes. "Floating in a pool." She could just almost feel it. "At night."

"A moonless sky up above," Grayson replied. She could tell just by the sound of his voice: His eyes were closed, too.

He breathed.

She breathed.

"Nothing but black," Grayson continued.

"Deep breaths, lungs filling to keep you afloat." Lyra *could* feel it now, her body and his, floating side by side. *Silence.*

And then, there really was nothing but black.

The calla lily.

The candy necklace.

"A Hawthorne did this."

He has a gun. Lyra couldn't breathe, but she didn't wake up. She sank deeper into the dream, deeper and deeper and deeper until there was no shred of awareness that it *was* a dream left in her.

"What begins a bet? Not that." She can hear the man, but she can't see him. There's silence, and then—a bang.

She presses her hands to her ears. She's a big girl. Not gonna cry. She's not.

Another bang.

Silence. She drops her hands from her ears. The flower falls to the floor. She twists and twists the elastic of the candy necklace around her fingers so tight it hurts, and then she hears something like the creaking of a door.

Suddenly, her feet are walking toward the stairs. Quiet, she thinks. She has to be quiet. She slips off her shoes.

Up the stairs. One step. Then another. Her foot sinks into something sticky and warm and red. It's red, and it's on her, and it's dripping down the stairs.

The walls are red, too. You're not supposed to draw on the walls.

A mewling sound. It's her. She's the one making the sound as she sees something at the top of the stairs.

Not something.

His face—he has no face. She can't scream. Can't move. Every-
thing is red. Everything.

And then there is a voice behind her, a woman's voice. "You poor
thing."

Lyra turns. At the bottom of the stairs, looking up at her, is a figure
dressed entirely in black.

Black cloak.

Black hood.

Black veil.

Black boots, coming up the stairs.

Black gloves gently touching her face. "You are a quiet one."

She can't scream. Her body is shaking and shaking and—

"You should not be here, little one."

Blood on her feet. The man doesn't have a face. And she shouldn't
be here. She trembles harder.

"You should not be here." A gloved finger brushes tears from her
face. "But who is to say that you were?"

A rustling of fabric.

Something is pressed to her lips. Drinking. She's drinking
something.

And then—bare feet on pavement. She's outside. She's running.
And she is alone.

Lyra woke frozen in her own body, like her bones and the blood
in her veins and the breath in her lungs had all turned to razor-
sharp ice. *There was someone else there.* Lyra tried to call to mind
an image of the woman in black—tried and *couldn't,* because her
brain just didn't work like that.

But she *could* hear the woman's voice: *You should not be here.*
But who is to say that you were?

Lyra might not have been able to see a damn thing in her mind, but she could remember: a cloak, a hood, boots. *All black.* Breathing hurt. Somehow, Lyra managed to roll onto her side.

Grayson was there, inches from her, and he was beautiful— far more beautiful in sleep than any man had a right to be. *Long lashes. Sharp cheekbones. Full lips.* There was hair in his face— not just one strand or two but enough for her to run her hands through.

She did, her touch light. He didn't stir. Lyra almost hated to wake him, but she had to.

You poor thing. Lyra could hear the voice so vividly now. "Grayson." Her voice came out quieter than she meant for it to. "Grayson, wake up."

He slept like the dead.

"I need you."

And just like that, Grayson's eyes were open and locked on to her face. "The dream?" He understood that much immediately. He sat up, pulling her toward him. Lyra wanted nothing more in the world than to lay her head on his shoulder and breathe in the smell of him. *Cedar and falling leaves.* But she didn't.

She couldn't.

"Not just the dream." The words felt like barbed wire in her throat. "It went further this time." Saying that out loud set her heart to pounding like a hammer driving in nails—or railroad spikes. "I saw more." She closed her eyes, knowing it was useless. "I *saw it,* and I can't see anything anymore, but I remember her voice." Lyra's throat hurt. "I remember what she said."

"What *who* said?"

Lyra opened her eyes to stare straight into Grayson Hawthorne's. "I never knew how they found me—the police or my parents or whoever it was that took me out of that house." She'd never been able to ask, not without admitting to her family what she had remembered. "I was alone with my father's body. I had blood on my feet—*blood on my feet, and I was alone.*" Lyra sucked in a breath. "And then I wasn't."

Grayson's hands made their way to the sides of Lyra's face. He cupped her jaw, cradling her head, his fingers gently massaging the back of her neck. Small movements, steady. He was there, and he wasn't asking a damn thing from her.

That, more than anything else, let Lyra continue. "She wore a black cloak, the hood pulled up." Lyra pressed her lips together. "Her face was veiled. She said I shouldn't be there. And then—it was like she was covering for me, for the fact that I *was* there. She fed me some kind of liquid, poured it down my throat."

"I've got you." He was still only touching her face and neck, but Lyra could feel Grayson's presence in every inch of her body, anchoring her like silver and steel. "I am here, and I have got you, Lyra Kane."

"Alice." Lyra said the name out loud. It was the only thing that made sense. *A Hawthorne did this*—and then, the woman in black was there.

"Breathe," Grayson murmured. He breathed, and so did she, and it was like running beside him all over again, a duet of sorts.

I am not alone. Lyra leaned in to one of Grayson hands, feeling the warmth of his skin on her cheek, and then there was a buzz at his wrist. *His watch.*

Grayson pulled back. He didn't blink, and from his eyes alone, she wouldn't have even thought he felt it—but he *pulled back.*

Grayson Hawthorne didn't pull back. Not when she needed

him. *Not like this.* Lyra's fingers locked around his wrist, her hand too small to make it more than halfway around the circumference. But she was strong enough to hold his arm in place, if only because he let her.

"That was your watch," Lyra said.

Grayson stroked the thumb of his free hand over her cheek. "My watch doesn't matter right now."

Lyra wanted to believe that. But..."My body knows yours." *Better than it should. Better than it has any right to.* She swallowed. "You carry the weight of the world on your shoulders, Grayson. There's tension in your muscles all the time, but there's a difference between *tension* and *tensing*." The tension that lived in Grayson's body was the tension of a bow with an arrow notched and at the ready. *He* was always ready. "You only tense for a reason."

Slowly, Lyra turned his arm over. She pressed her thumb to the inside of his wrist, knowing her technique was lacking but not willing to risk loosening her grip.

"What are you doing?"

Lyra would have thought that was obvious. "Taking your pulse." He looked so calm, so steady, but his heart—it was racing. "If I turn your wrist back over," Lyra whispered, "if I look at your watch, what am I going to see?"

She didn't wait for an answer. She tried to turn his wrist back over, and Grayson's free hand caught hers. For the longest time, the two of them stayed there in the bed, in a silent standoff, her hand on his arm and his on hers, neither one of them saying a word.

"Don't look." Grayson broke first—and so did his voice. "I am asking you not to look," he said, his entire body taut now, "the way that I asked Emily not to jump."

Lyra's heart twisted, but in the back of her mind, all she could hear was Savannah and her warning, a warning Lyra had set aside, a warning that hadn't come back to her even once since the yacht.

When all is said and done, when it matters most...

Lyra bowed her head to look.

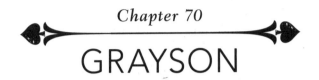

Chapter 70

GRAYSON

Grayson twisted his wrist, angling the face of his watch out of Lyra's view. He had no idea what the message he'd just received said, but the last messages he'd sent had indicated that Toby *knew*—and not just about Eve.

About Alice. Alice, whom if Lyra was to be believed—and he *did* believe Lyra Kane, body and soul—might have *been there* the night that Lyra's father had died. Grayson's mind went to Jameson saying that he'd been drugged, saying that his memory of what had happened to him in Prague was minimal, fractured—all feelings, few specifics. Grayson remembered thinking that Jameson knew more than he consciously remembered—the calla lily, for one—but Grayson hadn't made the connection between Jameson's splintered memory and Lyra's.

What if she didn't repress that night because of the trauma? What if someone repressed it for her?

Across from him, Lyra Catalina Kane was looking down, but

she still couldn't quite see the face of his watch—not yet. Grayson let loose of her arm and twisted his wrist as far as he could without fully breaking her hold.

"It's funny," Lyra said, bringing her amber eyes back up to his face. "Playing the Grandest Game, you start to get a sense for when you're missing something." She swallowed.

Grayson went to pull his arm back, and Lyra's grip tightened.

"Don't you dare," she said.

"Lyra." Grayson couldn't bring himself to say more than that. No more lies. No more half-truths.

"Show me what your watch says." Lyra's voice shook. "*Show me, Grayson.*"

Words threatened to lodge themselves in his throat, but he forced them out. "I cannot do that, Lyra."

She dropped Grayson's wrist. "You know something. Your brothers and Avery know something, don't they? About Alice. Back on the yacht, after you talked to them about the calla—I believed you when you said that it was nothing, that they knew nothing. I *trusted* you."

"I know." Grayson wanted nothing more than to touch her now. "If you will just—"

"Don't," she bit out. "Show me your watch, Grayson."

He'd asked her not to look. She had, but he'd twisted his arm before she could read the message. And now, *she* was the one asking, telling him what she needed.

Slowly, Grayson turned his wrist back over. A message stared up at them both: *O.M. LOCATED.*

Alisa had found Odette. The message itself was less damning than Grayson had feared it would be, but Lyra scrolled back.

"*Toby knows something,*" Lyra read. "Not about Eve, apparently.

So what exactly does your uncle Toby know, Grayson? Something about his mother? About *Alice*?"

I was trying to protect my family, and I was trying to protect you. Grayson knew that Lyra Kane would not thank him for that.

"And Odette has been *located*? Was she missing?" Lyra fired questions off, one after another. "I don't understand. Make me understand, Grayson." Lyra gave him a second—just one—to reply. "Why does your family consider me a liability? A threat."

"They do not think you are a threat." Grayson's voice stayed even, no matter the sensation in his chest: a tightening of muscles, a ripping of something at his core.

"If *I'm* not the threat..." The expression in Lyra's golden brown eyes shifted as she realized the full implication of that. "*Alice*. She's the threat. And I'm a liability because I know she's alive. I guess that makes Odette a liability, too, since she's the one who told us. And you—"

Grayson cut her off. "I," he told Lyra, his voice breaking, "am forever pulling people back from cliffs."

Lyra just looked at him. "I don't want your protection."

Grayson knew that. She wanted *him*. And though he knew exactly how this was going to play out, he could not stop his reply. "You have it nonetheless."

For the longest time, Lyra just stared at him, and then she left the bed and stood, her feet shoulder width apart, beside it. "I have a game to play."

For years, Grayson had not been capable of running to anything or anyone. The risks of losing someone else were too great. But this time, he was out of the bed in a heartbeat.

He went to Lyra. He ran to *her*. "*We* have a game to play," Grayson said.

For four or five excruciating seconds, Lyra stood there, saying absolutely nothing, and then she raised her eyes and looked at him the way she had the first time he'd ever touched her—in the ruins, his hand on her arm.

It was a warning look, electric and raw. "I'm not going to stop," Lyra said intently. "You know that, right?"

She wasn't going to stop looking for answers. She wasn't going to stop pushing.

"*I am not going to stop*," Lyra repeated, her intensity a match for any Hawthorne. "And when it comes down to it, if the Hawthorne family is on one side of this, and I'm on the other…" She pushed past him and out of the ballroom. "We both know that you won't choose me."

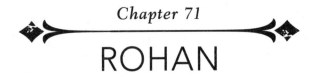

Chapter 71

ROHAN

Burn it all down. Rohan watched Lyra Kane from a distance. She was running, and she was alone. Perhaps his earlier warnings to her had finally paid off. Perhaps not. Either way, it wasn't personal. Strategy was strategy.

People were a means to an end, and that was all.

It made sense, from that perspective, to light another match, another fuse. After all, there was little else for Rohan to do in the hour remaining before *night* fell.

Clever Hawthornes and their clever little tricks.

Rohan followed Lyra, staying far enough away that she wouldn't see him immediately and close enough that she might feel him closing in. When she did, when she turned to glance back over her shoulder, Rohan disappeared into shadow.

Just a little while longer.

Just another few minutes.

And then he looped around, approaching her from the front. *Let her believe there's someone else on her tail.*

"I tried to warn you," Rohan called in greeting.

Lyra said absolutely nothing, and Rohan read in her silence and posture and eyes absolutely everything he needed to know. Some people wore devastation as armor and some as a veil. Hers was both, but her body—

The body gave her away. Lyra was tougher than most would have given her credit for, but she was broken.

Burn it all down.

"Grayson Hawthorne has a history, you know," Rohan told her, "of fancying himself in love with girls and failing to follow through. It's the idea of a person for him, not the actuality. You are, I'm afraid, one in a long line." True, not true—it hardly mattered. Sometimes, broken things were useful only if mended, and sometimes, they needed to be broken just a little bit more. "Less than seventy-two hours in, I'm not sure how you thought you were anything else."

"*Stop.*" There it was—more than just a hitch in her voice. A chasm, split open.

Burn it all down. "I'll see you at the tree at nightfall," Rohan told Lyra. It had been the fact that she and Grayson had retreated to the house for a nap that had let Rohan spot the trick in their latest clue, but *he* hadn't slept.

He hardly needed sleep once the switch had been flipped.

In fact, right now, all he needed was to find Brady Daniels. Savannah had doubtlessly taken the scholar's deal by now. *Time to burn that down, too.*

Rohan located the scholar in the ruins. Savannah was not with him, but as far as a deal went, that meant very little.

And Rohan wasn't here about Savannah. He was here for his dart.

"You again." Brady did not sound surprised.

"Me again." Leaving all of six feet between them, Rohan lifted his left wrist—his watch. "I wanted you to observe as I sent this." The message to the game makers was already partially typed. Rohan finished it off with no small amount of flourish. "A copy of your latest missive from your sponsor. I haven't the faintest idea what it means, but perhaps the game makers will."

Brady took a single step forward. "I can't you let you do that."

In his current state, Rohan truthfully felt very little, not even satisfaction at a move well made. "I know."

"Has it occurred to you what it means that I don't have to win this game?" Brady said with what Rohan recognized as an artifice of calm. "That all I have to do is take you down?"

"It would be egocentric of me," Rohan replied facetiously, "to assume that I am your only target."

"I don't want to hurt you," Brady stated. "But I will."

Rohan read the truth of that statement in the way Brady stood, feet shoulder width apart, weight slightly to the balls of his feet. *It means you have no incentive whatsoever to follow the competition's rules.*

Rohan was counting on that. To preserve his own place in the game, he could not attack first. He had to let Brady Daniels get in a couple of good hits—before he put the scholar *down*.

"Perhaps the game makers won't just disqualify you when they receive my message," Rohan said, his finger hovering over the screen of his watch. "Perhaps they'll call off the game. I wonder what your sponsor will do to your Calla if they do."

That did it.

One moment, Brady Daniels was standing perfectly still, and the next, his body was a blur. Rohan recognized immediately that Brady's goal was close combat—close enough for the weight he had on Rohan to be an advantage. Close enough to grapple. Close enough for choke holds and forceful strikes delivered with elbows, shins, and knees.

Rohan let him have that—for a time. He *let* himself be beat bloody, and then...

Push him back. Rohan did exactly that, without leaving a single mark, without drawing a single drop of blood. It hadn't taken him long to pinpoint the mix of styles Brady fought with. Unfortunately for Rohan's opponent, Rohan's strength as a fighter had always been that he had no style. Every move he made was calculated based solely on what his opponent was *about* to do. There were no restraints to the way Rohan fought. He was whatever he needed to be.

There was clarity in pain, and *clarity*—in a fight of this kind or any other—was always a matter of understanding one's opponent.

You're fighting like her life depends on it. Your sponsor made you believe that it does. In the labyrinth of his mind, Rohan could hear Nash Hawthorne telling him that he wasn't going to win the Grandest Game. *Our games have heart. It ain't gonna be you, kid.* But Rohan didn't need heart to win *this* fight. All he needed to do was take advantage of Brady's, to give the scholar an opening, one small enough that the intrepid and desperate Mr. Daniels would believe it authentic.

Rohan purposefully overswung. Brady ducked and charged—but Rohan was not as off-balanced as he seemed. He'd cut his teeth fighting in alleyways and palaces and everything in between. The best assaults were always masked with defeat.

He gave Brady a moment—just one—to believe that he'd gained the upper hand, and a fraction of a second later, Rohan was behind the scholar, his arm wrapped around his neck.

A choke hold. An arterial reflex. A sudden drop in blood pressure. A less-experienced fighter—or a more principled one—would have let go when Brady Daniels went limp. Rohan held on just a while longer. Not long enough to do permanent damage—not this time.

He hadn't even left a mark.

Beaten and bloody himself, Rohan lowered his fallen prey to the ground, and then unzipped the man's jacket, confiscating every object he had—including *two* golden darts. Brady hadn't even bothered to hide them.

"Some people never learn," Rohan told the scholar, and then, belatedly, he checked the man's pulse. *Steady. Strong.* It was just as well. Death was messy. This was a moment for precision.

Rohan lowered Brady's wrist, and his gaze caught on the tattoo he'd seen earlier, a spiral lined with letters on the inside of the man's arm. Dozens and dozens of letters, spelling nothing, a seemingly random assortment, and then Rohan realized...

Not random at all.

A potential meaning of the third message that Brady had received from his sponsor hit Rohan as solidly as any blow. *One out of three.* Every third letter.

Rohan started at the outside, spiraling in, but halfway through, he stopped and reversed course, starting at the center—with the *R*—and spiraling out.

R, *skip two letters, O, skip two letters, H*...

And there it was in black and white, a directive literally tattooed onto Brady's skin:

R-O-H-A-N-M-U-S-T-L-O-S-E.

Rohan must lose.

This was not a temporary tattoo. Based on the look and depth of the ink, it wasn't of the semipermanent variety, either. No, this tattoo was real, and it was fully healed. Brady Daniels had been one of the Hawthorne heiress's picks for the game. He would have had all of three days' notice of that, and yet, the man had clearly had this tattoo for at least a month or two.

You had a sponsor long before you received that invitation, didn't you, scholar? Long before the nature of this year's game was even announced. And that sponsor had not given Brady his most important directive directly. That sponsor had not sent Brady into this game knowing that his mission, above all, was to make sure that Rohan lost.

No, Brady's sponsor had only triggered *that* order much more recently—sometime after the bonfire but before the yacht. *Once it was clear that Savannah and I were still working as a team. Once it was clear just how formidable the two of us were.*

Rohan could only conclude that it would have been cleaner for Brady's sponsor if Brady never knew who his target really was, cleaner if Brady had simply been in position to win the Grandest

Game himself. But said sponsor had built in a fail-safe—one that, unlike a message written in invisible ink, could not be intercepted or stolen.

Was the scholar supposed to memorize this sequence? Did he have this inked into his own skin—or did you? Rohan silently addressed those questions to Brady's sponsor—the same sponsor who had equipped the man with information about the death of Savannah Grayson's father. *Gigi's, too.*

Had Brady been given leverage on any of the other players? It hardly mattered. What mattered most was the fact that this one message—this one directive—had merited different treatment. *Weeks before Brady was chosen as a player, he was given this code. Weeks before I became a player, someone knew I would.*

Someone had been playing the long game here, and *that*, as much as the way he'd been targeted, told Rohan exactly who Brady's sponsor was.

The Devil's Mercy was many things. A luxurious gambling club. A place where deals were struck and fortunes set. A historic legacy. A shadow force—like an invisible hand, guiding outcomes just so, one long game after another.

And there were only two individuals at the Devil's Mercy who would dare target Rohan like this. One was the Proprietor himself, and the other was the only person on this planet who *needed* Rohan to lose the Grandest Game. The person who stood to gain the Devil's Mercy if he did.

Like hell, Duchess.

Chapter 72

ROHAN

Thunder rumbled as Rohan made his way back to the forest, his golden dart held between his middle finger and thumb. A storm was coming, but there wasn't a storm in the world that could have kept Rohan away from a certain tree as night fell.

If Zella expected Rohan to fall prey to Brady Daniels—or Savannah—she was going to be sorely disappointed.

You played the long game, Duchess. I play a vicious one. Rohan knelt and stabbed the dart into the side of the silver plaque. This time, there was a click. *"Only at night,"* Rohan murmured, as the plaque rotated ninety degrees, revealing an opening underneath.

Rohan thrust his hand down and into it. His fingers locked around the leather cover of a ledger, and when he pulled it out, he heard the delicate clinking of metal. *Charms, attached to a ribbon on the book.* He helped himself to one—a tree, by the feel of it—then opened the ledger and pressed his watch to the page. The book lit up, allowing Rohan to see his name appear on the otherwise blank sheet. *First.*

There was a flash of brilliant light to his left, and Rohan turned to see an ultra-powerful spotlight shining up into the sky through a break in the canopy overhead. Rohan tilted his head back, taking in the result. Letters—three of them—appeared against the backdrop of the night, washing out the stars.

LIE.

And there's the next clue, Rohan thought. He did a thorough examination of the hidden compartment to ensure there was nothing further, and then he tossed the ledger back into the hole, locked his fingers around the golden dart again, and pulled it from the plaque. The spotlight didn't switch off, but the plaque descended, covering the compartment once more.

Rohan stood. There was a rustle in the woods about twenty yards away. Thanks to the spotlight, he was able to make out the full outline of Lyra Kane's silhouette as she made way toward him, toward the tree. She lifted her gaze to the sky, taking in the word that appeared there.

LIE.

"Some lies are beautiful," Rohan told his opponent, "for a time."

Lyra knelt next to the plaque, her gaze on the dart in Rohan's hand, leaving Rohan to wonder if she still had her own. Wasting no time, Lyra ran her hand around the edge of the plaque and found the hole, and then Rohan got his answer about the dart as Lyra withdrew hers from her jacket pocket.

Raindrops began to fall as she made use of it.

Soon enough, she'd signed the ledger and returned it to the compartment, and it occurred to Rohan that there was one more thing he could do to put distance between Lyra Kane and Grayson Hawthorne, between Savannah and himself. Perhaps he'd already pushed Lyra too far.

But perhaps not.

Lyra stood, and Rohan allowed his body to list toward hers. "If you find yourself in need someone to *despise*, Ms. Kane..." Rohan wielded his rogue's smile like a blade. "I assure you that I am most despicable."

Often, it was those who pushed the world away who had the strongest underlying need to be anything other than alone.

"I don't need your assurances," Lyra bit out. "I don't need anything from anybody."

That was, of course, a lie, and as Rohan considered his next move, the part of his brain that was always listening registered that they were about to have company. *Long strides, weight to the balls of the feet.*

Hello, Savvy.

Rohan let his eyes settle on Lyra's—brown, not that palest of blues and grays. After a long moment, he lifted his gaze to the clue in the sky, offering his face up to the rain as he did. "We're all liars, Ms. Kane."

"Knowing that..." Savannah announced her presence like he was not already well aware of it, making her way toward them. "Living it..." Savannah crouched next to the still-raised plaque and retrieved the ledger for herself, and then she looked up at Rohan and Lyra both. "That's the grandest game of all."

Chapter 73

GIGI

It had been hours since the Woman in Red had walked out the door, locking them in once more. How many hours, Gigi wasn't sure. Ominous words rang in her ears.

The time for watching *is done.*

For probably the hundredth time, Gigi tried to rouse Slate—and this time, he groaned.

"What happened?" His voice was gravelly and low. Golden hair, darker with sweat, hung in his face all the way down to his cheekbones. Through his hair, Gigi saw his dark eyes open—and focus.

On her.

"Do you want the extended version or the really extended version?" Gigi asked. "I also offer reenactments."

Eve rolled her eyes, thoroughly pretending that she hadn't been keeping vigil over Slate this entire time. "You got knocked out," Eve told him flatly. "And someone took the bait."

"Not in that order," Gigi added helpfully. "The person who knocked you out wanted to know about the Grandest Game. She called herself the Watcher."

The Lily. Calla. The Woman in Red.

Eve narrowed her eyes at Gigi. "You knew her." Eve sounded like she'd been biting back that accusation for hours.

"I knew *of* her," Gigi corrected. "She's supposed to be missing or dead or . . . something."

"I'm going with *something*," Eve replied.

Slate straightened, pulling against his bindings, his hair falling back out of his face, his posture almost leonine. "Will one of you *please* get this tape off me?"

"For the record," Eve told Gigi with another roll of her eyes, "that *please* was for you."

Gigi offered Eve her sweetest smile. "Full disclosure: I am still planning your doom."

"I'm still planning his." Eve eyed Slate. "It evens out."

Eve rounded to the back of the chair to work on his wrists, and Gigi approached from the front, squatting down in front of Slate and attacking the bindings on his ankles. Gigi didn't have nails as sharp as Eve's—but she *did* have teeth.

The duct tape made a satisfying sound as it tore, and within seconds, thanks to Eve's nails and Gigi's teeth, Slate was free. As he stood, Gigi popped back to her feet.

Dark eyes found hers. "Are you all right?"

To prove—to herself as much as to him—that she was, Gigi forced a grin. "Teeth like a beaver," she told him.

"Not what I was talking about," Slate replied, and then he turned. "Eve?"

Eve tossed her hair, which Gigi figured meant about the same thing as her own grin. "I'm fine," Eve said. "I gave our visitor what she wanted, and she left."

"What exactly did you give her?" Slate shot a *look* at Eve.

"Lyra," Gigi realized belatedly. "You gave her *Lyra*."

Gigi had no idea what anything Eve had said meant—*omega, lilies, Alice Hawthorne*—but Gigi *did* know what throwing someone under the bus sounded like. She also knew how her brother looked at Lyra Kane. She knew that a target on Lyra was as good as a target on Grayson himself.

First Savannah. Now Lyra and Grayson.

"No time like the present," Gigi said, and that was all the warning Eve got. Nobody expected a Tasmanian devil pounce—pretty much ever. As flying tackles went, it was a thing of beauty.

Slate gave Gigi a second or two, then hauled her off Eve. "Nicely executed."

"Thank you," Gigi replied. "But I'm not done yet."

"Easy there, sunshine."

Eve picked herself up off the ground. It took Gigi a second to realize that Eve was holding something in her hand. It looked like a coin of some sort but unlike any that Gigi had ever seen.

"How many of these is it going to take," Eve asked Slate, "to make you mine again?"

Mine. Gigi's brain latched on to that word. *Hers.*

"It was never just about the seals for me," Slate said, "and I think you know that." Something unspoken passed between him and Eve, the intensity in his eyes matched by a slight narrowing of hers.

Slate broke eye contact first, turning to Gigi. "And...*false*."

It took Gigi's scrambled mind a second or two to think back to the last True or False question she'd asked him. This was Mattias

Slater, telling her that he and Eve did *not* have the kind of relationship that involved making out.

Before Gigi could make heads or tails of that, the wall to her left parted.

Gigi whirled. Slate slid in front of her and Eve as the wall closed behind a woman who wore not a spot of red. She was tall and willowy in a way that should have made her look slight but didn't, her skin very nearly ebony—luminescent, *flawless*. Thick black braids of varying sizes streamed down her back.

She was one of the most beautiful, self-possessed, arresting women that Gigi had ever seen—and Slate slammed her back against the wall.

"Are you quite finished?" The woman's voice was familiar, but her accent was much stronger now. *The first woman in red. The one who was* playacting. *The one who used us to bait the other.*

"You're..." Gigi thought of about a thousand different descriptors that would have applied. "British?"

"When it suits me," the woman replied. "Zella," she introduced herself, like Slate didn't have her pinned to a wall. "Charmed. Now, I'm going to need at least one of you to tell me, word for word, what the Watcher said to you."

Chapter 74

LYRA

Lyra looked from Rohan to Savannah to the clue in the sky. She barely even felt the rain or the cold.

"It happened, didn't it?" Savannah said from the ground. "Just like I said it would. With Grayson."

Lyra refused to answer that and focused only on the word in the sky. *LIE.* The clue seemed to be mocking her. How many times had Grayson Hawthorne lied to her? What exactly did his brothers know?

About the lily.

And the three.

And omega.

"Did Eve offer you a deal, Lyra?" Savannah rose to her feet, looking so much like Grayson that it hurt. "You should have taken it."

Lyra needed someplace dry to think, but she couldn't go back to the house, couldn't risk running into Grayson. She had to work the puzzle. *For Mile's End.* She had to keep playing. It was dark. She was wet. And there were a limited number of places that offered coverage.

She ended up in the boathouse—and not on the roof this time. Alone, she walked to the very edge of the dock and stared out at the blackened ocean.

Come and get me, she thought. But her body sent up no warnings. Every instinct she had said that no one was watching her right now.

The great stone arches above her only did so much to the block the rain blowing in off the ocean, but it was better than nothing. It was enough for Lyra to be able to rage and seethe and hurt and *think.*

LIE. She paused, breathing through every single emotion that wanted to come. *An abbreviation?* She hit a wall with that line of thinking quickly enough. *An anagram?* With an *S*, she could have made *ISLE*, but the word wasn't *LIES.* It was *LIE.*

Unless it's not a word. Lyra turned that thought over in her mind. *A number?* The letter *E* wasn't a Roman numeral, so she discarded that possibility. *L* was the twelfth letter of the alphabet. *I* was the ninth. *E* was the fifth.

1295. Lyra tried as hard as she could to make sense of that number or any of its component parts, but she couldn't. She wanted to scream. She wanted to run until her muscles burned and her lungs threatened to combust, but even that had been ruined for her, because when Lyra thought about running, all she could think about was his body and hers, a synchrony like she'd never known.

The muscles in Lyra's throat constricted. She'd known better than to trust Grayson Hawthorne, known better than to rely on him in any way.

When I told you to stop calling . . . Grayson's voice echoed in her mind. *I didn't mean it.*

He'd let her down before, and Lyra had hated him for it, *hated* him even though she'd had no right to expect anything from him back then. They'd been strangers.

They weren't strangers anymore.

You don't fall. I do.

The thing that hurt most was that Lyra knew Grayson hadn't been lying—not about that. He'd manipulated her, and he'd lied to her, and maybe she should have been questioning whether any of it had ever been real, but she wasn't. Her body knew, and so did she.

It had been real, and it had been *beautiful*, and now it was done.

I am forever pulling people back from cliffs.

I don't want your protection.

You have it nonetheless.

Grayson Hawthorne was who he was. He'd been pulling her back from cliffs from the start. *And I don't have it in me to let him.* He'd known that. She had as good as told him that.

Lyra paced the docks beneath the massive stone arches: one enormous slip perpendicular to two somewhat smaller ones, a large platform in between.

1295. Lyra tried, as she paced, to concentrate on that, on the clue. *LIE.* But her mind just wouldn't let it go, wouldn't let Grayson Hawthorne go.

You don't fall. I do. His voice—even before these last few days, Lyra had never been able to forget Grayson Hawthorne's voice.

Breathe for me, Lyra Catalina Kane.

Lyra couldn't stop herself from remembering. She couldn't stop walking up and down the dock. Water was streaming down her face—rain and tears.

I've got you. I am here, and I have got you, Lyra Kane.

It hurt Lyra that she couldn't picture the way he had looked when he'd said it—not the lines of his face or the look in those unmatched blue-gray eyes. But her body remembered. *Your hands on my face. Your fingers combing tangles from my hair.*

Her body remembered: his lips and hers; strong arms holding her aloft, a chandelier overhead.

Pacing the docks, walking them again and again and again, Lyra desperately tried to turn her mind to something else—not the puzzle this time but the dream and the woman in the black cloak.

You should not be here. That voice—*Alice's voice?*—rang in Lyra's ears. *But who is to say that you were?* Lyra could feel herself running, running with bare and bloody feet, out into the night. She tried to remember more—if there *was* more.

And then she tried *not* to remember: A Hawthorne boy and a girl who had every reason to stay away from Hawthornes...

A brush of his hand at her temple.

Stepping out of time.

Her lips crashing into his.

Fingers trailed lightly along her jaw.

Their bodies, side by side in bed, floating off into nothing.

Lyra was nothing *but* memories, and all she could do was just keep walking—down the edges of the large dock and across. Up the platform, over to the smaller docks. And suddenly, she realized...

The docks.

Sometimes, words were words. Sometimes, letters were letters—but sometimes they were numbers. And sometimes, like an infinity symbol carved into a silver music box, letters or numbers were really just *shapes.*

Nearly all problems, Grayson's voice rang in Lyra's memory once more, *are a matter of perspective.*

Lyra walked backward until she was as far from the docks as she could get and still be beneath the roof of the boathouse. She reached for the ladder built into the stone wall, and then she climbed until the top of her head very nearly scraped the bottom of the roof.

She had a bird's-eye view now, and this time, she *did* see something.

The shape of the docks.

Lyra couldn't rotate the visual in her mind, but she *could* let go of the ladder with one hand and use it to trace the shape of the docks with her fingers. If you divided the platform between the slips in half, if you traced it twice...

Close. Lyra reversed the movements she'd just made, like she was teaching a dance class, standing in front of her pupils and mirroring the moves that they should make, going right for every left, her version of rotating the shape in her head.

And there it was, no space between the letters but clear as day. *LIE*.

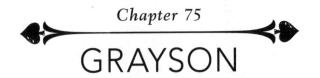

Chapter 75

GRAYSON

gnoring the rain, Grayson stood at the edge of the ocean, only a few feet from where Xander had hoisted Lyra up onto his shoulders the day before. *Gallus gallus domesticus en garde.* It was hard not to feel like the universe had given him a window, a very tiny window, into the way things might have been, if he and Lyra had been allowed to simply *be.*

His brothers and Avery would have liked Lyra. They would have welcomed her, if she'd been anyone else.

Damn Alice Hawthorne. Damn Eve for bringing Lyra into the Grandest Game not knowing what she was unleashing. Damn Jameson and his secrets. But above all...

Damn me. It took everything in Grayson not to walk right into the ocean, not to submerge himself in the bitterly cold water to swim and swim and push it all down. But he'd worked too hard and too long to give in to old habits now.

Don't fight it. Grayson's breath went jagged as he let it all come.

What he and Lyra could have been. What they should have been. *Why not me?*

"I should have told her everything." Grayson said the words out loud, every muscle in his body tense, his lungs screaming like each breath was an assault on his body. No matter his intentions, the truth had still come out in the end—enough of it, anyway, to ensure that Lyra would look and look and look for more.

Grayson should have known. He *had* known. The piper had to be paid either way.

This is all on me. It was Grayson's nature to carry failure with him—mistakes carved into hollow places he'd never been able to fill—but no part of him felt *hollow* now.

She filled him.

In his mind's eye, Grayson could see Lyra—stretching for a chandelier overhead, the lines of her body damn near impossible; amber eyes meeting his from behind a masquerade mask.

He could hear her. *Give me your jacket?*

She was probably never going to forgive him. She'd told him exactly what she needed and why, and he had still denied her the truth.

My mistake.

But Grayson *refused* to carry this one with him, *refused* to let this be one more regret, refused to stand by, frozen, while she was out there somewhere, hurting, when he could at least *try* to make it hurt less.

You just resisted the urge to say that Hawthornes do not try. Toby's voice rang in Grayson's mind, and Grayson thought about other things Toby had said—about his Hannah, about regrets. *Maybe if I'd learned to love differently, I could have loved her better. I certainly couldn't have loved her more.*

This close to the water's edge, Grayson could hear the waves. He couldn't see them in the dark, but he *felt* them breaking against stone, and somewhere in his mind, he heard Lyra's voice.

Maybe some of us need to break to be whole.

"Maybe some of us do," Grayson whispered. Maybe that was the secret to loving without reservation, without fear.

A broken man could *try*. And try. And try.

To love her differently. To love her better.

Grayson shuddered. He threw back his head, raising his face to the night sky, and he let it all out. There was a poem he'd always liked by Elizabeth Bishop about the art of losing things and people and dreams.

He'd lost.

And he'd lost.

And he'd lost.

And this time, he was not letting go.

Chapter 76

ROHAN

More than an hour after the spotlight had shined the word *LIE* into the sky, Rohan arrived at the boathouse to find that someone else had beaten him there.

"Think we're the first?" Savannah asked, her back to him.

It had taken Rohan far too long to figure out this clue. "*We?*" he said.

Savannah turned around. Lightning flashed over the mainland. Thunder came after a few seconds' delay, and Savannah seemed to take that as her cue. She walked toward him, the dim lighting of the boathouse doing nothing to disguise the set of her jaw, the tension between her upper and lower lips.

She stopped all of a foot away from Rohan. "I never gave you permission to be the one who ended things," she said, a queen to the last.

Rohan let the words slide over him, proverbial water off the duck's back—or a particularly wily fox's. He was on the verge of disregarding her altogether, as much as anyone *could* disregard Savannah Grayson, when she spoke again.

"You were listening when Brady made me that offer, weren't you?" Savannah was far too insightful for her own good. "I don't know how you could have been, but logic dictates that you were."

"Does it?" Rohan might have felt some level of admiration at her conclusion, if he'd been in the state to feel anything at all. "I suppose logic likes dictating things—as do you, Ms. Grayson."

"I do not care for being manipulated, Rohan. Not by you. Not by Brady Daniels or his sponsor. Not by Hawthornes. Not by Eve." This was a Savannah Grayson who'd had her fill—a dangerous Savannah Grayson indeed.

She held something up between her middle and index fingers. *The photographs.*

Rohan watched as Savannah walked slowly to the end of the largest dock slip, staring out at the storm, seemingly impervious to the water blowing in off the ocean. She lifted the hand that held the photographs of Calla Thorp and those damning invisible messages from Brady's sponsor, and then her fingers parted. "Take them," she told Rohan, as the photographs dropped to the dock. "If you want them. They'll improve your case against Brady."

The wind caught the edge of the pictures, and Rohan moved in a flash to catch them just in time.

"What game are you playing, Savvy?" Rohan had not meant to use the nickname, but there it was.

"All of them." Lightning flashed behind Savannah. "You thought I was going to take Brady's offer." Her voice was measured. "Given that, the most strategic move on your part would have been to bide your time and wait, to pull your enemy closer than any friend. But you didn't."

She was right. That was exactly what he *should* have done. What he would have done had it been even the slightest bit bearable to do so.

Savannah walked past him toward the shore and then turned back around, trapping him at the end of the dock. "I see you, Rohan." She smiled—a glittering, knife's-edge kind of smile. "Do you remember the lengths you went to, at the start of this game, to make me feel seen?" She tilted her head to the side, her eyes locked on to his. "Do you remember me telling you to save the wolfish smile and the quips and the charm and all the rest?"

He did.

"I am not a person you can manipulate." Savannah placed herself firmly in his way, though she had to be aware that was never a safe place to be. "And you do not *get* to decide," she continued, "whether or not I betray you."

All the cards were on the table now.

"All you get to decide," Savannah Grayson said, "is whether you are really that *scared*." That word was a fighting word. "Of me."

Rohan had never been able to resist parrying with her. "Hate to break it you, love, but I'm not capable of feeling much of anything at the moment." He meant that. He knew it to be true, knew that in his current state, there were no lines he would not cross.

And yet...he'd called her *love*.

"Oh really?" Savannah challenged, and then she walked toward him and past him, all the way to the end of the dock this time.

And then, she stepped off into the water.

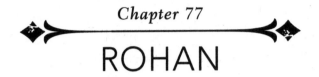

Chapter 77

ROHAN

She didn't come back up. It had been more than a minute and two strikes of lightning in the distance, and Savannah *had not come up.*

Rohan had done everything he could since the yacht to shove her into Brady's lap, to hasten the demise of their alliance, to give her the courtesy of the first betrayal, and in return, Savannah Grayson had given him the photographs he now held in his hands—the leverage she'd had, such as it was, over Brady.

I see you, Rohan.

He was the one who said things like that, the one who preyed upon the very human desire to be seen and recognized and *known.* He was the one who pulled the strings, the one who threw down gauntlets and backed opponents into corners.

Damn her. Rohan stripped off his jacket and tank top. The ocean was dark and undoubtedly cold, the water surrounding the docks of indeterminate depth. The last thing—the *very last thing*—that Rohan wanted to do was go in after her.

But she'd left him no choice.

He secured the photographs along with his jacket, and then he pulled the trigger, going in feet first. *Dark water.* His body plunged downward into its freezing depths. His ability to swim was strong enough for this, at least, but beneath the ocean's surface—*how is it so damn deep this close to shore?*—memories circled like sharks.

Like there was chum in the water.

The sound of gentle humming came first. The smell of his mother—and then the weight of stones tied to his ankles.

Strong arms grabbed him, pulled him up. Rohan sucked in air, the way he had so many times before, and that was when he realized: Savannah Grayson had just pulled him up and *under* the dock.

She treaded water beside him. "Aren't you going to sign the ledger?" she said, her voice echoing in the small expanse of space. It was well-lit in the hollow beneath the dock, and Rohan came fully back to himself—to the view of *Savannah*, wet and mostly submerged.

And triumphant.

Rohan followed Savannah's gaze to an open ledger, attached to the bottom of the dock. Keeping himself afloat with his legs, Rohan lifted the arm bearing his watch and pressed it to the page. His name appeared, the third in the ledger, after Savannah's, which appeared right under Lyra Kane's.

"I suppose that answers that," Rohan said. They weren't the first.

"Lyra beat us this time," Savannah replied, and the word *us* rang in Rohan's mind. "But I am going to beat you both to the end."

That was a promise, a familiar one, and Rohan thought about the way that Savannah had declared that he did not have her permission to end things. He'd pushed, and he'd pushed, cutting at the rope, *willing her* to walk away.

And still, she hadn't. She hadn't betrayed him. She hadn't even *tried* to.

You do not get to decide whether or not I betray you. All you get to decide is whether you are really that scared. Of her. She'd accused him of being scared of *her*.

Fear was weakness, as bad as affection, not nearly as dangerous as trust.

Being here, with Savannah Grayson beneath the dock, in dark and freezing water, their bodies wet and far too close together was a threat on many fronts.

Rohan looked past her, searching their surroundings until he found what he was looking for: the next clue. *No charm this time,* he registered, *just words.* They were written in glowing script on the underside of the dock.

> *Respect the grayest pile*
> *For the departed creature's sake*
> *That hovered there a while*

"When I win," Savannah declared forcefully, treading water beside him, her gaze locked on those same words, "I'll give you the money you need."

He would have rather she come at him with a knife. "Now why would you do a thing like that?" he challenged.

They were in freezing water—in a storm. Neither one of them had any business lingering there.

"Because," Savannah said, "a key part of my strategy for win-ning this—on my terms, *my* way and no one else's—is by wanting it *more.*"

Once upon a time, Savannah Grayson had told him that she didn't want things, that she set goals and achieved them, end of story. *Fair warning, love,* Rohan had told her, *I want it more.*

In the hollow beneath the dock, having said her piece, Savan-nah put her hands on his shoulders. Rohan's body tensed, preparing for her to push him under, but instead, Savannah Grayson raked her nails all the way down his back and brought her lips to his.

He kissed her back. *Damn me.* Damn him all the way to hell, he kissed her back.

"And the second I give that money to you," she said, her lips brushing his with every word, "*then* we're done." She pulled back. "I decide. Not you."

Her body rotated in the water, and she pushed off the bottom of the dock with her legs.

Have it your way, love. Rohan's gaze went back to the next clue. And then, he was off.

Chapter 78

GIGI

"Where is the remote?" Slate demanded. "The one that opens the door." As far as Gigi could tell, Slate's grip on their captor's throat hadn't wavered once since he'd slammed the British woman to the wall. "I want it. Now."

"You wouldn't be the first man to strangle me when all I wanted to do was talk." This woman—*Zella*, she'd said her name was *Zella*—had poise to rival a queen.

"You aren't the one calling the shots right now," Slate informed her, and then he glanced back over his shoulder at Gigi and Eve. "Get me what's left of the duct tape."

"There is no need for that," Zella declared. "Answer my questions, and you have my word that you will all be free to go."

Gigi raised her hand. "Skeptical. Me. Very. Again. What about the Grandest Game? Noninterference? Eve being an emotional bull in a china shop of your making?"

"Unless I am mistaken," Zella said, in the tone of someone who knew quite well that they were not, "the Grandest Game will soon be coming to its end. I have put in motion all I can on that front, and now it seems there are bigger games to play. Tell me what the Watcher said."

Slate stared her down for three full seconds—and then he dropped his hand and backed away. There was something unrecognizable in those dark eyes of his, and Gigi thought about his knife, about the number of horrible things he claimed to have done. *Fourteen.*

"Who is she?" Eve walked to stand toe-to-toe with Zella. "The Watcher. How did you know she would come? How do you know her?"

"We were sisters," Zella said, "once upon a time."

Gigi's eyes widened. And widened some more. "Calla is your *sister?*" Gigi thought back to the Woman in Red and her story about the seventeen-year-old girl she'd once been. She'd said something about Orion Thorp having a biological child, even though Calla was the one who'd borne the Thorp name.

"*Calla* is long gone." Zella let her disconcertingly calm gaze settle on Gigi. "Now, what did the Watcher want with you?"

With me. Gigi thought about the flower she'd found—the calla lily she'd been *sent.* "She wanted information about the game." Gigi had always excelled at trusting people who'd done nothing to deserve it, so why change now? "About Lyra."

"And what information did you give her about Lyra Kane?" Zella asked.

Gigi glanced pointedly at Eve. "*Someone* told her all sorts of things."

"Oddly enough," Eve said, crossing her arms over her chest, "I find I'm no longer in a sharing mood."

"Defy your mood," Zella replied, "and in return, I will arm you." One second, her hands were empty, and the next, she was holding a sheathed blade.

"My knife." Slate's voice was flat, even for him, and Gigi's sixth sense for broody boys told her that he was about half a second from going for that knife.

"Omega," Gigi blurted out. Her optimism had run desert-dry, and she wasn't taking any chances with that blade.

With Mattias Slater.

"That's what Eve told Calla," Gigi continued, trying not to sound like she was babbling. "Something about *omega*, something about *lilies*, something about *Alice Hawthorne*."

There was the slightest incline of Zella's chin. "That will give her the ammunition she so badly desires. She always was the ambitious one."

"Ammunition for *what*?" Gigi said, but all she could think was: *The time for* watching *is done.*

Zella spun the knife in her hand to grip it by the sheath and held the handle out to Slate, who took it. "If you're still keeping a tally," Zella told him, nodding to the knife, "you're not all the way gone yet." The elegant woman turned to Gigi and Eve. "As for the two of you, I will arm you with this: If the time comes that you see my *sister* again—or anyone like her—know that it is in your power to say no."

Gigi blinked.

"*No* to what?" Eve said.

"Regardless of how the question might be phrased or what pressure is brought to bear, it is an invitation, an ask. And *asks* may be answered, *invitations* declined." Zella turned back toward the infinity fountain on the wall, and a moment later, it parted.

Freedom.

Zella waited for them to take it. "Four miles, due north," she told Slate. "There's a bar. It's a rather seedy establishment, but if you take her there, someone Hawthorne-adjacent will come for her soon enough."

Chapter 79

LYRA

Respect the grayest pile—the words echoed through Lyra's mind as she walked through the remains of that once-great mansion—*for the departed creature's sake that hovered there a while.*

For Lyra, the clue called to mind a tombstone—or ashes, which was how she'd ended up back in the one place on the island where it was even harder not to think about Grayson Hawthorne: the ruins.

Lyra remembered walking this place with her eyes closed on day one. She remembered Grayson's hand on her arm—then forced herself to focus on the charred world around her. *Respect the grayest pile...*

At night, with no source of light but her watch, there was no reason for Lyra to close her eyes, but she did it anyway.

For the departed creature's sake... She found her way to what remained of the hearth. *That hovered there a while.*

Nothing lasted forever. That was what Lyra took from the words, no matter how hard she tried to see them as a riddle. All any human could hope for was to hover for a while, and then, in the blink of a cosmic eye, that person's life was over and gone and done, and the world went on.

Beside the hearth, Lyra sank to her knees, opening her eyes and running her hands over the ground. There was no floor to speak of, only what remained of the foundation, which was cracked and splintered, vines growing through it.

Respect the grayest pile...

Even the word *grayest* hurt—too close to his name. Lyra swept her hand out and over the rubble. Crawling forward, she did the same thing again and again and again, and then finally, she must have tripped some kind of wire or trigger, because delicate beams of light began to shine up through the cracks in the foundation, illuminating the ruins in a strange, piecemeal kind of way—a little unearthly and wholly unsettling.

If she'd thought this place had looked haunted before, it was downright eerie now.

Using the scant and scattered light, Lyra continued her search, feeling for something—anything—on the ground. *Nothing.*

Nothing.

Nothing.

"*Respect the grayest pile.*" She said the words out loud, her voice little more than a whisper. "*For the departed creature's sake that hovered there a while.*"

Lyra willed the clue to make sense. She'd been the first to it, but there was no telling how long she had before someone else caught up to her. It was still raining. She was soaked—from the rain, from the water. Her armor provided a decent amount of protection, but her teeth were starting to chatter anyway. And still, Lyra didn't have it in herself to give up.

That was the problem. That was the *whole damn problem*. She kept going, kept searching. There had to be something. *"Respect the grayest pile…"*

"For the departed creature's sake…" A voice—that voice, *his* voice—spoke behind her. *"…that hovered there a while."* Grayson, like Lyra, didn't know when to give up. "Emily Dickinson," he said.

Despite herself, Lyra rose and turned, and there he was, soaked to the bone, his pale blond hair stuck to his face in a way that should have made him look a little wild. Instead, Grayson Hawthorne looked like something out of a dream, the kind you ached for from the moment you opened your eyes.

"The clue." It took everything Lyra had to focus on what he'd said and not the way he'd said it. "It's a poem?"

"Ashes denote that fire was." Grayson's voice sounded deeper in the dark. *"Respect the grayest pile…for the departed creature's sake…that hovered there a while."*

"Grayson—" Lyra bit out his name with all the warning she could muster.

"Fire exists the first in light…," he continued.

"Stop." Lyra couldn't do this with him. She couldn't do *anything* with him right now. It took her a moment to realize that he'd heeded her command. "You stopped."

The rain was pouring down now, coating her face and his, pelting their bodies, but Lyra barely felt it.

"I know an order when I hear one," Grayson replied. "And it has never been my intention to force on you anything you did not wish to receive."

Lyra heard in those words a promise: If she asked him to go, he would go.

Leave me alone, she thought vehemently. *Go and don't look back. Forget it all. Forget me. Forget whatever this was.* Lyra's lips would not, could not form those words.

"You lied to me." That was easiest enough to say, though. "And *I know* that you were trying to protect me, but—"

"Not just you." Grayson bowed his neck, but his eyes found their way back to hers. "I was raised to put family first, always."

And there it was, the truth at last, slid between her ribs as effortlessly as any blade, and yet, Lyra could not help thinking about Grayson's definition of family. *People you would die for. People you know damn well would die for you.*

Loving fiercely was not a crime.

"Jameson already knew about Alice." Grayson's bowed head slowly rose, his shoulders squaring, rain streaming down his angular face. "He's known for more than a year."

Why was he telling her this *now*?

"Threats were issued," Grayson continued, a subtle but lethal quality in his voice marking those words as an understatement. "They made my brother bleed."

They. "There are always three." Lyra couldn't coax her mouth into saying anything else. All she could do was stand there and wait for his response.

Grayson's full lips parted, more words spilling out, a confession in full. "Jameson's memory of what transpired is full of holes, very likely for the same reason that your memory of your father's death is. But I've never seen him scared before, Lyra. Of *anything*."

Jameson is competitive, Lyra could hear Grayson saying. *Intensely and frequently reckless. Fearless to a fault.*

"What Jameson does remember," Grayson continued evenly, "is that he thought he was going to die—that they were going to kill him."

"What the hell is this?" Lyra said sharply. "All of it. *Any* of it."

She still couldn't tell Grayson to go, so *she* went—across the broken, uneven foundation, out onto the ruined patio with an ocean view. She walked right up to the edge, and this time, Grayson did not pull her back.

He stepped up even with her—beside her.

"I don't know." Those words cost him. Grayson Hawthorne was not a person with a high tolerance for *not* knowing. "But *this?*" His tone made it clear that he wasn't talking about Alice Hawthorne anymore—or Jameson. He wasn't talking about danger or threats.

He was talking about *them*.

"*This,*" Grayson said again, "is worth fighting for."

This. A ball of emotion rose in Lyra's throat. "The right kind of disaster just waiting to happen," she whispered.

"A Hawthorne and a girl who has every reason to stay away from Hawthornes." Grayson turned his entire body toward her, and Lyra's responded like they were dancing, like this was just another pas de deux, angling back toward him. Water streamed down their faces, and Lyra reminded herself that Grayson was who he was, and she was who she was, and there was no changing that—for either of them.

Some things were just not meant to be.

"I need to get back to the game," Lyra said. *I,* not *we*.

Lightning struck with sudden, electrifying force over the ocean. Seeing it out of the corner of her eye had Lyra's head whipping back toward darkened ocean waters she could not make out in the night, and for the first time since the helipad, she felt something.

Eyes on us.

The warning rose up like bile from the pit of Lyra's stomach and crawled down her spine.

"What is it?" Grayson said.

Lyra shook her head, then lightning struck again—close enough that it tore open the sky and lit up the world.

There was a difference between sensation and perception. It took a moment for Lyra to register what she'd seen in that blinding flash, and by the time she did, the ocean was pitch black once more.

Calla lilies. Hundreds of them. Floating on the water, washing onto the shore.

Chapter 80

GRAYSON

Grayson did not think, did not hesitate. He removed his jacket. Then shirt. Moving rapidly backward like a blade through the night, he calculated the exact trajectory needed and the exponentially small margin of error within which he would need to hit it.

And then he ran—straight for the edge of the patio, the edge of the cliff. His body anticipated the moment of liftoff, the way he *would* arc through the air to dive into the water a hundred feet below, narrowly skirting the rocks.

Then Lyra *threw* herself sideways—directly into his path.

Abort. Grayson couldn't manage a full stop, so he flung his arms around her and twisted, redirecting his momentum as best he could and praying that it would be enough.

They landed hard, all of an inch from the edge.

"Have you lost your mind?" Lyra was not one for raising her voice, but she was yelling now. She was also on top of him.

"Let me up," Grayson commanded.

Even at night, Lyra blazed. "What the hell, Hawthorne?"

"Let me up," Grayson repeated, but she pinned him down instead. "Let me do this for you, Lyra."

"Asshole." She was straddling him now, her hands locked on his wrists. "Do you really think that I am going to let you dive off this cliff and just *hope* that you manage to avoid the rocks?" Her chest heaved. "Do you really think that you're the only one who would do anything to protect the people who matter to you?"

Her voice broke on the word *matter*, and Grayson knew in that instant that he was going nowhere.

I matter. To you. This matters.

"I have spent years lying to my family because I knew that if they knew I was suffering, they would suffer, too," Lyra continued, the timbre of her voice powerful and deep. "And maybe lying to protect them and expecting something different from you makes me a hypocrite. Maybe I am every bit as much of a liar as you are, Grayson Hawthorne. But in this much..."

Grayson sat up, shifting her lower on his thighs, his hands making their way back to hers, his fingers interweaving with hers.

"In this much," Lyra said again, "we are the same." Her grip on his hands tightened, like she didn't trust him to stay put, like she'd put him right back down again if she had to.

We are the same. Grayson let those words roll over him. He committed them—and this moment—to memory, in case it was one of their last. But reality was a wolf at the door. "There's someone out there. I saw what you saw, Lyra."

Grayson's mind went to the letter *A*.

Lyra let loose of him and slid off his thighs, standing and orienting her body toward the water. "I don't feel anything anymore. Whoever's responsible for those flowers—they're gone."

Grayson was not sure which defied logic more: her certainty or his predisposition to believe it. He climbed to his feet. "I'll let my brothers know."

The image of calla lilies on the water, illuminated for less than a second by a lightning strike, was emblazoned on Grayson's mind. It felt, to him, like a warning.

A declaration of war.

He typed and sent the message, then looked back up at Lyra, who beat him to speaking.

"There is only one way that this is going to work," she said.

This. Grayson lingered on the word. *This. This. This.*

"I get to pull you back from cliffs, too."

Grayson felt the rise and fall of his own Adam's apple, then a tightening of the muscles in his throat and a loosening of the ones between his shoulder blades. *This.* "I accept your premise," he said, a Hawthorne striking a deal, "but I do not like it."

"Join the club," Lyra told him. "And no more lies. If there's something you can't tell me, just say that. You're entitled to secrets, Grayson. You are entitled to put your family first, to protect them, but if you *ever* lie to me or try to manipulate me again, this—us—we're done."

"No more lies." Grayson could agree to that much at least—for her. *Differently. Better.* "To that end, there is something that you need to know. You said that I would not *choose* you."

"I'm not asking you to—"

"You were wrong. I *would* choose you, Lyra—not over my family but as a part of it." Grayson thought about Nash saying that he'd known immediately with Libby, about the old man and his propensity for talking about the way that Hawthorne men loved.

"You can't mean that," Lyra replied. "It's only been three days."

"Try telling me again," Grayson suggested silkily, "what I can and cannot mean."

Before she could say a word, his watch buzzed. Grayson looked down at it, expecting a return message in response to the warning he'd sent, but instead, an image had taken over the face of the watch.

A diamond.

After three or four seconds, the diamond dissolved, only to be replaced with words. *A PLAYER HAS REACHED THE FINAL PUZZLE.*

"A player," Lyra said out loud, having received the same message. "A Diamond—Rohan or Savannah."

Grayson looked back out at the ocean. They could try taking the long way down, try to track a threat that was probably already long gone—or they could see this through, make one last attempt to give Lyra the ability to save Mile's End, one last attempt to save Grayson's sister from herself.

"Emily Dickinson," Lyra said, as intense and intent as any Hawthorne. "We're headed back to the house—to the library."

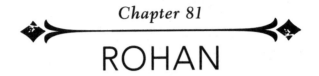

Chapter 81

ROHAN

Rohan ignored the buzzing at his wrist, not even blinking as he opened a leatherbound copy of Emily Dickinson poems. The pages inside had been hollowed out.

Sitting there, staring back at Rohan, there was a silver charm—a quill—and beside it, much larger, there was a gleaming, metallic gear. *Platinum.* Rohan removed first the charm, then the gear, and the moment he lifted the latter, he heard a compartment opening in the floor behind him.

He whirled. *The ledger.* Rohan had it in his hands in an instant. He flipped it open to a single name, the only player in this game who'd beat him here.

Savannah. Rohan could make out the places she'd dripped on the floor easily enough, and as expert as he usually was at locking memories away in the labyrinth of his mind, Savannah Grayson's words down on the dock haunted him.

I never gave you permission to be the one who ended things.

All you get to decide is whether you are really that scared. *Of me. When I win, I'll give you the—*

Rohan cut Savannah's vow off in his mind. Only a fool would rely on the promise of a woman he'd scorned. As he pressed his watch to the ledger, Rohan registered the message he'd received and ignored.

A PLAYER HAS REACHED THE FINAL PUZZLE.

Of course she had. Rohan did not know whether to be gratified or infuriated that the Grandest Game—and his future, the Mercy—was going to come down to this. To the two of them—on her terms, not his.

Rohan returned the ledger. The compartment closed, and as Savannah obviously had before him, Rohan descended the spiral staircase from the fifth floor to the fourth, from the fourth to third and then down one more story, to a door covered in gears of bronze, silver, and gold—but not *completely* covered.

There were gaps here and there—one fewer, Rohan would wager, than there had been before. He pressed his gear to the door, into one of those open spots, and the moment he did, all the other gears began to turn.

A lock clicked.

The door swung outward.

Rohan stepped across the threshold—and onto a ledger.

He added his name below Savannah's. *Where are you, love?* He assessed the rest of the room. The floor was made entirely of stained glass, a rainbow of tiles in every shade imaginable, no two squares exactly the same hue. Hanging from the ceiling were strings of sparkling jewels—dozens of precious stones and crystals, suspended midair in a room that seemed to be made of light.

It would have made for a dazzling finale, but Savannah was

nowhere to be seen, which meant that Rohan was still behind. *He hadn't reached the final puzzle yet.*

But she hasn't solved it. Rohan had to believe that all of the players would have been informed if Savannah had finished the game, and that meant that he hadn't lost yet. *I just have to catch up.*

Pacing the edges of the room, Rohan took in each and every string of jewels. *Different colors. Different sizes.* There was even a geode or two. He processed that—processed everything about this room, all at once, including the pattern of the water that Savannah had dripped onto the colored tiles. It looked like she'd traversed nearly the entire room. *Doing what?*

Rohan came to the spot with the biggest puddle, the spot where she'd stood dripping the longest. He knelt, examining the tile there. It wouldn't come up, but when he put his palm flat against it and pressed down, words appeared for a second or two.

PAY THE TOLL.

Rohan knew better than most: Everything came at a cost.

But what cost? He tilted his gaze up to look again at the riches dangling from the ceiling, a veritable maze of shining, sparkling things. *What toll?*

Refusing to even consider a process of trial and error, Rohan looked back down at the tile he'd found, indigo in color, perhaps eighteen inches by eighteen inches, translucent enough for light to shine through.

In fact... Rohan shifted, dropping his chest to the floor, bringing his eyes very nearly level with the tile. He depressed it again. No words this time, but enough light shined up through it that, for a split second, he was able to see through to what lay underneath.

The object in question lay coiled beneath the surface like a snake, and though Rohan could not make out much more than its silhouette, he recognized it immediately.

Savannah's chain.

Rohan knew then how she had paid the toll—with a form of payment that wasn't an option for any other player. For days, Savannah had worn that platinum chain wound around her waist, and then she'd opened this room with a gleaming, precious-metal gear, and when a toll had been requested...

She'd paid.

Rohan did not have time to dither, to wonder, to curse himself for not removing her advantage earlier. Unlike Savannah, he had no trump card to play here, no ability to shortcut this puzzle. He needed an answer. *What toll?* Rohan looked up again, scanning the items hanging from the ceiling, and then he stood, walking through them, zigging, zagging. *Which item?*

Which object?

It hit him—hard and all at once. *There is one object left in this game that has never been used in any way, shape, or form.* Rohan reached for his pocket, for his dice. He went back to the indigo tile and placed them on its surface. When that didn't work, he tried rolling them.

Still nothing.

Rohan did not have time for this. The Mercy hung in the balance. Promises were no harder to break than glass. He punched a closed fist into the indigo tile—not hard enough to shatter it but hard enough to *hurt*.

With pain came clarity. Rohan *needed* that clarity. To his surprise, the second time he punched the tile, another word flashed across its surface.

LOVELY.

Rohan's mind raced. *Pay the toll. Lovely.* He hit the indigo tile again and again and again until another word appeared. *ALLURING.*

Overhead, riches awaited, and these descriptions—they could describe *any* of them. *Lovely. Alluring.* Rohan would beat his knuckles raw if he had to, but it didn't come to that, because the next word to flash across the tile was *PRINCE.*

Rohan let out a low and rumbling chuckle. *Lovely. Alluring. Prince—*

"Charming," Rohan murmured. The jewels hanging from the ceiling were nothing but a *lovely* bit of misdirection. The dice were *not* the only objects left in this game. "The charms."

There was a sound behind him, then—turning gears. *Company, incoming.*

Rohan moved like lighting, dropping his charm bracelet and the attached charms onto the indigo tile. When that yielded no effect, he tore the charms off one by one.

The sword.

The clock.

The music note.

The tree.

The quill.

He dropped the charms—and only the charms—onto the tile, and the effect was immediate. The five bits of precious silver rearranged themselves, each pulled with what had to be some kind of magnetic force to a specific location on the tile.

Not silver, Rohan realized, *but steel.*

The door behind him opened, but Rohan didn't even look back. Together, the five charms now formed an arrow. The indigo tile dropped, causing his charms to fall into the compartment below—his toll, accepted, and the wall that the arrow had pointed to parted.

Rohan dashed through the opening, and the watch on his wrist vibrated, the same message as before.

A PLAYER HAS REACHED THE FINAL PUZZLE.

The wall closed behind Rohan, and he turned back just long enough to catch sight of Lyra Kane and Grayson Hawthorne.

How much did they see? Rohan dismissed the question. He did not have time for questions. Before him, there was a darkened staircase. Rohan resisted the urge to run down it and was rewarded when he noticed something—besides water—on the second step down. *Earbuds. Multiple pairs.* Rohan plucked a set up and plugged them into his ears.

As he descended the remaining stairs, the voice of Avery Grambs rang in his ears. "Biggest, smallest, white, red," the voice said. "Do you know the question yet?"

Rohan reached immediately for the dice in his pocket—red dice that rolled a six and a two, every time, for a total of eight. Savannah's *white* dice had yielded the same result through a slightly different roll—a five and a three.

Biggest, smallest, white, red. Do you know the question yet?

Rohan could do the Hawthorne heiress one better. He knew the answer. The code. Stepping off the staircase, Rohan looked for a way to input it. The room before him was plain. The floor was made of what looked like cement. The walls were white and bare. There was no keypad, no combination dial, no flatscreen on which to enter the code that Rohan *knew*.

The only object in the entire room was a small glass cylinder sitting on the floor, its circumference just slightly bigger than the breadth of Rohan's dice.

And that was when Rohan knew: The dice weren't just a clue to a combination. They weren't a code. The dice themselves were the key to one final lock—and he needed *both* pairs.

Biggest, smallest, white, red. Do you know the question yet?

Rohan thought back to words that Avery Grambs had spoken at the beginning of phase two. *Only one of you can win this year's Grandest Game, but in a very real sense, none of you are in this alone.*

"I knew it was going to be you." Savannah stepped out of the shadows, and in Rohan's mind, he heard yet another voice. *It ain't gonna be you, kid.*

Nash Hawthorne had predicted that Rohan was going to lose the Grandest Game, because Hawthorne games *had heart.* And to win *this* game . . .

Rohan looked from the dice in his palm up to another palm, holding another set of dice. *Savannah's.* From the room above, there was a rumbling sound—the wall at the top of the stairs, parting once more.

Rohan's watch buzzed. *Twice.* Lyra and Grayson had paid the toll, and Rohan *knew*, whether or not they'd mended things, Grayson Hawthorne would give Lyra Kane his dice in an instant.

Biggest, smallest, white, red. Do you know the question yet?

Rohan knew. He'd solved it. And it didn't matter. *Bloody Hawthornes and their bloody games.* There was no time. *No time to make a go at lifting your dice, love. No time for persuasion. No time for bargains.*

The Devil's Mercy hung in the balance, and there was no time for Rohan to do *anything* except the one thing that Nash Hawthorne had clearly not expected him to be capable of.

"Damn it all to hell and back." Rohan crossed to Savannah and pressed his dice into her hands.

Trust was weakness.

Affection was weakness.

Rohan was not wired to rely on anyone else, ever—not like this. But what choice did he have? He'd aligned himself with Savannah Grayson, and he'd pushed her away. He'd pushed and pushed and pushed, and the betrayal had never come.

Make your move, love.

Savannah did not hesitate. She *never* hesitated, was incapable of it. One after another, she dropped the glass dice into the cylinder: White dice first, the five before the three. Then the red six and the red two last.

Biggest, smallest, white, red. Do you know the question yet?

The second the last die was in the cylinder, music filled the air. *Church bells.* The ceiling parted. A flatscreen television descended, an obvious camera attached to its side. The screen flickered to life—but the light on the camera never came on.

On the screen, there were four chairs. One for each of the game makers, but those chairs were . . .

Empty.

Rohan's watch buzzed. He didn't look down, his eyes trained on Savannah. Behind him, Lyra Kane read the message they had all just received aloud: *"We have a winner."*

Savannah. She'd won the Grandest Game. But there was no one on the screen—no Hawthornes, no heiress, not even their lawyer. There was no livestream, no one to accuse.

"Where are they?" Savannah Grayson was fury and poise and best-laid plans come to ruin. "I *won*." Savannah did not raise her voice, but she might as well have been screaming for all the power and heartbreak in those words. *"Where are they?"*

Rohan had warned her. She'd never stood a chance without the element of surprise. *Should have taken Brady's deal, love.* But before Rohan could say that out loud, Grayson Hawthorne took a heavy step forward, staring bullets at the screen and those empty chairs.

"Something is wrong."

Chapter 82

GIGI

Four miles, due north. Gigi wasn't sure she was going to make it.

Here lies Gigi Grayson, her tombstone would read, *done in by cardio in the end.*

When the bar finally came into view in the distance, Gigi tried—and failed—to breathe a sigh of relief. This night was ending. This brief, absolutely bonkers chapter in her life was coming to a close.

"This is as far as we go," Eve told Slate. "We need to be long gone before anyone Hawthorne-adjacent comes for her."

That stung more than it probably should have.

"Stay out of trouble, sunshine."

A ball of emotion rose in Gigi's throat, but she *chose* to smile. Because she could. Because even after everything, she still had to believe that happiness was a choice.

"*Trouble* is my second middle name," she told Slate. "Juliet

Aurelia Trouble Grayson." Her smile wavered, but Gigi persevered, nodding toward the bar, which looked, even from a distance, every bit as seedy as advertised. "Think they sell mimosas?"

"No," Slate said. "I don't."

"True or false." Gigi met his eyes through the dark. "You'll miss me."

"Slate." Eve's patience was clearly evaporating.

Gigi decided not to wait for an answer that probably wasn't going to come. She set her sights on the building in the distance and made it all of three steps before Mattias Slater spoke behind her.

"Let's play a game," he said. "It's called You Don't Need to Prove a Damn Thing. To anyone. It's called You're Already Strong."

Gigi stopped walking, but she didn't look back. She didn't let herself look back. Still, she had to ask: "Were you ever out there?"

How many times in the past year-and-a-half had she hedged her bets, calling out into the night? *I know you're out there.* He'd been a figment of her imagination on so many nights—and maybe that was all.

Maybe if she turned around, she'd discover that he was already gone.

And then came a reply. "More than once."

Gigi nodded, and then she swallowed. *It wasn't all in my head.* She took the deepest breath of her life. "Good-bye, Mattias."

She started walking toward the bar again. The first two steps were the hardest. After five, Gigi forced herself to pick up the pace, as much as she could—for Savannah. Even if Zella had been right and the Grandest Game was ending, even if it was already over and Gigi was too late, she had to get to her sister. And now, thanks to

Eve and her big mouth, Gigi needed to get to Grayson and Lyra, too. At the very least, she needed to tell someone about Calla—*the Watcher, the Lily, the Woman in Red*.

Because whatever came after *the time for watching*? Even Gigi wasn't optimistic enough to think that it was good.

Chapter 83

LYRA

Something is wrong. Grayson's words hung in the air. Lyra should have been thinking about the fact that she'd lost, about Mile's End, but all she could actually think about, as she stared at the game makers' empty chairs on that screen, was calla lilies floating on water.

So many of them.

"Why would something be wrong?" Savannah said, her voice high and clear and sharp and jagged all at once. "Even when I come in first, I lose." Grayson's sister looked to the person who'd been her partner in this game, the one who'd given up his dice so she could win. "The house always wins, right, Rohan?" Savannah said.

The house. Lyra couldn't shake the question bubbling up inside of her like an ominous sense of premonition.

What if the game makers aren't the house?

Beside Lyra, Grayson was typing something on his watch, but before he could finish, all four of their watches buzzed with what Lyra could only assume were four identical messages.

REPORT TO HELIPAD FOR EXTRACTION.

—>•<—

"Something is very wrong," Grayson reiterated directly into Lyra's right ear as a military-style chopper touched down on the helipad. His assessment was immediately confirmed when one of the helicopter doors opened, and two passengers climbed out.

Men. Neither of them Hawthornes. It was obvious, just by looking at them, what these men were. *Security.*

"There were supposed to be five of you," one of them yelled over the sound of the chopper's blades.

"Brady Daniels," Grayson called back. He strode toward the men. "He must still be out on the island somewhere. Now, which one of you gentlemen is going to tell me what *precisely* happened?"

Something did, Lyra thought. *Something happened.* The Grandest Game was not a game that had been designed to go out with a whimper. This wasn't just about Savannah and Eve and their agenda, whatever it was.

Calla lilies on the water. The house always wins.

"You four," one of the men barked, ignoring Grayson's question and taking his life into his own hands, "in the chopper!"

"Allow me to rephrase," Grayson said. "Which one of you would prefer I not devote considerable time and resources going forward to making you regret *not* answering my question?"

The man on the right broke first. "We were told to secure all of the players and get you back to the yacht. Oren's orders. The heiress is AWOL."

A change came over Grayson's body, and Lyra felt a shiver crawl down her own spine.

"What do you mean," Grayson said, grabbing the man by the front of his shirt, "*the heiress is AWOL?*"

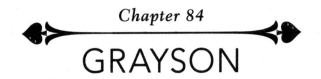

Chapter 84

GRAYSON

*A*very. *Completely off the grid. No sign of foul play—but missing.*
That was all Grayson had been able to extract from Oren's men. Now those men were searching the island for Brady Daniels, and Grayson and the rest of the players were en route to the yacht.

Grayson zeroed in on the helicopter pilot—also one of Oren's—and attempted to extract more information, but the pilot didn't know *more.*

Because, Grayson thought, *Oren's men don't know about Alice.*

Grayson wanted to believe that he was getting ahead of himself, that Avery's sudden disappearance might have nothing to do with *Alice,* but then Grayson thought about Prague—ash on Jameson's skin, cuts on his neck.

Threats were issued.

Grayson didn't even wait for the helicopter to touch down on the yacht before he leapt out of it. Two seconds later, Lyra landed a foot behind him, the result of her own leap from the chopper. It took everything Grayson had not to shut down and shut her out, but he knew from experience that he wouldn't do anyone any good like that—that he wouldn't do *Avery* any good like that.

This time, I will not freeze. Worst-case scenarios flashed through his mind, and Grayson let them come.

"We need to find Jameson," he told Lyra. "Or John Oren, Avery's head of security." Behind them, the helicopter had finished landing. Rohan and Savannah were climbing out of it.

And there's no one here to meet us. Grayson held Lyra's gaze for a fraction of a second, and then he took off, tearing through the yacht, knowing damn well that Lyra could and would match his pace. Jameson and Avery's suite was empty. Grayson wasn't certain where on the yacht security was being headquartered, so he went for the next best thing.

Alisa's office.

Grayson didn't bother knocking before throwing open the door. Inside, Alisa and Jameson stood huddled over Alisa's phone.

"And that's all?" Jameson was saying, his voice unrecognizable, his eyes locked on the phone like it was the only thing that mattered in the world. "That is, word for word, everything the Woman in Red said?"

The Woman in Red. Grayson filed that phrase away as the voice on the other end of the call replied: "Yes."

Grayson knew that voice. "Gigi."

Alisa glanced up at him. "Knox has her. She's safe and on her way here."

Gigi was safe, but Grayson knew just by looking at Jameson: *Avery isn't.*

Grayson went to his brother but addressed his next words to Alisa's phone: "Gigi. It's me. What do you know?"

Grayson's sister was fully capable of talking ten thousand miles an hour. A veritable avalanche of information poured out of Gigi. *A woman in red, Calla Thorp. Another woman, Zella.*

Eve telling the former that Lyra knew something about calla lilies, Alice Hawthorne, and omega.

A warning from the latter that if Gigi was asked a certain question, no matter how coercively it was phrased, she could say no.

And then there was the phrase that Gigi said most frequently—over and over and over again. *The time for* watching *is done.*

Before Grayson could reply to the onslaught of information, Jameson reached forward and ended the call.

Without even looking at Grayson, Jameson brought his eyes to Alisa's. "*Do something,*" Jameson told her, practically vibrating with intensity, like at any moment his earthly body might fail to physically contain the storm brewing inside. "*Now.* You heard Gigi. Calla Thorp. Calls herself the Watcher. Wears a red cloak."

"Brady's Calla?" Lyra, who'd been silent up until now, looked to Grayson. "A cloak, Grayson."

Grayson heard exactly what she was saying. "Your dream. Alice. You said she wore a black cloak."

"*Alice,*" Jameson repeated, his voice dangerously low. "I told you to stop saying that name, but you wouldn't." Jameson's head swiveled slowly, the motion more animal than human, his gaze coming to rest on Lyra. "You did this," Jameson told her.

Grayson put himself in front of Lyra. "What happened?" he asked. *To Avery.* Grayson didn't need to say that part out loud. Avery was the center of Jameson's universe, his *everything* in every way that mattered.

Jameson looked past Grayson and addressed his reply directly to Lyra. "You did." Jameson's eyes were wild and charged, his entire body like a live wire. "*You* happened, Lyra. Eve happened—and now Avery is *gone.*"

"Details," Grayson said, his voice every bit as low as his brother's and shot through with the kind of intensity meant to rattle bones. "Now. Est unus ex nobis, Jamie." *She is one of us.*

From very nearly the beginning, Avery had been one of them.

Jameson's head bent downward until his chin almost touched his collarbone, so much tension visible in his neck that the cords of muscle looked like they might snap.

I'm right here, Jamie. Just tell me.

"We were being *watched,*" Jameson said, his voice uncharacteristically dull as he parroted what Gigi had told them. "And now, the time for *watching* is over. You just had to push, Gray. You just had to keep right on saying that name."

None of them said it now. *Alice.*

"And you." Jameson raised his head again, locking feral eyes on Lyra's. "You opened your big mouth to Eve, and now—" Jameson cut off. Without warning, he put his entire body behind a punch delivered straight to Grayson's jaw.

Grayson went down, and the next thing he knew, Lyra had put herself directly between them, shielding his body with her own.

"Jameson." Alisa's voice cut through the air. "I need you to pull it together."

"This is me," Jameson told Alisa, staring down at Grayson on the floor, "pulling it together."

"I understand," Alisa told him. "Believe me, Jameson, I do. But keep acting like a liability, and I will have a discussion with Oren, and you will find yourself waking up locked in a storage unit somewhere with no way out while the grown-ups do whatever is necessary to get Avery back."

"Get her back." Grayson forced himself to say the words out loud. "From *them*."

"Odette said there are always three." Lyra's voice shook slightly—very slightly—as she addressed those words to Jameson and Alisa. "Alice Hawthorne was there the night my father died. She was wearing a cloak. Black. All black." Grayson could practically hear Lyra's mind churning. "And Calla's was red..."

Grayson knew that Lyra was thinking about the twisted game her father had laid out for her the night he'd killed herself. *Three pieces of candy on a candy necklace. A calla lily. A Hawthorne. And omega.*

"This is the last time that I am asking for details." His jaw still aching from Jameson's punch, Grayson climbed slowly to his feet.

Alisa preempted any reply that Jameson might have given. "Less than an hour ago," she told Grayson, "Avery shut down the cameras on the yacht, all of them, for a period of less than three minutes. She saw to it that Oren and his team were otherwise occupied. Based on the footage we do have, she was alone when she did it and gone by the time the cameras came back up. There was no sign of a struggle, no sign of anyone else with her at the time. And she left a note."

Alisa plucked it off her desk and handed it to Grayson—purple ink, scrawled over the back of one of her mother's old postcards.

I'm not missing. Don't look for me.
The press cannot find out that I am gone.
∞

"How long ago did you find this?" Grayson asked Jameson, knowing instinctively that Jameson was the one who had.

Jameson didn't answer.

"Thirty-three minutes," Alisa told Grayson. "Approximately fifteen minutes after the security outages. In that time, Oren and I have been completely read in. Multiple teams have been dispatched. Xander is trying to get ahold of Nash and Libby. Every shred of security footage we have is being gone over with a fine-tooth comb. Right before we talked to Gigi, I put in a call in with a very discreet contact at the Coast Guard."

Discreet. The muscles in Grayson's throat tightened as he looked back to Avery's note. *The press cannot find out that I am gone.* Grayson would have recognized Avery's handwriting anywhere. "What do we make of the lemniscate?" he asked.

"*We* don't make anything of it." Jameson's voice was like a beast uncaged. "Avery is none of your concern." He said Avery's name like it had been torn from his soul, and Grayson felt Jameson's statement like a sword through his heart.

Avery was *family*, and family had always been Grayson's concern.

"I want Odette's location," Grayson told Alisa. Hurting or not, his brain sorted through next moves at warp speed. "She knows something. And where's Toby?"

"He's been out looking for Eve for the last couple of hours," Alisa replied.

"What does he know?" Grayson asked Jameson. "About Alice."

"Nothing he's felt like sharing," Jameson replied, voice taut, jaw hard, eyes hollow. "And he's not answering our calls. But like I said, *brother*, this is none of your concern." Jameson looked from Grayson to Lyra and back again. "You have other concerns now."

It couldn't have been more obvious: *He blames Lyra for this. He blames me.*

"Blame me all you want," Grayson told his brother. "But est unus ex nobis. Nos defendat eius." Grayson said the full phrase this time. "Avery is one of us, Jamie. We protect her. We *will* find her." Grayson felt the force of that vow in every inch of his body.

"*I* will find her," Jameson replied. "Oren and Alisa and their teams will. Nash will. Toby will. But you?" Jameson turned back and looked Grayson dead in the eye. "As far as I'm concerned, you and Lyra can go to hell."

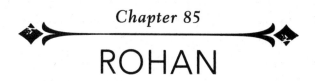

Chapter 85

ROHAN

Rohan could feel the labyrinth in his mind shifting, remade by a single new piece of information. *Avery Grambs, missing.* Without the heiress, there might well be no prize money—not immediately, at least. Not soon enough for Rohan to ascertain beyond any shadow of a doubt whether or not Savannah Grayson intended to keep her promise.

Why would she? Rohan did not appreciate being at anyone else's mercy. He had to find another way.

There was always another way.

The paths laid out before Rohan were many and varied, his opponent crystal clear. *This isn't over, Duchess.*

"What the hell is going on?" Savannah said, the first words she'd spoken to Rohan since she'd turned to him back in the final chamber and uttered the phrase *the house always wins.* "Why did they bring us back here?"

I'm the house, Rohan told himself. *There is no other choice. I have to be the house.*

"One might conclude," he told Savannah, "that there is a *situation*." Rohan made his way toward the front of the yacht, just to see if she would follow.

She did not.

My terms, Savannah Grayson had told him. *No one else's.*

"And when there is a *situation* of a certain sort . . . ," Rohan continued, pivoting to face her again, walking backward now. "The first thing you do is lock down every player on the board."

The helicopter that had brought them here had already taken off again, headed back to the island, no doubt, for Brady Daniels. *Even as we speak, there's a team flushing him out.* That was good.

For Rohan's purposes, Daniels was key.

Were you forbidden from interfering with the game, Duchess? Rohan had the photographs, but those wouldn't be sufficient to prove Zella's hand in any of this. *Did the Proprietor tell you that if the Grandest Game was called off, you'd be disqualified as a potential heir? Is that why you instructed Brady that the game* must *go on?*

The only real proof that Rohan had of Zella's involvement was tattooed onto Brady's arm.

Rohan continued walking backward, willing Savannah to follow—and finally, she did. *Not done with me quite yet, love?*

"You gave me your dice." Savannah said those words like an accusation.

Rohan spun again and took up position at the railing on the front of the yacht, fixing his gaze straight ahead. "It was," he said, "the strategic thing to do."

"You took me at my word," Savannah replied.

She really was going to make him say it. *Vicious, winter girl.*

"What choice did I have?" Rohan kept his tone light, and then, despite himself, he turned his head to look at her. "Right from the start, what choice did I have with you?" He added the nickname solely to annoy her. "Savvy."

"I despise that name, *British*, so here is my final deal for you." Savannah Grayson was made for moonlight—that platinum hair, those pale gray eyes, which narrowed at him in the most delightful fashion. "You may call me *Savannah*, and I will call you *Rohan*."

The sound of his name on her tongue really was something else.

"Very well." Rohan lifted a hand to her jaw—a strong jaw for a merciless woman. "*Savannah*."

"Ask me what my plan is now," she ordered.

"What..." Rohan anticipated the moment that her hand would grab his hair, and she did not disappoint. "...is your plan now?"

Savannah brought her lips very nearly to Rohan's. "My plan," she whispered, making certain he could feel that whisper on his lips, "is none of your damn business." She brought her mouth just a little closer, her lips parting—but she did not kiss him. Instead, Savannah Grayson let Rohan feel all the ways she *might* have kissed him, and then she pushed him back against the railing.

Ruthless.

Those lips of hers parted once more. "Good-bye, Rohan."

And soon enough, he was alone.

Chapter 86

ROHAN

Power came, always, at a cost. The only question was what the price was—and who was going to pay it. Fortunately for Rohan, there was clarity in pain.

And even more fortunately for Rohan, Jameson Hawthorne was a desperate man. He tracked Rohan down, the way Rohan had very much hoped that he would.

"I have an offer for you," Jameson said, his jaw hard.

The human body told stories, if you knew how to listen. Rohan assessed Jameson for a moment. The muscles in Jameson's jaw were just the beginning. *And there's my safety net.* Rohan had not pieced together exactly what was going on here—yet.

But he would.

"I need ten million pounds, and I need it in the next seven weeks," he told Jameson. "You appear to be down an heiress. You should have taken me up on my offer sooner."

Like power, Rohan's assistance would come at a price.

"I have money of my own." The story that Jameson Hawthorne's body was telling right now was a story of a dangerous, brutal, almost inhuman thing barely leashed. The man was broken. And Rohan had always had a certain fascination for broken things.

Putting them back together—or scavenging them for parts.

"Help me find Avery," Jameson said fiercely, "and the money is yours—what you need and more, every dime I have, no strings attached."

Yes, Rohan thought, the words a low, vibrating hum in his mind. *Yes. That will do.*

"And how precisely do you believe that I can be of assistance?" Rohan asked. Information, in times like these, was priceless.

"The duchess." Jameson's eyes narrowed to slits. "Zella. She knows something."

Of course she does, Rohan thought. His rival was a master of the long game—in all likelihood, more than one.

Taking her down would be a pleasure. *His* pleasure.

"I'll need the money before I can go back to London," Rohan told Jameson. "Technicalities. You understand."

"You'll get the money when I get Avery back."

Well, that could be a problem—but then, Rohan had always excelled at taking care of problems.

Without waiting for Rohan's assent, Jameson turned, walking away—stalking, really, like a desperate, broken, dangerous man with somewhere to be.

"Where are you going?" Rohan called. "Where will I find you, once I have the information you need?"

Jameson's stride never even broke. "Prague."

Chapter 87

GIGI

In the time it took Gigi's beloved-against-his-will former teammate to deliver her to Alisa Ortega on what appeared to be a yacht the size of a sprawling sportsball field, Gigi ascertained three things from He of the Grumpiest and Most Inscrutable of Pants.

One: Knox had looked for her. He'd *been* looking for her for more than a day.

Two: He'd been paid to do it.

And three: Even though Knox had heard every word Gigi had told Jameson and Alisa about the Woman in Red, even though Knox was the one who'd placed the call to Alisa in the first place, he clearly wasn't going to ask.

About Calla.

Gigi just kept thinking about the scar at the base of Knox's neck, the one he'd called a *Calla Thorp good-bye.* She kept thinking about the way the Woman in Red had insisted there was no Calla Thorp anymore.

"It appears our business arrangement is at an end," Knox told Alisa, handing Gigi over.

"Yes, yes," Alisa replied curtly, "you're heartless and driven only by greed and weren't worried about Gigi here in the least. Ridiculous premise accepted. I have another job for you, Mr. Landry."

"Not interested, Ortega."

"You will be."

Gigi felt a bit like she was watching two sexually repressed mountain lions playing Ping-Pong.

"I was just notified by security," Alisa continued, "that Brady Daniels has disappeared from Hawthorne Island without a trace. I can't help but wonder if he had help."

Knox scowled. "You think he's with Calla—or the other one."

Zella, Gigi thought.

"I think," Alisa told Knox, "that our business arrangement is not at its end."

Chapter 88

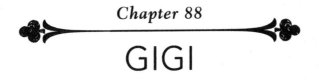

GIGI

igi found Savannah standing on one of the yacht's open decks between a hot tub and a pool. She stood with her back to Gigi, who still wasn't used to her twin's haircut, wasn't used to being able to see the back of her sister's neck—the tension in it.

"You won, didn't you?" Gigi said. That was such a nonsensical way for her to start, but she couldn't take it back now. "The Grandest Game."

"Winning rarely matters as much as I think it will." Savannah did not so much as turn. Gigi could tell just by the tone in her sister's voice that Savannah's walls were all the way up.

Solid ice.

Gigi was not without discretion or the ability to take a hint, but Savannah's walls were always highest when she was hurting most.

"I'm going to hug you," Gigi announced, walking toward her sister. "It's probably a very bad idea, but you're going to let me, because if you don't, I will be forced to find something else to do with my arms, and we both know that my arms and I should pretty much never be left to our own devices."

"Go away, Gigi." Savannah's voice broke, and that broke Gigi.

"It's okay if you hate me." Gigi's voice broke, too. In response, Savannah said nothing and nothing and nothing.

And then: "Believe me, Juliet. I've tried."

Tried to hate me. "Now." Gigi slipped her arms around Savannah. "I'm going to hug you now."

"Our father was murdered," Savannah snapped, "and you—"

"Our father was a murderer." Gigi felt the rise and fall and rise and fall of her sister's chest. "And I wanted so badly to protect you from that." Gigi had wanted *so badly* to be strong.

She thought about Mattias Slater telling her that she already was.

"It killed me, Savannah. Every time I saw you, it killed me." Gigi knew that she was on the verge of babbling, and she didn't care. "But I wanted to do for you what you did for me when you found out about Dad cheating. About Grayson. About all of it."

"You pushed me away." Savannah's voice was almost too calm as she said those words.

"I didn't mean to," Gigi whispered. She waited for Savannah to shrug off her hug, to push her away.

But it didn't happen. After an absolute eternity, Gigi's twin spoke again. "You're hurting."

Gigi didn't smile. She didn't grin. For once in her life, she didn't even try to make it hurt less. "He was our dad." She hadn't cried about this. She hadn't once let herself cry about it. "I know that I should hate him for what he did, but I don't. Men died, and there is nothing that I can do to make up for that, no matter how hard I try, and I can't even hate the person who killed them."

Savannah's arms wound around Gigi's shoulders. As hugs went, it was hardly expert, but it was enough.

"I was going to bring it all to light." Savannah's voice was quiet but not at all soft. "I was going to bring them down."

Was. Gigi knew her sister well enough not to read too far into that. Savannah was not a person known for changing course.

"But now," Savannah continued, "Avery is missing, and I don't even—" Savannah cut off mid-sentence. "You didn't know."

Gigi stared at her sister. "I am totally going back over a mostly one-sided phone conversation I had that is making a lot more sense now."

This is bad, Gigi thought. *This is very bad.*

"I know you care," Savannah said. "About them. About Avery."

"I care too much," Gigi told Savannah. "Always and sometimes inappropriately. It's kind of my thing—but you know what's really not my thing? Secrets. Keeping them. From you."

No more secrets, Gigi thought. "I might know something," she told her sister, "about what's going on." It all came pouring out—again: Slate and Eve, Calla and Zella, *the time for watching.*

"Back up to the part where you got kidnapped," Savannah said. "*Twice.*"

"And I didn't even get a T-shirt," Gigi quipped. Part of her wanted to ask—if they were okay, if *Savannah* was—but Gigi didn't get the chance.

Savannah turned suddenly, whipping her head left. It took Gigi a good three seconds to realize why. *Footsteps.* Coming toward them.

Rohan.

There were walls, and then there were *walls*. Gigi sensed the change in her sister immediately.

"You again?" Savannah raised her chin as Rohan wrapped his way around the pool toward them.

"Lower your hackles, love. I'm here with an offer." Rohan smiled, a wicked smile, a far-too-charming one. "For your sister." He turned to Gigi.

"Over my dead body," Savannah said. "Or better yet—over yours."

"Promises, promises," Rohan replied.

"Me?" Gigi blinked. And blinked again.

"I find myself in need of an accomplice who can go where I cannot," Rohan said, his gaze lingering on Savannah's for another second or two before it shifted back to Gigi once more. "And based on what I just overheard, you'll do quite nicely."

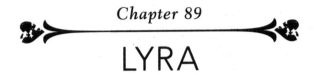

Chapter 89

LYRA

Lyra knew that Grayson was hurting, but in the hours since his brother had told them to go to hell, she wouldn't have been able to tell it.

Grayson was a man on a mission, and Lyra was right there with him.

"Bold move." Odette's long gray hair, with its black tips, was swept up in an elegant twist and held in place with what looked to be an antique pin. Her gaze was steady, and Lyra knew just by looking at Odette—the canny old woman's eyes missed nothing. "Holding a lawyer of my caliber against her will."

"The exit is right there," Grayson told Odette. The three of them were ensconced in a borrowed conference room in a luxury hotel. Lyra had half expected Grayson to try to leave her behind, but he hadn't.

For better or worse, she was in this now.

"Avery is missing," Grayson told Odette. He didn't mince words, nor did he provide any verbal elaboration. Instead, all Grayson did was place a single calla lily on the table separating him from Odette Morales.

The old woman's gaze lingered on the flower, but she said nothing. Lyra thought about everything Gigi had said, and she made the next move.

"What do you know about *invitations*?" Lyra asked. "About a certain kind of *ask*."

Odette stared at Lyra for a small eternity, and then, every inch the old Hollywood star, the old woman deigned to reply. "Less than I once wanted to and more than I should."

Grayson withdrew two objects from his suit jacket pocket— poker chips, borrowed from the yacht, one red, one black, both priceless.

He set down the red chip first. "A woman in red..." The black chip was next. "A woman in black..."

Lyra reached out to lightly touch the first chip. "Calla Thorp." She moved her hand to the black chip. "Alice Hawthorne." Lyra paused. "But there are always three."

Odette's eyes and demeanor gave away nothing. Not a single tell. Then slowly, deliberately, the old woman reached back and withdrew the antique pin from her hair, freeing her long silvery tresses.

Odette laid the pin—silver, with pearls at the head—on the table, next to the poker chips. One by one, she lightly touched the three objects. "Red. Black. White." Odette brought her hand back to the start and went through the sequence again. "The Lily."

The red chip.

"The Omega."

The black one.

"And the Monoceros."

The white. The term was unfamiliar to Lyra, and the sound of it didn't fit with the other two.

Across from her, Odette moved her hand back to the first chip. "The Watcher," the old woman said, then moved her featherlight touch from red to black. "The Hand." Finally, she touched the pearls at the head of her hairpin. "And the Judge."

Watcher. Hand. Judge.

Lily. Omega. Monoceros.

"There are always three," Lyra said quietly.

"Who are they?" Grayson demanded.

"Women, exclusively." Odette appeared for a moment like she might leave it at that. "They answer to no one but themselves and a great many answer to them. If you know where to look, history tells the tale."

"And what tale is that?" Grayson asked.

Seconds crept by. Lyra didn't even blink.

"Men ruin things," Odette said finally. "Not all of them. Not all the time. But often enough—and powerful men more than most. The group you're after—all I can tell you is that they believe that some situations require a gently guiding hand and others a gilded blade."

A blade. "Exactly how dangerous are they?" Lyra asked, so Grayson wouldn't have to.

"Dangerous enough that I stopped looking for answers fourteen years ago," Odette replied, "when I awoke in my own home to find a calla lily on my pillow. A warning."

Lyra thought about the calla she'd found near the helipad, the one that Eve had insisted she did not send. She thought about hundreds of calla lilies, washing onto the shore. And then she thought about the one her father had given her.

She thought about her father's blood—the feel of it on her feet, the *smell* of it.

Lyra leaned forward, her forearms on the conference table. "You called the Watcher the *Lily*. And the *Omega* is the Hand. What exactly does that second one mean?"

Odette said nothing, but Grayson filled in the blanks. "Omega," he said, "is the end."

The end. For the first time, Lyra wondered if her father had killed himself to prevent someone else from doing the job for him. *A woman in black. The Omega. The end. The Hand.*

A Hawthorne did this.

Lyra thought about a woman, calling her a poor thing. *You should not be here. But who is to say that you were?*

"What about the third?" Lyra said. "The Monoceros." The *Omega*—the Hand—had been hiding her from someone, and Odette had already been clear: These women answered to no one.

Again, Lyra's question received no reply, and again, Grayson filled in the blanks. "Monoceros," he said. "It's a mythical creature and a constellation and, it seems, the Judge." He looked back down to the chips. "Calla Thorp. Alice Hawthorne. Who's the third?"

"If I knew that," Odette replied, "I suspect that I would not have received a *warning* all those years ago."

"A warning," Lyra repeated. "A calla lily." She glanced at Grayson.

"What does it mean," he said, "if there are hundreds of them? Calla lilies."

This time, Odette's silence was not measured in seconds. Neither Lyra nor Grayson moved. Neither said a word.

"It means…" Odette reached for her pin and used it to fix her long hair back once more. "That something very big is about to happen."

AVERY

I woke up in a white room. White ceiling. White floors. White walls. The room had no windows. It had no doors. My first thought was of Jameson.

My second was of Alice.

And my third was that the white room wasn't just white. Etched into every surface, there were indentions—twisting, turning lines that connected just so.

It took me longer than it should have to realize what I was looking at. This room had no windows. It had no doors. And built into the walls and ceiling and floor, there was a very complicated maze.

ACKNOWLEDGMENTS

I am beyond grateful to the incredible team who helped me bring this story to life and to the readers who have given me the opportunity to dream (and plot) big as the Inheritance Games saga comes rushing toward its finale.

Thank you to my editor, Lisa Yoskowitz (to whom this book was dedicated). Lisa, working with you is such a joy at every stage of the process. Thank you for your insights, your support, and your passion for these books. They mean the world to me.

Thank you, Elizabeth Harding, for being my agent of more than twenty (*twenty!*) years now. With every new book, I think back on all the others and about how very grateful I am to have had you in my corner with each and every one.

I know I say this in one form or another with every book, but I feel like the luckiest author in the world to work with the incredible team at Little, Brown Books for Young Readers, led by Megan Tingley and Jackie Engel. I cannot imagine a more passionate, creative, and effective team or express how much I truly enjoy working with you all. Thank you, art director Karina Granda and artist Katt Phatt, for another *incredible* cover. Thank you, Danielle Cantarella, Leah CollinsLipsett, Rachel Nuzman, Allie Stewart, Katie Tucker, and the rest of the sales team, for your yearslong efforts to bring new readers to the Inheritance Games saga. Thank you,

Marisa Finkelstein, Andy Ball, Jen Graham, JoAnna Kremer, Mary McCue, Marissa Baker, Kimberly Stella, Becky Munich, Jess Mercado, Victoria Stapleton, Christie Michel, Orlane Dubreus, Margaret Hansen, Erin Slonaker, Jody Corbett, Su Wu, Janelle DeLuise, Hannah Koerner, and everyone else who had a hand in bringing this book into the world and getting it into the hands of readers.

Special thanks to Alex Houdeshell, whose editorial feedback on the first draft of this book was incredibly helpful in nailing down what I wanted *Glorious Rivals* to be; to Savannah Kennelly for all things social media (including cards, reveals, and riddles!); to Kelly Moran for (among *many* other things) helping *The Grandest Game* to become a Good Morning America Book Club pick; and to Bill Grace and Emilie Polster for working your marketing magic! I cannot tell you how much I enjoy working with you all. It is truly a dream.

While I was writing this book, I was lucky enough to be able to visit the United Kingdom and spend some time with my publishing team at Penguin Random House UK. It was so lovely to meet you all, and I am grateful to all of you for your work on these books as well. Special thanks to Anthea Townsend and Sarah Doyle for taking such good care of me while I was there, as well as to Michelle Nathan, Charis Lowe-White, Harriet Venn, and everyone else who has worked on this book!

At last count, the *Inheritance Games* books have been translated into more than thirty languages. I am so grateful for the support of my publishers around the world—for the beautiful editions you have published, for the innovative ways you've found of bringing readers to the series, and for your enthusiasm for the world and characters in these books. I very much wish my life allowed for more travel right now, because I would very much love to visit you all and to meet my readers around the world. A huge thank-you also goes out to all the translators who work tirelessly (and creatively!) to translate the puzzles, riddles, and codes into their respective languages. Every time I think I've written puzzles that won't be *too* diabolically hard to translate, I realize that actually, *this* puzzle—and maybe that one—are a little bit fiendish. Thank you for playing this grand game alongside me!

I also owe a huge debt of gratitude to my entire team at Curtis Brown! Thank you, Holly Frederick, for continuing to be such an advocate in film/TV; Karin Schulze, for helping me bring these books to readers around the world; and to everyone who has been helping me stay on top of all that goes into the business side of things, especially Jahlila Stamp, Eliza Leung, and Alexandra Franklin.

Large sections of this book were written while sitting across from my longtime friend, Rachel Vincent. I couldn't ask for a better friend and sounding board. Thank you, Rachel!

Finally, I am endlessly thankful for my family—for my husband, who doesn't bat an eye at holding down the fort when I am on tour or deadline; for my parents, who turn their house (the initial inspiration for Hawthorne House!) into a writing retreat for me whenever I need to make a big push for the finish line; and for my three boys, for endless inspiration.

Kim Haynes Photography

JENNIFER LYNN BARNES

is the #1 *New York Times* bestselling author of
more than twenty acclaimed young adult novels,
including the Inheritance Games series, the
Grandest Game series, the Debutantes series, *The
Lovely and the Lost,* and the Naturals series. Jen
is also a Fulbright Scholar with advanced degrees
in psychology, psychiatry, and cognitive science.
She received her PhD from Yale University in 2012
and was a professor of psychology and professional
writing for many years. She invites you to visit her
online at jenniferlynnbarnes.com or on Instagram
@auhorjenlynnbarnes.

Don't miss the thrilling conclusion
to the Grandest Game!

THE GILDED BLADE

Summer 2026